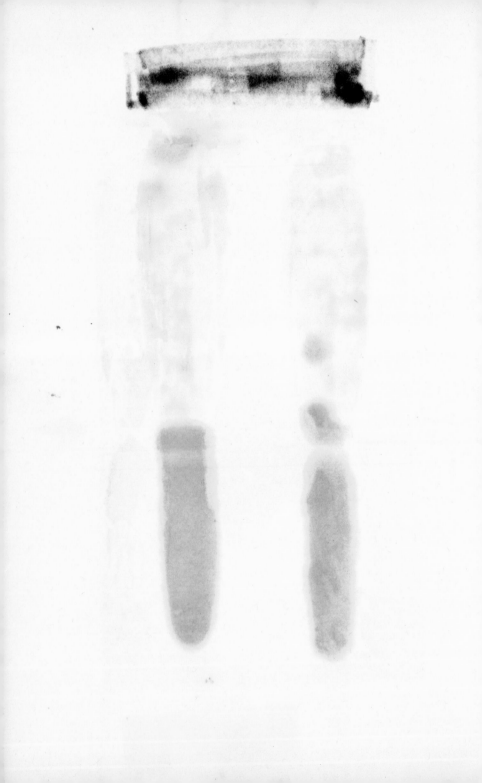

Mrs. Tim Carries On

Books by D. E. Stevenson

Mrs. Tim Christie
Mrs. Tim Carries On
Mrs. Tim Gets a Job
Mrs. Tim Flies Home
Smouldering Fire
Vittoria Cottage
Music in the Hills
The House of the Deer
The Young Clementina
Gerald and Elizabeth
Sarah's Cottage
Sarah Morris Remembers
The House on the Cliff
The Marriage of Katherine
Katherine Wentworth
The Blue Sapphire
Fletchers End
Bel Lamington
The Misgraves
Still Glides the Stream
Anna and Her Daughters
The Tall Stranger
Summerhills

Amberwell
Blow the Wind Southerly
Five Windows
Young Mrs. Savage
Kate Hardy
The Four Graces
Listening Valley
The Two Mrs. Abbotts
Celia's House
Spring Magic
Rochester's Wife
Alister & Co.
The English Air
The Green Money
A World in Spell
The Story of Rosabelle Shaw
The Baker's Daughter
Crooked Adam

Omnibus Volume
Miss Buncle *containing*
Miss Buncle's Book *and*
Miss Buncle Married

Mrs. Tim Carries On

D. E. STEVENSON

HOLT, RINEHART AND WINSTON

New York   Chicago   San Francisco

Library of Congress Cataloging in Publication Data

Stevenson, Dorothy Emily, 1892–
    Mrs. Tim carries on.

    I. Title.
PZ3.S8472Mo5 [PR6037.T458]   823'.9'12   72-91586
ISBN 0-03-007491-6

Printed in the United States of America

Contents

Author's Foreword
to the Story of the Christie Family

by D. E. Stevenson

The four books about Mrs. Tim and her family are being re-published during 1973 and early 1974, and the author has been asked to write a foreword.

The books consist of:

1. *Mrs. Tim Christie*
2. *Mrs. Tim Carries On*
3. *Mrs. Tim Gets a Job*
4. *Mrs. Tim Flies Home*

The first "Mrs. Tim" was written many years ago (in 1934). It was written at the request of the wife of a professor of English history in a well-known university who was a personal friend. Their daughter was engaged to be married to an officer in a Highland Regiment. Naturally enough they wanted to know what it would be like and what she would be expected to do.

There was nothing secret in my diary so I gave it to Mrs. Ford to read. When she handed it back, Mrs. Ford was smiling. She said, "I read it aloud to Rupert and we laughed till we cried. You could make this into a very amusing book and call it *Leaves from the Diary of an Officer's Wife*. It just needs to be expanded, and you could pep it up a little, couldn't you?"

At first I was doubtful (it was not my idea of a book), but she was so persuasive that I decided to have a try. The result was *Mrs. Tim of the Regiment* (recently reissued as *Mrs. Tim*

Christie). By this time I had got into the swing of the story and had become so interested in Hester that I gave her a holiday in the Scottish Highlands with her friend Mrs. London and called it *Golden Days*.

The two books were accepted by a publisher and published in an omnibus volume. It was surprisingly successful. It was well reviewed and the sales were eminently satisfactory; the fan-mail was astonishing. People wrote from near and far saying that Mrs. Tim was a real live person; they had enjoyed her adventures immensely—and they wanted more.

But it was not until the outbreak of the Second World War in 1939 that I felt the urge to write another book about Hester Christie.

Mrs. Tim Carries On was easily written, for it is just a day-to-day account of what happened and what we did—and said and felt. The book was a comfort to me in those dark days; it helped me to carry on, and a sort of pattern emerged from the chaos.

Like its predecessor, the book was written from my own personal diary but this time there was no need to expand the story nor to "pep it up" for there was enough pep already in my diary for half a dozen books.

It is all true. It is true that a German plane came down on the moor in the middle of a shooting party and the two airmen were captured. It is true that German planes came down to low level in Norfolk, and elsewhere, and used machine guns to kill pedestrians on the roads. Sometimes they circled over the harvest fields and killed a few farm labourers and horses. Why they did so is a mystery. There could not have been any military objective in these maneuvers. People soon got used to it and were not even seriously alarmed but just took cover in a convenient ditch like dear old Uncle Joe. Perhaps the German airmen did it for fun? Perhaps it amused them to see old gentlemen rolling into ditches?

An American friend wrote to me as follows: "Your Mrs. Tim has made us *think*. We have been trying to imagine what it would be like to have a man-eating tiger prowling around in *our* backyard."

She had hit the nail on the head for, alas, the strip of water which had kept Britain safe from her enemies for hundreds of years had become too narrow: The tiger was in our backyard.

To me this book brings back the past so vividly that even now —thirty years later—I cannot read it without laughter and tears. Laughter? Yes, for in spite of the sadness and badness of Total War, the miseries we suffered, and the awful anxieties we endured, cheerfulness broke through at unexpected moments— and we laughed.

When they were first published, these four books about Mrs. Tim were all very popular. Everybody loved Mrs. Tim (everybody except the good citizens of Westburgh who disliked her intensely). Everybody wanted to know more about her and her friends. But the books have been out of print and unobtainable for years. I was pleased to hear that they were to be republished and that they would all be available again. I was particularly glad because together they contain the whole history of the Christie family and its friends. Taken in their proper sequence, readers will be able to appreciate the gradual development of Hester's character and the more rapid development of Tim's. As the years pass by there is a difference in the children; Annie and Fred Bollings become more adult; Jack and Grace McDougall, having weathered serious trouble, settle down peacefully together. The Christies' friends are very varied but all are interesting and unusual. We are introduced to the dignified Mrs. London; we meet Pinkie, an attractive young lady whose secret trouble is that (although seventeen years old) she does not feel "properly grown up, inside." But, in spite of this, Pinkie makes friends wherever she goes. Her circle of friends includes all the young officers who are quartered at the depot and is enlarged by the arrival of Polish officers who have escaped from their war-shattered country and are billeted in Donford while they reorganise their forces and learn the language. There is a mysterious lady, swathed in Egyptian scarves, who is convinced that in a previous existence she helped to build the Great Pyramid. There is Erica Clutterbuck whose rude manners conceal a heart of gold, and two elegant American ladies who endeavour to persuade Mrs. Tim to go home with them to America so that they may exhibit her to their friends as "The Spirit of English Womanhood."

But the chief interest is to be found in the curious character of Tony Morley and his relationship with the Christie family. At first he seems to Tim and Hester a somewhat alarming personage. (To Tim, because he is a senior officer and fabulously wealthy: he drives a large and powerful car, owns a string of racehorses, and hunts several days a week. To Hester, because he talks irresponsibly and displays an impish sense of humour so that she never knows whether or not he means what he says.) Soon, however, they discover that beneath the surface he is a true friend and can be relied upon whenever the services of a friend are urgently needed. We find out how he uses his tact and diplomacy to smooth the feathers of a disgruntled cook and show her how to measure out the ingredients for a cake with insufficient weights. We learn how he helps Hester to save a naval officer from making a disastrous marriage and how he consoles and advises a young husband whose wife has deserted him. We are told of Colonel Morley's success with a battalion of raw recruits, how he wins their devotion, licks them into shape, and welds them into a satisfactory fighting machine by imbuing them with the necessary esprit de corps. We see him salute smartly and march off at the head of his battalion en route for the Middle East. Knowing his reputation for reckless courage,

Hester wonders sadly if she will ever see him again. But apparently Tony is indestructible. He has survived countless dangers and seems none the worse. He pops in, out of the blue, in Rome (where Hester, on her way home from Africa, is seriously embarrassed by her ignorance of the language). Tony Morley arrives in his usual sudden and unexpected manner. By this time he has become a full-blown general and, having learnt to speak Italian from an obliging enemy, is able to deal adequately with the situation. He also deals adequately with a little misunderstanding at the War Office where he sees a friend and pulls a string or two for Tim.

Meanwhile the Christie children, Bryan and Betty, are growing up rapidly. In fact they are "almost grown up," and, although they are still amusing and full of high spirits, it is obvious that they will soon become useful members of the post-war world.

We meet them at Old Quinings where their mother has managed to find a small house for the summer holidays. Here, also, we meet Annie and Fred Bollings, Grace McDougall and her boys, an old-fashioned squire with a pretty daughter, a school teacher whose unconventional views about free love are somewhat alarming, and a very good-looking young man who is studying medicine but is not too busy to open gates for a fair equestrienne. We meet the amiable Mrs. Daulkes and the far from amiable Miss Crease whose sharp eyes and caustic tongue cause a good deal of trouble to her neighbours. Another unpleasant visitor is Hester Christie's landlady, the wily Miss Stroude, who tries to bounce Hester and almost succeeds, but once again Tony comes to the rescue in the nick of time to defeat Miss Stroude and send her away "with her tail between her legs."

Betty says, joyfully, "This is the best holidays, ever" but Hester's pleasure is not complete until the arrival of Colonel Tim

Christie from Africa. Now, at last, she is happy with all her beloved family under one roof.

I cannot finish this foreword without voicing the grateful
thanks of Mrs. Tim to her many kind friends in America,
South Africa, Australia, and New Zealand who sent her parcels
to augment her war-rations. The parcels contained tins of fat,
packets of tea and sugar and dried fruit, bars of chocolate, and
boxes of candy for the children. These generous presents were
shared with friends and were worth their weight in gold.

Part 1

February—March 1940

Having said good-bye to Tim at the station and watched the train disappear from view I drive home in an extremely dejected condition. Discover Grace ensconced in the big armchair in front of the fire and am obliged to postpone the "good cry" which I had promised myself.

Grace says, "Well, has Tim gone? You aren't worrying, are you, Hester? There's absolutely nothing doing in France—nothing except concert parties."

Reply brightly and untruthfully that of course I am not worrying.

Grace says, that's all right then. She was afraid I might be, and Jack said she was to tell me that he knows where the 1st Battalion is and it's miles away from the front, and that, as a matter of fact, Tim will be much safer there than he would be at home. When asked to explain how this is possible, Grace replies that there are more people killed in the streets by buses and things than have been killed in France in the war, and Jack says that once Hitler starts bombing in earnest he's certain to drop some on the barracks. He knows exactly where the barracks are. Grace thinks that we really ought to move further away from the barracks in case a bomb, intended for the barracks, falls upon us by mistake.

I ask where she proposes to find a house, and she replies that *that* is the trouble, of course. Donford is simply crammed with people who have no reason to be here so the people who are obliged to be here cannot find houses to suit them. She adds that she wishes she and Jack could find a house in the country so that they could keep a dog for Ian—and perhaps a pony—but she sees no prospect of it at present.

I point out that it will be some time before Ian can enjoy a pony, and Grace admits that this is true. "It is really more on account of the bombs," says Grace earnestly. "I don't mind about myself of course, but I am rather anxious about Ian."

As Ian is not yet born but is due to make his appearance shortly, I feel bound to play the part of comforter and I assure Grace that it is common knowledge that the Anti-Aircraft Defences of Donford are most efficient.

"Oh!" exclaims Grace. "That reminds me—I want you to come to dinner tonight, Hester."

It is very kind of Grace, but I feel that a quiet evening at home is more in keeping with my mood, and I am about to refuse the invitation as tactfully as possible when the drawing-room door bursts open and Betty rushes in.

"Hullo!" exclaims Betty. "Has Daddy gone? Did you see him off? Do you think he has got to France yet? Will he have started killing Germans?"

"No," says Grace firmly. "Daddy won't *see* any Germans for months."

"Why?" enquires Betty with interest. "I mean why has he gone at all? Why couldn't he just stay here if he isn't going to see any Germans?"

"He has gone to France in case the Germans attack," declares Grace.

"Will they attack *him?*" asks Betty with round eyes.

"No," replies Grace.

"Why won't they?"

"Because he's there—because all our troops are there."

"But how do the Germans know . . ."

"Hester," says Grace, gathering up her furs and groping for her gloves down the back of the chair, "Hester, you will come tonight, won't you? I've asked the balloon man and I want you to come and talk to him."

"I'll come," cries Betty, hopping about with excitement. "I *love* the balloon man. He was standing in the gutter outside Woolworth's this morning. I like the red balloons best, don't you? I like the sausage-shaped ones. Annie gave me a penny to buy it, but it burst before we got home."

Grace explains that she does not mean "that horrid dirty man"; she means the officer in charge of the Balloon Barrage, Captain Baker. Betty, quite undefeated, says that *she* knows a man called Mr. Baker—she met him when we were staying with Mrs. Loudon at Avielochan—he's a darling, quite bald and full of funny jokes, and she can easily come to dinner and talk to him if Grace would like her to do so.

Grace lies back in the chair and shuts her eyes and says will Betty please go away before she (Grace) goes raving mad; whereupon Betty hugs her and exclaims rapturously, "I do love you so much. I think it must be because you are *so* beautiful."

Few women could resist such blandishment, and Grace immediately succumbs. "Am I really?" she enquires, opening her eyes and smiling at Betty in a fatuous manner.

"Yes," says Betty earnestly. "Yes you are. You're like Snow White you're so beautiful, and Mrs. Benson is like the Wicked Queen who tried to poison her."

This statement is too near the truth to be altogether comfortable, for Mrs. Benson, the wife of the Colonel of the 1st Battalion, is daggers drawn with Grace. I change the subject hastily and we talk about other matters until Annie comes for Betty and drags her away unwillingly to bed.

"Your daughter is a most extraordinary child," declares Grace, when the door has closed and we are once more alone. "I mean she is a most extraordinary mixture of imbecility and acumen. She's perfectly right about Mrs. Benson—the woman *would* poison me if she could do it without being found out."

"Grace, what nonsense!" I exclaim.

"I met her at Simpson's this morning," continues Grace, taking no notice of my interruption. "We were both trying on hats. I wish you could have *seen* Aunt Loo with one of those new soup-plate things perched on one eyebrow, it was a sight for the gods. But when she turned and saw me—when she *looked* at me—I didn't feel like laughing any more. It was awful, Hester. I felt a cold shudder run up my back. She hates me."

"No, oh no, Grace!"

"She does," declares Grace earnestly. "Perhaps nobody has ever hated you, so you haven't experienced hatred. I hadn't until now. It's a terrifying thing."

"If you would only take a little trouble to be nice to her . . ." I begin, but Grace does not listen.

"I wish she would go away," says Grace fretfully. "Why does she stay on here now that the 1st Battalion has gone to France and Frankie with it. I could do with her house very nicely— ours will be much too small when Ian arrives."

"Perhaps you would like this house?" I suggest, a trifle sadly, for I have suddenly realised that there is really no reason why I should remain in Donford either.

"That's *quite* different," says Grace. "Everyone likes having *you* here. I shall want you when Ian arrives, and the 'comforts' couldn't *exist* without you. For Goodness' Sake don't get silly ideas like that into your head."

The idea is there, and it is not really silly. Mamie Carter could run the Regimental Comforts Fund (and as a matter of fact Mamie ought to run it because her husband is commanding the Depot). I point this out to Grace, but Grace will have nothing to do with it.

"Heavens!" she exclaims in despairing accents. "You know perfectly well what would happen if Mamie were in charge, it would mean that Mrs. Benson ran it—Mamie is completely under her thumb."

"Well then, what about Stella?" I enquire. "It ought to be someone whose husband is actually at the Depot."

"It ought to be someone who can do it properly," replies Grace, "and neither Stella nor Mamie would be the slightest use. I shall never forget what I went through at Biddington with Mamie Carter. I found them a house and I moved them into it, and I had the nurse and the children to stay when the baby was arriving, and Mamie took it all as a matter of course. She even had the cheek to say that she wished I could have found them a house with three bathrooms!"

I agree that this was indeed the height of ingratitude.

"Herbert is a perfect saint," says Grace thoughtfully.

This leads us to discuss the strange anomaly of marriage—why is it that selfish wives nearly always have saintly husbands, and how is it that selfish husbands are usually provided with door-mat wives?

The clock strikes seven before we know where we are and Grace gets up in a hurry and says she had no idea it was so late. She has got the flowers to do and goodness knows what else. . . . "You *are* coming, aren't you?" she says persuasively as I follow her out to the gate.

"Honestly, Grace . . ."

"You *must*," she declares. "Hester, you simply must come. Dinner is at eight."

I hesitate for a moment, but I have had a long and very wearing day and I feel quite incapable of dressing up and going out to dinner. I explain this to Grace and remain deaf to her persuasions. Grace departs sorrowfully, saying that she always thought I was her friend.

I spend a solitary evening sitting by the fire, mending my stockings and writing up my diary. Have decided to keep a record of my doings while Tim is away as it will amuse him to read it when he returns.

FRIDAY 1ST MARCH

Very wet morning. Betty and I have breakfast together after which I despatch her to school, suitably clad in oilskins and Wellington boots, and hung about with her schoolbag and gas mask. As usual, when I slip the strap of the gas-mask container over my small daughter's shoulder, I experience a horrible sinking sensation and utter a fervent prayer that this precaution, insisted upon by the Government, may be unnecessary. My own gas mask does not trouble me in the very least and I can look it in the face without a tremor; it is only Betty's small but hideous protection which makes me feel sick.

"Jane forgot hers yesterday," says Betty as she settles the bulky contraption over her hip. "It was gas-mask drill, too— so she got a black mark."

"Poor Jane!" I exclaim.

"But she didn't care," says Betty. "She said she would rather have a black mark than do gas-mask drill."

"Do you mind it?" I enquire anxiously.

"No," replies Betty. "At least not much. It's a horrid chokey feeling, of course, but I just pretend I'm the man in the iron mask. . . ."

The small school, which Betty attends daily, is only about five minutes' walk from Winfield, so Betty is permitted to go by herself. She gives me a last hug and marches off sturdily into the teeming rain, and I return to the dining room where Annie has started to clear away the breakfast.

Annie has been with me for years and is a tremendous talker. She starts immediately and discusses the war news. Annie says that the war will be over quite soon now and the major will be back before I know where I am. . . . Cannot help feeling that Annie is a trifle too optimistic, but am comforted all the same, and repair to the kitchen in a cheerful frame of mind.

Cheerful feelings are soon dissipated. The kitchen is extremely warm, but the moral atmosphere is at zero. Mrs. Fraser, my large and terrifying cook, is waiting for me with a grim smile. I enquire in trembling tones whether anything has gone wrong. Mrs. Fraser replies that that depends. Having long and bitter experience of domestic catastrophes I am prepared for the worst, and glance hastily round the kitchen, but can see nothing calculated to cause alarm or despondency; the stove is burning brightly and without smoke, the copper boiler has not burst, neither has the ceiling fallen. Thus reassured I am able to face Mrs. Fraser with more confidence and to enquire further into the nature of the trouble.

Mrs. Fraser says that she has always been used to "good places" until she came here, places where the kitchen was properly furnished with everything necessary to hand. She wanted to make a cake today and what did she find? She found that there were no proper weights for the scales. How do I suppose she can weigh out the ingredients for her cake without proper weights?

As I have lived all my married life in furnished houses, amongst other people's belongings, I am neither surprised nor abashed to hear of this strange deficiency, and am about to soothe Mrs. Fraser by offering to go down to the ironmongers and buy a set of weights, when the kitchen door opens and Annie looks in with a beaming face. "It's Major Morley," she says, "only he's a colonel now, and he said was it too early."

I immediately abandon Mrs. Fraser to her fate and rush into the drawing room, where I find Tony Morley standing in front of the fire, looking very smart and soldierly in a brand new uniform. I have not met Tony since we stayed with Mrs. Loudon at Avielochan and am delighted to see him again.

Tony seems delighted too, "Hullo, Hester!" he says, shaking both my hands at once. "Here I am, back at the old game—a dugout. I had to look in and see you . . . hope it isn't too early."

I assure him that it couldn't be too early and ask where he has come from and what he is doing. Tony says he is in camp about two miles from Donford, and adds that they have given him the 4th Battalion to lick into shape.

There is a tremendous lot to talk about, because I want to know all his news, and he wants to know mine. He asks about Tim, and about Betty, and whether I have seen Mrs. Loudon lately and then enquires after the Regiment. He was in the Regiment himself, of course, but retired because his father was ill and wanted him at home to look after the property.

We sit down and chat. I explain that Herbert Carter is commanding the Depot, Lawrence Hardford is second in Command, and Tom Ledgard is adjutant.

"Ledgard!" exclaims Tony in amazement. "Couldn't they find somebody better than Ledgard? The fellow's an absolute fool. . . . Is he married yet?"

I cannot help smiling at this for Tom Ledgard is always complaining about his single state and urging his friends to provide him with a partner. Tony is also a bachelor, but shows little desire to change his condition. I reply to Tony's question by assuring him that Captain Ledgard is not yet married, nor even engaged, but that Grace MacDougall has taken the matter in hand and is trying to find a suitable wife for him.

Tony says it is to be hoped she will not succeed; Ledgard is the most devastating bore and he (Tony) would be profoundly sorry for any woman who had to live with him. "Fancy being tied to Ledgard for life!" says Tony in horrified tones. "Fancy seeing Ledgard's lean yellow face across the breakfast table every morning!"

Having thus disposed of Ledgard, we proceed to other matters of interest. Tony is so eager to hear Regimental news, that I begin to suspect he has found life pretty dull at Charters Towers and is glad to be back in harness again.

We are still talking hard when Annie comes in and says to me in a mysterious whisper, "What about the weights?"

Tony says, "Goodness, I never knew you had them in March! You had better give them a bob," and with that he extracts a shilling from an inside pocket and holds it out to Annie.

Annie looks at me in despair, and I explain to Tony that I must go and see what can be done.

"But what's the matter?" he enquires. "Can't you give them a bob and tell them to go away?"

"Who?" I ask in bewilderment.

"The waits, of course," he replies.

"But there isn't any, sir," declares Annie. "That's just the trouble, and she's in the most awful wax because she can't get the currants measured."

The misunderstanding is now cleared up and I am able to explain our difficulty. Tony says it's far too wet for me to go to the town this morning, and anyhow he wants to talk to me. He says he will interview the cook himself and see what can be arranged. Annie and I do our best to persuade him not to, but without avail, for Tony is one of those master-ful men who usually get their own way. We all repair to the kitchen (which fortunately is in apple-pie order) and Tony takes charge of the situation.

"Good morning, Cook," says Tony brightly. "I hear you want something weighed."

Mrs. Fraser is somewhat taken aback by the appearance in her kitchen of a real live colonel, armed to the teeth, but she pulls herself together and replies that nobody can weigh things without weights and that anyway she has never been used to working with old-fashioned balancing scales, but has always been provided with the kind that weigh things by themselves without fiddling little weights, which are bound to get lost.

"But *here* are the weights," says Tony.

"Not the right ones," replies Mrs. Fraser firmly. "Them weights are no use at all. I'm wanting to weigh out five ounces of flour for my cake . . . here's a seven ounce weight and here's a quarter pound and that's all there is."

Tony looks at the weights for a moment and then announces that there is no difficulty at all in the matter, and that Mrs. Fraser can weigh out any amount she wants.

"Not five ounces," objects Mrs. Fraser in incredulous tones.

"Five ounces is easy," says Tony. "First we weigh out two lots of four ounces . . . that's eight," says Tony, pouring the flour onto a square of paper; "we put the eight ounces of flour on one side of the scale and the seven ounce weight on the other . . . then we remove one ounce." He suits the action to the word and removes one ounce with a tablespoon. "There, it balances!" says Tony, with the air of a conjurer who has produced a rabbit out of a hat. "We now have seven ounces of flour on the scale and one ounce in the tablespoon, and all we have to do is to empty the seven ounces back into the bag, weigh out four ounces and add the ounce in the tablespoon, which makes five."

Annie and I are lost in admiration of Tony's cleverness, and even the dour Mrs. Fraser is impressed.

Tony now offers to weigh out all the ingredients for the cake, but Mrs. Fraser has grasped the principle and says she can manage now, and she proceeds to demonstrate how she can weigh out three times one ounce of currants. Tony says that's a very roundabout way of doing it, she can put the seven ounce weight on one side of the scale and the four ounce on the other and make up the four ounce weight with the currants, which will give her three ounces straight off. He plays about with the weights for some time, showing how various amounts of currants can be weighed with the least possible trouble until at last Mrs. Fraser loses patience with him and says he had better go back to the drawing room where he belongs and let her get on with her work.

We return to the drawing room and Tony says, "That's gratitude, Hester," in rather a dejected tone of voice.

SATURDAY 2ND MARCH

Receive a letter from Bryan who is at a preparatory school in Buckinghamshire. He says:

"My dear Mum, How are you getting on? I bet Dad will give the Germans beans. There was an air raid signal and Old Parker made us go down to the seller and then there was not an air raid after all, but we missed Latin so I was not sorry I can tell you and very few people were sorry. My marks are not so good this weak but I got 2 more for French than Edgeburton. Need I go on learning German because it is a horrid langwidge anyhow, but you will have to write to

old Parker and tell him because he would not beleive me.
How am I coming home I mean am I coming home by train
or how, you choose. Can I have 2 bob because Wonky is
leaving and all the people are giving her a present and I have
not got any money left except sixpence which is not ennough
and anyhow I owe fourpence of it to Edgeburton. Did Dad
take his sword? Edgeburton's father left it behind on purpose
because you do not get near ennough for swords. Edgeburton's
father is in the imagino line so why can't I know where my
father is? Some of the people have got colds but mine is better.
We found a baby pluvver and it was half dead so we brought it
back and put it in a barskit near the hot pipes and we gave
it some bread and milk and we thought it was O.K. but when
we came down in the morning it was dead. Mr. Fane says it
is very difficult to reer wild birds in capptivity so it would have
died anyhow. Love from Bryan.

P.S. Its a pitty I am not 9 years older because the war will
be over and I dont suppose I will ever have a chance of fighting the Germans which is a pitty because it would be grand
fun."

Grace arrives immediately after breakfast and is shown into
the drawing room, where I am hard at work answering Bryan's
letter, and trying to decide whether or not he is to continue
his study of the German language. Grace walks in with an
air of tragedy and announces that she has not slept a wink
for three nights. I try to appear suitably shocked and horrified,
but find it somewhat difficult, because Grace looks so extremely
fit and fresh that the statement is hard to believe.

"It's quite true," says Grace earnestly. "I lay awake for at
least an hour thinking about you and wishing I had not
said it."

"Said what?" I enquire in amazement.

"You needn't pretend," says Grace, shaking her head gravely. "You needn't pretend you didn't hear what I said. It was simply beastly of me after all you've done for me . . . and just because you didn't want to come to dinner and help me with the balloon man. . . . I told Jack and he said I had better come and apologise."

I realise now what it is all about and am able to assure Grace quite truthfully that I have never given her words a thought. She looks a little taken aback at this, and says, "That's all right, then"; but apparently it is not all right, but very much all wrong, and I become aware that Grace is annoyed with me for not being upset. It is all extremely silly, and at last I lose patience with her and take her by the shoulders and shake her gently and tell her not to be a goose. She didn't mean to be unkind, and therefore her casual words were nothing to bother about, and she knows quite well that we are the best of friends and understand each other's ways.

Grace smiles and agrees that of course we are and do, and adds that I am a perfect saint to bear with her.

We chat for a little about various matters and I show her Bryan's letter, of which I am somewhat proud. Grace says the letter is perfectly sweet and she is looking forward to the time when Ian will write letters to her from his prep. school. She is quite sure that Ian will write beautiful letters. Good handwriting is so important. She is going to make a special point and have Ian taught to write well.

I remove Bryan's scrawl from her clutches and reply that of course she should do so, and that Bryan used to write much better (his handwriting has degenerated in the most extraordinary way) and his spelling is disgraceful for his age, but what really matters to me is the gist of his letters: they are full of news and so like himself that they bring Bryan before my eyes so vividly that I could weep.

Grace says, "Darling! There I go again. I didn't mean to be catty a bit . . . I do really and truly think it's a sweet letter. It's just because I say things without thinking, and because I'm thinking so much about Ian just now . . . and if Ian is as nice as Bryan when he is eleven, I shall be perfectly satisfied."

This is indeed *amende honorable* and I am propitiated.

Grace takes the letter again and reads it more carefully, and repeats that it really *is* sweet. She likes the bit about the "pluvver", because it shows that boys are not naturally cruel nowadays. She thinks this fact augurs well for peace in the Future.

I agree somewhat doubtfully and forbear to draw her attention to Bryan's postscript.

Grace now becomes very serious and says isn't the War horrible, and do I think it is right for her to bring an Innocent Child into the World when the World is in this terrible condition. She was talking to Jack about it last night, but Jack did not seem to understand. As the innocent child is due to arrive in the world at any moment I feel that it is too late for anything to be done about it, and that he (or possibly she) will just have to make the best of it. Grace says that I don't seem to understand either. Sometimes she feels as if she couldn't bear the wickedness of it all another minute. . . . Her eyes are full of tears and I realise that she must be comforted, so I proceed to explain my own particular method of "carrying on". None of us could bear the war if we allowed ourselves to brood upon the wickedness of it and the misery it has entailed, so the only thing to do is not to allow oneself to think about it seriously, but just to skitter about on the surface of life like a waterbeetle. In this way one can carry on and do one's bit and remain moderately cheerful.

Grace says, "That seems rather a cowardly way of bearing things."

I agree that it may be cowardly, but it is the only way for me. It would do no good if I were to think seriously about the war, and it would do me a lot of harm; and I add that my family would suffer if I became a raving lunatic.

Grace looks thoughtful and says there's something in it. She wondered how I was able to behave in my usual cheerful manner and now she understands.

TUESDAY 5TH MARCH

A letter arrives from Tim. I pounce upon it with delight and tear it open, for this is his first letter from overseas. He says that he has arrived safely "Somewhere in France" and has been allotted a comfortable billet. "The Battalion is in good fettle"; continues Tim, "all the men fit and cheerful. Old Frankie is in tremendous form. He throws his weight about a good deal, but I must say he Gets Things Done. It is quite amazing, because he used to be such an old woman, terrified of the Powers That Be, and unwilling to shoulder responsibility. Everyone thought he would be quite hopeless to command the Battalion in war. It just shows that you never can tell. The old boy was quite nice to me when I arrived—everyone was, really, and it was good to see Preston again. We hadn't met since that time at Cawnpore. I got a parcel from Aunt Ethel containing unwearable socks and unsmokable cigarettes—fortunately my batman will wear or smoke anything. I have written to Aunt E. thanking her as warmly as I am able. If you have time you might go and see Mrs. Craven and tell her that I saw Craven in hospital. He had appendicitis, but has been operated on and is doing splendidly. He is being promoted and will make an excellent R.S.M. You can tell Mrs. C. if you like."

I decide to go down to the Barracks and see Mrs. Craven at once. She is an old friend—we have followed the drum together for years—and it is always pleasant to be the bearer of good news. Mrs. Craven's quarters are at the end of the row and I pass the time of day with several other women as I go along. They are all anxious for news of the Battalion. Mrs. Craven is busy dressmaking. I can hear her sewing machine buzzing as I knock on her door. She welcomes me warmly and is delighted at my news. Her kitchen is not as neat as usual and she apologises for "the bits and snippets" which are strewed about and explains that her daughter is being married on Tuesday, and that she is making herself a dress to wear at the ceremony. Am amazed to hear that Miriam is old enough to be married—I have not seen her for some time, but my recollection of her as a small peaky child with pigtails is perfectly clear—but Mrs. Craven says, "Aweel, she was set on it."

This speech sounds a trifle lukewarm and I enquire whether Mrs. Craven is pleased with the match.

She replies, "Och, aye, he's nice enough."

"Is everything all right?" I ask, doubtfully.

"Och, aye," says Mrs. Craven.

In spite of her words I have a strong feeling that everything is not all right. "You aren't worrying about your husband, are you?" I enquire. "He's getting on splendidly—Major Christie says so."

"Na, na," says Mrs. Craven. "I'm not worrying aboot *him*. He aye falls on his feet, does John. I'm real pleased he's got his promotion too."

"Well, what *are* you worrying about? Is there anything that I can do about it?"

"Och, it's just naething."

"Is it something about the wedding?"

"Na, na, we've fixed everything fine. We've fixed aboot the cake and all. It's all fixed."

"That's splendid!"

"Aye, and she's got a real nice dress. It's yon new colour, a sort o' greeny blue wi' a white collar on it."

"Lovely!"

"Aye, she looks real nice in it."

"You aren't worried about Miriam, are you?"

"Weel, maybe I am a wee bit pit oot . . . but it's naething."

"What is it? Do tell me, Mrs. Craven."

"It's naething *serious*," declares Mrs. Craven earnestly. "It's just that Miriam's taken an awfu' scunner at the man."

WEDNESDAY 6TH MARCH

I am doing my morning shopping and run into Mrs. Benson coming out of Simpson's. She is wearing a new hat—brick red and extremely modish—which does not suit her at all. In fact she looks so old and tired and dejected that my heart melts towards her and the hat seems pathetic rather than ludicrous. Mrs. Benson asks whether I have heard from Tim since he joined the Battalion and on being informed that I received a letter yesterday she enquires eagerly whether Tim "happened to mention the colonel". I have read Tim's letter so often that I know the contents by heart and am able to reply immediately that Tim *did* mention the colonel and said that he was extremely well and cheerful and that it was a great advantage to have such a capable C.O.

Mrs. Benson says, "Very nice indeed," and smiles quite amiably. She enquires for Bryan and Betty and asks if I will bring the latter to tea with her this afternoon. The invitation is rather a shock, for I am aware that Betty is never at her best with the colonel's wife—I remember the occasion of their last meeting and my heart sinks into my shoes. Fortunately, however, I remember that today is Wednesday and that Betty's dancing class is held this afternoon, so I am able to refuse the invitation with conviction.

Mrs. Benson says, "What a pity, I haven't seen the dear child for a long time. Is she still as shy as ever?"

This question is difficult to answer for Betty is not, and never was, shy. Her apparent bashfulness in Mrs. Benson's presence is due to dislike and disapproval. (I am now in the position of the unfortunate man who was asked whether he had left off beating his wife). I review the situation hastily and decide that it is much better for Mrs. Benson to remain in ignorance of my daughter's real feelings, and I am about to reply accordingly, when Mrs. Benson relieves me of the necessity to reply at all.

"Well never mind, it can't be helped," says Mrs. Benson. "You must just come yourself, Hester. Tea is at four o'clock, and we can have a nice little chat," and with that she disappears into Boots before I can think of an adequate excuse.

Am just getting ready for the ordeal when Grace appears and announces that she has come to tea with me and to be cheered up. She is feeling extremely low and I am the only person who can cheer her. Reply that I would willingly cheer and sustain her with tea and conversation, if I were not trysted to tea with Mrs. Benson.

Grace exclaims, "Mrs. Benson!" in tones of horror and disgust.

I endeavour to rouse Grace's better feelings by saying that the poor old thing is unhappy and requires cheering every bit as much as *she* does, to which Grace replies with a rude word. Try to look shocked, but am obliged to laugh.

We walk down the street together and part at Mrs. Benson's gate with regret.

Find a tall dark woman having tea with Mrs. Benson. She is clad in a loose brown garment and is hung about with Egyptian jewellery. Am introduced to her and discover that her name is Miss Browne Winters. She looks at me with an intent gaze and announces that we have met before. Am about to reply that I do not think I have had that pleasure when she continues that I may not remember but she remembers perfectly, it was in Toledo in the year twelve hundred and fifty-two. Begin to wonder whether Miss Browne Winters has escaped from the local lunatic asylum.

"Some Souls have little or no recollection of previous existence," declares Miss Browne Winters in bell-like tones, "but that need not necessarily indicate that they are New Souls. Sometimes a Soul, wrapped too closely in the meshes of the Present, loses contact with the Central Stream. One feels sorry for such a Soul for in losing such Contact, it loses the Best."

Feel inclined to reply that one life is about all I can cope with, and that sometimes even one life is a little too much, but Miss Browne Winters is so awe-inspiring that the words die upon my lips.

Mrs. Benson then enquires as to the circumstances of our meeting and Miss Browne Winters, who has been awaiting this question, replies that she was Alphonso X, surnamed the Wise and that, amongst other activities too numerous to mention, she improved the Ptolomaic Planetary Tables. I then ask whether I helped her in this great and useful work, and she replies that I was not far enough advanced, but was merely one of her mother's women. "Yes," says Miss Browne Winters, assuming a positively Delphian manner and drawing her long thin fingers across her eyes. "Yes, I remember it all . . . it is coming back clearly. I was interested in you for a time, but only in a temporal and superficial way. There has never been any Real Spiritual Bond between us."

Mrs. Benson looks a trifle alarmed, (perhaps she is afraid that her remarkable guest is about to define the nature of the temporal bond which existed between Alphonso X and his mother's handmaid) and she plunges into the conversation somewhat clumsily, "But it was the Great Pyramid you were talking about," she exclaims.

"Ah yes, the Great Pyramid!" agrees Miss Browne Winters. "That Marvellous Monument of Antiquity!"

"You were telling me about it," Mrs. Benson reminds her, and adds for my benefit, "Miss Browne Winters knows *all about* the Great Pyramid."

This seems rather a large order, but Miss Browne Winters does not disclaim her knowledge; she smiles a trifle wearily and says, "Ah yes, the Great Pyramid. Who should know more about it than I?"

"Were you there when it was built?" I enquire, for this seems the most likely explanation of her omniscience.

"I was there," she replies. "In fact I helped in the building of it. My duty was to measure the stones before they were put in place. How vividly I remembered it all when my father and I were in Egypt last year! How strange it was to lay my hand on a stone and to remember the placing of it! So vivid were my recollections that sometimes I had difficulty in coming back to the present . . . the Present was overlaid by the Past. My father became quite anxious about me and would not allow me out of his sight." Miss Browne Winters laughs and adds apologetically, "He was afraid I might Go Back."

Miss Browne Winters continues for some time in this strain, and builds up a picture of herself wandering about beneath a burning sun, living two lives at the same time, her unfortunate parent trailing after her. . . .

Eventually Miss Browne Winters says she must go. She rises and pronounces some words in a foreign language and declares that it is an Arabic blessing and means "May Allah protect you and give you children, numbered as the desert sands."— Feel that some other blessing might have been more suitable for Mrs. Benson and myself, as Mrs. Benson is too old to start a family of such proportions, and I find my family of two more than enough to feed, clothe and educate.

When she has gone, the conversation descends to lower levels, in fact it descends very low indeed. Mrs. Benson says that Miss Browne Winters is an interesting woman, but somewhat tiring, and now we can have a nice chat. She saw me with young Mrs. MacDougall the other day—how kind it is of me to take an interest in her, as, of course, we can have nothing in common!

Am aware that Mrs. Benson does not mean what she says, but something quite different and rather nasty.

"It is such a pity," continues Mrs. Benson, "such a pity when a young and promising officer like Jack MacDougall gets caught by a woman like that . . . No, don't interrupt, Hester, I know how loyal you are, but you and I, who have the Interests of the Regiment so much at heart, can discuss these things quite calmly."

I am feeling far from calm—in fact I am seething—and as I can find no effective rejoinder, I offer the bald statement that Grace is my friend. Mrs. Benson takes no notice of this, but proceeds to give me a resumé of Jack's history, qualifications, and parentage. His father commanded the Regiment and was "a dear friend of Colonel Benson's"; his mother was one of the Sinclairs of Auchenduchan; and his grandfather—a particularly fine man—was also in the Regiment and won his D.S.O. in South Africa . . . "Jack had the ball at his feet and he threw it away," declares Mrs. Benson sorrowfully.

(Feel that Jack should really have kicked the ball, but manage to refrain from saying so.)

"Sad!" says Mrs. Benson. "Very sad indeed. I have been talking to Colonel Carter about it and he agrees . . . he has promised to do what he can for Jack, to get him out of the rut, and give him an opportunity to show what he is made of."

This sounds somewhat sinister, and I feel bound to enquire what sort of opportunity Jack is to be given. Mrs. Benson says it is not our business to interfere, and that Colonel Carter is quite capable of running the depot without advice from anyone.

Once again Mrs. Benson's words convey an opposite meaning. She has been interfering—or trying to interfere. She has been "getting at" Herbert Carter and urging him to send Jack to France—and for all I know she may have succeeded in her endeavour. Soldiers are soldiers, of course, and must go where they are sent, but it would be cruel to send Jack *now,* with the baby due to arrive at any moment. If the 1st Battalion needs a captain, it is within Herbert Carter's power to send whom he pleases . . . and I can scarcely believe that Herbert who is a kindhearted creature (though admittedly a trifle flabby) would think of sending Jack . . .

Am so busy with these thoughts that I lose the drift of Mrs. Benson's conversation and come to myself to find her gazing at me with a baleful expression and obviously awaiting a reply.

"It is a bad habit to allow one's thoughts to wander," says Mrs. Benson firmly. "A very bad habit indeed, and one that is apt to grow upon one unless it is checked."

THURSDAY 7TH MARCH

Spend a miserable night endeavouring to weigh up Herbert Carter's character—his kind heart against his undoubted flaccidity. Dawn breaks and confirms my decision that Something Must Be Done. I hurry Betty off to school, rush down to the Barracks and demand to see the C.O. on urgent business. The Orderly Room Sergeant is a personal friend of mine, so I experience no difficulty in penetrating the defences. Herbert obviously is surprised to see me, but he invites me to be seated and asks what he can do for me. Somehow or other Herbert seems quite different from his usual genial self, much more dignified and unapproachable. I remember that he is the C.O., that he is commanding a large body of troops and that his responsibilities must be enormous. My courage ebbs rapidly.

Herbert says, "Come on Hester. What is it? You aren't frightened of me, are you?"

I reply, "Yes, I'm terrified. You're so grand and important, Herbert."

At this Herbert laughs and says that sometimes he is quite frightened of himself, and it's a funny world.

The ice thus broken I take the plunge and explain that I *had* to see him because there are rumours of Jack MacDougall being sent abroad, but that I hope he won't have to go until after the baby has arrived.

Herbert looks rather taken aback and says, "How on earth did you hear that?" But I am not to be drawn and reply firmly that it does not matter how I heard it as long as it isn't true.

"Are you sure he doesn't want to go?" asks Herbert.

To which I reply "Would you have wanted to go and leave Mamie to have her first baby?"

Herbert says, "No, of course not . . . and as a matter of fact I didn't intend to send Jack. They want a captain and a subaltern and I meant to send Wilson and Taylor. Then I happened to hear from—from a reliable source that Jack was anxious to go." He hesitates for a moment and then continues, "You know, Hester, it's not a bad thing for a young fellow to see some active service . . . Jack is a professional soldier and he's keen and ambitious."

I am aware that all this is true. Tim was pleased when he received his orders. He was sorry to leave me, but he wanted to go—he was as excited as a child going to its first party.

"Not now," I say, and I find the greatest difficulty in saying it, for there is a lump in my throat which feels like a golf ball.

"Well, perhaps not . . ." says Herbert doubtfully

I am hesitating whether to leave it at that or to drive home my advantage, when Herbert goes on, "It's very difficult for me. I want you to understand that."

"You can do what you like," I point out.

He smiles and replies, "Just imagine yourself in my shoes, Hester. The 1st Battalion asks for two officers and I've got to decide who's to go. Sometimes the choice is obvious—in Tim's case he was the only major available—but more often the choice lies between two or three fellows. I've got to decide. In one way they all want to go, and in another way none of them wants to . . . it isn't easy."

My anger is melting now; I can feel it running out like thawed snow.

He leans forward and continues, "So you see when Mrs. Benson said she happened to know that Jack was longing for Active Service . . ."

"So it *was* Mrs. Benson!" I exclaim.

"Well . . . in a way . . ." says Herbert uncomfortably. "I

happened to meet her, you see, and—and she happened to say . . . and so I thought . . . but of course I don't really let her interfere. You mustn't think that. Of course we've got used to—er—thinking of her as the colonel's wife, and—Oh curse it, you know what the old lady is like."

Yes, I know what she is like, but unfortunately the only word which describes her must not be allowed to pass my lips. I extricate myself from Herbert's presence and walk home boiling with rage.

FRIDAY 8TH MARCH

I awake suddenly in the early hours of the morning and hear the horrible moaning of the Donford siren. The sound chills my blood, and, for a moment, I find myself incapable of movement. Then I pull myself together, leap out of bed, and rush round the house waking its inhabitants. This is our first night alarm, and I am not at all sure how my household will take it, but I find that I need not have worried. Everyone is perfectly calm. Annie has Betty up and dressed in half no time and Mrs. Fraser emerges from her room clad in a siren suit of enormous proportions and with her head swathed in a pink woollen scarf. We have already agreed that the brush cupboard (which is large and commodious and is situated under the stairs) is to be our Shelter. The brushes are flung out and rugs and cushions are fetched. Mrs. Fraser says that the windows in the house should be "opened a wee bit" and comes round to help me in the task.

All is now ready, and we go into the brush cupboard and sit down.

"We should have had it *done*," says Mrs. Fraser. "We should have been prepared. It's a daft-like thing not to be prepared."

Annie agrees and says she will scrub out the cupboard tomorrow.

Mrs. Fraser says that will be fine, and the brushes can be kept in the kitchen cupboard. She will make room for them.

I pinch my leg to see whether I am dreaming. Is this really Hester Christie sitting in the brush-cupboard in the middle of the night, waiting for a bomb to fall? The pinch hurts quite a lot, so I am forced to believe that I am awake. I look round at my companions and feel a strange impulse to laugh, but manage to stifle it at birth.

We chat about various matters in a friendly manner. I have never liked Mrs. Fraser very much, and have been under the impression that Mrs. Fraser disliked me, but tonight I positively love the woman. She sits there, looking like something out of the Arabian Nights in her siren suit and her pink-swathed head, but she is as calm and as firm as a rock. After about half an hour, during which nothing whatever can be heard, Mrs. Fraser announces that she is going to infuse tea—Hitler or no—and we can just wait there till she brings it. I remonstrate with her, but without success. I feel that I ought to go with her and share the dangers of the kitchen, but Annie and Betty do not want to be left. Presently Mrs. Fraser returns with a tray of tea and biscuits and says she went out and had a look round, but there's nothing to be seen.

Betty remarks in a disappointed tone, "Perhaps they aren't coming after all!"

She has scarcely spoken when we hear several dull thumps. It is a strange sound, for, although the thumps are not very loud, the house seems to shake slightly. It reminds me of an earthquake which occurred when Tim and I were in India.

Betty says, "What's that?" and Mrs. Fraser replies that it is the kitchen door banging.

"But didn't you shut it?" enquires Betty.

"How could I?" says Mrs. Fraser. "I was carrying the tray and I've not got three hands on me."

This intrigues Betty and she asks whether Mrs. Fraser would *like* to have three hands, to which Mrs. Fraser replies in the affirmative.

Betty says what would she *do* with three hands.

Mrs. Fraser says, "There's whiles I could do with six hands. They would be gey useful when I'm dishing up the dinner."

We now hear two more thumps, slightly louder than before, and Betty (who is no fool) says that *she* thinks they are bombs, and can she go out and see if there are any German aeroplanes about.

Everyone replies in chorus that she must remain where she is.

Nothing more happens and in another half hour the "All Clear" signal is heard and we all go back to bed. Betty is in great form and I can hear her asking Annie whether we can have another "Siren Party" soon.

Annie calls me at the usual hour and I arise feeling as if I had had no sleep at all. Decide to let Betty sleep as long as possible—Annie agrees with this. I enquire whether Annie has heard whether any damage has been done, but everyone seems to be late this morning—even the butcher's boy—so no news of the raid has come to Winfield.

While I am having breakfast the telephone bell rings loudly, and Annie comes in with eyes like saucers, and says, "It's Captain MacDougall, and will you come at once and speak to him."

I ask Annie what is the matter and she replies that she doesn't know, but Captain MacDougall said it was very important and she thinks it is the Germans. She adds that the milk hasn't come, nor the post neither . . . she wonders what has happened. . . .

I rush to the telephone and clamp the receiver to my ear and murmur "Hullo!" in trembling tones.

Jack's voice sounds distraught, he says it has been an awful night; he hasn't been to bed at all; he thought at one time it was all up; nobody knows what it's been like.

I have visions of German Soldiers, landing on the coast, and enquire in still more tremulous accents how far they have got.

Jack says, "They're here. It happened at five o'clock this morning. Of course we were prepared in a way, but I never thought it would be so frightful. Grace has been marvellous. . . ."

Am now so terrified that my knees give way altogether and I sink down on to the floor still clutching the telephone and pressing it against my ear.

Jack says, "Are you still there, Hester? Oh, I thought perhaps they had cut us off. You heard the bombs, of course . . . yes, that was the beginning of it. You had better come round here and stay with Grace. I've got to go to the Barracks at once."

This is impossible, of course, for my first duty is to my own children, and their safety is my paramount concern. I point this out to Jack and add that if only I could get Betty to a place of safety I am prepared to remain with Grace and sell my life as dearly as possible. I have two shot guns and a small revolver and ammunition for a prolonged siege. . . .

Jack says, "I don't know what on earth you are talking about."

I reply, "The Germans of course. You said they had landed."

Jack says, "Good Lord, it isn't the Germans; it's twins."

"Twins!" I echo incredulously.

"Yes," says Jack, "Yes, *twins*. I thought Grace was going to

die. I was terrified. It's been the most ghastly night. I don't
know why people ever *have* children, it's wicked—positively
wicked."

I pull myself together and endeavour to readjust my outlook
. . . but somehow or other it isn't easy . . . Jack is still hav-
ering at the other end of the line. I can hear him saying that
Ian arrived about five o'clock in the morning and his brother
followed him into the world about twenty minutes later; the
doctor and nurse were both there in plenty of time and showed
no signs of anxiety—"Absolutely heartless, both of them," declares Jack indignantly.

I sympathise with him and say that I will go round and see
Grace shortly.

"Yes," says Jack, "yes, you had better come *at once*. I don't
know what they are playing at. The doctor has gone home, the
nurse is wolfing bacon and eggs in the dining room, and the
twins are bawling their heads off. The whole house is topsy-
turvy. It's driving me mad . . ."

Find Grace lying in bed surrounded by masses of flowers
which Jack has ordered on his way to the Barracks. Grace
is looking remarkably well—all things considered—and seems
comfortable and cheerful; she says she is delighted to have
twins because they will be such nice companions for each
other. They will do everything together, of course. The only
thing that worries her is that she does not see how she and
Jack can possibly afford to send them both to Eton . . . and it
would never do to send one and not the other.

I suggest that she should leave the future to look after itself.

Grace says she *likes* thinking about the future and making
plans—even if the plans don't come off—and perhaps if Jack's
old aunt dies in time they will be able to manage it all right.
The old aunt is "over ninety and quite queer", so Grace
does not feel that it is wrong to envisage her end.

Ian and his brother are now displayed by the proud nurse. They are exceedingly small, but seem quite lusty. Nurse says, "Aren't they pets, Mrs. Christie?" I agree that they are.

Grace says she thinks she will call the second one Alec . . . "Ian and Alec," says Grace dreamily, "My boys, Ian and Alec!"

I suggest that I must go now, but Grace says she must tell me about her dream—it was a lovely dream. She dreamt that she was walking across the field at Lords with the two boys, one on each side of her. She was wearing a new frock with pale blue ribbons, and they were in Etons with lovely shiny top hats—they looked adorable.

Nurse now interferes and says that Grace must have a nice sleep, so I depart, but am called back and given a list of things which are wanted for the twins. Nurse follows me out to the door reiterating requests for Johnson & Johnson's Baby Powder and the best olive oil.

Enquire, a trifle fretfully, why these things are not already in the house, to which Nurse replies, "Well, they *did* come a bit before time. It was the siren did it, and the fuss of getting up, and then the bombs. Have you heard where the bombs fell, Mrs. Christie?"

Reply that I have had no time to ask anyone.

Nurse says, "Well, it was the Vegetable Man told *me*. He said the first lot were on the shore, and the second lot on the golf course. He said one of them fell just in the very place where the committee had marked out a new bunker. It's saved the club three hundred pounds, the Vegetable Man said . . . not that I believe all I hear, do you, Mrs. Christie?"

MONDAY IITH MARCH

Am sitting by the fire feeling somewhat blue when The Child is shown in. The Child is an extremely large subaltern with extremely large and innocent brown eyes. His correct name is William Taylor, and some of his intimates call him "Bill".

The Child says he has received a letter from Tubby Baxter and he thought I might like to hear what Tubby says about the Major, and that's why he came. I assure him that I am delighted to see him, and that it was a very kind thought.

"Well, here's the letter," says my visitor, "You can't read it of course, because . . . well . . . because you can't. I'll read bits of it to you." He produces a bulky epistle, spreads it out and clears his throat importantly.

" 'My dear Bill, How are you, you old—er—. I am in quite decent digs and the Mess is O.K. A French cook and fizz practically ad lib. So far so good and it—er—makes your—er—mouth water—but there are some pretty large flies in the—er—ointment. You say you want Active Service—well, you ought to be here. We are active all right, digging like—er—er—moles but haven't seen much of the—er—Boche so far. It's funny how this sort of show affects people and shows them up for what they are. People that one thought were no—er—use are doing splendidly and people that one thought were absolutely O.K. are—er—er—awful.' "

Bill pauses to straighten out the paper and remarks that Tubby's handwriting is difficult to read, but we are coming to the interesting bit soon. I assure him that I am finding it *all* most interesting, especially the bits that he does not read, and add that I can fill them in for myself with the greatest of ease. Bill says he bets I can't, and continues as follows.

" 'Major Tim has arrived and seems in great form, everyone is—er—er—pleased to see him except the—er—shirkers. They know they'll get his boot—er—er and serve them—er—right. It was about time someone gave them—er—er. Talking of girls'

—no, you wouldn't be interested in that, I'll go on to the next bit."

I assure Bill that I shall be most interested in Tubby's reaction to Mademoiselle, but Bill says "No," quite firmly, and turns over the page.

"This bit is all about the Colonel," says Bill, smiling to himself. "The old boy seems to be having a pretty good time now that he has managed to get away from old Mrs. B. I don't wonder either; Loo is a bit stultifying, isn't she?"

I enquire what Tubby says about the Colonel, and Bill replies, "I've told you most of it," which is palpably untrue. The only other piece of news I can extract from Bill is that "the old boy sings in his bath".

"That's about all," says Bill, "except for the Limerick—there are two, really, but one of them is a bit—er—silly."

Tubby Baxter is the Regimental poet, and sometimes shows a neat turn of phrase, so I am all ears for the Limerick, which runs as follows:

" 'There *was* a gay Colonel called Benson,
Who said, "Now you chaps; pay attention;
If Loo comes to Vimy
Please don't let her see me,
But just have her put in detention." ' "

"Rather neat, isn't it?" says Bill, chuckling. "Of course you have to say 'Benshon' to make it rhyme; but I daresay there isn't much difficulty in that if fizz flows like water," adds Bill reflectively.

Having given me all the news, Bill folds up the letter and stows it away carefully. There is an uncomfortable pause, and I look at him and note that he is sitting on the very edge of his chair and twisting one of the buttons on his tunic, as if his one aim in life were to tear it from its moorings.

Bill is usually a very self-possessed sort of person and—as I have reason to know—full of initiative and resource, so I am quite astonished at this sudden attack of nerves. I ply him with encouraging conversation, but he answers in monosyllables; I offer him a drink, but he refuses. At last I come to the end of my patience and demand point blank what is the matter with him, whereupon he swallows nervously several times and says, "You know the Bradshaws?"

I reply that I do. The Bradshaws live at Hythe and keep open house for the Army. They were exceedingly kind to us when we were stationed there. As I am aware that Bill has been at Hythe quite recently, indulging in a Small Arms Course, I put two and two together and arrive at the obvious conclusion. I enquire how Elinor Bradshaw is getting on, and whether she is doing anything warlike.

"No," says Bill, "she seemed all right. It wasn't *her* exactly. I mean, of course, I saw her too . . ."

"Who was it then?" I enquire patiently.

Bill leans forward, picks up the poker and proceeds to demolish my fire. (As it is obvious that he is upset and therefore not responsible for his actions, I endeavour to bear the calamity with all the fortitude at my command.) "It's Pinkie," says Bill, poking fiercely. "It's Pinkie . . . you know . . . the niece . . . she lives there. She said she knew you."

Do I know Pinkie? Yes, I remember her now—Elinor's niece from India, a small mousy child with thin legs and lank hair and a gold band across her front teeth. Poor little Pinkie, of course I remember her.

"I thought perhaps you might ask her to stay with you," says Bill, gritting out the amazing request through clenched teeth.

"You thought what?" I demand, unable to believe my ears.

"Well, I just wondered . . ." says Bill miserably. "You're

always so sporting, Mrs. Tim, and there isn't anyone else. She's staying with a schoolfriend at Perth—and—well—she could easily come over here for a few days. I could fetch her if it came to that. She hasn't anywhere else to go, so she would just have to go home unless . . . and—well, I just wondered . . ." He drivels on in this strain until I interrupt him by asking what on earth I should do with the girl if she came here. She is too old to play with Betty.

Bill agrees, but says that he thought perhaps I might be feeling dull and Pinkie would cheer me up.

"Why isn't she at school?" I enquire.

Bill says she *was* at school in Paris, but of course they brought her home and it is frightfully dull for her at Hythe, so won't I please ask her, if only for a weekend, because she talked about me a lot and he knows she would like to come and he is quite sure she won't be a bother. The conversation continues for some time and eventually my resistance is worn down, and I agree to write to Pinkie and invite her . . . I agree chiefly because I am certain that she will not come.

"Oh, Mrs. Tim, you *are* sporting," declares Bill beaming at me gratefully. "Oh, Mrs. Tim, will you write the letter *now,* and I'll post it on my way back to the Barracks."

I write the letter with Bill breathing heavily down the back of my neck and he departs with the precious missive in his pocket.

WEDNESDAY 13TH MARCH

I arrive at the Mob. Store, one corner of which has been partitioned off, and here the "Comforts" for the Troops are collected and despatched. In theory the officers' wives take it in turn to perform the necessary duties, but in practice it works out differently. Mamie Carter is to be my sole companion this morning, for Grace is exempt at present, and Stella and Evie have telephoned to say that they are in bed with colds.

Mamie is seated by the stove, smoking a cigarette (which is contrary to regulations), she says there were so many parcels to open that she did not know where to begin. I look at the pile of parcels and realise that I shall probably be there all day. Enquire whether Mamie would prefer to open parcels or write out receipts, whereupon she replies that she would rather write out receipts, but she has not brought her spectacles, so she supposes she had better open parcels. She adds that both Stella and Evie were at the pictures last night—she saw them with her own eyes—so it's nonsense to say they can't come and help us with the "Comforts"; and Herbert is having a few hours' leave this afternoon, so *she* won't be able to stay very long. If anyone had a good excuse for not turning up this morning it is *she* (continues Mamie) because Baby is teething, but *she* isn't the sort of person to let other people down.

By this time I have opened two parcels and written out the forms which we despatch to donors. Mamie lights another cigarette and says, "Oh dear, more socks! Why can't people send gloves or helmets?"

Am about to reply somewhat tartly when the door opens and Tony Morley walks in. He seems surprised to see us and says he is looking for the Quarty and *is* this the Mob. Store, or isn't it. I assure him that it is, and explain that we are allowed to use it for "Comforts".

Mamie gets up and gushes at him, but Tony hates being gushed at; he asks what she is supposed to be doing, and advises her to get on with her job (Strangely enough Tony seems to be able to say these things without giving mortal offence). Then he comes over to the table and picks up a sock and says, "Who made that? Is it intended for Fan M'Kool?" I enquire who Fan M'Kool may be, and Tony replies that he was an Irish giant who lived in the 18th century and was in the habit of eating a whole sheep for his breakfast. Tony then tries on a helmet and a pullover, and surveys himself as best he can in the cracked mirror which hangs over the stove and has "Schweppes Tonic Water" written across it in blue letters. He seems quite pleased with his appearance, so I tell him that he may have the garments if he likes, whereupon he removes them as though they were red hot.

Mamie asks him how he is getting on and whether he likes his Battalion, and Tony replies that the men are grand stuff, but completely raw, and he would give a thousand pounds for a couple of N.C.O's. who really knew their job.

"How long will it take you to train them?" enquires Mamie, looking at him with large and innocent eyes.

Tony opens his eyes wide too, and replies that if Mamie will give him five years, he guarantees to make the Grenadiers look like a Sunday School Treat . . . "Five years," says Tony thoughtfully, "Yes, I could *just* do it. The last six months would be the worst, because we should be practising the hollow square."

I suggest that the hollow square is an obsolete formation, but Tony says it is obsolete only because of its difficulty. *He* will use it for Drum Head Courts Martial, and it will be the very thing for Hitler's trial.

Mamie is completely bewildered at all this (she does not know Tony as well as I do). "Five years!" she murmurs in horrified tones, "but surely the war will be over long before that!"

"Oh yes," agrees Tony. *"This* war will be over, of course, but my Battalion will be ready for the next war—the war of 1945—unless by some unhappy chance it is disbanded by the Peace Treaty."

I enquire, somewhat pointedly, whether the Battalion is capable of training itself, to which Tony replies, "Dash it all, Hester, d'you want to get rid of me? I'm waiting to see the Quarty. I want to wangle some stuff out of him. I *told* you . . ."

At this moment the door opens and a small thin woman with a brightly painted face peeps in. We all look at her in surprise, and then at each other . . . none of us knows her.

"Is this the place I'm looking for?" she asks.

Tony, who is never at a loss, replies that it all depends upon what place she is looking for. If she is looking for the Officers' Mess or the Headquarters of the A.T.S., this is not the place she is looking for, but if she happens to be looking for the Mob. Store, this is it. Far from being dashed, the woman brightens and bridles, and, opening the door wider, she comes in, showing herself to be attired (to match her face) in brightest pink and crimson.

"This *is* the place," she declares. "Ha, ha, I can see wool! I want to make socks for the dear soldiers. Everyone should do their bit, shouldn't they?"

Mamie asks whether she is connected with the Barracks and has a pass, to which questions she replies in the negative, adding brightly that they wouldn't let her in at the big gate, so she went round to the side gate "and slipped in when the soldier wasn't looking."

Mamie exclaims, "Good Heavens!" in a scandalised voice, and Tony laughs uproariously. Mamie says to Tony (somewhat tartly) that she does not see anything to laugh at, and Tony wipes his eyes and declares that is the funniest thing he has heard since the war started, and he would give a good deal to see Herbert's face when Mamie tells him about it.

Mamie says doubtfully, "Well, he *ought* to be told," at which Tony laughs again, louder than before.

Meanwhile I am busy making up a parcel of wool for the

woman (she certainly deserves it) and I provide her with a printed leaflet describing the way in which we like our socks made. The woman reads the leaflet with the help of a lorgnette and remarks, "Oh, I see you need four needles for these."

I assure her that socks are usually made on four needles.

"Cast on twenty stitches on each of three needles," reads the woman. She looks up and adds, "That's what it says here, so I only need three needles after all!"

It takes some time to convince her that she will require four needles for her labour of love, but at last she says, "Well, I suppose you must know . . ." and takes the parcel which is now ready and prepares to go. Mamie offers to accompany her —explaining in hurried undertones that for all we know the woman may be a German Spy, and Herbert would not like her to be let loose inside the Barracks and that anyhow she (Mamie) must go now because of Herbert's half day's leave, so she may just as well walk down to the gate and see the woman safely off the premises.

It is now half past eleven and only four parcels have been opened. I explain this to Tony and suggest that he should leave me to get on with my task in peace.

Tony says, "What? You don't mean to say you've got to do all those parcels yourself! You'll be here all day . . . hold on a minute and I'll get Symes."

I enquire who Symes is, but Tony has vanished.

He returns a few moments later with a tall young man in battle dress, whom he delivers over into my keeping with a few words of explanation. "This is Symes," says Tony. "I've got to go now, or I would give you a hand myself, but I'll lend you Symes. He's my batman and driver and a most useful chap . . . You'll give Mrs. Christie a hand, won't you, Symes? . . . That's right . . . Symes will see you through."

Having been used to regular soldiers I feel a little doubtful whether Symes—for all his apparent keenness—will be of much service to me, but after a few moments conversation I discover that in private life Symes works in the packing room in a large London store. I immediately take advantage of his superior experience and invite him to organise the proceedings. He organises them rapidly and efficiently. "You want method," he says. "You want everything set out in its proper place before you begin. You want the table cleared . . . I'll put it over here because the light's better . . . you sit here, Miss . . . that's right. You can enter up the ledgers and write the receipts. I'll open the parcels and count the garments."

In half no time the table is cleared and the ledgers are open, and the receipt forms are in a neat pile close to my hand.

We work away cheerfully—what a comfort it is to work with someone who knows *how* to work—I have time to glance up occasionally and see his hands flying, such dexterous hands they are. The parcels are opened, the garments sorted out into piles, and the wool which we despatch to working parties is divided up and parcelled with incredible neatness and rapidity. Symes and I are close friends by the time the job is finished. Symes has heard all about Tim and Bryan and Betty, and I have heard all about Symes's girl friend who sold stockings at Marshall and Snellgrove's, but who joined the Wrens at the outbreak of war and is now a telephonist at Portsmouth.

"Her name is Miss Ebb—Miss Gertie Ebb," says Symes gravely. "Perhaps you would like to see her photo." He produces a small photograph from his pocket, and I look at it with interest. Miss Gertie Ebb is a very nice-looking young woman with a pleasant open face.

"Pretty, isn't she?" says Symes, looking at it reflectively. "Doesn't do her justice, this doesn't—she's got a lovely skin and lovely big brown eyes."

I congratulate him warmly upon his good fortune.

"Yes," says Symes, "and it isn't only her looks. She's a little bit of all right, Gertie is. Clever and smart . . . and yet not too smart, *you* know."

When Tony returns to collect his batman, he looks round approvingly and says, "Good work! I thought Symes would see you through. You can have him for an hour every Wednesday morning if you like."

I accept this noble offer with alacrity.

THURSDAY 14TH MARCH

Betty is doing her "prep". As a rule she races through this unpalatable duty and demands a game of snakes and ladders before going to bed, but tonight she is deeply engrossed in her work. Her head is bent so low that her curls are falling over the exercise book; her feet are twisted round the legs of the chair. After some time Betty sighs deeply and looks up, "Mummy, did you like nessies when you were a little girl?" she enquires.

"Nessies?" I repeat in dubious tones.

"I like them," says Betty, nodding. "I like them awfully."

"I don't think I ever had them."

"I like them better than sums or French or spelling. I don't like spelling *at all*."

"I know, but you must learn it."

"Nessies are rather fun," says Betty, smiling to herself.

"What are they, Betty?"

"Just nessies," replies Betty. "Well, they're sort of stories, really. Miss Clark gives them to us. She said today, 'Write a nessy on *My Fav'rite Game*,' so I'm doing it." Betty giggles and adds, "D'you know what Jane said when Miss Clark said that? Jane said, 'But I don't know what your fav'rite game *is*, Miss Clark.' Wasn't Jane silly?"

"She was rather," I agree, hiding a smile, for Jane Carter is very like her mother and seems to have inherited her mother's sheeplike nature. In addition, Betty—the little wretch—has copied poor Jane's bleating tones with amazing success, and this is an entirely new accomplishment.

"Yes," says Betty, a trifle smugly, "yes, Jane *is* silly. Of course I knew what Miss Clark meant when she said that. She meant we were to write nessies on *our* fav'rite games."

Nessy is such a delightful word that I am loath to correct Betty's mistake, but I realise that it would be the act of a foolish doting mother if I allowed her to continue in error. I explain it to her carefully.

"Oh!" says Betty, wrinkling her brows, "Oh, I see. I'll have to remember that or the others would laugh. It's an essy and not a nessy . . . I don't think it's nearly so nice."

I agree that it is not, and add a request that she will refrain from sucking her pencil.

"Teddy *always* sucks it," replies Betty quickly. "His mouth is black all round whenever we have sums—and it hasn't poisoned him yet."

"You are not to suck yours," I declare firmly.

"It helps me to think . . . and I've got to think *hard* because it's got to be a whole page, you see. Would you like to read it?"

This is what I have been longing to do for the last ten minutes, so I stretch out my hand for the "nessy" without more ado.

MY FAVRITE GAME

My favrite game issunt a game at all reelly. Its playing with my bruther. I dont mind what it is. I dont mind being a horce or a wilde beast. When I am a tiga I hide in the bushes and he storks me. He can shute me two. I dont like being a bosh, but I can bare it if he lets me play. I can clime trees two. I can clime as hie as Bryan neerly. Well I can clime as hie as Atha ennyhow. Its maw fun playing with boys even if there ruff. Girls dont have to mind it if they want to play with boys and I do. Well thats my favrite game.

"D'you like it?" enquires the author eagerly. "D'you think it's a good nessy? Is the spelling right? I wrote it three times so as to get it neat. You see Miss Clark said the best nessy—I mean essy—would get a prize and I *think* it's a little pig that you blow out and it dies squeaking—a sort of tiny wee balloon-thing—I saw it on her desk. D'you think she'll think mine's the best?"

These questions are impossible to answer, for I have no idea of the standard to which Betty's form has attained. I am aware that my child is backward for her age, for this unpleasant fact has been presented to my notice by all her teachers. It is true that we have moved about from place to place in our endeavour to follow the drum, and Betty's education has suffered accordingly, but this is not the only reason for her backwardness; most of her reports point out that "Betty could do better if she tried," and that "Betty should pay more attention"; and one report lamented somewhat fretfully, "Betty does not seem able to sit still!"

"D'you like it?" enquires Betty again.

"Yes, I like it very much, but of course I don't know whether Miss Clark will like it."

"No," agrees Betty.

"The writing isn't very good, is it? You can write better than that."

"But not when I'm thinking," replies Betty promptly.

"The spelling isn't very good either."

"Oh dear!" says Betty, shaking her head. "Oh, dear, that's a pity. I s'pose it wouldn't be fair if you told me, would it?"

"Not if it is for a prize."

"No," says Betty, shaking her head again, "No, it wouldn't really. It wouldn't be *fair*. It wouldn't be fair even if you just said which of the words were wrong and I could have another try at them, I s'pose?"

"No, I'm afraid not."

"Oh well, we'll just have to leave it . . . I wonder what Jane will write about. I believe she'll write about dolls. You couldn't ring up Mrs. Carter and *ask,* could you?"

"No, I don't think I could."

"No," says Betty sadly. "No . . . well, I s'pose I'll just have to wait. I hate waiting, don't you?"

"Yes, but it's good for us to have to wait for things, some-times."

"It isn't good for me," says Betty firmly. "I mean I don't s'pose I'll sleep *all night* wond'ring about it."

Fortunately for my peace of mind I am aware that this is an empty threat, and that my daughter will fall asleep the moment her head touches the pillow, and will not stir until Annie wakens her in the morning.

MONDAY 18TH MARCH

A letter arrives from my old friend Mrs. Loudon saying that her son, Guthrie, is in hospital at Donford and will I go and see him and report upon his condition. She is in bed with a bad attack of lumbago and can't move hand or foot. I immediately put on my hat and coat and walk down to the hospital, and, after some little trouble occasioned by red tape, I am ushered into a small ward, where I discover Guthrie in bed. He wel-comes me with cries of delight which allay my anxiety a good deal. The nurse, who is red-haired and extremely pretty, places a chair for me, warns Guthrie not to get too excited, and goes away.

Guthrie says his wounds are nothing—a bullet through his leg and a splinter in his hand—and he will soon be as fit as a fiddle. He seems in excellent form and gives me a spirited account of the naval action in which he received his injuries. "It was great!" says Guthrie with shining eyes. "Gosh, it was the most exciting thing that ever happened."

"Were you frightened?" I enquire—for Guthrie and I are old and well-tried friends, and I can ask him anything—

"No-o," says Guthrie thoughtfully. "No, Hester, I wasn't exactly frightened . . . but I tell you this: it was a most awfully queer feeling when I gave the order to open fire. Somehow it seemed all wrong to fire at a real live ship with men aboard. It seemed a perfectly frightful thing to do. I'm sure the gun crews felt the same. I was standing on the deck and they looked round at me . . . I just said 'Carry on'. Once we began to get some of their stuff dropping round us, the chaps settled down to it and did simply splendidly. There was no *trouble*, you know. It was just a feeling we had . . ."

"But Guthrie . . ." I begin.

"Yes," says Guthrie smiling. "Yes, I know what you're going to say. You're going to say it was a natural feeling, a right and proper feeling. So it was, really, but we jolly well had to get over it."

"It seems so awful, Guthrie."

"All war is awful," says Guthrie. "It's a wrong and horrible thing, war is, but we don't need to worry about the rights and wrongs of war. We tried our best for peace. We tried for peace to the absolute limit of honour . . . but you can't have peace when a pack of ravening wolves gets loose . . . Let's talk about Avielochan."

I am delighted to talk about Avielochan for Betty and I

spent a holiday there with Guthrie and his mother, and enjoyed ourselves enormously, so I agree at once, and we talk about it. Guthrie says, "D'you remember the day we walked over to the laundry and got lost in the woods? What a lovely day it was! I often think of that day when I'm watch keeping;" and I reply that I remember it well, and return the ball by reminding Guthrie of the picnic at Loch Darroch when we saw the ghost.

As we talk the peaceful atmosphere of Avielochan seems to fill the bare hospital room, and once more I seem to see the upstanding hills, the placid lochs with the pine trees reflected in their bosoms, and I seem to feel the cool sweep of the hill wind, and to breathe the clear sparkling air.

Presently Guthrie asks me if I will write to his Mother for him, because his hand is swathed in bandages and he is unable to write himself, so I find a piece of paper and a pencil and prepare to take down his words.

"Oh dash it!" says Guthrie. "I can't *dictate* a letter. Just tell her I'm all right—you know the sort of thing. . . . Ask her how her lumbago is getting on. Tell her not to come here—she's a lot safer at Avielochan—and I'll come there when I'm better. Tell her I shall probably get a fortnight's leave, and I want her to ask Hester Christie to come too."

I shake my head at this and inform Guthrie that it is quite impossible for Hester Christie to desert her post.

"Well, tell her, anyway," says Guthrie, smiling.

I am most unwilling to convey the message, for I know that Mrs. Loudon will do all she can to persuade me to fall in with Guthrie's wishes (she holds a strange and quite erroneous theory that I am "good for Guthrie") and I know, also, that Mrs. Loudon usually manages to get her own way, for she has an extremely forceful personality.

"But why not?" enquires Guthrie in a wheedling tone. "It

would be lovely—just like old times—we could fish all day long."

"No, Guthrie."

"Yes, Hester . . . think how nice it would be for Betty! It would do Betty all the good in the world. We could have some more picnics; we could walk on the moors. Please, Hester."

I reply, with all the firmness at my command, that I have certain duties to perform. They may not be spectacular, but they are my small contribution to our war effort . . . and Betty must be educated. . . .

Guthrie says, "Why must she be educated? I hate well-educated women, they are always boring."

As I have started the day by visiting the sick I decide to continue in my good works by dropping in to see Grace, and taking her a novel from the library. Grace looks comfortable and happy. I am not surprised at her air of well-being, for, on looking back at my own experience, it seems to me that the happiest and most comfortable times in my own life were after my own babies arrived. One feels one has done a good job of work to the best of one's ability, and one glories in the rest and the attention and in all the kindness and consideration. There one lies, a luxurious prisoner, in an atmosphere of cosy comfort which nothing is allowed to disturb.

Grace's prison smells faintly of milk, and of warm flannel, and the smell arouses memories and longings in my breast. The babies are quite adorable now, they have improved tremendously, though it is only a week since I saw them last. I declare that Grace is a lucky woman, and she laughs and agrees.

The babies are now removed, and we settle down to chat. Grace informs me that she has gained tremendous kudos in Jack's family by presenting it with two male representatives at one blow. Jack's elder brother has three daughters, so Ian and Alec are the first grandsons, and costly presents have been arriving for them by every post. This is all the more satisfactory because Jack's parents have never liked Grace, and on several occasions (to my certain knowledge) they have been distinctly unpleasant to her. Grace says that of course her sister-in-law will dislike her more than ever, but *that* doesn't matter. Indeed, far from depressing Grace, the thought of her sister-in-law's added dislike seems to give her a good deal of satisfaction. Grace is almost smug, and, because I am really very fond of her, I endeavour to bring her to a better frame of mind.

She smiles at me and says, "Darling, I know I'm hateful and I don't deserve my good fortune, but I can't help enjoying it."

"But of course you *should* enjoy it!" I cry.

"Yes," says Grace nodding. "I should *enjoy* it, but you think I shouldn't enjoy it so blatantly. Well, you may be right, but I can't help it." She looks thoughtful for a moment and then continues, "Good things come in waves. This is one of the times when *everything* goes right . . . then there are times when everything goes wrong. That's my experience of life."

It is mine too, and I murmur agreement.

"If I were to go to Monte just now," says Grace raising herself on her elbow in her excitement, "if I were to go to Monte (only I don't suppose the place is open) I should break the bank with the greatest of ease."

I assure her that I believe her.

"Of course you do, darling, because you've had the same feeling—the feeling that nothing can possibly go wrong, you've had it, haven't you?"

"Yes, I have."

Grace sighs. "It *is* a pity I can't go to Monte," she says regretfully. "Nurse has put ten bob on 'Thunderer' for me, and I've taken a ticket in a raffle at the Church Bazaar, but I feel I ought to make more *use* of my luck while it's in."

I agree that she should.

"It isn't only *things* that are turning out luckily," continues Grace somewhat vaguely. "It's people too. Everyone is so *nice*. Even Mrs. Benson seems a pleasant sort of person."

"Mrs. Benson!" I exclaim.

"Yes," says Grace. "She came in yesterday and admired the boys and brought them each a pair of woolly boots which she had made herself . . . the woman was really quite human."

Somehow or other I don't like this at all. It doesn't ring true. I remember the Latin tag about the Greeks bearing gifts and murmur, "Timeo Danaos et dona ferentes" at which Grace, who has had the benefit of a classical education, raises herself on her pillows and gazes at me. "My dear, I thought you doted on the woman!" she exclaims with quite unjustifiable exaggeration.

"Doted on her!" I echo in annoyance. "Who said I doted on her?"

"Well, you have always stood up for her," says Grace. "You have always said that she wasn't really such a bad old stick—"

"I was wrong."

"What do you mean?"

"Just what I say," I reply, groping for my gloves. "I was wrong about her. She *is* a bad old stick. You had better be careful of her."

"What has she done?" cries Grace. "You can't go now without explaining. You have spent hours beseeching me to be nice to her and now, when I feel that I *can* be nice to her, you swing round and warn me against her like a Delphic Oracle or something . . . Hester, don't go!"

Fortunately Grace is in bed and can neither prevent my departure nor follow me. It is most important that I should go now—immediately—for I am aware that if I remain a moment longer, I shall blurt out the whole story of Mrs. Benson's duplicity and the fat will be in the fire. Grace must never know . . . nobody must ever know . . . the whole affair must remain a secret, locked up for ever in my own breast. The secret is so leaden that I would give a good deal for a confidante, to whom it might safely be revealed.

I hasten away, deaf to all Grace's appeals, blandishments and threats.

Part 2

April–May

Good resolutions anent keeping a diary already broken as I find I have written nothing for a fortnight. Easter has come and gone, but as it is so early this year the children's holidays do not start until tomorrow. Have had several letters from Tim, and from what he says there seems to be very little fighting—except in the air—and, thank heaven, very few casualties. Have decided not to mention the war in my diary—or at least only to mention it as it affects me. Diary is to be an escape from war (if possible). Domestic affairs much smoother now. Mrs. Fraser is settling down and is not nearly so alarming, and she and Annie seem to be getting on better. . . . Have been obliged to speak to them about the kitchen wireless which has been blaring at full pitch from early morning to late at night. Remonstrances taken very well and immediate improvement noticeable. Have made up my mind that I *must* keep the household up to the mark while Tim is away—I am too apt to let things get slack. This will not do at all, and even though I don't care what I eat, and would rather bear small deficiencies than complain about them, I must insist upon everything being properly done . . . it will be easier in the holidays because Bryan will be here and he enjoys good food.

WEDNESDAY 3RD APRIL

Bryan returns home for his Easter holidays. He seems somewhat subdued, is unnaturally polite and replies to all questions in monosyllables. Feel worried about the child and ask him whether he is feeling quite well. He replies in the affirmative. Ask him whether he is tired and would like to spend the day in bed. He replies in the negative. During the day Bryan's good manners wear off a little and he becomes more like himself. He makes friends with the boy next door and invites him to come and play in the small burn which flows through the back part of the garden. They play there the whole afternoon and Bryan comes in to supper extremely wet and dirty. He announces, at supper, that this garden is much better fun than the garden at Biddington—it is smaller of course but there are better trees in it and the burn is simply marvellous.

Personally I have always thought the burn somewhat uninteresting, it is a small trickle of water flowing between banks about three feet high. Betty shares my opinion of it. She says "But Bryan, it's a rotten little burn, you can't sail boats in it or anything. It's too shallow to be any fun."

Bryan does not reply, and I am just congratulating myself upon having the burn—which will keep Bryan happy during the holidays—when Annie comes in and says "Please Ma'am, will you come. There's water pouring under the back door and the kitchen's ankle deep!"

I look at Bryan, and, noting his expression of guilty dismay, realise immediately that he is the author of the flood.

By this time it is dark and cloudy. I rush into the hall, seize my waterproof, my Wellington boots, a torch and a spade.

Bryan says "Can I come? I want to see if my boat's all right."

I reply sternly, "Come? Of course you must come. Hurry up and get ready."

Bryan and I sally forth together. It is so dark that I can see nothing, but I am aware that a stream of water is flowing along the path to the back door. Bryan keeps close to my side. He says "I *am* sorry, I meant to be so good . . . with Dad away and everything."

Feel my heart melting within me but make no reply.

Just as we reach the bank of the stream the clouds part and a beam of moonlight shines forth. It shines on to a large pool of water which stretches from bank to bank, a pool which brims to the lip of Bryan's dam and ripples gently in the breeze.

"Oh!" exclaims Bryan in amazed admiration of his handi-work, "Oh golly, what a dam!"

It is indeed a masterpiece of engineering, and despite my annoyance and vexation I cannot but admire it. The water in the pool is not rising now but remaining at the same level. Bryan points this out and explains that it is because he made an overflow. "You see I built it exactly like it said in my book," says Bryan gravely. "I made the overflow . . . and the dam itself is convex so the strain is taken by the banks. Arthur wanted to make it concave, but I was right."

I feel that Bryan is getting too pleased with himself, so I point out as sternly as possible that it was a very silly thing to do, and has occasioned a great deal of trouble for everyone.

Bryan agrees remorsefully. "Yes," he says. "Oh yes . . . but I never thought it would fill up so quickly—neither did Arthur —we thought it would take all night." He heaves a sigh and adds "We'll have to bust it, I suppose."

Most certainly we shall have to bust it, and the sooner it is busted the better. I hand Bryan the spade and he prepares him-self for his task. "I had better let it out gradually, hadn't I?" he says, "I mean we don't want it to rush down and do some damage below."

This seems a sensible suggestion and I agree to it, but Bryan's efforts to "let it out gradually" are doomed to failure. He makes a small opening with his spade and the imprisoned water does the rest; it pours like a torrent through the gap, widening it, deepening it, sweeping away rocks and stones and tightly packed turves in its mad rush to be free.

There is nothing to be done, nothing that we could do would stop it; we stand there silent and somewhat awed. In a few moments the brimming pool has vanished and in its place is the usual narrow turgid stream of water flowing over its usual stony bed.

We walk back to the house—still without speaking. I have no intention of punishing Bryan for his deed. He knows that he has been foolish and that is punishment enough.

As we reach the kitchen door—the step of which is covered with a thin layer of mud—Bryan heaves a sigh. "I wish Edgeburton could have seen it," says Bryan regretfully.

SATURDAY 6TH APRIL

Return home to lunch somewhat jaded after a morning's shopping and am met at the door by Annie who says that the young lady has arrived, and she is unpacking, and was it all right to put on a fire in the spare room because it felt a bit dampish.

I enquire in bewilderment, "What young lady?"

Annie replies, "She said you expected her. I thought perhaps you'd forgotten to tell me . . . I didn't know what to do."

I enquire again—this time in some irritation—"What young lady, Annie?"

Annie says, "It's Miss Bradshaw . . . and cook sent out for another cutlet and she's making a chocolate pudding."

Words fail me. I make my way upstairs and open the door of the spare room. As a rule this room is a bare, somewhat austere apartment with a cold and slightly fusty smell, but Annie's fire has cheered it up and my guest's clothes, strewn all over the chairs and bed, give it a friendly air. There are silver brushes on the dressing table and tissue paper all over the floor and kneeling before an open trunk is my guest herself—a large fair young woman with golden curls and a peachy complexion. She looks round as the door opens and, scattering paper in all directions, she rises and flings herself upon me with cries of delight.

"Darling Mrs. Tim . . . how lovely this is!"

I am so overcome with astonishment that I murmur feebly, "Oh Pinkie . . . how you've grown!"

"I know," says Pinkie, shaking her head. "I know . . . it's simply frightful. I don't suppose you would *know* me, would you? Nobody *does* know me. Of course I'm far too big all over," declares Pinkie, stroking herself all over at the words. "I *know* I am . . . and of course I ought to diet . . . but I simply can't." She hugs me again, and then continues: "You didn't expect me to *write,* did you? You knew I'd come, didn't you? I can't tell you how excited I was when I got your letter. I would have come right away but I'd promised to stay and help with a beastly bazaar . . . so I had to. I came as soon as ever I could."

I reply, somewhat breathlessly, that if she had let me know the date of her arrival I would have had the room prepared and could have met her at the station, but Pinkie brushes all this aside and declares that it didn't matter the least bit in the world. "Annie was sweet to me," says Pinkie, "she had the fire going in no time—though I told her I didn't need a fire—and I got a taxi at the station, it was the oldest taxi in the world and it chugged along exactly like a steam roller. Oh dear, how lovely it is to see you again! *You* haven't changed a bit, not the tiniest little scrap . . ."

It is quite impossible to be annoyed with Pinkie—or at least to be annoyed with her for more than a few seconds. My annoyance has vanished into thin air and I am able to welcome her warmly and sincerely and to enquire after all her relations.

Pinkie says, "Well I haven't seen Aunt Elinor for more than

a month but I expect she's all right . . . and Father may be coming home from India. I haven't seen *him* for two years. He took me to the school in Paris and left me there . . . I expect he'll get a bit of a shock when he sees me again. I loved being in Paris and I didn't want to come home, but it's quite fun being grown-up. Seventeen really *is* grown-up, isn't it? It's about ten years older than sixteen . . . I felt quite different the moment I was seventeen, wasn't that odd? . . . I suppose you think I'm simply enormous?"

I reply hastily that she is by no means enormous, but that she used to be so small, hence my surprise, and looking at her more carefully I perceive that her figure—though somewhat exuberant for present day fashions—is beautifully proportioned. I take in at a glance her skin, her teeth, her hair, her finely chiselled features and decide that she is without flaw, a veritable goddess . . . only her eyes are human, they are gentian blue, kind and friendly and trustful.

"Pinkie," I say sternly, "Pinkie, what's all this about being enormous? You know quite well that you're an exceedingly attractive young woman."

"Oh well!" says Pinkie, blushing to the roots of her hair. "Oh well of course . . . I mean you can't help knowing when people like you . . . and it's fun, really, in a way. But I'd give anything," says Pinkie earnestly, "I really would give *anything* to be small and slim, with dark hair and brown eyes.'

MONDAY 8TH APRIL

I receive quite a sheaf of letters this morning. Tim's letter has priority over the others and I open it eagerly. It is a short letter and contains little news. He says they are digging like beavers and making everything nice for Brother Boche. The men are suffering from blistered hands so will I send out all the gloves available from the "Comforts Fund". There are a good many Jerry planes about but they don't do much harm.

There is also a letter from Mrs. Loudon saying that her lumbago is better and she wants to come and see Guthrie. Can I find her lodgings in Donford? She adds in a postscript, "You needn't think you have to ask me to stay with you for I wouldn't dream of it."

This is so like Mrs. Loudon that I have to laugh.

Betty asks why I am laughing and I reply that Mrs. Loudon is coming to Donford.

Betty says, "Oh, let's go and stay with her instead. It would be much nicer. Bryan can come too . . . Bryan would love it, wouldn't you Bryan?"

Bryan agrees that he would.

I point out that we have not been asked to stay at Avielochan and that Mrs. Loudon is coming on purpose to see Guthrie.

Betty says, "What a pity!" in a disappointed tone.

As I am aware that Mrs. Loudon always says exactly what she means, and that if she has made up her mind to refuse my hospitality nothing less than a seventy horse power tractor will move her to change it, I sally forth to find rooms for her in the town. It is not an easy task, for the town is full of "evacuees" and soldiers' relations and I trail from house to house without success. Some of the houses look clean and comfortable, but have no rooms to let, others have rooms to let but are dirty and unkempt. At one house, which seems suitable, and has a couple of pleasant rooms vacant, I am informed that "the lodger would need to get her own breakfast", at another there is only one bathroom and the hot water is strictly rationed, and at a third I am interviewed and turned away by a peroxide blonde who says that she prefers gentlemen.

At first these adventures are somewhat amusing, but after a little they become far otherwise. It is late in the day before I succeed in finding a bedroom and sitting room which I think will suit Mrs. Loudon's requirements. The house seems clean and comfortable and the landlady amiable and willing to please. She informs me that she does not take lodgers, she has never had to do such a thing—"never thought on it"—but she is willing to oblige by offering hospitality to a paying guest. To Mrs. Macphail the difference is of immense importance. She assures me that Mr. Macphail would turn in his grave if she were to take a lodger, but apparently he will continue to rest in peace if she takes a paying guest. I promise to write to Mrs. Loudon and make the point perfectly clear.

"She's an old lady, you said?" enquires Mrs. Macphail.

I have not said so, for it would never occur to me to call Mrs. Loudon an old lady. To me an old lady conjures up the vision of a placid plumpish lady dressed in rustling silk with a large cameo brooch upon her bosom and a white shawl over her shoulders. An old lady sitting by the fire with her feet on a cross-stitch footstool, talking about "the old days" in a tiny threadlike quavery voice.

"Well, she isn't young," I reply, somewhat doubtfully.

"She'll not have Breedge Parties and burn the electreecity?" enquires Mrs. Macphail anxiously.

"No, I'm certain she won't do that."

"And she'll not smoke in bed?"

"No, I can promise that."

"Ooh well," says Mrs. Macphail, and the thing is settled.

I engage the rooms provisionally for a week and send off a wire to Mrs. Loudon.

TUESDAY 9TH APRIL

As I have been bidden to dine with the MacDougalls tonight and have accepted the invitation I ring up Grace and explain that I have a guest. Grace says, "Bring her too and I'll get the balloon-man, he was rather sweet. As a matter of fact he was a professor at the University before he went into the balloons."

I enquire whether she is sure it will not be too many, but Grace assures me that she is in tremendous form and is looking forward to the party with keen anticipation. "Nurse has gone," says Grace. "Of course she was a perfect gem but—well—I don't mind telling you I feel like a person who has just come out of jail . . . Yes, I *do* know how they feel because I feel like it, you see . . . and Jack feels like it too. We're going to have fizz to drink the boys' healths and Jack says if it were not for the black-out we would have fireworks. . . . Yes, we're both on top of the world."

We arrive at the party rather late because Pinkie has taken such a long time to dress, but I am bound to admit the result of her efforts is exceedingly pleasing. Her gown is made of soft white crepe and moulds her figure like a sheath, and there is a wreath of shining green leaves in her hair. As she follows me into Grace's drawing room there is a sudden hush —a tribute to her loveliness—and I go forward to shake hands, feeling like the duck who hatched out a swan. Bill, who is standing at the fireplace drinking a cocktail, looks round and sees us. His face goes the colour of a tomato, and his glass falls from his nerveless fingers and crashes on to the tiles.

Jack says, "Leave it . . . doesn't matter a bit . . . Woolworth's . . . quite all right, Bill."

Meanwhile Grace, who is always at her best as a hostess, is welcoming us cordially and making the introductions. Miss Browne Winters, Captain Ledgard and Captain Baker complete the party. Miss B. W. looks even more peculiar than before. Her hair is cut in Egyptian fashion with a straight fringe, and her clothing is composed of tightly swathed scarves.

Grace says dinner is ready and we'll go in; as we troop through the hall, she seizes my arm and says, "Where did you find Brunhilda? She's gorgeous!" but there is no time to reply.

Dinner is an enjoyable meal. The food is excellent—as it always is in Grace's house—for Grace despite her somewhat slapdash manner is a very good housekeeper. Everyone is talking about the German invasion of Norway and Denmark and of our promise to help the Norwegians. Jack MacDougall declares that it is the best thing that could have happened and that Hitler has overshot himself completely, but Captain Baker is not nearly so optimistic and seems to have a much higher opinion of the enemy's strength. He was in Germany for a few weeks last summer 'before the war started and assures us that Hitler has everything planned to the last button and will stop at nothing to attain his ends.

Jack says, "What *are* his ends?"

Captain Baker replies, "World domination. Anyone who reads *Mein Kampf* must realise *that.*"

I am finding the conversation most interesting and am annoyed when Miss Browne Winters puts an end to it by saying in a loud voice that it makes her feel quite ill when people talk about the war. Jack enquires (quite reasonably, I think) what she likes to talk about, to which Miss Browne Winters replies that there are many subjects upon which civilised people can exchange ideas with profit to themselves and each other. This pronouncement produces an alarming silence—for my part I am racking my brains in the endeavour to find a subject which will attain the high standard demanded by my fellow guest. The silence is broken by Pinkie who remarks suddenly and ecstatically, "Oh, I do love chocolate ice pudding!" This releases everyone from constraint and the situation is saved.

Captain Baker, who is sitting on my left, is an exceedingly

pleasant person. He tells me that he was at school with Tim and had a great admiration for Tim's prowess in the cricket field. They lost sight of each other when Tim went to Sandhurst. . . . I am quite sorry when Grace gives the signal for the females to withdraw as I am aware that I shall never hear the end of a most exciting innings in which Tim and Captain Baker piled up an immense score and saved the school from defeat.

Conversation in the drawing room is of an entirely different order and is conducted by Miss Browne Winters with an occasional remark from Grace. Pinkie and I are obliged to listen—or at least to pretend to listen—to a long dissertation upon Roman Law—a subject with which Miss Browne Winters has made herself familiar. I can see Pinkie struggling with yawns and am immediately assailed with the infection. Fortunately our male companions do not tarry very long, they come in laughing and talking cheerfully. Jack produces a card table and enquires if anyone would like some contract, and, after a good deal of discussion, he and Captain Baker, Miss Browne Winters and Captain Ledgard sit down to play. Bill maneouvres Pinkie onto the sofa at the other end of the room, and Grace and I are left to talk by the fire.

Grace enquires in a whisper who the girl is, and where I met her and adds that Bill is an extremely eligible young man. His father has a big place in the Midlands and a flat in London and his mother is one of the Winkles of Wersh. Grace is a born matchmaker and is never happy unless she is pairing people off, but I am not so reckless; I explain—also in a whisper—that Pinkie is a mere babe and that I am responsible for her, and add that I do not want any complications to arise while she is in my charge.

Grace says that is nonsense, they make a splendid couple and for her part she intends to encourage them as much as she can. Bill is a darling, but he needs a steadying influence, and marriage—to the right sort of girl—would be the making of him. She adds that it is high time we left off calling him "the child". She then lowers her voice still further and asks what I think of Ermyntrude.

I reply that I do not know anyone of that name.

Grace glances in the direction of the Bridge table and nods meaningly.

I realise that Ermyntrude must be the name which was given to Miss Browne Winters by her godfathers and god-mothers at her baptism, and reflect that for once they have chosen well. The name suits her admirably—or she suits the name—and indeed it seems to me that I might have guessed her name if I had given thought to the matter.

"What do you think of her?" enquires Grace again.

I murmur that she strikes me as being "very intense".

"Exactly," says Grace nodding. "She's extremely clever and ambitious and her Views About Life are most unusual. In fact she is the very person for Tom Ledgard."

"Do you think so?" I ask in amazement.

"Yes," says Grace. "Yes I do. Don't you?"

I point out that Captain Ledgard is rather stupid, has no views of any kind and (as far as I know) no ambition beyond having as good a time as he can afford.

Grace says, "Ermyntrude will change all that."

I reflect, not for the first time, that Grace is an optimist.

The two young people come over near the fire, and we make room for them. Pinkie says she was cold. Bill enquires anxiously whether he shall fetch her a shawl . . . or her fur coat . . . or his own scarf which is no further away than the hall, but Pinkie says she isn't cold now, in fact she is quite warm. It was only the draught from the window. Bill asks if she is quite sure she has not caught a chill and suggests to

Grace that Pinkie should be given a small glass of cherry brandy, or, failing that, a hot cup of tea, but Pinkie refuses all these offers quite firmly. Bill then insists on feeling her hand to see if she is *really* warm now, and holds it a good deal longer than is necessary. He is obviously head over heels in love, and the disease affects him like an overindulgence in champagne. It is said that all the world loves a lover but poor Bill must be an exception to the rule. Bill is usually amusing without effort, but tonight he makes an effort to shine and does not succeed (He is talking too much and laughing hilariously at his own jokes). I feel very sorry for Bill and wish that I could get him alone and tell him to be quiet; I wish I could put his head under a pump . . . Pinkie laughs at his jokes, for she is a kindhearted creature, but I can see that she is not quite so amused as she would like to be . . . she is a trifle puzzled as to why she is not amused at Bill's efforts to entertain her.

Suddenly I feel that I can bear it no longer and I rise and say that we must go. Grace is horrified and declares that the night is young but I adhere firmly to my decision.

WEDNESDAY 10TH APRIL

I hurry through my housekeeping and go down to the Barracks. Find Stella Hardford there and explain that I have heard from Tim and the Battalion wants gloves. Stella is inclined to be difficult and says that if gloves are required they should have been indented for in the usual way. Take no notice of this but begin to search for gloves.

Stella says, "How do we know they really need gloves?"

I reply that we know they need gloves because Tim has said so.

Stella says, "I don't feel that we can take the responsibility of sending them without a Committee Meeting."

This annoys me, and I reply that I am quite willing to assume all responsibility for sending gloves, and add that I am used to responsibility by now.

She enquires what I mean, and I point out that since the "Comforts Fund" was started I have run the whole thing with very occasional help from herself and Mamie.

Stella is somewhat taken aback—as people usually are when a worm turns—she says, "Oh! . . . Oh well . . . but you haven't anything else to do, have you? I mean I thought you liked doing it."

I make no reply but continue my search, and Stella, after a moment's hesitation, comes over and helps me. We turn out all the boxes but can only find thirty pairs.

Symes now appears upon the scene and asks if I want him. I reply that I want him very badly so he takes off his coat and goes away to hang it up. While he is away Stella asks who he is, and where I found him and whether it is necessary to have him, to which I reply that he is Colonel Morley's batman and I find his help invaluable. Symes is now ready to work so I inform him of our problem and he tackles it in his usual efficient manner.

"But we've plenty of mitts," says Symes, "and they're just as good. Why, there must be nearly four hundred pairs in that cardboard box I packed last Wednesday."

He brings out the box and we count them and find that he is right.

Am somewhat amused at the "play" between Symes and Stella. They dislike each other at first sight and are up against each other at every turn. Stella orders Symes about as if he were a galley slave, but Symes is a match for her, and, though perfectly respectful and polite, he gives her to understand that he takes his orders from me. We spend the morning packing a large box of gloves and mittens for dispatch to France.

As we come away Stella asks if I have met "that awful Browne Winters woman". *She* thinks the woman is a witch. The mere sight of the woman gives Stella cold shivers up her spine. Do I think there is anything between the woman and Tom Ledgard, because if so he ought to be *warned*. We don't want a woman like that in the Regiment.

Am exceedingly guarded in my replies to these questions as I am aware that Stella is a dangerous person in whom to confide.

FRIDAY 12TH APRIL

The 4th Battalion is encamped in a meadow near the sea on the outskirts of Donford, and, having been invited to tea by Tony Morley, Pinkie and I put on our best bibs and tuckers and set off in good time. We have decided to walk along the beach because Pinkie says she does not get nearly enough exercise and adds that it is a nice day and the sea breezes will be good for us.

The tide is out and the sands are brown and firm; they stretch for miles but their monotony is broken by masses of tumbled rocks. There are no living creatures to be seen—except the graceful white seagulls—the sun is golden, the sea is incredibly blue and the little white frills of waves splash and ripple to our feet. A day like this is a gift from God—or so it seems to me—and it seems all the more precious when it comes at the end of a long dark dreary winter. I am thinking of this as we walk along in companionable silence when Pinkie suddenly remarks that it's glorious, isn't it? . . . and do I mind if she goes mad? and, before I can reply to this somewhat alarming question, she takes a short run along the sands and turns three Catherine Wheels without stopping.

The spectacle of a large and beautifully dressed young lady turning Catherine Wheels upon the sands is so preposterous that I am seized with sudden and uncontrollable laughter, and am obliged to sit down upon a convenient rock to recover myself. Pinkie returns and sits down too. She is in such magnificent fettle that she is breathing no faster than usual, nor has she a hair out of place. Her hat, a plate shaped device of the latest fashion, is still resting upon her golden curls at the same angle as before—in fact the only sign of her recent activities is that her hands are covered with golden brown sand.

"Aren't I awful?" she says, as she takes out her handkerchief and wipes them carefully. "I *know* I'm awful, but I can't help it really. A day like this gets into my bones and makes me quite mad . . . I hope nobody *saw.*"

"Only the sea gulls," I reply in a trembling voice.

"Yes," says Pinkie, looking round, "and they aren't interested. I wonder why I feel like that. Do you think it's because I'm not really properly grown up? Are you awfully fed-up with me?"

Far from being "fed-up" I am astounded at her skill, and I compliment her upon her performance.

Pinkie brightens at once and allows that she "isn't half bad at Catherine Wheels" but beseeches me not to mention it to anyone. "You see, darling, it's so *childish,*" says Pinkie, looking at me with her wide dewy eyes. "I mean it takes me all my time to be properly grown-up and keep my end up with people . . . and if they ever suspected that I wasn't properly grown-up inside . . . well then . . ."

I assure her that I understand, and add that I do not think there is any need to worry. Many people, far older than she is, have the same feeling—the feeling that they are not properly grown-up inside.

"Yes," says Pinkie gravely, "but then they *are* properly grown-up outside, so it doesn't matter, you see. I mean they *look* absolutely grown-up. . . ."

Tony Morley is waiting for us; he has provided an excellent tea in his comfortable hut, and has also provided a large pink subaltern to entertain his younger guest. Pinkie—as ever—allows herself to be entertained with gratifying indulgence and the tea party is a great success.

I can see that Tony approves of his younger guest, but is not taken in by her assumption of sophistication. There is a latent twinkle in his eye as he looks at her and he treats her with the marked respect and consideration due to a woman of advanced years.

"I suppose you've known Hester for years?" he enquires as he hands her the scones.

"Years and years," agrees Pinkie, as she selects the largest. "It was at Hythe that we first met—that was before I went to France, of course."

"You know France well?" Tony enquires.

"Paris," says Pinkie. "I love Paris. It's a marvellous place—but you have to know your way about."

The twinkle in Tony's eye becomes more pronounced, but he agrees quite gravely that to enjoy Paris it is most essential to know one's way about. Young Craddock (the subaltern) murmurs something about "Moulin Rouge" but it is obvious from his manner that he has never been there.

Pinkie has now demolished most of the scones and is being plied with chocolate cake by Mr. Craddock. "It's so good," she remarks, apologetically, as she accepts a third slice.

Tony says he adores it too. His Mother sends him an enormous one every week so there is no need to spare it.

Pinkie points out that she is not sparing it, and adds that Colonel Morley would require at least three chocolate cakes a week if she came to tea with him often . . . to which Colonel Morley replies with his usual gallantry that, if Miss Bradshaw will honour him by coming to tea with him often, he will write to his mother and ask her to send four chocolate cakes a week. . . .

"Tell them about the general, sir," says Mr. Craddock, smiling.

"Why don't you tell them about the general?" enquires Tony.

"Because you would do it so much better, sir," replies Mr. Craddock promptly.

"Oh well . . ." says Tony, smiling, "it was one of those things that seem funnier in retrospect than they do at the time. He was a fat pompous little general, and he came down to have a look at us—not a proper inspection, but just to see how we were getting on. He was one of those spit and polish enthusiasts, didn't take any interest in musketry or machine gun drill, but was all out for smart turnout, shining boots and neatly packed haversacks . . . Don't think he knew there was a war on, do you, Craddock?"

"Hadn't the slightest idea of it," Craddock agrees.

"Well, the fact is," says Tony, "we've got one or two men in the Battalion who seem quite unable to put on their puttees in the orthodox manner. We've striven with them valiantly but they just can't grasp the principle. We've several like that, haven't we, Craddock?

"Yes, several," says Craddock, "but chiefly Fraser who is in my company."

"Mark that," says Tony gravely, "for on that hangs the whole sorry story, chiefly Fraser, who has the inestimable advantage of being in Craddock's company."

"And the odd part is he's an awfully decent fellow," declares Craddock earnestly. "He's one of the best, Fraser is. He's keen and intelligent and smart—except for his puttees, of course—he tries very hard but somehow or other he just can't manage them. He says it's the shape of his legs," adds Craddock in an apologetic manner.

"Well, perhaps it is," says Tony thoughtfully. "Now that I come to think of it his legs *are* a peculiar shape . . . but, be that as it may, when Fraser marches for any distance his puttees invariably descend and twine themselves round his boots."

Craddock flings himself back in his Roorkee chair and says "Oh Lord, I shall never forget that day!"

"Nor I," agreed Tony. "It was one of those days that live forever in the memory of man. I knew we were in for it when the general mentioned the word 'drill'. He mentioned it at lunch if you remember, Craddock."

Craddock says he remembers, and adds that it had the effect of making his favourite pudding taste like sawdust.

"The reason for our dismay," continues Tony; "the cause of our alarm and despondency was the fact that the only two men who could be trusted to act as markers were in bed with 'flu' . . ."

"And the R.S.M., sir," puts in Craddock.

"*And* the R.S.M.," agrees Tony. "The R.S.M. tried to get out of bed when he heard what was afoot. His temperature was 103° and he had to be held down by two orderlies . . ."

"Three orderlies, sir," says Craddock quickly.

Tony accepts the amendment. "Three orderlies," he says; "the R.S.M. is a very powerful man and had been having instruction in unarmed combat—I'd forgotten that . . . Well, I did my best to persuade the general that what he wanted to see was a spot of bayonet practice, but to no purpose. He wanted to see the Battalion on parade, 'and just a little simple drill, nothing very elaborate' . . . Ye gods!" says Tony, "Ye gods and little fishes, he saw something worth seeing! I don't suppose he had ever seen anything the least like it before. I certainly hadn't. It was worse—much worse—than I had expected, and I had expected it to be pretty bad."

"They started none too badly," Craddock reminds him.

"Yes," says Tony, "but they degenerated rapidly, didn't they? And at last they were so flustered that they didn't know their right hands from their left . . . the climax came," says Tony, and his voice quivers with laughter so that he can hardly speak, "the climax came when Fraser tripped over his puttees and fell heavily to the ground . . . and then . . . and then . . ." says Tony between his spasms of mirth, "and then the man in the next rank fell over him, and two more men on the top of *him*. It was exactly like a rugger scrum."

"Nobody laughed," says Craddock, shaking in his chair. "That was the awful part of it . . . nobody laughed . . ."

"I thought we were in for it," continues Tony, wiping his eyes. "I was beginning to wonder where I'd stored my bowler hat . . . I was composing a letter to Moss Brothers asking what they were prepared to offer for a colonel's uniform and equipment, camp-bed, bath and washing basin. I was doing that as we walked back to my hut where the old boy had left his scarf. There was tea ready when we got here—Symes had it all prepared—so I offered the old boy some tea. He sad 'No' but not very convincingly. Somehow or other we got him into a chair and a large cup of steaming tea into his hand . . . but it was a near thing."

"The chocolate cake did it," declares Craddock, helping himself to another piece. "Nobody can resist Lady Morley's chocolate cake . . . it's so gooey . . . it melts in your mouth. I don't know how many pieces the general had, I just went on feeding it to him . . ."

Pinkie and I walk home together across the sands. The tide is coming in and the waves are chasing each other, and overtaking each other, and scuttling back again. The sun is shining as brightly as ever and the sky is blue and cloudless, but Pinkie shows no desire to turn Catherine Wheels; she walks along by my side very sedately and is somewhat distrait. I cannot help wondering whether it is the effect of the chocolate cake, for I am aware that if I had eaten half as much as she has I should be feeling decidedly unwell . . . but apparently her malaise arises from a totally different cause. After a little Pinkie enquires what I thought of Mr. Craddock, and I reply that I thought him charming.

Pinkie says, "Yes, he's a perfect darling. He asked me to go to the Pictures with him—you don't mind, do you?"

"Of course not," I reply.

Pinkie hesitates and then says, "It isn't very kind of me, I suppose."

I assure her that I am delighted that she should go to the pictures with Mr. Craddock, but Pinkie is still uncomfortable . . . "It's Bill, really," she explains.

The situation is now perfectly clear, but I am unable to cope with it.

MONDAY 15TH APRIL

Mrs. Loudon arrives today. Am quite thrilled at the prospect of seeing her again and make arrangements for my family to lunch without me, so that I shall be free to meet Mrs. Loudon at the station at 1:15. No sooner have I done this than a wire arrives from Mrs. Loudon saying tersely, "Do not meet me."

Pinkie says why not ignore this command and meet her as arranged, but Pinkie does not know Mrs. Loudon. I decide to obey Mrs. Loudon's wishes.

Pinkie says, "Well, let's put flowers in her room—she hasn't said you aren't to do that, has she?"

This is an excellent idea. We go out together—Bryan and Betty too—to carry it into effect, and find that the daffodils have come in and are blowing like the bugles of Spring in the flower-shop window.

Mrs. Macphail is quite pleasant about the flowers and provides vases and jugs to put them in. She informs us that when she lived at Troon she had a garden full of flowers "not to speak of a maggie-nola", but that only hardy plants will grow here. "It's the east," says Mrs. Macphail gravely. "The east is aye colder than the west . . . excepting India of course."

Betty says, "India's south. It's south on my map anyhow, and the equator goes through it and keeps it warm."

Bryan says, "D'you think the equator is a hot water pipe or what?"

Betty says, "No, I know what it is just as well as you do. It isn't anything at all—so there!"

Mrs. Macphail has not followed this exchange, she is still harping on about "the east." India is east, declares Mrs. Macphail, and she ought to know, because she has a cousin who was a steward on a ship and he brought her a cup and saucer with a picture of a temple on it. "A sort of pagoda, it was," says Mrs. Macphail. "I'll let you see it one day when you're in . . . I'd let you see it now if I could mind where I put it."

Betty says she would like to see it very much.

"He's not a steward now," says Mrs. Macphail, referring to her cousin. "He joined up the very first day and they made him a photographer. I thought at the time it was a daft sort of thing to have a photographer in the Air Force—that's what he's in—but they seem to keep him busy. I never lift a paper but I see pictures of soldiers and tanks and aeroplanes and such-like."

Pinkie, who has finished doing the flowers, says quickly, "But your cousin will be taking aerial photographs . . ."

"He'll just need to take whatever he's told," declares Mrs. Macphail, "and he'll do that, for he's a sensible fellow and not one to stick at anything."

I can see that Pinkie is prepared to argue, but time is getting on and it would take too long to unravel the tangled skein. Indeed I doubt whether anyone could ever unravel it. I collect my family and, having warned Mrs. Macphail of the approximate hour of her guest's arrival and given strict injunctions regarding fires, hot water bottles, and thoroughly aired sheets, we return home to lunch.

During the meal Pinkie announces that she is going to the pictures with Mr. Craddock and will not be in to tea. She adds that it is just as well because Mrs. Loudon is coming and it will be far nicer for us to be alone.

Betty says, "But they won't be alone because we'll be here."

Bryan says, "Couldn't *we* go to the pictures too? We needn't go with Pinkie because they wouldn't want us and anyhow it would be far more fun by ourselves. It's *The Wizard of Oz*," adds Bryan persuasively. "All the people at school have seen it and I want to see it awfully. Betty would love it."

Betty jumps up and down shouting, "Oh, do let us! Oh, do! Oh, please do!"

I am not very keen on letting them go alone, but I am aware that Tim likes Bryan to be independent. In fact Tim warned me before he left that I was not to keep Bryan in cotton wool— so, after some hesitation, I agree to let them go if they promise to be sensible. Bryan promises faithfully to take the greatest care of his sister—especially crossing the streets—and they walk off together very sedately.

They have no sooner disappeared than Mrs. Loudon arrives. She seems to bring with her a breath of hill air. She has changed very little (except that her hair is a trifle more grey) and is as full of energy as ever. I realise afresh what a splendid person she is—blunt and downright, tenderhearted and generous. It is the pleasantest thing in the world to see her sitting in the shabby chair, to be pouring out tea for her and offering her scones and listening to her conversation.

Mrs. Loudon says she has seen Guthrie and there seems little wrong with him. "He was sitting up in a chair daffing with a wee red-headed nurse," says Mrs. Loudon. "Did you see that nurse, Hester? A limmer if ever there was one. She gave one look at me and fled as if the fiend himself was at her heels."

I reply that I did happen to see a nurse with red hair but had not realised she was dangerous.

Mrs. Loudon says she was up to no good or she wouldn't have fled, and adds that she is terrified of any woman who *looks* at Guthrie now. She had always comforted herself by the reflection that Guthrie had some sense, but ever since the time at Avielochan when he nearly married that cat-faced creature she has lived on tenterhooks.

I assure her that there is no need for her to be alarmed, but Mrs. Loudon says it's no use talking, if Guthrie had any sense at all he would have known from the very beginning what like the creature was—"not his style at all," declares Mrs. Loudon.

"It was a lesson to him," I point out.

Mrs. Loudon says it's to be hoped that Guthrie's learnt it. She is not so sure. She wishes Guthrie would find a wiselike girl and marry her and be done with it.

To change the subject I enquire whether her rooms seem comfortable and she replies that they are very comfortable indeed, and that "the woman" seems a kindly sort of body though she talks too much. "I was not in the place half an hour before I knew her life's history," declares Mrs. Loudon roundly. "It appears she's come down in the world and *that* through no fault of her own. Well, it's a common enough story and I did her the credit of believing it, but if you'd asked me where she hailed from I'd have told you Pollokshields."

I enquire what sort of place that is.

"Genteel," says Mrs. Loudon. "Oh, I listened to the whole story, but when it came to diseases and operations I could thole it no longer, so I put my hat back on my head and went off to the hospital. Disease is a subject of conversation I never could thole." She hesitates a moment and then adds, "I'll need to think of some way of stopping her tactfully."

The idea of Mrs. Loudon being tactful is so ludicrous that I cannot hide a smile.

Mrs. Loudon smiles too. "Oh, yes, I know," she says, "I know what you're grinning at. The fact is I speak first and think afterwards and by that time I've walked into the mire with both feet. It's my nature and I can't change it."

The time passes rapidly. At six o'clock we listen to the news and are informed the British Forces have landed in Norway. Mrs. Loudon says it's to be hoped we'll send enough troops to take the country and hold it—though she doesn't see how we can spare them at the moment. I tell her what Captain Baker said at dinner the other night and she says, "No doubt he knew what he was talking about." Mrs. Loudon sounds so gloomy that I enquire what she really thinks about the war, and after a moment's consideration she replies, "It'll be a long and weary job, but we'll just need to go through with it."

Pinkie returns from her afternoon's outing with shining eyes and cheeks like wild roses, and it is obvious that she has enjoyed herself. Mrs. Loudon—who has not seen her since she was ten years old—is amazed at her appearance and says so in her usual forthright way . . . and, when Pinkie goes upstairs to take off her things, Mrs. Loudon seizes my arm in a vice-like grip and says in a loud whisper that she thinks Pinkie would do for Guthrie.

I point out that Pinkie has provided herself with a young man and seems to have enjoyed her afternoon in his company.

"Has Guthrie seen her?" enquires Mrs. Loudon. "Just tell me that—*Has Guthrie seen her?*"

I reply that Guthrie has not seen her, but that she can be taken to the hospital and shown to him if Mrs. Loudon so desires.

It's all very well for you to make fun of me," says Mrs. Loudon. "Just you wait till Bryan starts looking at girls."

TUESDAY 16TH APRIL

Mrs. Loudon arrives at 10 o'clock in the morning and announces that she is on her way to the hospital to see Guthrie and she thought she would just look in and see how we were getting on. As the hospital is situated at the opposite side of the town, this statement cannot be taken at its face value. I enquire whether Mrs. Loudon would like me to accompany her to the hospital but she says no, she would not dream of taking me away from my household duties at this hour. She knows what it is to run a house, and how everything goes wrong if you're not there yourself . . . but maybe if Pinkie has nothing special on she would like the walk.

Pinkie says she has nothing to do unless I would like her to do the shopping . . . but Mrs. Loudon interrupts her and says, "Hester is quite capable of managing her own affairs."

This trenchant remark surprises Pinkie a good deal—as well it might—but, being a good-natured creature and always willing to oblige, she goes and gets ready to accompany Mrs. Loudon to the hospital. I cannot help smiling to myself as I watch the two figures walking down the road together. One is old and the other young but both are tall and straight—there is something alike in their easy gait and proud carriage.

Pinkie returns to lunch but has little to say anent her visit to the hospital and I am obliged to wait until the afternoon, when Mrs. Loudon comes, to hear the result of the expedition.

It is not Mrs. Loudon's way to beat about the bush and with her first breath she says, "It was useless, Hester. The girl sat like a dummy and Guthrie never let his eyes fall upon her."

She is so depressed by the unsuccess of her scheme that I feel sorry for her and sympathise with her.

"Oh well, it's no use crying for the moon. Love's a queer thing . . ." says Mrs. Loudon with a sigh.

FRIDAY 19TH APRIL

Annie asks if she can speak to me for a moment. I reply that she can and lead the way to the drawing room with a sinking heart. I know quite well what is coming; I have seen it approaching for some time. I sink into a chair and look at Annie, but Annie does not look at me. She stands before me, twisting a corner of her apron, and is obviously at a loss how to begin.

"Well, Annie," I say at last. "I suppose you want to get married—that's it, isn't it?"

Annie says that it is and it isn't—if I know what she means —and if it wasn't that Bollings had been made a sergeant and got impatient she wouldn't be standing here, but would be clearing the breakfast, as she ought to be doing this very minute.

I listen to this and my heart sinks lower than before, for I have had Annie for years. She came to me at Biddington as housemaid and stayed on as Betty's nurse, and now she combines the two posts and has become invaluable. In addition to this I have become very fond of Annie, and am aware that she is fond of me—we have shared many vicissitudes and understand each other's ways. Tim has vanished into some unknown part of France and now Annie is going—I shall be absolutely bereft. "Oh Annie, I *am* sorry," I murmur feebly.

Annie says it's very difficult. It's Bollings being so impatient. Bollings says he's tired of hanging about and he won't hang about any longer . . . "and I'm twenty-six now," says Annie, "and if I don't take this chance I mayn't get another, and I wouldn't like to get left on the shelf."

This seems such a strange point of view that I am incapable of making any rejoinder. I gaze at Annie helplessly.

"So that's 'ow it is," says Annie, and I perceive that she is very near tears.

I dash hastily into speech and say that of course I have known for some time that she and Bollings would be getting married, and that Bollings is a particularly nice man—as well as being extremely lucky—and that I am sure they will be very happy indeed. Now that Bollings has got his promotion there is no need to wait any longer, as they will get a comfortable quarter and can settle down . . .

Here Annie interrupts me to say in a choked voice that she isn't going to leave me, not for a hundred Bollingses she wouldn't, not even if he was a R.S.M. which he never will be if he lives to a centipede, and how could she look the major in the face if he came back and she wasn't here, and she couldn't look herself in the face neither, and anyhow there's no saying but what Bollings won't be sent to France next, or Egypt most likely, and most likely killed, and where would she be then? . . . So if I don't like the idea of her getting married then it's off, and Bollings can find someone else, and she's told Bollings the same to his face—more than once she's told him—so I don't need to worry . . . and with that Annie turns and blunders to the door.

But this won't do at all, so I call her back and explain that it won't; and presently I find myself trying to persuade Annie to marry Bollings, which of course is the last thing I desire. We are both so upset by this time, and so muddled and confused, that we talk for some time without getting any further. Annie is weeping quite openly and her aitches are flying in all directions. "Not unless I can stay" she sobs, dabbing her eyes with the corner of her apron, "Not unless I can stay . . . and that's my last word . . . Bollings is all very well in 'is way . . . and I don't say as what I'm not fond of 'im . . . but if it means I've got to go . . . and leave you and Betty . . . and the major away . . ."

Suddenly I see a ray of light and my heart bounds with relief, for here, of course, is the solution to the apparently insolvable problem . . . and this is what Annie has been trying to make me understand. "You mean," I begin, "you mean you want to marry Bollings and stay on with me?"

"Not if you don't want me to," sobs Annie.

Now that I have grasped the idea I cannot imagine why I have not grasped it before; I explain this to Annie and add that I had never thought of it, but that it seems an excellent plan. "What does Bollings think about it?" I enquire anxiously.

Annie replies that it was his idea, really, and on further investigation I discover that the details of the plan have been thoroughly examined and nothing but my sanction is required. Bollings will spend his nights beneath my roof, except when he is on duty at the Barracks, and this will be an advantage, rather than a disadvantage, to me, for Bollings was Tim's batman before we went to Westburgh, and I know him to be a steady decent creature, with a domesticated turn of mind. I enquire what Mrs. Fraser will say, and Annie replies that

Mrs. Fraser has been sounded and has signified her willingness to fall in with the arrangement. "She likes a man about the place," explains Annie, "and Bollings knows just 'ow to take 'er."

The thing is settled to our mutual satisfaction, and Annie smiles with delight and declares that it is a weight off her mind. It is a weight off my mind also, and I repair to the kitchen to interview Mrs. Fraser, feeling that the world is slightly more secure.

MONDAY 22ND APRIL

Tea has just been brought in when Bill appears; he looks round the room and is obviously disappointed to find that I am alone. I invite him to stay and share my meal, but he seems doubtful and enquires whether Pinkie is likely to be back soon. I reply that Pinkie has gone to play tennis with George Craddock, and add that there is no need for Bill to stay to tea if he does not want to.

Bill says, "Oh, Mrs. Tim, of course I want to—it's only—I mean, I'm feeling so rotten that I'm no use to anyone . . . No, I'm not the least bit ill. I wish I were. Perhaps if I were very ill she would be sorry for me."

As there is now no need to beat about the bush I ask him straight out whether he is in love with Pinkie.

He says, "You know I am. I want to marry her."

I look at him across the table (for he has now taken a seat opposite to me and is eating bread and margarine in an abstracted manner) and I note that his face is well formed and his eyes are steady and sincere. Perhaps his appearance of extreme youth may be due to his honey-coloured hair which sweeps across his forehead in a thick swathe.

"I want to marry her," says Bill again; "but Pinkie doesn't

want it. Pinkie wants to go on just as we are . . . just being friends."

I point out that Pinkie is very young.

"It isn't *that*," says Bill earnestly, "I mean that isn't the reason. As a matter of fact Pinkie says I'm too young."

"You're both too young, Bill."

"No," declares Bill. "No, we've argued that out . . . I'm six years older than she is . . . and so I'm exactly the right age for her, but she doesn't seem to see it. Oh dear, I don't know *what* to do!" declares Bill, seizing the last three pieces of bread and margarine and wolfing them ravenously. "I don't know *what* to do."

I suggest that he should have a serious conversation with Pinkie and clear the air.

Bill says, "I've tried, but it's no use. She just says we're friends. She said that from the very beginning—she said that we were to be friends and no silly nonsense, and I thought it was a good idea—but now I don't. I see now that it was a silly thing to agree to."

"But Bill—"

"That was at Hythe," says Bill. "That was at the very beginning. I thought she was just a kid—an awfully nice kid and awfully amusing and good fun. . . . I say, there isn't any more bread and butter. Have I eaten it all?"

"Have some cake," I suggest.

"No," says Bill somewhat sadly. "No, thank you. I don't seem to have much appetite really . . . and then," says Bill, continuing his tale, "and then you see I got to know her better, and I began to see her as she really is. She is *so* different from other girls, isn't she? She's so innocent and good . . . she's so pure," says Bill earnestly. "I can't help thinking about her all the time. She looks lovely and she *is* lovely. Don't you think so, Mrs. Tim?"

He is quite right about Pinkie, of course, and I tell him so, but add that if Pinkie has told him that all she wants is his friendship it would be better to accept her decision or else to put her out of his mind altogether. Bill does not listen to this eminently sensible advice; he interrupts me in the middle and explains at length all that he feels about Pinkie, repeating that she is so different from other girls, and that he thinks about her all the time . . . nobody really knows Pinkie (except Bill, of course), nobody understands how marvellous she is—how sweet and clever and amusing—nobody knows what a sad life she has had . . . he wants to take her away from all her relations (who don't appreciate her at all) and make her happy forever and ever.

"Yes," I say, "Yes, but Bill—"

"If only she'd let me!" exclaims Bill. "If only she'd trust me! You see I love her so much that I *know* it would be all right."

"But Bill, I don't think Pinkie is ready yet, do you?"

"Not ready?"

"No, she's just a child, really. She ought to grow up quite a lot before she thinks of marriage."

Bill does not agree with this—I hardly dared to hope that he would—he says it's quite obvious that I don't understand Pinkie either . . . he wonders if there is Someone Else . . . perhaps young Craddock . . . what do I think about it.

At this moment the door opens and Pinkie appears. She greets Bill in a friendly manner and kisses me fondly. "Hester darling!" she exclaims, "We've been asked to a sherry party at the Donford Arms—we're going to get a really proper invitation, of course, but George told me about it. The officers of the 4th Battalion are giving a party, won't it be fun?"

Bill enquires whether Pinkie has had some good tennis, and she replies that it was not particularly good tennis, but she enjoyed it thoroughly—"You're much better than George," says Pinkie, smiling at Bill in her usual friendly way.

"Am I?" enquires Bill, brightening visibly.

"Yes," says Pinkie. "Your service is so terrifying, you see. George is really better at golf than tennis."

"But you like tennis best," says Bill earnestly.

"Only because I'm better at it—that's all."

There is silence for a moment and then Bill gets up. "What about tomorrow?" he enquires. "I mean could you play tennis if I got Alister and his sister for a four?"

Pinkie cogitates for a few moments and then says that she can—though not till after tea—and Bill goes upon his way rejoicing.

THURSDAY 25TH APRIL

Pinkie and I are sitting in the drawing room waiting for lunch to be ready, when the door bursts open and Betty rushes in. I am about to reprove her for her mode of entry when I see her face and realise that something has happened.

"It's Bryan . . ." she gasps. "He fell out of the tree . . . Bryan's dead . . ."

Pinkie is off like an arrow from a bow and I follow as fast as I can. We arrive at the scene of the accident to find Bryan rising from the ground and dusting himself with his cap. To all appearances he is perfectly sound; my fright turns to anger —as fright so often does—and I demand in stern accents why Betty thought it necessary to alarm us.

Betty says tearfully, "But Bryan *said* he was dead."

Bryan says, "How could I say I was dead, you nitwit?"

Betty says, "But you did. I said, 'Have you hurt yourself?' and you said 'I'm dead, I'm dead,' so I ran to tell Mummy."

Bryan says, "I didn't at all. You said, 'Have you hurt yourself,' and I said, 'My head, my head!'" He adds a trifle shame-facedly, "It was dashed sore for a minute or two."

I now behold a lump the size of a pullet's egg rising upon Bryan's forehead, anger melts into sympathy, and we take him into the house to apply antiphlogistine, which is my remedy for most ills of the flesh. When this has been done we suggest that he should go to bed, or lie on the sofa, but Bryan assures us that he feels absolutely O.K. Cannot help wishing that I shared his sense of well being.

Pinkie, who has been most capable throughout, says, "Darling, you look frightful!"

Reply that I cannot look much worse than I feel.

She rushes off and returns almost immediately with a bottle of brandy and a glass. Annie also appears upon the scene. They pour some brandy into the glass and urge me to drink it, assuring me that I shall feel better in a few minutes. Feel so peculiar that I drink it without demur. As there is no immediate improvement in my condition I am supported to the drawing-room sofa and laid out upon it and more brandy is administered. Feel queerer than before. Can hear Annie's voice asking whether she shall ring up the doctor—voice sounds a long way off—murmur faintly, "No, don't want doctor." Feel glass held against my lips and murmur faintly "No more," but it is forced upon me and I am obliged to swallow it to prevent it running down my neck.

Feel worse and worse. Faces seem to float in mid-air. Voices seem far away. Endeavour to say "Don't leave me," but find great difficulty in forming the words. Whole room goes up and down as if in a storm. When I shut my eyes it goes round and round as well. Begin to wonder if I am going to die.

Suddenly Major Shaw, the Regimental Doctor, appears. His face floats into my line of vision wearing a puzzled, anxious expression. He feels my pulse and asks to see my tongue. Pinkie's face (white as a sheet with enormous blue eyes) gazes at me over the doctor's shoulder. Make a frightful effort and say, "Don't worry . . . feel mos' 'strawnry . . . better soon."

Major Shaws says, "How much brandy did you give her, Miss Bradshaw?"

Pinkie says she doesn't know and adds, "She looked so awful that we were terrified . . . we gave her *lots.*"

Major Shaw says, "You've made her drunk." He is struggling not to laugh. I can see his somewhat dour face quivering as he wrestles with the spasms.

"Drunk!" exclaims Pinkie in horrified tones.

"Tight as a lord!" says Major Shaw. His voice breaks and laughter overcomes him like a flood . . . he laughs and laughs.

Presently as if by magic a large cup of black coffee appears before my eyes. I am raised from my cushions and encouraged to drink it. Everyone very helpful and sympathetic; Pinkie almost tearful with remorse. Begin to feel slightly better, and assure Pinkie that no harm is done. Major Shaw is most reassuring and declares that I shall be perfectly all right in a few hours. He writes out a prescription for a corpse reviver and Bryan is sent to the chemist on his bike. Find I can speak now and murmur faintly that, if that's what it's like to be drunk, I can't imagine anyone doing it for pleasure. I never felt so awful in my life.

Pinkie says, "Are you *sure* she'll be all right?"

Major Shaw replies that he is perfectly certain of it, and adds that he is a specialist in my complaint. He goes away, but promises to return later and see how I am.

I recover slowly and by dinner time I am able to eat an adequate meal, which completes my cure. Pinkie and I have a good laugh over the affair—though it seemed far from humourous at the time.

"No," says Pinkie. "It wasn't funny. I was terrified . . . and Major Shaw says it was a dangerous thing to do. Major Shaw says you should *never* give people brandy without a doctor's permission. I shall never do it again, that's one thing certain."

FRIDAY 26TH APRIL

Receive a letter from my brother, Richard, inviting Bryan to come and spend a few days in London on his way back to school. Richard says he and Mary have not seen Bryan for ages and would enjoy having him. They will take him to the Zoo and to the Tower and give him a good time. I need not worry about air raids, as they never have any in London.

Bryan says, "Gosh, how marvellous! May I? Oh Gosh, how gorgeous!" and the matter is settled.

Bryan now wishes to know all particulars about his prospective host and hostess and I discover—somewhat to my distress—that he has no recollection of them whatsoever. When questioned more closely Bryan says, "Well, how *could* I know about them? I was only a kid when Uncle Richard came to stay . . . I wouldn't know him from Adam . . . Oh yes, I know he's awfully decent and sends me money for my birthday, but I don't know anything *about* him. What does he do?"

I inform Bryan that his Uncle was in business in London, but is now a Captain in the Gunners. He is on sick leave at the moment, having fallen over a limber in the dark and broken his arm.

"How can he write letters then?" enquires Bryan instantly.

This has not occurred to me, but now that I think of it

I am forced to the conclusion that Richard must have broken his left arm.

Bryan accepts this explanation, "Yes, that must be it," he says. "Will Uncle Richard be in uniform? I *do* hope so. It would be so splendid to go about London with him and see everyone saluting us."

"They would be saluting Uncle Richard," I point out.

"What sort of a house do they live in?" Bryan enquires.

I reply that the house stands in a square with gardens in the middle and add that it used to belong to my parents and that Uncle Richard and I were born there.

Bryan says, "Oh, it's a very old house then."

I remain silent, hoping that the catechism is at an end, but it is only beginning.

"Uncle Richard is your brother, isn't he?" says Bryan.

"Yes."

"Just like Betty and me."

"Yes."

"Has Daddy got a brother?"

"No."

"Well, who is Uncle Joe?"

I explain that Uncle Joe is Daddy's uncle and therefore Bryan's great-uncle, and add, "Surely you remember Uncle Joe and Aunt Posy—we went to stay with them in Essex. It was near the sea."

Bryan screws up his face and says, "Oh yes, I believe I do. I fell into the stream and there was a donkey, wasn't there? Has Uncle Joe still got the donkey?"

"I don't know."

"Oh well, . . ." says Bryan, "and that's all the relations we've got. Why haven't I got a grandfather—some people at school have two. Edgeburton's grandfather is frightfully decent."

"Is he?"

"Yes," says Bryan. "If Edgeburton wants some extra dibs he's only got to write a letter to his grandfather and he gets a postal order for five bob by return . . . he doesn't ask for it, even."

"I hope not."

"No," says Bryan. "He doesn't *need* to ask. Edgeburton just writes and says 'How are you?' and that sort of thing and the money arrives."

"Edgeburton must write a very good letter."

"Well, he doesn't, really," says Bryan gravely. "As a matter of fact I write it for him sometimes—he always gets more when I write, because I make it interesting. Last time I told him about the plover, and Edgeburton got a whole quid. The letter said, 'Your handwriting is much worse and your spelling is deplorable, but you seem to have grasped the idea that a letter should be informative, and should convey to its recipient some idea of your activities.' He uses *very* long words . . . we had to look them up in the dick. . . . I made Edgeburton give me five bob," adds Bryan reflectively.

These revelations are somewhat startling and I remonstrate with my son. "But why is it wrong?" he enquires. "Edgeburton's grandfather liked my letters and we liked getting the money, so everybody's pleased."

MONDAY 29TH APRIL

Betty and I go to tea with Grace. We have been invited on purpose to inspect the twins and, as Betty has not seen them before, she is full of curiosity and excitement. The twins are now seven weeks old, and are extremely attractive and pretty. They are as like as two peas and Betty wishes to know—amongst other things—how Grace knows which is which. Grace replies that they are entirely different, and are even more different in character than in appearance. Alec, although the younger, has a more forceful personality and is destined to be the leader in all their games. Ian's nature is very unselfish.

Betty looks at them again and says, "How do you know?" and Grace replies that a mother always knows, and that some day when Betty has dear little babies of her own, she will understand.

Betty says, "I shall have triplets—three babies all the same age—two boys and a girl. The girl will be called Marjorie, but I haven't decided what the boys will be called."

I am pleased to see that Betty is very gentle with the babies. She is allowed to hold Alec on her knee, and sits in a large armchair with her legs straight out in front of her and cuddles him with serious satisfaction. Alec seems quite contented in her care and gazes up at her with wide-open blue eyes.

"He's so soft and warm," says Betty. "He's so sweet and cuddly, I think he knows me quite well. He can't talk yet, of course, but I'm sure he thinks things."

Grace is delighted at this, and says that Betty is perfectly right, it is the Child Instinct. I ought to cultivate this Instinct, and not allow it to be crushed and overlaid by Wordly Cares. I ask Grace, quite humbly, how she thinks I should go about it, but she seems unable to give me any definite advice . . . "Ermyntrude would know," says Grace, after a moment's thought.

"I thought The Great Pyramid was her forte."

"Oh, she knows a lot about other things as well—her interests are very wide. Child Psychology is one of the subjects she has studied. She's given me most valuable advice about the boys."

I am wicked enough to murmur the well-known saying regarding old maids' children, but Grace refuses to see the joke against her latest friend—"Ermyntrude is different," declares

Grace, "and I think busy people like you and me should be glad to take advice from someone who has the time and the brains to study. Her knowledge of children isn't just theoretical; she has practised psychology with the greatest success. She was telling me about her sister's little boy—it was most interesting."

"Did she practise on him?" I enquire.

"She *cured* him," replies Grace. "He was very frightened of horses, and his parents were terribly distressed about it— they are great hunting people—so Ermyntrude analysed his psyche and discovered the cause. What do you think it was?" enquired Grace, looking at me with wide eyes.

This riddle is child's play to me, and I reply instantly that he was bitten by a horse in a previous existence.

"How did you know?" asks Grace suspiciously.

"I guessed it."

"You can't have guessed it!"

"I'm rather good at riddles."

Grace looks at me sadly and says it is a pity that I do not take Ermyntrude seriously, because she could help me so much. Psychology is a science, there is no "guessing" in psychology. It took Ermyntrude three weeks to discover the Cause of Fear, and when she had established the Cause, she had to Go Back and eradicate Fear by suggestion. It was a long process and Ermyntrude was quite exhausted after it. Unfortunately her sister was not properly grateful—not even when she saw the results with her own eyes. Ermyntrude said it was one of the best moments in her life when the child climbed onto his pony and rode round the paddock—her eyes were full of tears.

Grace is so much in earnest that I have not the heart to tease her any more, so refrain from suggesting that the unfortunate child may have preferred to ride his pony rather than undergo further ministrations from his Aunt.

Betty breaks into the conversation and announces that she will now have Ian on her knee, because Ian might be jealous if she didn't, and she adds that Alec knows her now, and she wants Ian to know her too. Grace sees nothing funny in this, and makes the exchange at once and without comment. We settle down again, and are all quite comfortable and happy until Jack arrives upon the scene, and looks at Betty in amazement and says what on earth is Grace thinking of.

Grace says, "Thinking of?" in a surprised voice.

Jack says, "Yes, what are you thinking of to allow Betty to handle the child? If Betty dropped him on his head, he might be an idiot for life!"

Betty exclaims indignantly, "But I wouldn't dream of dropping Ian; he likes me holding him," Grace points out that it is quite impossible for Betty to drop Ian out of the chair—as indeed it is.

This does not satisfy Jack, however. He says Betty might jump up suddenly, or let go of the child for a moment, and he gives Grace no peace until she removes the baby from Betty's arms. This annoys everybody. Ian screams, Betty sulks, Grace is angry and sarcastic, and I am made to feel that, somehow or other, it is all my fault for consenting to the arrangement. I cannot help reflecting that Jack is a very unsettling sort of person, and very annoying at times. Jack and Grace are obviously fond of each other, and Jack is always buying Grace costly presents which he can ill afford, but they are not partners—as Tim and I are—and they pull in opposite directions.

The twins' Nannie now makes her appearance and invites Betty to come and see them bathed. When they have gone Jack sits down and says he has had a frightful day, and he can't think why all the senior officers at the Depôt are soft in the head. Carter is the worst C.O. in the world, he is incompetent and mulish, and he is so terrified of anything going wrong that he badgers everyone to death. You never have a moment's peace, and you can't get on with the really important things because Carter is always plaguing you about details . . . "If it isn't one thing it's another," says Jack gloomily.

Grace enquires what has happened today—what particular detail has gone wrong—and Jack replies that he has spent hours trying to trace fifty rounds of ammunition which cannot be accounted for. "Fifty rounds!" says Jack in disgust, ". . . and there's a war on! Carter doesn't seem to know there's a war on. How many rounds do they lose in France, I wonder."

"Where can they have gone?" enquires Grace—an unwise question which, in my humble opinion, is unlikely to soothe the savage breast.

"Where can they have gone?" echoes Jack in furious tones. "I should think someone's been shooting rabbits . . . or someone's bagged them to have a pot at Carter . . . perhaps that's why he's in such a flap. Oh hell, I wish I could get out of this place and see some Active Service!"

"Jack!" exclaims Grace in dismay.

"Well, I'm a soldier—not a blinking clerk," says Jack firmly.

It has been difficult for me to know where to look during this heated exchange, for it is always extremely embarrassing to be present on occasions of this nature, and now it is more than ever impossible to look my host in the face, for if it had not been for my unwarranted interference in his affairs he would be on Active Service at this very moment. I rise and collect my reluctant daughter, and hasten home.

TUESDAY 30TH APRIL

The date of Annie's wedding is now approaching and Annie is extremely preoccupied. She goes about with a dazed expression upon her usually serene countenance; she jumps if anyone speaks to her suddenly; she forgets to give us knives and forks with which to eat our food; she forgets to waken us in the morning. As I can sympathise with Annie's feelings, I bear with the small inconveniences in patience and spend a good deal of my time rushing round the house and remedying the deficiencies. It has been settled that Annie shall have a holiday to correspond with her future husband's leave, and they will go south to Annie's parents—who live at Hounslow—and be married there. Meanwhile a substitute for Annie has been found for me by Mrs. Fraser, who recommends her to me by saying, "She's young and daft-like, but I'll see to her."

I present Annie with some extra money and a frock, which is slightly tight for me across the back. It will fit Annie quite well, and she is delighted with it. She takes it and goes away and, a few minutes later, she returns wearing the frock and says she thought I would like to see how nice it is. I *do* like to see it, and compliment her upon her appearance. It suits Annie far better than it suited me.

Annie tries to see her back in the mirror and says, "I've a good mind to get married in it," and I agree that she might do worse. "It's good," says Annie, "that's what I like about it, and nobody's to know but what it isn't new . . . Oh dear," says Annie with a little sniff, "Oh *dear,* I 'ope it's the right thing to do . . . me getting married I mean . . . such a plunge, it is . . . not but what Bollings is a nice fellow."

I reassure Annie as best I can.

"If it wasn't that it was all arranged I'd back down," declares Annie frankly.

I assure Annie that a lot of people feel like that as their wedding day approaches.

"Yes," says Annie. "Mrs. Fraser did too. Mrs. Fraser says it's like 'aving a tooth out. You're sorry you ever came when you find yourself in the dentist's chair, but you're all the better for it afterwards."

WEDNESDAY 1ST MAY

Annie leaves in the morning and her substitute arrives in the afternoon. Mrs. Fraser brings her into the drawing room and says, "This is her," and goes away. She is a small plump girl with round brown eyes, and is neatly dressed in a tailored coat with a fur collar and a scarlet beret. She says her name is Florence Mackay, but I can call her Florrie, if I like—"lots o' folks do." It is a little difficult to know what to say to this, so I leave it and proceed to outline her duties, but I have not got far when she interrupts me.

"There's nae need for that," she announces. "They'll just be the usual things. I ken fine whit's wanted in a hoose."

"You've had experience?" I enquire, somewhat surprised, for Mrs. Fraser has led me to believe that her experience is extremely limited.

"Lots of it," replies the girl firmly. "I can dae the hoose, and the table, and I can dae the cooking when the auld wumman's oot."

There is no more to be said, so I declare the interview at an end, and suggest that Florence (or Florrie) should go upstairs and change her dress. Pinkie and I congratulate ourselves on the fact that Annie's substitute knows her job, but unfortunately we congratulate ourselves too soon, for if Florence has had any experience, it has not been gained in a house like mine. It would have been better—from our point of view—if she had had no experience at all, for in that case she might have been willing to listen to reason. It would be *very* much better —from our point of view—if Florence were not so full of unbounded confidence in her own abilities, or so certain that in all matters of domestic procedure she was right and we were wrong. Mrs. Fraser sums up the situation in her usual trenchant manner. "The gurrl wouldna' be sae bad if she would take a telling," says Mrs. Fraser.

THURSDAY 2ND MAY

Am invited to go to tea with Mrs. Loudon at her rooms, and set off in good time, as I am aware that she likes her guests to be punctual. Mrs. Loudon is so pleased to see me that I feel quite sorry for her, and I ask whether she is feeling very bored here, and why she does not go home. She replies that she *is* bored, for there's nothing on earth to do except visit Guthrie at the hospital, but as he is better and likely to get leave soon she has decided to wait for him and take him home with her. I suggest she should go on in advance, and Guthrie could follow when he gets his discharge, but she replies somewhat cryptically, "I daresay he could, but would he? It's safer to wait and take him with me. Come away in and have some tea."

It is curious to see Mrs. Loudon in these rooms, for they do not suit her personality at all, and she has made no attempt to alter them, but is abiding amongst Mrs. MacPhail's goods and chattels like a person in a waiting room at a railway station. I have been forced to dwell amongst other people's belongings all my life, but I have always managed to make a home amongst them. The first thing to do, on arrival at a new house, is to remove the plethora of useless and tasteless objects with which people who let rooms and furnished houses clutter the available space, but Mrs. Loudon has removed nothing—not even a small round red plush footstool from the hearth rug, not even the antimacassars from the backs of the chairs.

"Yes, it's an awful place," says Mrs. Loudon, following my eyes round the room. "That blue vase gives me the shudders whenever I look its way—and the pink cushion—and yon antimacassar with the dragons. Oh well, I'll be glad when I can get home and no doubt I'll appreciate it the more."

I suggest that the offending objects should be removed.

"I've thought of it," admits Mrs. Loudon nodding at me gravely over the tea pot. "I've thought of it once or twice—but she might be hurt. She's a dwaibly sort of creature and I wouldn't care to hurt her feelings, Hester. She worked the antimacassar herself, poor body, and she put yon footstool there for me because I'd had lumbago—though how the footstool could help me I fail to see. She brought the thing up and put it there with her own hands, and if I've fallen over it once I've fallen over it a dozen times. And yon wee bamboo table with the fern, it gets in my road whenever I open or shut the window. Dear knows how it's survived! I'll be glad when I get out of the place with a whole skin—but never mind that. Have a cookie, Hester."

I accept one.

"Now then!" says Mrs. Loudon, sitting up even straighter than usual in her plush-covered chair, "Now then, I've something to ask you. Will you and Betty come to Avielochan for a visit when Guthrie's better—and Bryan too, if he's still at home—it would do you all a lot of good to have a wee change."

"It's very kind of you, but I'm afraid I can't."

"And why not, may I ask?"

"Because I've got work to do," I reply, smiling at her.

"Pooh!" exclaims Mrs. Loudon. "Somebody else could take a hand at it, and high time too. You need a holiday, Hester."

"No, I can't leave just now. There's a lot to do, and nobody to do it. I might come later on when Grace MacDougall is better—"

"It's now I want you," declares Mrs. Loudon. "Now, when Guthrie's at home. I'm not at all sure he's not hankering after that red-haired nurse—"

We argue for several minutes, but I have made up my mind and Mrs. Loudon's persuasions will not move me. I have interfered once before in Guthrie's love affairs, and although it is true that my interference produced the desired result, I am determined not to repeat the experiment.

FRIDAY 3RD MAY

Grace rings up and enquires whether Pinkie and I will go round after dinner for a chat. She explains that she would ask us to dinner if she could, but her servants have both left to go into munitions, and she has not been able to get anyone else . . . "It seems so awfully mingy to ask you *after* dinner," declares Grace apologetically; "but the only thing I can make really well is a soufflé, and I should have to be in the kitchen when you arrive—watching over it like a guardian angel—and my hair would be standing on end, and my nose would be red and shiny . . . so you see."

I appreciate Grace's difficulty at a glance, and assure her that there is absolutely no need to ask us to dinner, and that Pinkie and I will dine at home and come round afterwards. . . .

Having accepted the invitation on the spur of the moment, I begin to have qualms as to whether I should have done so without consulting Pinkie, for it is quite likely that she may have made other arrangements. Pinkie has settled down as if she belonged to the family, and I am delighted to have her as long as she can stay. She is an easy guest, for she requires no entertainment, and she has the rare virtue of being at hand when wanted, and of disappearing for hours when her hostess is busy or tired. Bryan and Betty adore her, and the servants are her willing slaves—it is like having a grown-up daughter in the house. I have encouraged her to make her own plans, for it is so much better for us both to be free. Pinkie goes out to tennis, and sometimes to the pictures, and I have my own friends to visit. In this way we have more to talk about when we are together. I notice that the subalterns drop in more frequently than usual, but am not deceived by their unwonted anxiety as to how I am getting on. Bill, who was Pinkie's first friend, pursues her indefatigably, but does not seem to be making much headway. She is nice to him, of course, but Pinkie is nice to everyone—she distributes her smiles with fine impartiality. Young Craddock is another constant visitor, and is often accompanied by his colonel. It is all very cheerful and amusing, and if Tim were here I should be completely happy . . . but alas, Tim is not here.

I discover at teatime that Pinkie has made a "date" with young Craddock, so she will not be able to accompany me tonight. She offers to put it off, but I see no need for this, it will be more amusing for her to go to the pictures than to come to the MacDougalls' for a quiet chat.

"It's *Rebecca,* you see," says Pinkie; "so if you really don't mind . . . but if you *do* mind the least bit . . . or if you don't like the idea of walking down to the MacDougalls' by yourself in the black-out . . ."

I assure her that I don't mind at all, and that I am quite capable of looking after myself.

"Take your torch," says Pinkie, "and be *very* careful crossing the road."

It is a fine night and the walk is quite enjoyable. I have been out so little since the war started that it is quite a pleasant change. The black-out in Donford seems fairly satisfactory, and except for an occasional slit of faint light at the edge of a window, the darkness is complete.

Jack opens the door and ushers me into the drawing room, where Grace is discovered reclining in a large armchair. She is looking less soignée than usual, and seems somewhat fretful. "My dear, I'm nearly dead," says Grace. "I seem to have spent the whole day washing dishes. Nannie helps, of course, but she hasn't much time . . . we shall both be thankful when the new cook arrives. I don't mind anything except the dishes, but they go on all the time, and no sooner have you got them all nice and clean than they are all dirty again. People use far too many dishes—far more than they need— and as for spoons and forks—"

"Well, you can't eat rice pudding with your finger," says Jack firmly. "I defy anyone to do that—especially when it is the consistency of soup—"

Grace replies that it was quite a good pudding, and that he could have eaten it with a spoon only, and not used a fork as well, which makes it clear that there has been some unpleasantness between my host and hostess.

"I like to sit down for a little after my meals," explains Grace. "I like to digest them peacefully with a cigarette, but the mere fact that there is a large pile of dishes waiting to be washed makes it quite impossible to digest my meals in peace . . . washing up dishes is my idea of hell," adds Grace thoughtfully.

It is mine also, so I can sympathise with her.

"Yes," says Grace. "I could have given Milton a few tips

when he wrote *Paradise Lost*. My hell will be washing greasy dishes in insufficient lukewarm water. The dish towels will be damp and slimy, and the pile of dishes will grow and grow until there's no room to put them *anywhere*."

"Dust would be worse," declares Jack—and I can't help smiling, for dust is Tim's pet horror and aversion—"Dust would be infinitely worse. My hell would be full of dust and germs, and I should have to sweep it with one of those old-fashioned brooms that people used before vacuum cleaners were invented—horrible unhygienic things they were!"

"That's a sort of nightmare," declares Grace; but Jack does not agree. "A nightmare is quite different," he replies. "As a matter of fact I had a most awful nightmare last night. I dreamt I was in the orderly room with stacks of papers to deal with and the sun was shining brightly outside. I wanted to get out, but I knew I had to deal with all the papers before I went, and the papers kept on increasing and increasing in a mysterious kind of way, and at last they were all round me and all over me and I was smothering in them."

I make sympathetic sounds, but Grace, who has obviously heard the story before, is eager to recount her pet nightmare, which she invariably experiences if she is so unwise as to eat anything cheesy for dinner. She is trying to pack her clothes in a hurry, so as to catch a train, and she has not enough trunks or suitcases in which to pack them . . . and, every time she thinks she has finished her task, she pulls out another drawer and finds it full of clothes. We discuss nightmares in general terms and Jack enquires whether I ever suffer from a nightmare—the kind of nightmare which returns and returns and haunts one during the day. I reply, somewhat reluctantly, that I do, but I am not particularly anxious to recount my nightmare, for it is so horrible to me that I prefer not to think of it. Strangely enough my reluctance has the effect of whetting

Jack's interest, and he urges me to tell them about it, and continues to urge me until I realise that it will be easier to comply with his request than to refuse. Before describing my nightmare, I premise that it is difficult to define the horror of it to other people, so, if they are expecting something startling, they will probably be disappointed. My nightmare begins in a very ordinary sort of way: I wake up—just as I wake every morning—to find Annie in my room with my morning tea. She puts it on the table beside my bed—just as she always does—and then she says something to me; I can see that she is telling me something very important, but I can't understand a word she says. The frightful part of it is that I am aware that I shall *never* be able to understand what *anyone* says. Tim speaks to me too—and I can't understand a word. Tim and Annie speak to each other—and I can't understand a word. Other people come in and talk to me and gesticulate—"Wah wah ditchy wen, ditchy wen waddy wah wah," says everyone earnestly . . . and I wake up dripping with heat and trembling in every limb.

Grace says, "My dear, it's perfectly frightful! It's the *most* frightful nightmare I ever heard of. I wonder what it means. Perhaps Ermyntrude would know, she knows all about dreams and things—they all mean something."

I feel that I would rather not know what my nightmare means, but am too cowardly to say so.

At this moment the front door bell rings and Jack goes to answer it, and returns with Bill Taylor. He is evidently expected, for Grace says, "Oh, here you are! I thought perhaps you weren't able to get away."

"Well, it wasn't easy," replies Bill. "But I managed to get someone to take my duty . . ." his eyes stray round the room and he adds, "I thought you said . . ."

"I know," murmurs Grace. "I hoped she was coming tonight."

It is quite obvious that Pinkie is the mysterious "she" and that Grace's scheme has gone awry. For some reason I feel somewhat annoyed with Grace—she has no right to poke her fingers into this particular pie—and I am quite glad that Pinkie has not come. We chat for a little, but Bill is restless and after about a quarter of an hour, during which he has been extremely distrait he rises and says that he must be off. Jack offers him a whisky and soda, but he refuses the solace, saying that he will go back to his quarters, and do some work, and that he can work better without the aid of stimulants. This surprises Jack a good deal, and he declares—as he escorts Bill to the door—that it is quite impossible for him to make any serious mental effort without an occasional whisky and soda to jolly up his brain.

When they have gone Grace turns to me and says, "You must do something, Hester. You must take a firm line with Pinkie."

"Why should I?" I enquire.

"She's making poor Bill miserable," replies Grace in indignant tones.

It seems to me that Bill is making himself miserable, and I point this out to Grace, adding that I have no intention of interfering in Pinkie's affairs.

Soon after this I take my departure, and Jack walks home with me to my gate.

SATURDAY 4TH MAY

Today is the day of the Sherry Party at the Donford Arms and as Pinkie and I have received an invitation and replied, in the usual and somewhat absurd phraseology, that "Mrs.

Christie and Miss Bradshaw accept with much pleasure etc. etc." we are now engaged in preparation for the event. Pinkie has a flair for clothes which was cultivated during her sojourn in Paris. She refuses to allow me to wear my best hat—which, to tell the truth, has seen a good deal of service—but ransacks my cupboard for something more stylish, and finding an old velour she strips off the trimming, turns it inside out, sticks several pins into it and places it upon my head. "Wear it just like *that*," says Pinkie firmly.

I rush to the mirror expecting to see a figure of fun, but am utterly confounded; the result of Pinkie's slapdash treatment is so incredibly good that I agree to wear it "just like that". Pinkie herself is extremely smart in black and white—a truly Parisian ensemble which has the effect of making her look a good deal older than usual. The long mirror in the hall which we consult before leaving home assures us that we can pass muster.

Donford High Street is full of cars and the Donford Arms seems to have gone all Military for the evening. There are sentries outside the door, and stewards to open the door, and the hall is full of officers' batmen dashing about with trays. Symes has been given the task of announcing the guests and he is doing it extremely well—announcing them loudly and clearly.

The large room is already comfortably full of officers and guests when Pinkie and I walk in. We are warmly welcomed by George Craddock, who looks like the advertisement of an officers' tailor in a new and perfectly fitting tunic and a shining, chestnut-coloured Sam Brown. His face is pinker than ever and his hair has been cut so short as to be almost invisible to the naked eye. "Here you are!" he cries delightedly. "Here you are! Splendid! Two sherries, Waddell . . . that's right . . . where are the biscuits and things? The colonel said I was to tell him when you came."

"Where is he?" I enquire, trying to discover Tony's tall figure amongst the crowd.

"Over near the fireplace," replies George. "That's a general he's talking to—the fat one with the red face—so I don't want to butt in. I wonder what I'd better do—he said I was to tell him when you came in."

It is impossible to advise George, not only because I am ignorant of the proper procedure, but also because we are suddenly separated by an influx of new arivals.

One of the new arrivals is Captain Baker; he smiles at me in a friendly manner and seems delighted to renew our acquaintance. "I feel a bit of an impostor here," he says confidentially. I enquire whether he has gate-crashed, but he replies that on the contrary he received a very large card printed in gold letters inviting him to the feast.

"Then why do you feel like an impostor?" I ask with interest.

"Because I'm not a real soldier," replies Captain Baker. "I was too young for the last war and I'm too old for this one. . . . Oh yes, I know I'm in uniform, but fine feathers don't make fine birds."

It is true that soldiers predominate here, but, whether or not they are all real according to Captain Baker's standard, it would be difficult to say. I can sympathise readily with Captain Baker's feelings, because I have often felt like a fish out of water in an assembly of civilians. Captain Baker seems surprised to hear this, and says that he had no idea that there was any feeling of that kind in the country. "Are you sure you did not imagine it?" he enquires.

"Perfectly certain," I reply firmly. "I don't say that the feeling was general, but in some parts of this country—before this war—there was a tendency to look down upon soldiers and their wives and to treat them as if they belonged to a lower order of beings. . ."

"Well, you've got your own back now," declares Captain Baker a trifle grimly.

"I don't want my own back," I cry. "I mean I hate to see the whole population turning itself into soldiers. I'd rather be treated like a leper all my life. . ."

Jack MacDougall is suddenly forced between us by pressure from the crowd, "Hullo!" he says. "Have I interrupted you? What do you think about Norway?"

"Bad," says Captain Baker. "We shall have to evacuate—at least it looks like that."

A voice behind me says, "Hester, is it you?" and turning round I find myself face to face with Mrs. Loudon. It is surprising to see her here, for sherry parties are not in her line, but she explains her presence by saying that Colonel Morley asked her to come and she thought it would be pleasant to have a crack with him . . . "but I might have stayed comfortably at home for all the talk I'll get with *him*," adds Mrs. Loudon, surveying her fellow guests in great disgust.

"How's Guthrie?" I enquire, for I have not visited the invalid lately and am feeling conscious of my neglect.

Mrs. Loudon replies that Guthrie is perfectly well and is likely to be discharged from the hospital shortly. She goes on to say that she is wearying for Avielochan and the peaceful hills, but for some reason Guthrie is not.

"Guthrie is not!" I echo in surprise.

"No," says Mrs. Loudon. "He seems perfectly content to remain in hospital. I can't understand it at all—unless it is that nurse. What do you think I should do, Hester?"

The room is now much too crowded to talk with comfort—or even to think—and the noise of chatter and laughter, the clink of glasses, the human waves and eddies caused by the passage of stewards with trays of tempting savouries and biscuits make consecutive conversation impossible. Before I can reply to Mrs. Loudon's question, she is swept away and disappears behind a broad khaki back. Pinkie has vanished completely, and I am alone in the crowd. Snatches of conversation reach my ears from various directions:—

"But, my dear girl, we can't spare more troops for Norway . . ."

". . . it burst in the road and broke all the windows. . ."

". . . so I told the butcher that he shouldn't have taken *all* the coupons, and he said. . ."

"Holland will be the next. I don't mind betting you that's the reason for our withdrawal. . ."

". . . so I said well of course, if you want to go and make munitions. . ."

". . . I was *terrified,* my dear. It ran under the dresser. I said to John, you must get a trap. . ."

". . . and I haven't had a letter from him for a fortnight . . ."

". . . no, she's in the Wrens. She's doing coding. . ."

". . . but they prefer an eleven inch foot. You cast on sixty stitches. . ."

". . . in hospital at Grimsby, but Edith heard yesterday. . ."

The crowd divides for a moment, and I have a glimpse of Grace; she is talking with animation; her eyes are bright with excitement, her hat is tilted at a becoming angle upon her neat dark head. Almost at the same moment, I recognise Mrs. Benson's brick red hat, and realise that it is coming in my direction. I turn to flee and bump into Miss Browne Winters and upset her sherry on to the floor. . .

"But it does not matter in the least," declares Miss Browne

Winters in answer to my abject apologies. "It is merely one of those trivial accidents which have no importance in the Scheme . . . such things are only important if we allow them to disturb us."

I assure her that it has disturbed me, and apologise again for my clumsiness.

". . . but it has *not* disturbed *me,*" says Miss Browne Winters firmly.

This statement—and the tone in which it is uttered—leave me without anything further to say, but I am not satisfied with the conclusion and I continue to work it out in my own mind. If—as Miss Browne Winters declares—the accident is only important in so far as it disturbs our equilibrium, it must be important because it has disturbed mine; and is it not a trifle selfish of her to be so completely undisturbed by my distress? By the time I have reached this point in my meditations Miss Browne Winters has managed to stop a passing steward and has substituted her empty glass for a full one from his tray. I am about to congratulate her on her cleverness, when we are separated by a large fat woman saying "Excuse me" and pushing between us, and by the time we have found each other again it seems scarcely worth while to reopen the subject.

The band has now started to play, which adds to the noise. Miss Browne Winters leans towards me and enquires in a ringing tone, "What are they playing, Mrs. Christie?"

"I don't know," I shout in reply.

"It seems to strike a chord of memory, I wish I knew where I heard that tune before."

A voice behind me announces, "Say it over and over again . . . over and over again . . . never stop saying you're mine." The voice is the voice of my host, Tony Morley, and I am aware that he is replying to the question which has just been put to me by Miss Browne Winters, but it is obvious from her startled expression that she has not grasped this fact. I therefore seize her by the arm and say, "That's what it's called. May I introduce Colonel Morley . . . Miss Browne Winters."

"How do you do, Miss Withers," says Tony. "It's a silly tune, isn't it? Frightfully silly . . . and yet there's something in it, you know. 'Never Stop Saying You're Mine.' I shouldn't have known what it was called if I hadn't happened to see the programme. Can't keep pace with all these new tunes. Perhaps you can."

Miss B.W. replies promptly that she does not try. She finds the past more interesting than the present, and she is about to produce reasons for her preference when Tony interrupts her by saying "It has been *such* a pleasure to meet you, Miss Withers. You *will* excuse us, won't you. I've promised to introduce Hester to Lady Neckley," and before I know where I am, Tony has me firmly by the arm and is steering me through the crowd.

Now that Tony has taken charge I feel less like an unclaimed parcel at the lost luggage office, but I still feel somewhat dazed. I am introduced to the general's wife (Lady Neckley) and listen meekly while she tells me about her grandchild; I am rescued from her—again by Tony—and several officers of the Fourth are introduced to me; I find Pinkie and lose her again; I have another scrappy conversation with Mrs. Loudon; I speak to Herbert Carter; I run up against Grace and enquire after the twins. Suddenly I look round the room and discover that the company is thinning rapidly, and that it is time to go. Pinkie is easily found now—but not so easily detached from a large red-haired captain, with whom she is exchanging pleasantries.

As we walk home together Pinkie exclaims in rapturous

tones, "Oh, what a lovely party it was! I *did* enjoy it, didn't you, Hester?"

"Yes," I reply a trifle doubtfully. "Yes, I did . . . but I don't know *why* I enjoyed it."

"You enjoyed it because you looked so *nice*," declares Pinkie, squeezing my arm. She is silent for a few moments after uttering this profound piece of psychology, and then she enquires a trifle differently, "Did you notice that I called you 'Hester'?"

"No, I didn't."

"That's all right then," says Pinkie, smiling, "if you didn't notice, it means you didn't mind."

MONDAY 6TH MAY

Guthrie is convalescent and has been given a fortnight's leave, so he and his mother depart to Avielochan. Their train leaves at 9:15 and Bryan's at 11:30, so I spend most of the morning dashing backwards and forwards to the station and seeing people off. Bryan is much excited at the prospect of his visit to London, and listens to my instructions with some impatience, but, as I am extremely anxious for my son to make a good impression upon Richard and Mary, I continue my efforts feverishly.

We are on the platform now, awaiting the arrival of the train, and I spend the last few minutes reiterating the principal points of conduct befitting a gentleman of Bryan's years, "They have no children of their own," I remind Bryan, "so they aren't used to boys."

"Oh yes," says Bryan. "You told me that before."

"Be sure to wipe your feet on the mat . . . and change your shoes if they're muddy."

"Oh yes, of course," says Bryan.

"Remember to wash your hands before meals," I adjure him, "and be sure to wash them thoroughly before you dry them on the towel . . . and get up out of your chair when Aunt Mary comes in."

"Oh yes," says Bryan. "I know all of that."

"Don't throw the bathroom towel on the floor," I continue earnestly, "and don't scatter your cap and gloves all over the hall, and don't forget to use your table napkin. . ."

"Oh Mum," says Bryan reproachfully. "Oh Mum, why *are* you worrying? You know quite well I can behave beautifully when I like."

As this is perfectly true, there is nothing more to be said.

Return home to lunch feeling extremely flat. Pinkie is also somewhat depressed and the meal is taken in silence save for an occasional remark by Betty between mouthfuls of food. After lunch Pinkie suggests that she and I should go to the pictures to cheer ourselves up. I enquire what Bill is doing, or young Craddock, but Pinkie says she would rather go with me.

We walk down to the Picture House and take our seats, but unfortunately the film is by no means cheering. It is an American film of the worst type, with frequent close-ups and glycerine tears. The story is centred round a small child whose father and mother misunderstand each other and decide to get a divorce. The child loves them both and is torn between them. Its poor little heart is broken, but it suffers in silence and presents a brave front to the unsuspecting world . . . we see the child growing thinner and paler before our eyes, but apparently its relatives are blind, for they go on their ways oblivious of its dwindling strength . . . eventually the child dies (I have been dreading this climax for the last two reels) and the parents are reunited over its dead body.

Pinkie and I emerge into the sunshine with blotched faces and smarting eyes. Pinkie squeezes my arm and says, "Wasn't it *beastly*? I don't know why I cried . . . it was false all through. The man was horrible. His hair was permed and I'm sure he used scent."

Enquire with interest how she could possibly know of this depraved taste on the part of the man.

Pinkie says he was that sort of man . . . and the woman was worse if anything . . . as for the child it was positively disgusting, don't I agree?

I agree wholeheartedly.

"It has made me feel that I need a bath," says Pinkie gravely, "and I believe that's just what I'll do."

Pinkie bathes and, emerging pink and cheerful from the steam-filled bathroom, she declares that she feels much better now and adds that nobody could commit suicide after a nice hot bath.

I enquire whether she felt like suicide before and Pinkie replies that she did, everything was beastly and the film put the lid on.

WEDNESDAY 8TH MAY

I am just changing my shoes to go out when Annie's substitute knocks loudly upon my bedroom door and says in a hoarse voice, "It's Lady Morley."

"On the telephone?" I enquire.

"Naw, she's *here*," says Annie's substitute. "She's wanting tae see you, but she wouldna' say whit she wanted . . . she's gey and auld and she's got ane o' they furry capes . . ."

By this time I am half way down the stairs, for heaven alone knows what Annie's substitute has said or done to my distinguished visitor. I had half expected to find her languishing on the doorstep in the rain, but luckily she has been allowed to come into the hall. I welcome Lady Morley and say how glad I am to see her, and Lady Morley explains that she is staying at the "Donford Arms" for a few days because she wanted to see Tony—and it seemed quite impossible for the poor boy to get leave—and Tony suggested that she should call on me while she was here.

I repeat that I am delighted to see her.

"You stayed at Charters Towers, didn't you?" says Lady Morley a trifle doubtfully.

I reply that I have had that pleasure.

"Yes," says Lady Morley. "Yes, I was sure I had seen you before."

I have managed to get her into the drawing room by this time—fortunately it seems fairly tidy—and I introduce Pinkie, who has been indulging in forty winks on the drawing-room sofa and arises therefrom, surprised and dishevelled but beautiful as ever. It is obvious that Lady Morley is struck with Pinkie; she raises her lorgnette and looks at Pinkie intently and murmurs to herself, "Very nice indeed."

It is now incumbent upon me to invite my visitor to stay to tea and I endeavour to do so cordially, though cordiality is somewhat difficult to achieve, because there are only three scones in the house and the remains of a madeira cake. In addition I am aware that Florence has no idea where my best lace tea cloths are kept, and I feel sure that her ministrations will compare unfavourably with those of the butler at Charters Towers. Lady Morley hesitates for a moment and my hopes soar high . . . then she accepts the invitation, saying that it is very kind, and hotel teas are so unappetising. Feel even more doubtful whether the three scones and the piece of stale madeira will meet with Lady Morley's approval.

We sit down and talk, and, while we are talking Pinkie

vanishes. Her defection annoys me a good deal, for I have been counting upon her to help entertain my guest. The truth is that Lady Morley and I inhabit different worlds and have so little in common that it is almost impossible for us to find subjects of conversation. Lady Morley does not help very much, for she is used to being entertained. She takes off her sable cape and waits for me to entertain her. I enquire whether she has been out to the camp, and whether she has seen Tony's quarters, and she replies that the hut is very draughty. I remark that Tony looks well, and she agrees—though very reluctantly—that he does. We decide that Tony's robust health must be due to the fact that Donford is a healthy place. Now that we are on the subject of health, I enquire for Sir Abraham, and Lady Morley replies that he is better. She makes this admission grudgingly, and adds that she does not know why he is better because the Specialist said Rest Was Essential and, now that Tony has gone, the management of the Estates has devolved upon Sir Abraham. I suggest that doctors are not always right and Lady Morley agrees that even Harley Street may make mistakes. We are still discussing Harley Street—a subject upon which I am entirely uninformed —when the door opens and tea appears . . . a magnificent tea, which, to my startled eyes, seems like a vision from the Arabian Nights. I lose the thread of my visitor's conversation completely, as I behold scones and cakes and plates of thin bread and butter—or is it margarine—being laid out upon a snowy embroidered cloth.

Pinkie strolls in and says, "Oh, is tea ready?" but her nonchalant manner does not deceive me, nor do I require the wink which is conveyed to me behind Lady Morley's back, to inform me who is the author of the feast.

Betty has been promoted to drawing-room tea (owing to the absence of Annie) and as she has not come down I make my excuses to Lady Morley and go upstairs to find her. It will be just as well to get hold of Betty and see that she is clean and tidy before she makes her appearance . . .

I find Betty sitting on the nursery floor with her legs stretched out in front of her and large tears pouring down her cheeks. "I'm paralysed," says Betty with a sob. "My leg is paralysed—I'm like that little boy that goes to school—and can't walk—"

"Betty darling!"

"I didn't scream—because there's a lady in the drawing room —I just bore it—"

"Darling!" I cry, hugging her. "Darling you *can't* be paralysed all of a sudden like that."

"But I *am,*" wails Betty. "I *am,* I tell you. I can't move my leg at all."

"Where does it hurt?" I enquire, feeling the injured limb— and in spite of all that I can do to remain calm my hands tremble—

"It doesn't hurt," she sobs, "It doesn't *feel*—Oh, dear, I shall be like Freddie, I shan't be able to walk ever again—"

"But what were you doing?" I ask. "When did you find it had gone like that? Can you bend your knee? Do try to be sensible, darling."

Betty tries to be sensible and chokes back her tears. "I was sitting on the floor," she says with a little catch in her breath. "I was sitting just here, playing with the doll's house— and when I tried to get up—and I tried to stand—my leg was like cotton wool—and now it's full of fizzy lemonade—"

Just for a few moments I was frightened (and moments like these add years to one's age). I had envisaged doctors, and wheel chairs, and a ghastly iron boot—but now I perceive that my alarm was needless—"Don't cry," I beseech Betty. "It's

quite all right—it's nothing the least serious. Your leg had
gone to sleep, that's all . . . look, I'll rub it for you."

I rub her leg briskly and after a few moments she smiles
and says it has wakened up now, so we had better go down
to tea, and when her face has been washed and her hair
brushed, she seems none the worse of her alarming experience.
Together we descend the stairs and now that my anxiety is
relieved my thoughts return to my visitor—I have left her
for hours (or so it seems to me) and have left poor Pinkie to
entertain her, but I soon find that I need not have worried, for
the two of them are talking with animation.

Pinkie turns to me and says, "Oh Hester, we just went on
with tea—you don't mind, do you?" and turns back to Lady
Morley and exclaims, "Oh, but I like Adrian *much* better."

Lady Morley replies, "But Rupert is brilliant, and a very
fine rider to hounds. My daughter has a great admiration for
Rupert."

It is obvious from this exchange that my guests have discovered mutual friends and, as I pour out Betty's milk and
spread honey on her scone, I hope devoutly that the family is
numerous and diverse and that much remains to be said about
them.

"Will you have a sandwich, Lady Morley?" enquires Pinkie,
handing her a plate of delicious tomato sandwiches.

Lady Morley refuses at first, but, when pressed, she changes
her mind; whereupon Betty, who has been silent up to now,
says in a loud voice, "You don't need to have one if you don't
like them, because we can easily finish them up."

This pointed remark, from a hitherto dumb child, startles
her ladyship considerably, and makes Pinkie choke. It startles
me also, for I now perceive that Betty is suffering from a
reaction to her recent experience, and is feeling on top of the
world. Her cheeks are very pink and her eyes are shining,

and she is ready to take an active part in the conversation.
When Betty is in this mood she may say or do practically
anything—and for all I know Lady Morley holds the opinion
that children should be seen and not heard. I grasp at the first
straw of conversation I can think of, and find myself telling
Lady Morley that Betty's nurse has left to be married, so Betty
is having tea with us.

Lady Morley says that is very nice, but obviously does not
think so.

Betty says, "Yes, she's being married *today* and she's going
to send us some of her wedding cake—and then she's going
for a honeymoon with Bollings—and then she's coming back—
and when she comes back she isn't going to sleep with me any
more—she's going to sleep with Bollings—and they're going
to have the big room in the attic—Annie and Bollings are—
and it's been painted and papered—and the paper has got pink
roses on it, and that's Annie's fav'rite flower—and Annie will
be called Mrs. Bollings ever after—and Mrs. Bollings will be
written on her letters instead of Miss Wilkes—I should think
the postman will get a surprise, don't you?"

Lady Morley is too dazed to make any reply, and there is a
short, but somewhat strained, silence.

Pinkie says, "Will you have a piece of cake, Lady Morley?"
and she accepts it like a woman in a dream.

Betty opens her mouth for further revelations, "Annie has
got a lovely new—" she begins, but I interrupt her hastily
and say that we don't want to hear any more about Annie
just now—Lady Morley would not be interested.

"Why not?" enquires Betty, looking at Lady Morley in surprise. "Why wouldn't she be intrusted? I think Annie is a *very*
intrusting person . . . I wonder if she will have twins!"

I reply with conviction that she will not, and endeavour to
change the subject by offering Betty a chocolate biscuit and

asking whether she has done her prep., but Betty is not so
easily put off.

"How do you know?" she enquires eagerly. "People always
have babies when they've been married, so why shouldn't
Annie have twins like Mrs. MacDougall? I think it would be
lovely if Annie had twins, because I could look after them
for her while she washed the dishes. I think we ought to get
two babies' cots and have them all ready just in case they come
suddenly in the middle of the night when Annie isn't expecting them. It would be awful if we had no beds for them."

Pinkie tries to damp Betty's ardour by saying that Annie
won't have any babies for a long time, and I assert my authority by telling my daughter to go on with her tea and not talk
so much.

Betty says, "All right, I won't talk any more—I just wanted
to *know* . . . and I don't see why Annie shouldn't have twins
tomorrow . . ."

Pinkie says, "How lucky it is that you have got such nice
weather for your stay in Donford, Lady Morley. The camp is
splendid, isn't it? I can't think how they manage to get the
tents in such regular lines."

I say, "Yes, we were over at the camp the other day, and we
thought the lines remarkably regular. Of course Tony is so
clever and capable—"

Pinkie says, "Yes, but don't you remember he told us that
the tents were put up for them before they arrived?"

I say, "Oh yes, how stupid of me to forget."

By this time Lady Morley has recovered a little; she says
it is time for her to go, because Tony is coming to dine with
her at the hotel and she always rests before dinner. I press
her to stay, but not very convincingly; for I feel that I require
rest as much as she does. Pinkie seizes her sable cape and puts
it over her shoulders; I retrieve her gloves from beneath the

table and her bag from beneath the chair. We accompany her to the door—still talking somewhat feverishly—and watch her as she hastens down the path to her large Daimler and is driven away.

THURSDAY 9TH MAY

A letter arrives from Bryan.

"Dear Mummy, How are you getting on? I am getting on O.K. I got here safely and Uncle Richard met me it was dark because of the black out. There were no lights at all except the cars it was not like London but of course it was. It is very nice here and I have got your room that you had when you were a little girl with bars on the windows. It is all like you said I mean the gardens in the middle of the houses and all that. Well we went to a film and it was not in the afternoon either it was at night so you can ammagine how nice it was. It was Gone with the Wind and it lasted a long time but we had choclate creams to eat. we got a taxy and drove home and it was dark like the night I came. I think they must be rich because the house is so big and they have three servants and a basement and never mind about how many taxies or anything like that and you should just see how many pairs of shoes Uncle Richard has much more than Dad and soots too. I did not look but just saw them when I was in his dressing room and the door was open I mean the wardrope so I think they must be rich. It is jolly good food. Aunt Mary thinks I have nice maners because she said so and she is not so pertickuler as you thought but very nice and just puts a clean towel when its dirty I mean the bathroom one but I do try. We bought some more collers because they get dirty in a minnit almost. It is because of the soot. Aunt

Mary liked buying them with me but I payed out of the two pounds so then she bought some choclate for me so I scored. At the restaron where Uncle Richard took us we had lobster and he said you pay the same and it does not matter whether you eat it or not so I was glad he said that at the beginning. Then he said it was worth taking somebody who injoyed their food, so I said well anybody would enjoy lobster. There were people dancing too and we did not go home till half past nine but other nights I go to bed erly to make up. It is his left arm so we were right. She has just come in and said tell Mummy you are a very nice gest so I am telling you. So you dont need to worry. I shall have lots to tell people when I go back to school speshully Edgeburton. It will make a lot of diffrance I mean Edgeburton wont be so cocky. Heed better not.

Please give my love to Pinkie and Betty and love to you too. Your loving Bryan."

WEDNESDAY 15TH MAY

The last few days have been anxious ones for everyone; Pinkie and I have listened to so many news bulletins that we are becoming quite dazed. Pinkie makes the sensible suggestion that we should ration ourselves, and only listen two or three times daily, and I agree, but somehow or other we don't seem able to keep this resolution, and continue to listen whenever we can. Pinkie says she would not feel so awful if she could do something, and enquires whether I think she could get into the Wrens. When I ask, "Why Wrens?" Pinkie replies, "Well, the Navy's so marvellous, isn't it?" We make enquiries about Wrens and find that they will have nobody under eighteen, which rules out Pinkie's hopes for nearly a year. There is so much War News in News Bulletins, in Newspapers, and so much talk about the war that I do not intend to write about it in my diary. Indeed my diary is a sort of escape from the war . . . though it is almost impossible to escape from the anxieties which it brings.

Have just written this when Mamie rings up and says, "Oh Hester, Sergent Major Craven has been killed and Herbert says I must go and see Mrs. Craven . . . I thought perhaps *you* would go. You know her better than I do."

I reply that I will go tomorrow and enquire whether Herbert has any news of the Battalion, but Mamie knows nothing.

SATURDAY 18TH MAY

It is a pleasant custom in Donford for morning shoppers to meet in Ye Olde Tea Shoppe at eleven o'clock and partake of coffee and conversation. Before the war we used to chat about clothes and children and the delinquencies of our servants, but when the war started we talked about the war. Stella Hardford's nephew is in the R.A.F. and we heard a good deal about his exploits; Mamie Carter's cook had a cousin who was scullery maid at No. 10 Downing Street, so Mamie was the possessor of Inside Information; Grace MacDougall is always in the know, and was willing to enlighten her friends . . . but soon there was a change in our attitude, for we were told that we were surrounded by spies. Hitler's agent might be hiding behind the partition which screens the service door; Mussolini's myrmidon might be lurking beneath the settee. It must be admitted that conversation languished when the war was ruled out as a topic to be discussed in a public place— some of us tried to recapture a little of our pre-war interest in domestic matters, but it was a halfhearted attempt.

Most of the usual coffee drinkers are already present when

I slide into my chair. Stella and Mamie are here to represent the Regiment, and Mrs. Huntley and Mrs. Marsden to represent the town. Mrs. Huntley is talking about food cards, but, as we are all familiar with them and somewhat bored at the extra trouble which they occasion, nobody is very interested in what she is saying, and it is with a feeling of relief that I see the swing door open and Grace MacDougall appear, for Grace usually can be depended upon to enliven the proceedings.

"Hullo everyone!" exclaims Grace, as she pulls out a chair and seats herself upon it, "Hullo Mamie, how's Jane . . . what do you call those?" she adds, producing a packet of labels from her shopping bag and placing them on the table.

"Labels!" cry several of us in surprised chorus.

Grace nods, "Yes, labels," she says, "but they call themselves luggage tags—"

We now perceive that the packet, which Grace has placed upon the table, bears the words "luggage tags" written upon it in large black letters.

"Luggage tags!" says Grace again. "Why luggage tags? Can anyone tell me why? It's longer, it's uglier, it isn't even more descriptive."

"It isn't only labels," says Mrs. Marden thoughtfully. "They are altering the names of almost everything, and altering them for the worse."

"Footwear," I suggest, for this particular paronym has always annoyed me profoundly.

"Yes," agrees Grace, immediately. "Yes, footwear. What's the matter with *shoes*—a good, sound, solid, English word—footwear, indeed!"

"I went to buy a petticoat and they offered me an underskirt!" cries Mrs. Muntly.

"I wanted a pair of pyjamas," says Stella, "and they showed me slumber-suits!"

"Dental Cream instead of tooth paste," puts in Mamie eagerly.

The list grows longer and longer, as we all rack our brains and try to out-do each other in suggesting further examples of homologous names. "Neck wear" and "foundation garments" are suggested and condemned.

Yes, Grace has started a hare which provides good sport, and if Hitler's agent is lurking behind the screen he will be vastly disappointed.

TUESDAY 21ST MAY

Return home from a shopping expedition, and discover that various disasters have befallen my household during my absence; the meat has not arrived in time to be cooked for lunch; Mrs. Fraser has mislaid the key of the store-cupboard, and Annie's substitute has dropped a valuable cut glass bowl and smashed it to atoms. The bowl was a present from Tim's uncle and aunt—Uncle Joe and Aunt Posy—and I have always taken the greatest care of it. We have moved fourteen times since our wedding day and the bowl has survived, but Annie's substitute has been too much for it. What annoys me even more than the actual breakage is the fact that Florence shows no regret and expresses no apology whatsoever—

"What were you doing with it?" I enquire, as I view the shattered remains. "Why didn't you leave it alone?"

"I was having a wee look round," replies Florence cheerfully.

"There was no need to *move* the bowl. It was on the top shelf."

"Aye, that's where it was, I just thocht I'd take it doon and have a luik at it and it slipped oot o' my hand. You'll easy get anither."

This is adding insult to injury, and I reply, "Indeed I can't. It was a valuable bowl!"

Florence smiles in a superior manner, "Oh away!" she says. "It was just a wee glass bowl. Woolworth's is full o' wee bowls like yon . . ."

Words fail me—which perhaps is just as well—and I turn and walk away. I seem to have carried out this manoeuvre several times in the last few days. (I seem to be constantly turning and walking away from Florence) but the fact is she annoys me so much that I cannot trust myself to remain in her vicinity . . . Thank Heaven Annie will be back on Friday, I say to myself, as I go upstairs. . . .

The tale of disasters is not yet complete, for, as I am about to remove my hat, I become aware of strange thumpings and rattlings emanating from the bathroom. My first induction is that Mrs. Fraser has heated up the boiler again (she has a habit of piling on fuel to such an extent that the water boils in the pipes and, on several occasions, we have exchanged bitter words on the subject), but no, this noise is different, it is a human noise (so to speak). I rush to the bathroom door and find it locked.

"It's me!" cries Betty from within. "Mummy, it's me—I'm in here and the lock has stuck—I can't get out." She bumps and rattles and bangs at the door in her efforts to liberate herself, and I realise that her imprisonment is driving her quite mad.

"Betty, don't!" I cry, "Don't bang on the door. Try it slowly. Hold the key with both hands."

"I've tried *every* way," she declares. "I've tried and tried . . . so now I'm just banging."—and with that comes the sound of a soft but fairly solid body being hurled against the unyielding wood.

"Betty, stop it at once," I cry. "There's no need to be frightened. I'll send for the plumber and he'll take off the lock."

"How long will he be?"

"Not very long. Can't you pretend that you're a lion in the zoo?" I enquire anxiously.

Betty says, "I don't think so—it's difficult to pretend things all by yourself—and I'm so *lonely.*"

It is obvious from her shaky voice that Betty is very near tears, and I decide that I cannot leave her in solitary confinement until the plumber can be fetched, so I go outside and examine the window with a view to climbing in. Mrs. Fraser follows me expostulating loudly, and declaring that I shall break my neck ". . . and that'll be anither disaster in the hoose."

"We've had three already," I reply.

"Aye, but I've found the key," she declares. "It wis in the pocket of my other apron . . . so there's only been two . . ."

It would be a major disaster if I broke my neck, but there is no reason to anticipate such an occurrence, for if the steps are brought and reared against the wall I can climb on to the roof of the wash house and from thence to the gable. The bathroom window is large enough to admit me and will open from the bottom. Mrs. Fraser is unconverted by this simple explanation, and continues to make objections—"You'll never do it," she declares. "It's a daft-like thing altogether. I'll not have hand nor part in it. We've telephoned auld Growther and he'll be here before very long."

"He won't he here for at least half an hour," I reply.

"Send the gurrl," whispers Mrs. Fraser, nodding towards the pantry window, where Florence's head is visible.

This idea does not appeal to me at all, and I point out that *she* might break *her* neck, but Mrs. Fraser doesn't seem to think that this would matter.

The steps are brought and reared against the wall, but unfortunately they are too short for my purpose. I can reach the edge of the roof with the tips of my fingers, but am unable to pull myself up.

"There!" says Mrs. Fraser, with a sigh of relief, "there, ye'll no can do it. We'll need to wait for auld Growther after all." But by this time Betty's sobs are distinctly audible, and I refuse to be beaten. We carry out the kitchen table, and put the steps on the top of it—they are amply long enough now—and I prepare to make the ascent.

"I doot ye'll fall," murmurs Mrs. Fraser. "It's a daft-like affair—I gave Annie my word I'd look oot for you while she was away—she'll no be best pleased gin she comes hame and finds you've broken your neck—"

By this time I have mounted the table and have put my foot on the steps. Mrs. Fraser is holding them, but, in spite of her efforts to steady them, they wobble uncomfortably. I look up and take a grip of the ivy on the wall, and assure myself that I can do it easily—

"Here, stop!" cries a voice in peremptory tones, "Hester, come down . . . what are you doing? Wait! Hold on a moment!"

It is Tony Morley, and he is approaching rapidly—running up the path from the gate and waving his arms and shouting—Mrs. Fraser grabs my skirt, so I am obliged to wait, and when Tony arrives at the base of operations, she proceeds to enlighten him. It is obvious that she regards Tony as an ally, and a valuable one at that, perhaps she is remembering the assistance he rendered her in weighing out the ingredients for her cake . . . "I'm thankful you've come," she declares, "I'm just *thankful*. Maybe you can do something with her . . . she'll break her neck, and if I've tellt her once, I've tellt her hawf a dizen times, but when she's set on a thing, she's neether to hawd nor to bind . . ."

"I know," agrees Tony gravely. "I can sympathise with you, cook. The mule has a plastic nature compared with Mrs. Christie."

Betty's face now appears at the bathroom window; there are tears on her cheeks, but she is smiling through them so cheerfully that it looks as if a rainbow might suddenly spring to view. "Oh, are you going to climb up?" she enquires. "Oh what fun! I'm like the princess in the tower—you know the story—'Rapunzel, Rapunzel, let down your hair'!"

"Well, let it down, then," says Tony, looking up at her.

"But I can't, because it's too short," replies Betty chuckling.

"Then I'll have to do without, I suppose."

Tony has mounted the table, and is about to climb the ladder when it occurs to me that Betty has recovered very rapidly from her tears, and being of a suspicious nature I call to him to wait, and take a firm grip of his tunic to make sure that he obeys the command.

"Why is he to wait?" asks Betty. "Oh, do let him come. It's such fun—Oh do let him, Mummy!"

"Is the door still locked?" I enquire in tones which will brook no prevarication.

Betty's face changes. "Well . . . no," she says reluctantly. "As a matter of fact it's open now. I put my toothbrush through the handle of the key and it turned quite easily."

SATURDAY 25TH MAY

Tony Morley and young Craddock drop in to tea. The latter is in tennis kit, and asks if Pinkie will come down to the courts for a game. I am somewhat surprised that Tony does not want to play too, as he is a good player and extremely keen. The young people go off in great form, and Tony and I watch them from the window. It has now become obvious that Tony is not himself, he is grave and silent and replies shortly to my attempts at conversation and, when I ask if anything is the matter, he evades the question and enquires if I have any idea where the Battalion is. This is so unlike Tony that I feel my heart sinking . . . it is a definite physical sensation.

"It's no use worrying," says Tony, "but still . . . I mean if you have any idea where they are . . ." and he adds that he wishes to goodness he was there, in the thick of it, instead of sitting here at home trying to instil the elements of soldiering into a lot of half-baked farm labourers and shop assistants.

This is still more unlike Tony, who is really and truly very proud of his Battalion and proud of its progress and its esprit de corps. I seize his arm and demand an explanation.

"I ought to be there," says Tony. "They need everyone, and need them *now.*"

Although I have listened to the news bulletins and read the papers assiduously, it has never occurred to me that the situation in France is desperately grave. It has never crossed my mind that our Army could possibly be defeated. I explain this to Tony, and he replies that it may be all right, but even our fellows can't do much against such overwhelming odds. The enemy have taken Boulogne . . . he doesn't like that, somehow . . . he didn't mean to alarm me, but he just wondered if I had any idea where the Battalion was . . .

"Tony!" I exclaim. "You simply must explain the whole thing. I'm a perfect fool, of course, but I believe I could understand if it was explained to me . . . I'll get a map." After some persuasion Tony agrees to give me an idea of the situation. We sit down at the table with the map between us, and he points out the position of the various forces engaged. The "gap", of which we have heard so much in the last few days, has increased in width and German armoured divisions have penetrated to our rear. Unless the gap can be closed, and closed quickly . . . "but perhaps they'll be able to close it," says Tony without much conviction.

I am still poring over the map, and now that I understand the position I wonder how I can have been blind to the danger—"How will they get away?" I enquire, and there is a horrible sick feeling in my breast.

"Get away?" says Tony. "It hasn't come to that . . . not yet."

Part 3

August—September

It is over two months since I wrote anything in my diary . . . two months which have seemed like two years. I do not think that any two months in the whole history of the world have been so full of terrible events. Holland, Belgium and France have all fallen victims to Germany's lust for power. Her armies have swept over Western Europe like a tidal wave, bringing misery and terror and destruction to millions of innocent people.

The retreat of the Expeditionary Force and their evacuation from Dunkirk are past history now. Our Battalion was evacuated and has now reformed somewhere in England . . . but Tim has not come back. There has been no news of him—either good or bad—he seems to have vanished off the face of the earth. Sometimes I feel hopeful—I feel it is impossible that anything could happen to Tim without my *knowing* it in my very bones—and sometimes I am crushed with despair. Oh Tim, where are you? You can't have gone away and left me here in this horrible, terrifying world alone!

My heart is like a stone without any feeling in it at all. I go on doing things just the same—eating and drinking, counting socks, ordering food, talking to people in the street and replying to their questions—but it is not really Hester who does these things; it is a sort of robot who looks like Hester and carries on in her place.

Pinkie is a great comfort to me and shows great understanding. She is kind, but not too kind. She does not worry me as some people do. It worries me when people stop me in the street and ask for news. They turn their eyes away when I reply, "No, I have no news of him . . . not yet," and I can see that they are sure he will not come back. Letters come from all sorts of people asking for news. Some of the writers are sure that Tim is dead—they don't say so, of course, and their conviction is hidden beneath a false veneer of hopefulness— Others assure me that he is a prisoner in German hands; they are quite certain of it, but can give no reason for their belief. There is a letter from a medium offering to put me in touch with Tim—or, failing that, with one of Tim's comrades who has Passed Over. There are letters which urge me to be brave and face up to it, and letters which are one long moan about the causes of the war, and our unpreparedness, about the collapse of Belgium and the rottenness of France, and the incompetence of our leaders. (Pinkie says "Don't read them, darling, they're just silly, and they make you miserable," but I have to read them.)

There is only one letter which strikes the right note and brings me a feeling of relief. It is from Tim's Uncle Joe, who lives in Essex—near Cobstead. Like all the Christies he was a soldier, but when his father (Tim's grandfather) died, Uncle Joe sent in his papers and retired to Winch Hall, the old family place. He was a gay dog—or so says the family legend—but he never married, and his sister lives with him and keeps house for him. Perhaps the reason that Uncle Joe's letter does not jar me, as the others do, is because Uncle Joe is very fond of Tim, so he is able to understand my feelings . . . "We are both very sorry for you," writes Uncle Joe, "and it would be foolish to say don't worry. We are worrying quite a lot ourselves and nothing seems worthwhile, but we both have a strong feeling that Tim is all right, and that he will come back soon. From what I hear France is in a desperate muddle, people are still drifting back in various ways, and will continue to do so for some time. You will let us know if you hear anything from Tim. Alice joins me in sending love to you and the children. It would be nice if you could all come and stay with us during the holidays—we are getting old, and we have not seen you for a long time—but perhaps before we make any plans we had better wait a little and see what Hitler is going to do next. It looks as if his Blitzkreig on England may start pretty soon, and we are in the Front Line here."

I pass the letter to Pinkie, and Pinkie reads it through. "That's what I call a sensible letter," she declares. "They must be nice—why don't you go and stay with them for a bit?"

"Because . . ." I begin and then I stop.

"I know," says Pinkie. "You can't leave here because Major Tim might come back . . . or you might get a letter telling you where he is. No, of course, you can't go." She hesitates for a moment and then enquires, "but I thought Uncle Joe's sister was called Aunt Posy?"

"We call her Aunt Posy," I reply, "but her real name is Alice. Tim used to go and stay with them when he was a little boy, and it was he who called her Aunt Posy. She is plump and smiling like the plump and smiling aunt in the story of Little White Barbara."

Pinkie does not respond to this explanation, and I realise, in some surprise, that she is too young to have been brought up on the little green books which were our delight when we were small.

MONDAY 5TH AUGUST

I am sitting at the open window trying to read a book when Tubby Baxter is shown in. His sudden appearance is unexpected, for, although I am aware that he came back from Dunkirk, I had no idea that he was in Donford. Tubby is an old friend of mine—he and I have shared some odd experiences—and when I see him walk in, I feel that I am going to cry. It seems such a long time since those carefree days at Biddington, and Tubby has changed. He looks older and more responsible; his round, cheery face has bone in it now, and his jaw is more in evidence. Fortunately I am able to control myself, and to welcome him in a sensible manner.

"It's about the major," says Tubby, sitting down and looking me straight in the face (what a relief, after those turning-away glances to which I have become accustomed). "It's about the major . . . only you mustn't think I know very much, because I don't. It was all such a muddle you see . . . but I just thought you'd like to hear what little I *do* know, and that's why I came."

"It's very nice of you, Tubby."

"No, it isn't" says Tubby firmly. "It's just—well—quite an ordinary thing to do—besides I wanted to see you. I saw a good deal of the major during the retreat," continues Tubby. "We all saw a good deal of him—in fact he seemed to be everywhere at once. He was full of beans. He was simply splendid—and I'm not just saying this to you—everyone said he was splendid. We marched and marched. You got dazed after a bit and just went on marching—it was a job to keep the Jocks from falling out—some of them were pretty footsore. The major was here and there and everywhere, joking with them and chivvying them along, and when jokes didn't work he gave them hell. I don't believe half the Battalion would be here if it hadn't been for the major. I could tell you more about it if I hadn't been so dazed . . . looking back it all seems like a dream; not a very nice dream, either. Well, I've tried to remember the last time I saw him and I'm pretty certain it was at a funny little village; I don't know what it was called, but it was rather like an English village, there were

trees about, and a sort of green in the middle. We fell out
there for a meal and a few hours' rest. I lay under a tree on
that green I was telling you about. I knew we couldn't stay
long, because the Boche was pretty close behind . . . so after
I'd had a bit of a rest I got up and went round to collect the
Jocks. I passed the major sitting on a doorstep putting on his
puttees, and he looked up and grinned at me—he was cheerful
as anything—'Hullo, Tubby!' he said, 'Hullo, Tubby, are you
enjoying yourself?' Of course I said I was. We talked for a
minute about the men, and then I asked him where he thought
we were going. You can ask him things like that. I knew he
wouldn't mind, and I knew he wouldn't tell me unless he
thought I ought to know. I said, 'Where d'you think we're
making for, sir, and what'll happen when we get there?' He
smiled and said, 'Dunkirk, and you'll have to swim, Tubby.'
So then I said, 'That's all right, sir. I just wanted to know. It'll
be a change from walking, anyhow.' He laughed quite a lot
. . . So then I said something about seeing him in mid-channel
—damn silly of course, but everything seemed pretty silly,
somehow—and he looked up at me with a funny sort of look
. . . it was a *serious* sort of look . . . and said, 'No Tubby,
you won't see me in mid-channel. I haven't got fins.' I said, 'I
suppose you're going to fly, sir?' and he shook his head and
said he hadn't got wings, either. I didn't like to say any more,
but I just waited, and he finished rolling his puttees and stood
up, and then he said, 'Perhaps I'll stay on a bit with the
Froggies. I love the Froggies, don't you, Tubby? It would break
my heart to leave them in such an unceremonious way.' . . . Of
course he didn't *mean* it," says Tubby earnestly. "He didn't
mean that he loved them, because he doesn't, but he *did* mean
something."

I have followed the story with breathless attention, and now
that it is ended, I am a trifle disappointed and more than a

trifle puzzled. I enquire what meaning Tubby attaches to Tim's enigmatic statement.

Tubby says, "The major talks like that sometimes, and it sounds like nonsense, but it really means something."

"What could it mean?" I enquire.

"I'll tell you what I think," says Tubby gravely. "I think he has been given something to do—some sort of job—and he's doing it, and he'll come back when he's done it. That's what I think."

I look at Tubby, and Tubby looks at me—straight in the eyes.

"Oh I know it sounds a bit fantastic" says Tubby apologetically, "but the whole thing was fantastic—you wouldn't believe half the things I could tell you . . . Germans dressed as British Staff Officers waiting for us at cross roads, and giving us orders, telling us to take the left fork and retake a village. Yes, it's perfectly true. We jolly nearly did it, too, and, if we had, we'd have walked straight into a neatly prepared trap . . . But that's a different story," says Tubby, "I'll tell you about it sometime. Let's get this straight about the major first."

"But we can't get much further, can we?"

"No," says Tubby, "but he *did* mean something. I know him awfully well, because he was my company commander for ages, and I know the sort of things he says. I remember one day in Mess; we were having tea, and he took my cup and pretended to read my fortune. He said, 'Oh Tubby, I see a journey for you, here,' and he went on and told me all about my journey—it was dashed funny—everyone in the Mess was in fits over it, and I was, too. But, whereas the others thought it was all nonsense, I knew quite well what it meant—and he knew that I understood. You see the fact was he knew I wanted leave awfully badly, and he had fixed it for me, and that was his way of telling me."

I am silent, for the story is so typical of Tim that it has given me a lump in my throat.

"It's the same sort of thing," continues Tubby earnestly. "It really is . . . you see it, don't you? So you won't worry about him, will you, Mrs. Tim, because I don't mind betting that he'll come through all right."

A drowning man clutches at a straw, so perhaps this is why I cling to Tubby's story and am somewhat comforted. We talk for a little longer, and then Tubby gets up to go and I accompany him to the gate (for, to tell the truth, I am loath to part from him). Fortunately, as he turns away, I happen to notice a roll of manuscript in his pocket and have the presence of mind to enquire whether he has written anything lately.

"Nothing much . . ." says Tubby in an embarrassed sort of voice, "at least I mean I have, really . . . but you don't want to be bothered with it . . . and . . . well, it's probably awfully rotten . . ."

I cut short these incoherencies by removing the manuscript from Tubby's pocket, and saying that of course I want to read it.

Tubby says, "Oh well . . . but I don't see why you should bother . . . it isn't funny or anything . . . just an idea I had . . . quite footling . . . at least the idea wasn't exactly footling, but I've made a hash of it. Well . . . thanks awfully . . . you'll . . . you'll tell me what you think . . . I mean . . . well . . . thanks awfully, Mrs. Tim."

DUNKIRK 1940.

We were not broken men, we were betrayed
O'ercome by cruel odds but undismayed.
Out of the fog of treachery came we
In Regiments, in Companies or one by one.
We stood half dazed and looked upon the sea

And, in the glory of the setting sun
Amongst those rosy clouds beyond the foam,
We dreamed that we could see the shores of home.
The Israelites, in wondering surprise,
Saw the sweet peace of Canaan's fertile parts;
Our land was hidden from our longing eyes,
Yet it was clear and living in our hearts.
Oh England, island home, fair as a star
How near you seemed that day—and yet how far!

When Israel escaped from Pharaoh's might
The Red Sea lay before them, in the wind,
And Pharaoh's chariots, spoiling for the fight,
Came rolling up behind.
God wrought great things for Israel that day.
He plucked them safely from the tyrants' hands
The sea rolled back and left a narrow way
And Israel went dryshod to happier lands.
Did others think as I? Did other men
Long for that wonder to be wrought again?

Oh that these waters, bounding with the breeze,
Could suddenly divide
And leave a narrow path between the seas
With towering walls of foam on either side,
So we (like Israelites in days of yore)
Might gain a happier shore!
A miracle there was, but not as I had prayed,
God stretched His hand and "Peace be still" He said.

And lo, this channel 'twixt unquiet seas,
Fretted by tides that never rest nor sleep,
Excited by the winds, stirred by the breeze,
Plagued by the currents' sweep;
This restless water hemmed by rocky land

Lies still beneath the shadow of His hand.
Calm lie the waters now, the winds have died;
No wave, no swell, no undertow is here.
Calm lie the waters and the ebbing tide
Laps gently as a sheltered English mere.
And now from England's shore our brothers come
To bring us safely home.

Amidst a storm of fire—a very hell—
Comes yacht and ferry-boat and collier barge,
Come sloop and ketch and dancing cockleshell
Comes little boat—and large.
A double miracle to set us free—
Lion-hearted men, calm sea.

FRIDAY 16TH AUGUST

Pinkie bounds into my room before breakfast and says that she heard the butcher's boy telling Annie that we got a hundred and sixty-nine German aeroplanes yesterday, and isn't it simply splendid. I agree that it is marvellous, but add that I cannot help thinking about the German airmen's mothers.

Pinkie says, "But you mustn't think of them, darling. We've got beyond that. It's a case of them or us."

I realise that Pinkie is right. There is no room for sentiment now.

The post is late in arriving, and after breakfast, when I am sitting in the drawing room adding up accounts (and wondering somewhat sadly why it is that large sums of money seem to melt away so quickly in a lot of small sums), Pinkie comes in with a letter in her hand. "It's from Aunt Elinor," she says. "Aunt Elinor wants me to go home." (Her expression is lugubrious in the extreme.) "And it isn't the first letter," says Pinkie. "I mean she's been writing and writing, but I took no notice because I didn't want to go, and now—for some reason or other—she seems to be a bit fed-up. Isn't it silly of her?"

"But Pinkie . . ."

"Of course I've been here for ages," continues Pinkie. "You asked me to come for a few days and I've stayed for months— Aunt Elinor says it's awful of me. She doesn't know what I'm thinking of . . . she says I'm to go home tomorrow."

I look at Pinkie, and Pinkie looks at me. Pinkie says, "It's for you to decide, Hester darling. It's like this, you see, if you want me to go, I'll go, but if you want me to stay, a thousand wild horses won't drag me away—that's all, really."

The situation might have been delicate, but it isn't, for Pinkie is so frank and straightforward and sensible that we can thrash out the matter quite comfortably. I explain that I don't want her to go at all, and that if she goes I shall miss her horribly, but perhaps she ought to go back to Aunt Elinor. Pinkie owes a good deal to Elinor Bradshaw, and must remember that . . . so if Aunt Elinor wants her . . .

"But she doesn't," declares Pinkie with conviction. "She never wants me. I'm no use to her at all. She treats me as if I were seven years old, and never tells me anything . . . why, you treat Betty much more reasonably than Aunt Elinor treats me."

This is amazing, of course, because Pinkie is a whole person, and an extremely interesting and amusing companion.

"It's true," says Pinkie—quite unnecessarily, for I know her too well to doubt her word.

"Then why?" I enquire, in a somewhat puzzled manner.

"Oh, because she thinks I'm a nuisance," says Pinkie frankly. "I'm a nuisance to her, so she thinks I'm a nuisance to you.

She explains all that quite clearly in her letter. Am I a nuisance, Hester? You had better say quite honestly."

Far from being a nuisance, Pinkie is the greatest comfort to me, and I tell her so in no uncertain terms.

"I knew it," says Pinkie, hugging me so tightly that I am nearly throttled. "I knew it all the time, only I had to ask you, hadn't I? . . . I should know at once if I was a nuisance to you . . . anybody would know, wouldn't they?"

"Almost anybody would," I reply in a strangled voice.

"Almost anybody," agrees Pinkie. "And anybody like me (who had been brought up by people who didn't like them much and only had them in the house because they hadn't got a mother, and their father was in India, and they had nowhere else to go) would be one of the very first to know they were being a nuisance."

"Oh Pinkie!" I exclaim in distress.

She hugs me again, "It's all right," she says. "I'm not moaning about it . . . I hate people who moan, don't you? And as a matter of fact, it's only since I have come here and . . . and been with you . . . that I realise what it was like before . . . It's so lovely to be *wanted*," says Pinkie, earnestly.

Her face is very close to mine, her skin with its fair fine texture, the hair which springs from her forehead like living gold. I put my cheek against hers and say, "I want you awfully badly, Pinkie."

"We want each other," Pinkie says, "so it's simply perfect." She gives me another hug, and then rises and shakes herself into a more sensible frame of mind. "So that's settled," says Pinkie, "and I can go and write to Aunt Elinor this very minute and tell her that I'm not coming."

I implore her to be tactful, and she promises that she will be, and goes upon her way rejoicing.

SATURDAY 17TH AUGUST

It is nearly midnight, and everyone else has gone to bed, but I am still sitting by the open window in the drawing room. This has been one of my bad days, I have carried a load of misery upon my shoulders since early morning, and nothing I could do would lessen it—how curious that some days should be so much worse than others! Hope is like a fitful flame that springs up and flickers and wanes without visible cause.

How quiet it is! The moon is shining so brightly that there are no stars to be seen. I have the feeling that everyone in the world is asleep—but I know that it is not so. All over Europe there are people—men and women—keeping watch. There are aeroplanes, laden with death, speeding across the sky; there are sailors on the lookout; there are thousands of women like me who cannot sleep because their hearts are torn with anxiety . . . all over Europe the shadow of suffering lies.

I sit and think about it, and in some strange way it is a relief to give way to misery. It does nobody any harm, for there is nobody to see. Just for a few moments I can take off the mask of cheerfulness. Just for a few moments I can allow myself to think. Despair rolls over me like a breaking wave . . . despair, not only for myself, but for us all . . . and the tears which wet my cheeks are for all wives and mothers . . .

Suddenly I am startled by a loud knocking which resounds through the silent house and, realising that it is someone knocking on the front door, I rise and go through the hall to open it and see who is there; but when I reach the door I pause with my hand on the key. Is it wise to open the door at this hour of night without knowing who is outside? I am hesitating and trying to decide what to do when another volley of knocks makes me jump and sets my heart racing . . .

the knocking is so peremptory that the stout oak door rattles and groans upon its hinges.

"Who's there?" I enquire as firmly as I am able.

A voice says, "Hester, is that you? For goodness' sake open the door . . . I've been ringing the bell and knocking for ages . . . I thought you were all dead."

It is Tim's voice—there is no doubt about that—it is Tim . . . my hands tremble so that I can scarcely undo the bolts, but at last the bolts are undone and the key turned and the door flies open.

"Tim!" I cry, as I fling myself into his arms.

"Hester!" cries Tim, almost squeezing me to death.

"Tim!"

"Hester!"

"Tim!"

We keep on saying "Hester" and "Tim" for several minutes in the most idiotic manner. I have to feel him all over with my hands to convince myself that he is real and whole; and, when the door is shut and the light turned on, I still have the uncomfortable sensation that I may be dreaming, for he looks so unlike himself, and so different from what I expected. His hair is long—much longer than I have ever seen it—and his military moustache is gone, and instead of being clad in Service Kit, or battle dress (garments in which an officer returned from the field of battle might reasonably be expected to appear), Tim is arrayed in a pair of baggy blue serge trousers and a navy blue jersey with a high neck. He sees my surprise and laughs—"But it is really me," he says.

"I know," I cry, hugging him. "I know it's you . . . only I'm so afraid that I'm dreaming."

"You've been worrying," he says. "I couldn't let you know I was safe—it must have been pretty beastly for you."

I assure him that it was, and add that if it had not been for Tubby I should have gone quite mad.

"Tubby been holding your hand?" enquires Tim, smiling.

"Not exactly. He told me what you had said—that you had been detailed for a special job."

Tim looks at me in surprise. "What?" he enquires, "Tubby said what?"

I repeat the conversation between Tubby and myself (it made such a deep impression upon me that I find no difficulty in repeating it practically word for word), and Tim listens and nods and says, "Yes, I remember that little village," and, "Oh yes, Tubby was all right . . . very good value Tubby was," and, "Yes, it was a bit of a job hustling the Jocks along," but when I come to the end of my story, Tim looks at me in blank amazement and exclaims, "Great Scott, did I say that? I suppose I must have said it . . . Tubby couldn't have dreamt it, because we never got any sleep."

"What do you mean?" I ask him.

"I suppose I said it," repeats Tim. "As a matter of fact I'm beginning to have a faint recollection . . . but I didn't mean anything at all. It was just nonsense."

"It was just nonsense!"

"Absolute nonsense . . ." declares Tim. "You see I talked so much. All through the retreat when we were marching here and marching there I just went on talking and talking and walking and walking. I talked to everybody, and I talked all the time, and said any nonsense or rubbish that came into my head. It kept people cheery, you see."

I find myself gazing at Tim with eyes like saucers . . . it was just nonsense . . . it had meant nothing . . . but it had kept me sane for weeks.

"Great Caesar's Ghost!" exclaims Tim. "Of *course* I meant to come back with the others. You don't catch me staying in

France a day longer than I need. I never want to see the place again—neither in war nor peace."

By this time Tim is seated at the kitchen table, and is busy demolishing the remains of a cold chicken, and I am making cocoa on the gas ring. ". . . the adventures I've had!" he continues, "the crazy hare-brained adventures! You wouldn't believe half of them, Hester. They would sound like a story out of one of those frightful tuppenny papers that Bryan loves. I was hiding in a barn one day and a German Officer came in— it was him or me, and I felt that it ought to be him,—I socked him on the head pretty hard—it was enough to keep him quiet for some time—and I covered him up with hay and left him there . . . but that was afterwards, of course."

"After what?" I ask.

"After a lot of things," Tim replies. "After I'd left the old woman's house and was trying to make my way to the coast. It was the old woman who gave me these clothes—marvellous, aren't they? They belonged to her son, and it was lucky for me she had kept them because she had burnt my clothes and I hadn't a rag to wear . . ."

"She *burnt* your clothes!" I exclaim, pausing in my stirring of the cocoa to stare at Tim.

"Look out, it's boiling over!" says Tim. "Yes, she had to burn them—it was safer. If the Boche had found them it wouldn't have been too good. She was a decent old thing—I wouldn't be here now if it hadn't been for her—she had only one tooth in her head and it was as yellow as a guinea."

I am feeling quite dazed now, "Where would you be?" I enquire.

Tim says, "Oh, if it hadn't been for her I should be languishing in a German Prison Camp—at least, I expect so. But I'm telling you this all wrong . . . this cocoa is dashed good, have some yourself."

I pour out some for myself—just to please him, for I am neither hungry nor thirsty. "Go on," I urge him. "Tell me how you were taken prisoner—tell me everything."

"It would take all night," he replies. "Tell me about everyone first—Betty, Bryan, how are they? Where are they? What are they doing? Tell me how things are on the Home Front. Are you getting plenty of food? Are you getting bombed? I haven't heard any proper news for weeks."

I tell him all he wants to know in a few words, for there is not much to tell, and then I enquire further into his—far more than interesting—history. "Do tell me," I implore him. "Do tell me what happened . . . How were you taken prisoner? . . . unless you're tired and would rather go to bed."

Tim says he isn't tired.—"I'd like to tell you, but it's all such a muddle," he declares, "and especially the last week or ten days, when I was wandering about sleeping in barns and behind hedges and trying to find some way of getting home. The difficulty was to know whom you could trust—some of the villagers were very bitter against us, and others were willing to do what they could as long as they didn't get into trouble. I got food from them sometimes, and one man gave me a bed in his cottage for the night . . . then there was another man who betrayed me, and I had to make a dash for it. After that I was pretty careful and hid in the woods . . . but that wasn't getting me any nearer home. I was almost in despair when I happened to run across a Belgian fisherman who was going out to have a look at his lines . . . but that's the *end* of the story," says Tim, pulling himself up with a jerk. "I must begin at the beginning. The story really begins with my knee."

"Your knee?"

"Yes, you know that loose cartilage of mine that always chooses the most inopportune moments to come adrift? Well,

it broke all previous records—it surpassed itself—by coming
adrift when its owner was taking part in a retreat."

"Tim!"

"I know," agrees Tim. "It was a pretty nasty moment when
I felt it go. We had spent a few hours in a village, and I had
just watched the Battalion march out."

"But wasn't there anyone with you?"

"Not a soul," replies Tim, helping himself to a week's
supply of butter and spreading it with a lavish hand on to a
thick slice of brown bread. "Not a single solitary soul. I was
always about the last person to leave a village, because I made
it my business to have a snoop round and see that nobody had
been left behind. On this occasion nobody had been left behind—which was unlucky for me. I was hurrying down the
village street when I put my foot on a loose stone and the
beastly cartilage went click, and down I went like a shot
rabbit—you know the way I do. It was a nice thing to happen,
wasn't it? I tried to get my leg straightened but I couldn't—it
was extremely painful—sickeningly painful. I was still wrestling with my leg when a tank came lumbering down the
street—a German tank. I had known there were some in the
vicinity, but I hadn't known that they were quite so near. I
couldn't do anything, of course, there was nothing I could do
except surrender. . . . The tank stopped and an officer got out
and came and looked at me, and asked what was the matter
with me in perfectly good English, so I told him what had
happened. He said, "I too, have a loose cartilage." It was damn
funny really; I thought so at the time, and I've often thought
so since . . . there we were—two deadly enemies who would
shoot each other without the slightest hesitation—comparing
notes about loose cartilages. He asked me whether it was the
outer or the inner cartilage—his was the inner, and it gave him
a lot of trouble. I said that mine was the inner too, and added

that it always seemed to choose the most awkward moments to let me down. He nodded and said he could well believe it. I said this was the most awkward moment so far. He appreciated that . . . 'You are my prisoner,' he said. I replied that I had suspected as much from the beginning . . . he had disarmed me, of course.

"Several other tanks rolled up and stopped and two more officers came over to where I was lying. There was a lot of talk and jabber. They asked me how long I had been lying there, and where my Regiment had gone, and which road they had taken, and how far ahead they were. I didn't tell them much, and what I did tell them—most reluctantly—was quite untrue. Then I lay back and said I felt ill. There was more talk . . . I could see that they didn't know what on earth to do with me. They were moving forward rapidly, and didn't want to be bothered with prisoners—on the other hand I was a major, and therefore quite a valuable prize. Eventually they had decided to leave me where I was until the transport came up. The first officer, who spoke English, explained that it would not be very long—they left a man on guard, climbed back into their tanks and moved off. There were about twenty tanks—great monstrous creatures—and they made a hellish noise.

"After they had gone it was very quiet. There was nobody about the place, because all the villagers had fled—they always did when they heard the Boche was coming—I remember a cat ran along the wall and jumped over into a garden . . . it's funny how you remember things like that. I lay and wondered what I could do, but I couldn't think of anything. My guard was quite young—a mere boy—and he sat on the step quite near me with his rifle across his knees. I wondered what he was thinking about—what he thought about the war . . . it would have been interesting to know. Then an old woman appeared; she was very small and old—a mere wisp of a creature—and she came shuffling down the empty street in a tottery kind of way. It looked as if she had scarcely the strength to put one foot in front of the other. My guard pricked up his ears and looked at her . . . and then settled down again. She passed quite near me, but took no notice of me at all . . . just shuffled past very slowly and disappeared into the house opposite—it was a cottage, really, and a dirty, unkempt sort of place.

"Nothing more happened for ages. There were planes flying overhead, but otherwise it was very quiet. My guard got up once or twice and looked down the street. (He seemed a bit restless—perhaps he expected the transport to come.) Then he turned and said something to me in German. I didn't understand, so I just lay still and shut my eyes. I wasn't feeling too good, and I thought there was no harm in letting him think I was rather worse. He stooped and looked at my knee—I had managed to get the cartilage back into place, but my knee was like a football. He grunted to himself. I opened my eyes to see what he was up to, and when he saw I was looking he made signs—pointing to himself and pointing down the street —'Brot,' he said. I realised what he was getting at, of course: he was hungry and he was going to forage for food. He had satisfied himself that I couldn't move, so there wasn't much harm in leaving me for a few minutes. I just lay there with my eyes half shut and said nothing; so, after hesitating, and looking up and down the street, he made off . . .

"Well, no sooner had he gone than the old woman appeared; *she* looked up and down the street, and then she nipped across to me—no shuffling or tottering about her—she was across that street like a flash of greased lightning, and she was waving her arms and jabbering and spluttering with excitement. I couldn't understand a word, but I didn't need to; I got up and stood on my good leg and, half hopping and half leaning on her, I made pretty good time across the street and into her house. She had taken up the floor boards in the back room, and I lay down under the floor. It was all white powdery dust, but I wasn't particular—in fact I thought it was a good idea. She put down the boards and rolled back the carpet, and I heard her moving the furniture about. There was air coming in, and it wasn't too uncomfortable, and that was lucky, because I was there for *hours*. I heard people coming in and clumping about, and I heard a lot of talking . . . then there was silence for a bit . . . then more clumping about and more talking . . . then silence. I didn't know what had happened, and I began to wonder if they had got the old woman—taken her away perhaps—and I should be left there to rot. It wasn't a pleasant thought.

"I was just thinking of trying to get out myself, trying to shove up the boards, when I heard the furniture being moved and the boards were lifted and there was my friend, grinning all over her ugly face, and her one tooth gleaming at me . . . I was so pleased to see her I could have kissed her! By that time I was feeling pretty rotten—what with the pain of my knee, and fright and hunger—and she was awfully decent to me. She explained that the 'sales Boches' had gone, but they might come back, and I had better get into bed. It was difficult to understand what she said, because she spoke a sort of patois, and the fact that she had only one tooth didn't help—my French is a bit sketchy at the best of times—however, we managed somehow. She warmed up some soup for me and helped me to undress and get into bed . . . if anyone came she would say I was her son, and I must pretend to be very ill—'très malade.' I nodded and said I would. As a matter of fact it wasn't difficult because I was feeling like nothing on earth.

"I was in bed for days—I don't know how long, really—and there was a constant rumble of tanks and guns and transport waggons going through the village. The noise scarcely ever ceased. It was a horrible noise—horrible in itself and even more horrible to me, because I knew what it meant—all those tanks and guns—rumbling past—I knew where they were going. There was no news to be got, so I didn't know what had happened. I didn't know whether—whether our fellows had got away—I didn't see how they *could*. I was ill in bed and I could do nothing—I nearly went mad. Honestly, Hester, it was the most awful time I have ever been through . . . and still those tanks went on and on, rumbling past; there must have been thousands of them . . . tanks and guns and waggons full of men . . . I used to get up and hobble to the window and peep out at them, but the old woman didn't like me to do it, because they might have seen me—she was right, of course. Sometimes a Boche would come into the house and question the old woman, and she would jabber and jabber like a monkey—and they would go away in despair, not having understood a word—sometimes they came and looked at me, but by this time my beard had grown, and I looked an absolute tinker . . . I suppose they believed that I was the old woman's son. At any rate they didn't bother about me.

"All this time the old woman was kindness itself; there wasn't much in the way of food, but she managed to scrape up food from somewhere, she foraged round the empty houses in the village, and of course there were vegetables in the garden at the back. There was a couple of goats, so we had milk—it was cheesy sort of stuff, but I wasn't particular.

"The old woman told me a bit about her history—I managed to gather that her only son had been killed in the last war, and one of her daughters had been murdered by the Germans that was why she hated them so. She hated them like poison.

It was almost terrifying to hear her when she got on the subject—and it was a subject which, under the circumstances, was bound to crop up fairly frequently. 'Les sales Boches,' she would mutter, and her eyes would flash and her whole body would shake with sheer hatred! I asked her why she had remained in the village when everyone else had gone, and she replied that she was 'trop vieille pour les sales Boches.' I think she meant that they wouldn't bother about her—and of course they didn't, so she was right . . ."

Tim has got thus far in his story, and I am sitting at the table, listening to him and watching him eat and enjoying every tone of his voice and every movement of his hands, when the kitchen door opens very slowly and quietly . . . and Pinkie appears. She is clad in a pale blue dressing gown, her hair is standing on end, and her eyes look half dazed as if she had just wakened from sleep.

Tim turns round and says, "Heavens, who's this?"

"Oh!" exclaims Pinkie, "Oh, I thought it was parachutists . . . *Oh, it's Major Tim!*" Her voice goes up in a squeak with excitement and delight.

After that we all seem to be talking at once, Pinkie is repeating that she thought it was parachutists, but now she sees that it isn't parachutists, she will go straight back to bed, because of course we won't want her; I am trying to explain to Tim who Pinkie is, and at the same time to explain to Pinkie that there is no need for her to return to bed; and Tim is declaring with vehemence that he has no recollection whatsoever of having met Pinkie before, but that it doesn't matter in the least because she is obviously nice to know.

Suddenly, in the midst of all this muddle, and for no reason at all, the tears pour down my cheeks—I can't help it, and it is a ridiculous way to behave, but it seems to have the effect of clearing the air. Tim pats me on the back and says, "It's all

right, darling. Everything's all right . . . it's all right, Hester,"
and Pinkie cries, "Hester darling . . . and you've been so
splendid . . . it's because you're hungry, that's all . . . it's
just that you're hungry," and Tim says, "Yes, of course . . .
that's what it is. You're hungry . . . and I've been gorging
food . . ."

It appears that we are all hungry—Tim seems to have forgotten that he has consumed half a chicken—so we raid the
store-cupboard and open tins of tongue and baked beans and
carrots and peaches, and we sit down to a solid meal. It is a
most hilarious meal for we are all so happy. Pinkie declares
that it is the nicest meal she has ever eaten in all her life, and
Tim agrees that he feels the same about it. I say very little, but
I look at Tim . . . and look and look again . . . I feel as if I
could not take my eyes off him for a moment. He is the old
Tim—my darling Tim come back to me—but there is something new about him . . . I can't quite make up my mind
what it is.

FRIDAY 23RD AUGUST

Now that Tim has come back the purpose for which I
started to write my diary is completed, but I have decided to
continue my record of events for my own satisfaction. There
are days when nothing of interest happens, or when I am too
busy to write, but there are other days when my pen flies over
the paper without the slightest effort, and I see no reason why
I should not write when I feel inclined—except perhaps the
shortage of paper.

Tim is living at home. He has been attached to the Depot
and is likely to be here for some time and if it were not for
the war, which lies upon one's spirit like a black cloud, everything would be perfect. To have all my dear ones together

under one roof—that is all I ask of life, and I have got my heart's desire.

Bryan and Betty are delighted at Tim's return. Betty is not old enough to understand what has happened, but Bryan is just the right age for hero worship. He sits and gazes at his father with an expression of awe upon his face, and I feel sure that the story of Tim's adventures on the field of battle will be retailed at length to Edgeburton, and will lose nothing in the telling.

"Tell me again, Dad," is a phrase which is frequently to be heard upon Bryan's lips. "Tell me again about the day the Germans nearly caught you, and you had to jump out of the window . . . tell me more about the time you hid in the woods."

Tim is wonderfully patient with Bryan and nearly always complies with his requests. Perhaps he realises how much it means to the boy, and realises, too, that Bryan is of an age to remember all that he is told.

There is one story which Bryan likes better than any of the others, and he declares it is the most thrilling story of all. . . . "Tell me again," says Bryan. "Tell me about the time when you spent the night in that village which was full of Germans."

"But I've told you so often," objects Tim. "I've told you about it at least three times, and it wasn't anything much. Lots of people had far more exciting adventures than that—you can read about them any day in the papers."

"I know . . . but *they* don't belong to *me*," says Bryan seriously. "It's because you belong to me, you see, and I feel as if I had been there myself, almost."

Tim smiles, "Oh well, if that's how you feel . . ." he says, and plunges into the story for the fourth time.

"It was in the retreat," he says. "I had stayed behind with a small detachment from A. Company to do a bit of scouting,

and as we were hurrying on to rejoin the Battalion we suddenly found that we were cut off. Some German Infantry
had arrived in the village and taken it over. We walked slap
into them before we knew where we were—at least, we walked
slap into the sentry. Fortunately we managed to stop him from
giving the alarm, and we made for the nearest house. It was
a good-sized house standing in a small garden. Dark had fallen
by this time and we did not know where the Germans were,
nor how many of them were in the place, so Tubby Baxter
took a couple of fellows and had a scout round—he discovered
that we were surrounded on all sides."

"But they didn't know you were *there*," says Bryan eagerly.

"They didn't know where we were," agrees Tim, "but they
knew we were somewhere about. The only thing to do was
to stay put, and to make ourselves as comfortable as we could
for the night."

"You piled up the furniture," says Bryan. "You made the
house into a kind of fort—didn't you? You made places at the
windows for firing out of, and you kept watch all night."

Tim agrees that all this was done.

"And all night long," continues Bryan excitedly, "all night
long you kept on going round the house to see that everything
was all right—and you told the men that if the Germans
attacked they were to fire like mad so that the Germans would
think that there were a lot more of you than there really were
—and one time when you went round some of the men had
heard Germans talking in the garden—quite near, they were
—but nothing happened—and then, in the morning, the enemy
attacked you."

"Yes," agrees Tim, laughing at Bryan's excitement. "Yes,
you seem to know as much about it as I do."

"No," says Bryan. "I don't, really, because every time you

tell me about it you tell me a little bit more. *Do* go on, Dad. I won't interrupt you again."

"They attacked just as dawn was breaking," says Tim. "They attacked on three sides at once, but fortunately the windows were well protected and none of our chaps were hit. We kept up a pretty hot fire and they drew off."

"Did you kill lots of *them?*" enquires Bryan, gazing at his father with eyes like saucers.

"I don't know," replies Tim. "You've got to kill people in war, but I prefer not to think about it . . . They drew off after about ten minutes. It seemed a good deal longer than that, but Tubby had timed it on his watch. Tubby is a cool customer. We didn't know why they had drawn off—it might have been a ruse, or they might have been waiting for tanks, or for a gun to blow the house to bits. We just had to wait and keep our eyes skinned—that was all we could do . . . and then, while we were still waiting, we suddenly heard the sound of firing at the other end of the village, and we realised that it must be some of our own fellows—"

"It was the Guards!" cries Bryan, unable to contain himself a moment longer. "Hurrah, it was the Guards! You got your fellows together and you unbarred the door, and you rushed out and took the enemy in the rear . . . and they thought it was reinforcements arriving . . . they didn't know there were only thirty of you . . . they didn't know that you had scarcely any ammunition left. You dashed into the battle shouting and firing and the enemy broke and fled," cries Bryan. "Oh Gosh, it must have been grand—it *was* grand! Oh Gosh, I wish I had been there too!"

Tim roars with laughter at this and says that there was nothing "grand" about it, and will Bryan kindly remember not to refer to it as a "battle." It was a skirmish in a village,

quite an unimportant affair, and will Bryan go and read the
Wizard now and leave him in peace.

The story of Tim's adventures—part of which I heard on
the night of his arrival—is continued in little snatches from
day to day; and, putting it all together and thinking about it,
I begin to get an idea of what he has been through. His bodily
adventures have been grim enough, but it is the adventures of
his spirit which have left the deepest impression upon him,
for he has said to me several times, "the worst part of it all
was when I was laid up in that old woman's house and heard
the tanks go rumbling past . . . it was frightful, Hester . . .
I nearly went mad."

Now that I have had time to observe Tim, I have discovered
what the *difference* in him really is—the "something new"
which I noticed in him on the night he arrived home. Up to
now I have always felt that I was older than Tim—not older
in years, of course, but older in spirit. I have felt that Tim was
my junior partner, a sort of large child to be humoured and
managed and loved, but now our relationship has changed
and, all of a sudden, Tim is the elder. He has borne tremendous responsibilities; he has met and overcome desperate
dangers, and in the course of a few weeks he has endured a
lifetime of suffering. When this is understood it is easy to
see why he seems older.

TUESDAY 27TH AUGUST

Jack and Grace come round after dinner for a chat, they
want to hear about Tim's adventures, but Tim has told and
retold the story so often that he is sick of it, and refuses to
play. Grace says, well what was the strangest thing that happened to him—surely he can tell them that much, and Tim
replies that the strangest thing that happened to him was

coming home and finding everyone going on just the same as before. It is quite obvious, says Tim, that nobody in this place knows there's a war on. Grace retorts, somewhat indignantly, that she does not know what he means, we have air-raids, don't we? Tim says she would know what he means if she could see Belgium. Grace says we are doing our best—she and Jack have given up having late dinner except when people are coming; she is cutting down her staff and making do with last winter's coat. She hasn't been able to take up any war work because of the twins, but she intends to start going down to the Depot very soon. If Tim will tell her what else she can do, she is willing to do it.

"That's just it," declares Tim. "There's something wrong somewhere. The inequality of sacrifice is what worries me. I agree that you can't do anything if that's any comfort to you."

Jack says, "It wouldn't help if we made ourselves uncomfortable."

"No, it wouldn't *help*," replies Tim, "but personally I should feel much more comfortable if I were more uncomfortable. Sometimes I feel as if I ought to sleep on the floor."

"But you've done your bit!" exclaims Grace.

"That's another thing that worries me," says Tim. "It's the attitude of people in this country; the satisfaction shown by the average person over Dunkirk. They look upon it as a sort of victory, whereas in reality it was a defeat. I grant you the evacuation was a magnificent show, but the fact that we were obliged to evacuate was a defeat, and a blow to our prestige that won't easily be countered."

"But look here," cries Jack. "That's just our strength. We're so damn sure we can't be beaten that we don't *notice* a defeat. We're like a chap that's been knocked out and gets up again and comes on for more. One of his eyes is bunged up completely and his nose is bleeding, but there's lots of fight in him

—he hasn't been defeated, has he? Lord, you *can't* defeat a chap like that!"

Grace says she knows nothing about boxing, and she thinks we have talked quite enough about the war . . . "Have you heard the latest?" she enquires.

Tim asks if she means the one about the padre and the cow, because, if so, he's heard it six times, and he can't laugh at it anymore. Grace replies that she did not mean that at all—it's a silly story anyhow and unsuitable for Hester—she meant had we heard the latest news—the news about Tom and Ermyntrude? Tim says he doesn't know either of them, so why does Grace think that news about them will interest him? Grace says, of course he knows them, it is Tom Ledgard and Ermyntrude Browne Winters, and they are engaged; Ermyntrude came round this morning on purpose to tell her. Grace thinks it will be splendid to have someone like Ermyntrude in the Regiment. It will liven us up, and she will be an antidote to Mamie who becomes more ovine daily.

Jack says he never cared for Ledgard, but he must say he's sorry for the fellow.

Grace says, "Why?"

Jack says, "Because you've saddled him with that woman, of course. If you had a down on Ledgard you could have made a wax image of him and stuck pins in it, or put arsenic in his food. It would have been kinder."

This annoys Grace, and she insinuates that Jack has not sufficient intelligence to appreciate Ermyntrude, to which Jack replies that he has sufficient intelligence to perceive that Ermyntrude is mad.

To change the course of the conversation, which is becoming more heated every moment, I enquire whether Captain Ledgard and his future wife have met in a previous existence. Grace says they have—Ermyntrude remembers perfectly, and

Tom is now beginning to remember. She is helping him, of course. Ermyntrude hopes to awaken Tom's Conscious to a realisation of the Higher Values, so that he may become part of the Great Life Stream.

Jack says that he too hopes she will be able to waken Ledgard's conscience, because he's one of the most irresponsible officers in the Regiment. Jack is willing to take off his hat to Ermyntrude if she can wake the fellow up and make him a bit more conscientious over his musketry returns—doesn't Tim agree?

Tim says he never thought much of the fellow.

Grace sighs, and says she wishes some people understood plain English—and none of us know the real Tom—perhaps, someday, we shall know him better and appreciate him at his true worth.

When our guests have gone, I put my arm through Tim's and ask why he was so grumpy with the MacDougalls, and he replies that he did not *intend* to be grumpy, but, somehow or other, Grace always annoys him—he does not know why it is, but it is an uncontrovertible fact—as for Jack, it would do Jack a lot of good to see some Active Service . . .

THURSDAY 29TH AUGUST

Meet Miss Browne Winters on my way home from the town and stop to congratulate her on her engagement, and to assure her that we are all delighted to hear she is "going to join the Regiment." She thanks me quite pleasantly, and says that Regimental Life will be a new experience for her, as she has never been associated with warriors. She then goes on to say that she and Tom are now fulfilled, the wheel has come full circle, and explains this cryptic statement by giving me a short résumé of the previous existences in which she met Tom and the circumstances of their meetings. We walk along together as she talks, and the odd thing is that her talk is extremely interesting. I cannot bring myself to believe that she has lived so many different lives—far more than any self-respecting cat —but she herself believes it, and she knows so many curious little details about those lives of hers that she makes them sound extraordinarily real. The first time they met—she and Tom—was in the days of the Building of the Great Pyramid, and from then on they continued to meet in various centuries and climes.

"We met and parted," declares Miss Browne Winters, fixing me with her intense gaze. "Sometimes we merely glimpsed each other like ships that pass in the night; sometimes a transient friendship was allowed us—sweet as the scent of honeysuckle in the early morning sun. We met . . . and parted, for we were not ready to come together. We were not worthy of happiness."

I murmur that they seem to have been very unfortunate.

"Oh, but you don't understand," she replies at once. "If we had been allowed to come together too soon, the flower of love would not have been so brightly coloured, nor would the fruit have been so sweet . . . Now we have grown to full stature. Now we are ripe for mating."

It is easy to agree with this, for it is an understatement— personally I am of the opinion that the fruit has been too long upon the tree. Early marriages are sometimes foolish, but when people have reached the age of Miss Browne Winters and Tom Ledgard they have become set in their ways and it must be extremely difficult for them to adjust themselves to each other. There are people, of course, who will remain forever young and adaptable, but Tom and Ermyntrude are not of these . . . to tell the truth I cannot "see" them married to each other, and their future seems fraught with dangers. I am so sure that they are unsuitable partners that just for a moment I am tempted to utter a warning, but fortunately, before I have found the words in which to utter it, I realise the absurdity of attempting to interfere in their affairs.

Suddenly Miss Browne Winters halts in the middle of the street, and announces in her clear resonant voice, "Mrs. Christie, I feel you are ready!"

"Ready for what?" I enquire, taking her arm and hastening her on—for several people have turned to stare at us, and two nurses with prams who have been walking behind us have been obliged to stop too—

"Ready for Knowledge," declares Miss Browne Winters. "Ready to receive enlightenment. I feel that if you were to devote a few hours daily to contemplation, the Past would unfold itself to you."

I murmur feebly that I have not much time . . .

"Time!" she exclaims. "What is Time?"

The question (I feel) is merely rhetorical, and this is fortunate, for I cannot tell her offhand what time is.

"Time!" she says again in a scornful tone. "A year, a week, an hour—it is all the same when you have lived for three thousand years or so."

I agree that that may well be.

"Believe me it is," she says earnestly. "Now let me see. I am studying Sanscrit at the moment, but I could give you two hours every morning. We could go back into the Past hand in hand."

This offer, though extremely kind, fills me with dismay, and I assure her that I could not think of causing her so much trouble. As this fails to put her off, I am obliged to fall back upon my previous excuse and plead lack of time. "My housekeeping," I murmur, "and housekeeping is so difficult just now, what with ration cards and one thing and another . . .

and then I have the 'Comforts' to count and pack and all the accounts to do . . . and then there's Betty, you see . . . and of course Tim has come home, you know . . . Bryan's holidays . . ."

She looks at me pityingly and says, "So earthbound!"

By this time we have reached my gate, and it is only polite to invite her to come in, but fortunately she is on her way to have lunch with her soul mate and cannot accept the invitation. She is turning away—having bidden me good-bye—when she suddenly turns back. "Your dream!" she cries, hitting herself on the forehead, "Your dream, Mrs. Christie! I had almost forgotten to mention it. Grace told me of your recurring dream, and it interested me profoundly."

"Yes," I murmur, "but I would rather not know what it means. It's very cowardly of me . . . but if it means something horrid I would rather . . . just . . . leave it."

"Strange!" she says, looking at me as if I had two heads. "Very strange! That shrinking from Knowledge is typical of a New Soul . . . and yet I feel sure that you are one of us. The meaning of your dream is easily read, and there is nothing alarming about it. You refuse to Go Back when you are awake and master of your mind, but when you are asleep your Conscious is free to return to happier days. You return to Ancient Greece; or to Mediaeval France where the language is different from the strange jargon misnamed modern English. It is when you are awakening, returning to the Present, that the two worlds impinge upon one another and create the hallucination which you find so distressing."

"Yes," I say meekly. "Yes. Thank you. It's very interesting."

I don't believe a word of it, of course—how could I—and yet this explanation of my dream has robbed it of its horror. As I walk up the path to the house I realise that if I am visited again by my haunting dream I shall be able to snap my fingers at it . . . strange, very strange, as Miss Browne Winters would say.

MONDAY 2ND SEPTEMBER

Pinkie comes back from the town laden with parcels and announces in accents of delight that "Donford is full of Poles."

"Poles?" enquires Grace, who is paying a morning call.

"Polish officers," says Pinkie, "the place is teeming with them."

I am not surprised at this news, because Tim has already informed me that Polish Troops are coming to Donford, but I am somewhat surprised at Pinkie's excitement which seems excessive.

"They're marvellous, my dear!" says Pinkie. "They're so tall and good-looking—so romantic-looking—and they've got such perfect manners! I met one coming out of the Post Office and he opened the door and bowed—it was absolutely *thrilling*."

Grace rises and says she must go—just lately I have noticed that she has become a trifle impatient with Pinkie. She has no sooner gone than Pinkie seizes my arm and exclaims, "Darling, I've done something frightful. I don't know *what* you'll say!"

"What have you done?" I enquire.

"Well," says Pinkie, "Well . . . well, the fact is I've asked two of them to tea tomorrow . . . two Poles, I mean . . . I simply couldn't help it, they were so sweet."

Naturally I am surprised, and ask Pinkie how she made their acquaintance. She replies, "Oh, *quite* easily, darling. They just spoke to me—they aren't a bit shy."

"How did they—"

"They speak French," explains Pinkie. "There's no difficulty at *all* in speaking to them, because they speak French."

"But Pinkie—"

"Darling, you aren't annoyed about it, are you?"

"No, of course not, but—"

"You'll simply love them!" cries Pinkie. "I know you will
. . . There's something *different* about them, something that
I can't describe . . . you're sure you aren't fed-up?"

"No, Pinkie, but the only thing is—"

"I couldn't help asking them. I felt—I felt I wanted to do
something for them, and there was nothing I could do—
nothing."

"I know, Pinkie, but you see—"

"They've lost everything," declares Pinkie, looking at me
with wide eyes. "They've lost *everything,* Hester."

I try to explain to Pinkie that I share her eagerness to do
something for them, but that I am doubtful whether they will
enjoy a tea party, especially when they discover that their
hostess is incapable of communicating with them. I have not
spoken a word of French since I was at school—and that is
not yesterday.

"It will be all right," replies Pinkie. "I'm sure they'll enjoy
it. We'll get along splendidly—you'll see. Even if you can't
talk to them you'll be giving them tea and you'll know that—
and they'll know it—I just wish I could do something for
them."

"Perhaps you'd like to make a cake for them," I suggest—
it is a somewhat feeble suggestion, but I can think of no other
on the spur of the moment—

"Oh *yes!*" cries Pinkie. "Oh Hester, what a marvellous idea!
. . . and I'll go and buy all the ingredients myself so that it
will really be *my* cake. You don't mind, do you?"

TUESDAY 3RD SEPTEMBER

Pinkie and I spend a busy day preparing a sumptuous re-
past for our prospective guests. Pinkie is full of excitement and
continues to assure me that I shall simply love them and that
their manners are too marvellous for words. Personally I am
in some doubt as to whether they will come, but Pinkie has no
doubts whatever on the subject.

They arrive as the clock strikes four, and I am bound to
admit that the eulogies which have been bestowed upon them
are not undeserved. Annie shows them in, and they bow and
smile and shake hands, and introduce themselves as Captain
Something and Lieutenant Something Else—it is quite impossible for a mere Britisher to pronounce either of their names,
and I do not intend to try. The captain is tall and dark with a
tragic face and haunting brown eyes, and the lieutenant is fair
and blue-eyed and extremely cheerful. I discover that I need
not have worried over conversational difficulties for the lieutenant can speak English, and is delighted to air it; he explains
that he has been learning it for two and a half months and,
when I compliment him upon his progress, he says gravely,
"But I am a vairrie diligent boy." I cannot help smiling at this,
and he immediately throws back his head and laughs, displaying a set of beautifully strong white teeth. "Ha, ha, ha, I have
said something foony!" he exclaims in delight.

It is good to find that he can laugh at himself, but I assure
him again that he speaks remarkably well.

He replies, "But we have come from Burnfoot, and there we
have lessons every day from an English Priest with window
glasses." (He makes a pair of spectacles with his fingers and
thumbs and holds them up to his eyes, so I am left in no
doubt as to what he means.)

I ask him how he got out of Poland, and he replies that his adventures would take too long to tell. He shows me pictures of his home—a lovely old place surrounded by trees—and explains that it is on the outskirts of Warsaw . . . "I have heard it is ruin now," he says with a sigh, "but my mother manage to escape and my little sister too. They are in France and I have a letter from them, but now no more letters. Perhaps they are still there, but perhaps they are left; I not know where they are . . . *He* not know either," continues the lieutenant, nodding in the direction of his comrade. "He not know where is his wife and his little childs. He is vairree sad not knowing."

I agree that it is dreadful.

"War is dreadful," he replies. "Our beautiful Warsovina is ruin—all heaps of stones—but we like that better than give it to the enemy as a present." (His eyes flash as he speaks and I realise he is thinking of Paris.) "Yes," he says firmly. "Yes, it is better . . . and you are the same. Your countree is made of rock."

I ask him to explain what he means by this, and he waves his hands and says, "But yes, I explain what I mean. It is treachery over there, and not knowing if your friend is your enemy, but here in your countree it is solid ground. I feel the rock under my feet when I step on shore."

"You must have been glad to get here!" I exclaim.

"I was glad," he agrees; "but now I desire to go back. I am doing nothing here. What is the good of me?"

It is easy to understand his feelings but, as he seems to be getting somewhat excited, I endeavour to strike a lighter note, "You couldn't fight the whole German Army singlehanded," I point out, smiling at him to show that this is a joke.

"Fight!" he exclaims with flashing eyes. "Yes, I will fight. You put me across the sea and I will fight. I will dead fifty Germans before they dead me . . . then I will dead happy."

While we are talking Pinkie and the captain are entertaining each other with great success. The captain has no English at all, but, as he can speak French and Pinkie has been at school in Paris, they have no linguistic difficulties with which to contend. When tea appears the conversation becomes general. I am so wound up by this time that my diffidence has vanished, and I try my French on the captain and find that I remember more than I expected. I can see Pinkie looking at me in surprise, and this spurs me on to further efforts—feel exactly as if my tongue were tied in a knot—

The lieutenant, who has recovered rapidly and is quite cheerful again, shakes his head and says, "My Comrade will nevaire learn English if all the peoples speak French to him. He is vairree lazy."

Pinkie says she wants to learn Polish, so the lieutenant points out various objects in the room and tells us what they are called, and the captain joins in the game and tries to make us pronounce the words correctly. Our desperate efforts to copy the unfamiliar sounds and to get our tongues round the syllables causes great amusement to ourselves and our guests. At last Pinkie says it is hopeless, and she thinks her tongue must be quite a different shape. The lieutenant asks if he may see her tongue, and when she puts it out at him he laughs uproariously. Pinkie says "Well, is it a different shape or not?" and he replies that as far as he can tell it is exactly the same shape as a Polish tongue.

We are just finishing tea, and full justice has been done to the carefully prepared feast, when Betty appears. She has had her tea, of course, but is willing to try a piece of Pinkie's cake, and anything else that is offered to her. I can see the captain looking at Betty somewhat sadly, and, after a few minutes, he explains that his little girl has fair hair and blue eyes and is just about the same age . . .

This statement is translated to Betty, who clasps her hands and says, "How lovely! Why didn't you bring her with you? Does she like climbing trees?"

The lieutenant is somewhat amused at this and translates it into Polish for the benefit of his companion, and after a short conversation in that language he turns to Betty and says, "My comrade say his little girl like climbing trees vairree mooch and sometimes tear her dress, and she would like coming to play with you, but it cannot be till after the war is over. She is in Poland—see—and the bad Germans not let her come."

Betty looks at him with wide eyes, "Oh!" she exclaims, "Oh, how dreadful! You tell him . . . tell him that my Daddy will go and fetch her and she can come and live with me."

This invitation is translated and causes tremendous éclat. The captain rises and bows to Betty and makes a short speech in Polish, whereupon Betty—far from being embarrassed—announces that she will kiss him if he would like her to do so. The lieutenant translates again, and the offer is accepted. Betty kisses the captain fondly and he puts his arm around her waist and draws her on to his knee, where she nestles down comfortably and with obvious satisfaction. The little scene gives me a lump in my throat and, as everyone else seems to be likewise affected, there is a long pause in the conversation. It is broken by the arrival of Tim, who has returned from the Barracks earlier than usual on purpose to meet our guests. He, of course, has no knowledge of what has occurred and his cheerful natural manner puts an end to the strain. Tim's French is even more sketchy than mine, but he is willing to do his best, and by dint of signs and gesticulations he manages to carry on a somewhat halting conversation with the captain.

Pinkie now asks if they may have the wireless, and, as the B.B.C. is supplying dance music and the hall has a parquet floor, there is only one thing to be done. We roll up the rugs and the young lieutenant slips his arm round Pinkie's waist and off they go. There is no need to worry about them any more, for they will be happy as long as the music lasts, so I return to the drawing room in time to hear Tim making laborious enquiries about the gunfire which has been loud and constant for the last two days.

"Est-ce que c'est vous qui—er tirez sur le—le . . . what's 'hill,' Hester?" says Tim.

I murmur, "Colline," and Tim says, "Oh yes, of course,— *colline.*"

The captain who—quite miraculously—seems to understand, admits that it is his unit which is making all the noise.

"Vous tuez moutons?" enquires Tim, laughing to make it perfectly clear that this is a joke. "Vous tuez beaucoup de moutons, eh?"

The captain laughs—it is a good joke—and holds up three fingers.

"Three!" exclaims Tim,—"Lord, I suppose you've got to pay for them . . . vous payez la—le berger?"

The captain says that they pay for them—"mais naturallement"—and sometimes have a piece of mutton for their dinner. He adds that they are practising with new guns which have just come over from America. This is a bit beyond Tim, so I translate the information, feeling extremely proud of myself for being able to do so.

Tim says "By Jove, how interesting! Ask him what kind of guns they've got, and whether they are calibrating—ask him if they use visible targets—ask him—"

Unfortunately this defeats me altogether, but Tim refuses to be defeated. He kneels down on the floor and emptying a box of matches on to the carpet he proceeds to illustrate his meaning. The captain enters into the spirit of the game. He seizes a cushion—to represent the shoulder of the hill—and alters the position of the matches. Tim points to three matches arranged in a row and says gravely, "Boom, boom, boom."

The captain nods excitedly and shows the trajectory of the shells with his finger . . . "Boom," he says, making a large dent in the cushion where the imaginary shell has fallen.

"Howitzers, are they?" says Tim, "Now look here. Supposing your guns were down here—Vos canons sont ici—"

I leave them playing quite happily and go upstairs to put Betty to bed. Pinkie and the lieutenant are still dancing in the hall, and Pinkie smiles at me as I look at them over the banisters. "My feet are cleverer than my tongue," she says in a dreamy voice.

Her partner waves his hand to me as they pass and cries, "We have make a great discovery—yes—we dance in the same language!"

THURSDAY 5TH SEPTEMBER

Am busy doing my morning round of shopping when I meet Mamie Carter coming out of the grocer's with a bursting shopping bag and a doleful face. "Oh Hester!" she exclaims, in what Grace so aptly describes as her bleating voice, "Oh Hester, poor little Jane wants a painting book, and I can't get one *anywhere.*"

"Try Woolworth's," I suggest, for, having had occasion to visit Woolworth's this morning to buy a piece of oil cloth for the kitchen cupboard, I remember that I saw a stack of painting books on the toy counter.

"Oh no!" cries Mamie. "I couldn't go *there.* It's always so crowded and I hate crowds. I never go inside the *doors* . . . It's dreadful," she continues drearily. "I don't know what's going to happen. I can't get *onions,* Hester . . . and Sprig hasn't any marmalade at all."

"There's a war on," I reply briskly. "Quite a big war in its way. Perhaps you hadn't heard."

"You're always *joking*," Mamie complains; "you're always making *fun* of everything. Perhaps you don't *like* marmalade . . . Herbert always says breakfast isn't breakfast without marmalade."

I reply that I agree with Herbert—for once—but that there is no need to forego one's favourite preserve because it cannot be purchased in the grocer's shop. I have just bought three large grapefruit, and with these and one sweet orange and a few pounds of sugar (which I have saved up for the purpose) I intend to brew my own special brand of marmalade—a brand which is hard to beat.

Mamie listens to this with unrelieved gloom. "But we've got no *sugar*," she moans. "We eat up all our sugar. I'm sure I don't know where it all goes to, but we never have any left by the end of the week . . . it's really dreadful . . . and Mr. Sprig can only let me have half a pound of cheese."

Mamie deserves to have her head punched, and, unless I can escape from her soon, she is in danger of getting her deserts (It would be unfortunate not only for her, but also for me if I were goaded into punching Mamie's head in the Donford High Street, for, even if the judge were to take a lenient view of my action, it would be exceedingly difficult to live down the disgrace), but Mamie is a difficult person from whom to escape. She dislikes her own company. She follows me into the butcher's and listens to me ordering a gigot of mutton for our Sunday dinner; she pursues me into the baker's and watches me choosing cakes; she accompanies me into Boots' library and tries to influence me in my choice of reading matter. This is the last straw—or very nearly the last—for I feel sure that Mamie's taste in literature is different from mine, and I point out that it is quite impossible for her to help me in my choice,

and ask her as politely as I can to leave me to make my own
selection.

"Oh, you *must* read *this*," says Mamie, picking out a book
entitled *Her Prince At Last* and trying to push it into my reluctant hand. "You *ought* to read it, Hester. It's such a sweet
story."

"I don't like sugar in stories nor in tea."

"But you'd like *this*," Mamie assures me. "It's by Janetta
Walters, so you can be certain that there's nothing nasty in it.
You don't want one of those horrid modern books lying about
when you've got a young girl in the house, do you?"

This is true, of course, and it strikes home all the more forcibly because the last book I had from the library was an exceedingly nasty book—and because I found that Pinkie had
read it before I had time to read it myself and discover that it
was unsuitable for the young—but by this time I am so annoyed with Mamie that I refuse to recognise any sense in what
she says; I reply, quite untruthfully, that I like nasty modern
books, and, picking up one at random, I walk out of the
library. Mamie has the strange effect of annoying me more
quickly and completely than anyone else I know—save only
the redoubtable Florence Mackay. I have been quite rude to
Mamie now, but she does not seem to mind and she is still at
my elbow when I emerge into Donford High Street. Our
ways home lie in the same direction and unless I can get rid
of her now I shall find myself walking home with her . . .
and my patience is spent.

Donford High Street is usually full of acquaintances at this
hour of the morning, but today as I gaze wildly up and down
I can see no friendly face . . . and Mamie has started to bleat
again. This time because it is impossible to procure sole for
Herbert's dinner, ". . . and he *does* love sole," says Mamie,
mournfully, as she struggles along at my side. "He likes it

fried in deep fat and garnished with lemon . . . and I can't get lemons, either."

"What have you got in that bag?" I enquire.

"What have I got . . ."

"Yes, what have you got in that bag? It's bursting with food, isn't it?"

"Oh!" says Mamie, "Oh, I see what you mean. I suppose we ought to be very grateful that we aren't short of food . . . but we were going to have Irish Stew. A stew isn't really a stew without onions—that's all I say."

"Put in leeks!" I exclaim, and with that I turn and rush into Woolworth's.

TUESDAY 10TH SEPTEMBER

Tim has always insisted that Bryan shall be free to come and go as he likes during the holidays, and for this reason he enjoys a good deal more liberty than most boys of his age. So far Bryan has not abused his privilege, but in the last three days we have scarcely seen him at all, except for meals, and at mealtimes he has worn a faraway expression as if his thoughts were elsewhere. He is off again now—I hear the front door bang—so I open the drawing-room window and call to him. He stops at once and comes over to the window, "Want a letter posted?" he enquires.

"No, thank you, I just wanted to know where you were going. You've been out a lot lately, haven't you?"

"Yes," agrees Bryan, "yes, I have. You don't mind, do you?"

This makes it a little difficult, and I decide to beat about the bush. "You know why you're allowed so much freedom," I suggest.

"Oh yes," replies Bryan cheerfully. "It's because Dad was kept like a prisoner when he was my age, that's why."

This is not quite what I meant (though it is absolutely true, and provides a curious problem for the psychologist—will Bryan's son be chained to the doorpost, or will he be a free man like his father?). "Yes," I reply a trifle doubtfully, "yes, but you see—"

"I know," interrupts Bryan. "I've got to use my privilege properly—and not abuse it. That's what Dad said, but this is something rather special."

"As long as it isn't anything wrong—"

Bryan shakes his head, "It isn't," he declares, "I'm quite sure it isn't. It's been rather fun having it as a secret, but I meant to tell you soon. I meant to tell you today, really, because—well, as a matter of fact I want a bob."

"You want a bob for the secret?" I enquire, hiding a smile.

Bryan nods gravely.

I find a shilling in my bag and hand it over and Bryan pockets it with expressions of gratitude. "I'll tell you," he says. "It's a new friend I've got . . . well, he's a Polish soldier really . . . not an officer, you know. I'll tell you all about it," says Bryan, climbing on to the window sill so that he can tell me about it more comfortably.

I sit down on the window seat and prepare to listen, for if there is one thing I enjoy more than another it is a heart-to-heart talk with my son. We do not indulge in them very frequently—indeed there seems to be little opportunity for such indulgence—Bryan's holidays coincide with Betty's and the house always seems full of people coming and going. I have often thought that "staggered holidays" would be an excellent arrangement for one would have much more good of one's children if one had them singly.

"I'll tell you," says Bryan confidentially. "I was out on my bike, you see, and I saw him sitting on a seat by himself, with no girl or anything. He looked a bit down in the mouth, so I

said "gin-dobray" to him—it means good-day, you know—so
then he waved to me and said a lot that I couldn't understand.
Well, then I got off my bike and came back. We could hardly
talk at all, because he only knew a few words of English, but
we tried to talk and we pointed to ourselves and said our names
and laughed like anything. He's grown-up, of course," says
Bryan naively, "but he doesn't *seem* grown-up. I mean he
doesn't seem any older than me—if you know what I mean.
He's awfully jokey."

"What do you do if you can't talk to him?" I enquire a
trifle anxiously.

"I'm teaching him English. You'd be surprised if you could
see how he's getting on. Perhaps you'll laugh," says Bryan, producing a red exercise book from his pocket and displaying it
a trifle diffidently. "I mean perhaps you'll laugh at the idea of
me teaching somebody—but it's really tremendous fun."

I assure Bryan that I have no inclination to laugh and ask if
I may see the book. He hands it over at once.

On the cover is written in large letters:

WOJCIECH KOWAL

"That's his name," says Bryan proudly. "It took me a little
time to learn to say it properly, but I made him say it over
and over again until I got the hang of it, because—well, because I thought it would make him feel more at home if I
could say his name exactly right."

"I expect it does. How do you say it?" I enquire.

"Voicheech," says Bryan, pronouncing the last "ch" as in
"loch" . . . "Voicheech Koval—that's his name. Koval means ·
blacksmith, but of course he isn't a blacksmith any more than
anyone here who is called Smith . . . now I'll show you how
I teach him."

As I have had no experience of teaching languages I cannot judge the merits of Bryan's system, but it seems original and amusing. The book is full of little drawings and beside each drawing is an English phrase.

"He draws the pictures," says Bryan, eagerly explaining, "and I tell him what the things are called. It was the only way we could do it as far as I could see. I mean it wasn't like a master teaching you French and saying, 'the cow—la vache,' because neither of us knew what the other called it."

"Very difficult!" I murmur.

"Yes, but *fun*," declares Bryan. "That's his house in Poland, you see. It's a little cottage on a farm and he lives there with his mother—at least he used to live there. That was the first thing he drew, and I taught him to say, 'This is my house,' then I went on and taught him to say 'this is my arm' and 'this is my leg'—he can say all that *beautifully* now . . . here's a plough," says Bryan, turning over the pages feverishly, "that's a plough, you see, and that's him ploughing . . . and that's him milking the cows."

The drawings are somewhat primitive, but quite unmistakable. They remind me a little of those very modern drawings which appear crude and childish to the uninitiated, but are supposed to be the height of sophistication.

"I must go now," says Bryan, leaping down. "He'll be waiting for me, you see . . . and thanks awfully much for the bob, I thought I'd give him a treat and take him to the circus . . . you don't mind, do you?"

I enquire whether Bryan's pupil is sufficiently advanced to enjoy the circus, but Bryan points out that the circus is an entertainment which can be enjoyed even by someone who is ignorant of the language . . . "he won't understand the jokes," says Bryan a trifle sadly, "and that's a pity because he loves jokes . . . but he'll be able to *see* the clowns tripping each other up and throwing things at each other, and he'll be able to see the animals . . . he's mad about horses . . ."

The circus, which visits Donford once a year for three hectic days, is not what one might call a very polished performance, but considering the fact that it spends its whole existence travelling from place to place, erecting the Big Top and taking it down again as often as three times in one week, it is a performance to be admired. Bryan dashes through his dinner and is off like a rocket to collect his new friend; Betty and Pinkie and I follow more slowly. We join the stream of townsfolk and soldiers which is wending its way towards the common where the circus is encamped—it is such a noble stream that I begin to wonder a trifle anxiously whether there will be sufficient accommodation for us all. Unfortunately Betty is not at her best. She was anxious to go with Bryan—instead of with Pinkie and me—and I was obliged to put my foot down firmly. She walks along between us brooding upon the injustice of fate, and it is not until we approach the tents and hear the band playing that her interest in life begins to revive.

The lions are in large cages on wheels; we pass them on our way to the Big Top, and I am glad to see that the poor animals look healthy and well cared for. In front of us there is a woman with two children whom she is incapable of controlling. They climb upon the shafts of the carts and pay no heed to her shouts. Betty watches them with interest, and I can see that she admires their defiance of authority and would emulate it if she dared. The woman shouts louder, and finally grips them by their legs and cries, "Come doon, ye wee de'ils! I'll gie ye tae the lions for their denners."

This threat has no effect upon the imps at all—for they are inured to empty threats—but its effect upon Betty is remarkable. She seizes my hand and cries in accents of dismay, "Oh

Mummy, don't let her—don't let her, Mummy!" It takes several minutes to convince Betty that the children's mother has no intention of feeding her offspring to the lions.

By this time we have arrived at the Circus Tent, and are shown to our seats by a dwarf attired in green satin. He is about the same height as Betty, and has a round cheery face. Betty asks in a loud whisper whether I think he is "out of Snow White"; the dwarf, overhearing this, chuckles delightedly and tells Betty that he has been given a holiday from the diamond mines so that he can take part in the circus. Betty would fain continue this interesting conversation, but the dwarf is too busy.

Having settled ourselves comfortably (or as comfortably as the hard benches will allow) we can look round and enjoy the fun. The circus has not started yet, but there is plenty to see. The Big Top is astonishingly large and well-lit and the circle of green grass in the middle, which is really a piece of Donford Common, is an excellent arena. Just along from where we are sitting I see Mamie Carter and her nurse and children, and Stella Hardford is with her. Stella wears a bored expression and obviously is in no mood to enjoy a childish entertainment such as this.

Pinkie says suddenly, "Look, there he is . . . look, over near the pillar!" and I look across the ring and see Bryan and his new friend. They have chosen seats as close to the magic circle as possible so that nothing that happens shall escape their notice. The young Pole is large and sturdily built with curly fair hair and blue eyes. I observe him carefully (for to tell the truth I have been a trifle anxious about this friendship) but his face is open and honest and very young, and I can believe that Bryan feels him to be a contemporary . . . I am still looking at him when he turns towards Bryan and smiles with real affection, which is pleasant to see. Bryan's face wears an expression of sheer bliss, and I realise that this is probably one of the happiest moments of his life, for, not only is he prepared to enjoy the entertainment himself, but he is giving enjoyment to his friend . . . they are laughing together now, and Bryan is pointing to a clown who has tumbled into the arena and is rubbing his head and pretending to be very angry . . . the clown has baggy trousers and a red nose and a small green hat with a feather in it.

The band strikes up and the circus starts in earnest, and it is a good deal better than one might have expected. There are conjurors and acrobats and tightrope-walkers; there are horses and bears and performing dogs. There is a real live elephant; there are lions.

The audience is an appreciative one, and it looks to me as though Stella Hardford is the only person in the tent who is not enjoying the fun. Her face remains coldly disdainful, and whenever I look in her direction she seems to be yawning. Why has she come, I wonder. What did she expect to see? The turns are not very wonderful, perhaps, but they are by no means feeble, and apart from the actual performance there is so much to see that it is almost inconceivable that anyone could be bored. The children's expressions—astonished, exultant, hilarious, as turn succeeds turn—are an entertainment in themselves.

There is so much to see; it is such a human sort of affair; it is a glimpse into a life which is entirely different from one's own life, and yet is lived by people very like oneself. Take "Rose Killarney" for instance. She is a nice-looking woman of about my own age and is attired in a pink satin ball dress. She climbs a silver pole and walks the tightrope with a little parasol to balance herself . . . a strange life! Is she happy, I wonder. Does she like wandering about the country? What is she really like? What does she feel? Is she proud of her accomplishment, or is she sick to death of walking the tightrope in a pink satin dress? Then there is the clown who is the laughingstock of the show; he is the butt of everyone and succeeds (very cleverly) in getting in everyone's way . . . is he really a butt, or is he a respected member of the little society to which he belongs? The "Dolly Sisters" who ride upon a fat old horse and jump very neatly through paper hoops are really mother and daughter. The daughter is a bit of a minx and enjoys showing off. The mother is a trifle stiff in the joints, and there is a little crease of anxiety and apprehension between her brows. . . She is wondering what will happen to her when the day comes —the dreaded day—when she finds that she cannot jump through any more hoops, when her limbs refuse to obey her will, or her nerve fails her.

There is a circus within a circus here. The lion-tamer, a cat-like man in smoothly fitting tights, makes eyes at the Dolly Daughter as she canters out of the ring . . . what gossip, what scandal, what chatter there must be amongst the people of this little world. How they must watch each other! How they must scheme and love and hate! Their little world is so circumscribed, it moves on an axis of its own and the people in it can have little contact with the larger world outside.

I avoid Stella and Mamie as we squeeze our way out through the crowd, for I have enjoyed myself and have no wish to listen to their criticisms of our afternoon's entertainment. We meet Bryan outside the gate and walk home together very cheerfully.

Pinkie enquires, "What *are* you thinking about?" and I reply that I am thinking that the circus is very like a Regiment . . .

WEDNESDAY 11TH SEPTEMBER

After a long morning at the "Comforts Depot," Grace and I decide to walk along the shore. We have done this before with great benefit to body and soul, and there is no reason why we should not repeat the prescription.

"I think we should do this every Wednesday," says Grace, and I agree that we might do worse.

It is a brilliant day with a rough wind; the sea is deep blue flecked with white horses.

"Gorgeous!" exclaims Grace somewhat breathlessly, as she seizes her hat and jams it more firmly on to her head.

"Simply splendid!" I reply.

We struggle along until we reach the shelter of the cliffs, and here we pause for a few moments to admire the view. The tide is out, and the sweep of firm brown sand stretches for miles, but the war has brought changes even here, for the shore is dotted with strong posts sunk in concrete, and there are concrete pill-boxes and coils of barbed wire hidden amongst the rocks. Personally I think that these evidences of conflict spoil the beauty of the view, but Grace says she can shut her eyes to them and see the view exactly as if they were not there. It only requires a slight effort of concentration to perform this feat, says Grace, and she adds that she wishes Jack were here instead of cooped up in the Orderly Room with a lot of dusty files . . . "Jack would appreciate the beauty of it," says Grace.

My acquaintance with Jack has not led me to believe that he has much eye for the beauties of nature (I have always thought him essentially practical), but I agree with Grace that it would be lovely if Jack and Tim were here.

I have scarcely spoken when we come round a high point of rock and find ourselves in a small secluded bay, and in the

middle of the curve of sand we behold our two husbands struggling together—apparently in mortal combat. The sight is so
unexpected and alarming that we stop dead in our tracks, and,
at that moment, Jack is lifted in the air and flung heavily on
to the ground. This breaks the spell. Grace and I rush forward
shouting "Jack" and "Tim" respectively, but by the time we
reach the scene of battle Jack has risen and Tim is brushing
the sand from his tunic and enquiring with solicitude whether
he is hurt.

"Were you *fighting?*" asks Grace in breathless tones.

Jack says, "Yes," and Tim says, "No," simultaneously. Then
they look at each other and laugh.

"Well, what on earth *were* you doing?" asks Grace.

At first they refuse any explanation of the incident, and then
they tease us by offering us various wild and obviously untrue
interpretations of its meaning. (Tim declares that he lent Jack
five bob and Jack refused to repay it, and Jack declares that he
discovered Tim was selling secrets to the enemy.) But eventually, by persevering in our endeavours, we discover that our
husbands have been practising "Unarmed Combat" in a purely
friendly spirit, and that Jack has had the worst of it.

"Tim is marvellous!" declares Jack. "He chucked me about
as if I were made of straw," to which amazing statement Tim
modestly replies "We did quite a lot of the stuff in France."

Now that they have started to talk about it they seem to have
plenty to say on the subject, and Grace and I are informed that
there are no rules at all . . . "You can kick or hit or squeeze,"
declares Jack gravely. "You can trip the fellow or swipe him
with your tin hat or poke him in the stomach, or gouge his
eyes . . . it's grand sport."

Tim says it's the wrestling that interests him. They had an
instructor attached to them; he was quite small and slight, but

he could throw the beefiest brawniest man in the Battalion without turning a hair.

I enquire whether Tim and Jack came out with the express intention of practising Unarmed Combat upon the shore, but Tim scouts the idea. "Good Lord, no," he replies. "We haven't time for that. We came to have a look at the defences—the pill-boxes and barbed wire. They're dashed good, as a matter of fact, aren't they, Jack?"

Grace and I are delighted to hear this report, but Jack is far from satisfied; he says that in his opinion the defences of Donford Bay are far too good. Nobody in their senses would attempt an invasion. It would be better policy to encourage the enemy to land in this country . . . then we should have him by the short hairs.

Tim enquires how Jack would encourage the enemy to land, does he suggest sending Hitler an invitation? To which Jack replies, "No, of course not, that would defeat our purpose. We should pretend that we're frightened."

As we turn and walk back together Grace tries to get Jack to admire the scenery. She points out the glorious colour of the sea, and adds that the wide sweep of sands is tinged with purple, but Jack refuses to see the purple tinge in the sand, and declares that sand looks brown to him, because it *is* brown. Grace immediately retorts that the water in the sea is not really blue, so she supposes that the sea does not look blue to Jack.

"I'm not an artist," says Jack, begging the question, "and if my family hadn't insisted on my going into the Service I should have been an engineer. I should have been more useful as an engineer, I'm certain. I've got ideas," declares Jack earnestly. "I've got a flair for engineering. Look at this enormous bay, for instance. Why don't we build a dam across the entrance and make all that waste space into profitable land?

That's what they've done in Holland, but we haven't got the initiative."

Tim looks at the bay and murmurs that there might be something in it.

"Hundreds of acres!" declares Jack, waving his arms excitedly. "We should have hundreds of acres of profitable land for growing food instead of this barren waste, which is no good to anybody."

Grace objects to this and says that the stretch of sand is useful because of its beauty. We need beauty in our lives. She quotes a proverb or saying (I think it is Chinese) which advises its hearers that if they have two loaves they should sell one and buy a flower. Jack allows that that might be quite a reasonable thing to do if you could be certain of getting another loaf before your remaining loaf was finished, but, if not, it would be sheer madness. . . "You couldn't admire a flower if you were hungry," adds Jack with conviction.

THURSDAY 12TH SEPTEMBER

Pinkie does a good deal of telephoning (but not at our expense, for she is almost invariably the recipient of the call) and as the telephone is situated, most inconveniently, in the hall her conversations are audible to the entire household. "Yes, Nick. . ." she is saying, "yes, of course I could. Yes, it is a lovely day for it . . . three o'clock? Yes, that will suit me splendidly . . . Oh, Nick, hold on . . . will you call for me or what? . . . All right . . . yes, three o'clock. . ."

It is difficult—in fact it is almost impossible to keep track of Pinkie's friends, but I feel that it is my duty to try, and as "Nick" is an entirely new name to me I feel justified in making enquiries about him. Pinkie is not of a secretive nature, and is only too ready to enlighten me; she explains that Nick

is the Polish lieutenant who came to tea. His name is quite
unpronounceable and, as it begins with "Nick", she has asked
and been granted permission to use the sobriquet. . . "and he's
going to call me Rose Marie," adds Pinkie, smiling. "It will be
rather nice because nobody *ever* calls me by my proper name.
Nick says it is such a pretty name—much prettier than Pinkie."

"Yes," I reply, a trifle doubtfully, "Yes, I see."

"We're going to walk along the shore to the Hermit's Cave,"
Pinkie continues cheerfully. "I told him about it the other day
and he wants to see it. You don't mind, do you?"

It is poor fun to be a spoil sport, but the idea of Pinkie and
her latest friend setting forth upon a solitary walk to the
Hermit's Cave is somewhat alarming. I consider the matter
hastily and decide that I must be firm.

Pinkie does not understand my tactful objections—"But you
liked him, darling!" she exclaims.

"I liked him immensely, but we know nothing about him
. . . he might misunderstand."

"Oh, he often does, poor lamb!" declares Pinkie, with a
chuckle, "That's half the fun, really. You see he can't speak
French, so our only means of communication is his lame English . . . sometimes we have to draw pictures to make each
other understand."

"I didn't mean *that*," I explain, sticking to the point tena-
ciously. "I mean he might think it odd if you went for a walk
with him by yourself. I don't suppose his sisters—if he has any
—would be allowed to go for a walk alone with a man."

Pinkie is no fool. "Oh, I see," she says, "Yes, I daresay they
have different ideas. It seems silly when there's a war on."

"It does, rather," I agree.

Pinkie considers the matter. "How would it do if you came
with us?" she enquires.

"Me!" I exclaim in amazement.

"Yes," says Pinkie, warming to her plan. "Yes, it's a marvellous idea. You'd like the walk, wouldn't you? Nick was awfully keen to see the Hermit's Cave . . . and if you came too . . . well, that would make it perfectly all right, wouldn't it?"

It would, of course, but I am extremely doubtful whether Nick would be as enthusiastic as Pinkie at the presence of a third party and, as I am not at all keen on playing gooseberry, I raise every objection that I can.

"But he *likes* you!" cries Pinkie. "He says you are 'full of attractiveness' so of course he will be pleased. How could anyone not be pleased to see you, darling?"

The argument continues throughout lunch and at two o'clock is still unsettled, when the telephone bell rings. I suggest that Pinkie shall answer the telephone, as it is probably for her, and she rushes away to do so. . . "Yes," says Pinkie, "Yes, it is. . . Oh Goodness, I'd forgotten! . . . Yes, oh yes, of *course*. No, it would never do. . . Well, as a matter of fact I'd forgotten about it . . . yes, but it will be all right."

The receiver is replaced, and Pinkie returns somewhat crestfallen, "I've done an awful thing," she declares. "I'd promised Bill to play tennis and he's taken the court and arranged a four . . . I'd forgotten, you see."

"Awkward for you," I suggest, feeling like a reprieved criminal.

"Very awkward," Pinkie agrees. "I'll have to go, I'm afraid, so would you mind seeing Nick when he calls for me, and explaining about it?"

It is not until Pinkie has departed with her tennis racquet that I realise what I have let myself in for. The matter is delicate, and the greatest diplomacy will be necessary, but how can one use diplomacy when one is hampered by linguistic inadequacy? The more I think about the prospective interview the more alarmed I become, until I finally determine to go out myself and leave Nick to his fate. I gather my knitting together and stuff it into the bag, and am about to rise and beat a hasty retreat when I hear the front door bell ring violently, and realise that the decision was reached too late, and that my line of retreat is cut.

Nick comes in smiling—he really is a most charming person —and, when we have greeted each other and shaken hands politely, I invite him to be seated.

"Rose Marie is nearly ready?" he enquires.

"No," I reply, "No, she is very sorry she cannot go this afternoon. She made a mistake—a muddle, you know—she forgot she had promised to play tennis and so—"

"You not allow," he says, shaking his head sadly. "No, I thought that. You not allow."

"She made a muddle of her arrangements," I tell him, trying to speak very slowly and clearly.

"Yes," agrees Nick—I am obliged to call him Nick, for I have no other name for him—"Yes, it is me make the muddle. I should not ask Rose Marie, no?"

"It was very good of you to ask her."

"Good?" he enquires in a puzzled voice, "but yes, it is true, I would be very good. Still you do not allow that she come —no?"

"She forgot," I explain, trying not to shout. "She did not remember that she had promised to play tennis."

"It was to walk not tennis that she promise," declares Nick firmly, "and I have said yes, I will be good. So you allow that she come, yes?"

"No, I can't, because she is not here."

"Not here?" he enquires in surprise, "But she promise to walk."

"She forgot about the tennis."

Nick shakes his head. "I do not know what mean this about tennis," he declares hopelessly.

I feel quite hopeless too, and we look at each other for a moment or two without speaking.

"Rose Marie is not here?" he enquires at last; "She has gone out with another friend—she forgot she promise to walk with me, yes?"

"No," I say firmly and shake my head, "No, she did not forget. She is very sorry."

"She is very sorry?" he enquires hopefully.

I nod and say, "Yes, very sorry indeed."

Nick sighs, "Oh dear!" he exclaims, and the old maidish exclamation sounds very droll from his lips. "Oh dear, it is pity! I *cannot* understand. It is like I walk in a fog . . . all the time the fog is there. You are not cross, no?"

"No, of course not."

"I do not mind, then," says Nick, with a delightful smile. "I do not mind that I cannot understand. It is all one . . . you permit that I talk to you, yes?"

"If you want to," I reply, somewhat amused.

"I would *like*," he declares earnestly. "We will talk about Rose Marie . . ."

SATURDAY 14TH SEPTEMBER

"I do love Bryan," says Pinkie, producing a small crumpled piece of paper and laying it beside me on my desk. "I do think Bryan is the most engaging creature—what do you make of that?"

The piece of paper is smoothed out for my inspection. On it is written in Bryan's well known scrawl:

KICK ATHER HARD.

HIT HIM ON THE HEAD WITH A TENIS BALL HARD.

The memo—if that is what it is—is written so fiercely and boldly that in some places the pencil has gone through the paper and left a ragged hole. . . .

Pinkie and I look at each other and smile. "Is it a threat?" enquires Pinkie. "Is it a sort of warning—like the Black Spot? —What do you think it is?"

I cannot elucidate the problem, but suggest that we should ask Bryan to solve it for us . . . "Poor Arthur," I add, a trifle sadly.

"Not at all," says Pinkie firmly. "I'm not the *least bit* sorry for Arthur. He must have done something extremely unpleasant—you can see that Bryan was furious with him—I don't mind betting you sixpence that Arthur thoroughly deserves it." She stands there for a few moments looking at the scrap of paper with her dimples coming and going in the most delightful way. "Dear Bryan . . ." she says, "I never knew much about boys before, but now . . . I think it would be lovely to have boys and when I'm married . . . if I ever do marry."

This seems a good opportunity to bring up the subject of Pinkie's young men friends—it is a subject which has been causing me some anxiety, and especially just lately. She has so many friends (their name is legion and there is safety in numbers, of course), but all the same I feel that I ought to know what her feelings are, for I am responsible to Elinor for her well-being. I have never been afraid of Bill, for he, poor soul, is merely a friend and has been told as much in so many words; I flatter myself that I know Pinkie better than he does, and am aware that what Pinkie says, she means. Young Craddock seemed a hot favourite at one time—though to do Pinkie justice, she treated him with the same friendliness which she extends to all her friends—but now there is Nick, and Nick is a different matter altogether. He is handsome and charming and has a romantic air about him—not to speak of a romantic background—Nick is the sort of young man who might turn any girl's head . . . I have been seeking an opportunity to speak to Pinkie seriously, and here it is. I must seize it and use it to the best advantage. . . .

"What *is* the matter, darling?" says Pinkie suddenly. "There's a faraway look in your eyes . . . and I've asked you twice whether you want me to take your watch to Mackay's to have it mended. You had better tell me what's the matter."

I reply that there is nothing the matter with me, but that I am worried about her, and add that, although she may not be aware of the fact, she is playing havoc with the affections of her admirers.

Pinkie opens her eyes very wide and says, "Oh *no*, Hester darling. You don't understand. I'm not that sort of person at *all*. I *hate* that sort of thing. I always *have* hated it—I mean at school and—and everywhere—"

"But Pinkie, I know you don't mean—"

"They're just *friends*," says Pinkie earnestly, "just friends, that's all. I like having *lots* of friends."

"But what about *them?*" I enquire.

"They understand," she replies. "They like being friends with me, you see. They ask me to play tennis or badminton, or go to the pictures, and of course I enjoy it—and they do, too. They wouldn't ask me if they didn't, would they?"

"Are you sure they understand?"

"I'm sure of it, perfectly certain," declares Pinkie. "I've told them, you see."

"You've told them?" I echo, somewhat puzzled by her words.

"Yes," says Pinkie gravely. "I tell them all—at the very

beginning—or, at least, as soon as they begin to get very friendly—I tell them that I like being friends with them, but I don't like any silly nonsense—so they couldn't possibly *not* understand, could they?"

"No-o," I reply doubtfully.

"No, of course not," says Pinkie firmly. "Things are different now. You can go about and have a good time together, and it doesn't mean anything except that you like each other —and you both know that, so it's all right. Everything is perfectly clear and—well—aboveboard, if you know what I mean . . . and anyhow, they're far too young."

I enquire somewhat anxiously whether they are *all* too young, and Pinkie says "Yes." She hesitates for a moment and I have a feeling that she is going to say something else, but when she does eventually open her mouth it is only to add that they are all mere children. When she marries—if she ever marries—it will be somebody much older than herself, somebody *quite old*. I ask Pinkie how old her ideal husband will be, and she replies "Oh, at least thirty."

Pinkie goes away after this, and I have just risen from my desk, and am peering into the mirror, trying to count my wrinkles and to number my grey hairs, when she comes back into the room and says in a conspiratorial tone, "Don't let's *mention* it to him, Hester. It might be—well, I mean it might be sort of private. Don't you think so?"

"Who, what?" I ask, gazing at her blankly.

"Bryan," breathes Pinkie. "That Black Spot affair . . . he mightn't like it if he knew that we knew about it."

I agree to remain silent upon the subject—though I am pretty certain that Bryan would not mind in the least—and Pinkie vanishes once more. . . . Spend the rest of the day worrying over our conversation, and trying to think which of Pinkie's friends has reached the ripe age of thirty.

MONDAY 16TH SEPTEMBER

Tim returns from the Barracks with the news that Tony
Morley has offered him a day's shooting . . . he has managed
to get leave, so that's all right, and, if only it's a nice day,
everything in the garden will be lovely. Pinkie and I are
invited too, and Tony will take sufficient food for us all. It
isn't a drive, because there aren't any beaters, so we shall have
to walk *miles,* but as Tim walked miles and miles in Belgium
he is in excellent training and it won't worry *him.* If Pinkie
and I get tired we can sit down somewhere and get picked up
on the way back.

Pinkie says she bets she can walk as far as Tim can, to which
Tim retorts, "How much?" Pinkie says, "Well . . . a bob,"
and Tim says, "Your bob is as good as lost."

To change the subject, I enquire whether the shoot is far
off and, if so, how we are to get there—our petrol ration for
the current month having been used already. Tim explains
that the moor belongs to a young subaltern called Craddock—
or, to be exact, to young Craddock's father—and Morley said
it was about ten miles away, but Morley is taking us in his
car, so we don't need to worry. There's a rattling good grouse-
moor and some fields where we may find some partridges.
Craddock père is a big bug, and owns a large estate, but he's
very seldom there because he's been given some important job
in London.

Pinkie has listened to all this in silence and now she enquires whether "old Mr. Craddock" is to be there tomorrow.
Tim says no, he doesn't think so. Pinkie says, "Oh, but I
suppose George Craddock is coming?" Tim says yes, he believes he is, and adds—quite unnecessarily of course—that

young Craddock is in Morley's Battalion and Morley thinks a lot of him. Pinkie says, "Yes, he's awfully nice."

I feel that Pinkie has shown a good deal of interest in the Craddock family—but young Craddock is more like twenty-three than thirty!

Tim is quite excited at the prospect of a day's shooting, he gets out his guns and spends the evening taking them to pieces and putting them together again.

TUESDAY 17TH SEPTEMBER

Two large cars pull up at the gate as the clock strikes the half hour—fortunately we are ready in good time and troop down the path carrying bags and guns and mackintoshes and other impedimenta.

Tony says, "Hullo, you're all ready—good show? It's going to be a lovely day." Symes hastens forward to open the gate. Young Craddock leaps out of his car—which is just behind Tony's—and salutes us smartly. There is a good deal of talking and laughing until Tony puts a stop to it by saying that time is valuable. "Hop in," says Tony. "You can all come in my car and Craddock can take Symes. Craddock's car is full of dogs and baskets."

Mr. Craddock looks somewhat crestfallen at this arrangement, and says that there's room for Miss Bradshaw in front and Symes could go in the back with the dogs, but of course if she would rather—and Tony says, "Oh, just as you like," and Pinkie solves the problem by making a beeline for George Craddock's car and getting in.

Off we go. It is a lovely autumn morning with a little nip of frost in the sparkling air, and the hills stand out in bold relief against the violet blue sky. Far over the sea there is a band of bright saffron on the horizon and, as we reach the

top of the hill, I turn and look back and am just in time to
see the sun rise out of the sea. No wonder the ancients wor-
shipped the sun for his appearance changes the whole scene
. . . before his coming the morning was painted in soft tones
of yellow and violet blue, but now in a moment it springs to
life and colour. The trees—all red and golden in their autumn
dress—are touched with the magic flame, and their long
shadows sweep across the road like pointing fingers. Our way
lies north and west, first along the cliffs which edge the bounding sea, and then inland towards the rounded hills. We climb;
we descend; we catch glimpses of farms, or cottages, of lochs
nestling in the folds of the hills, and all the time the sun rises
higher in the sky and the colours in the landscape brighten
and deepen. Now we are amongst the hills; they rise fold upon
fold around us, and the road twists and turns across the moors.

George Craddock's car is leading, for he knows the way,
and suddenly, in the middle of a stretch of moorland road, he
signals that he is going to stop and draws on to a grassy plot
at the roadside. Tony follows suit, and he has scarcely done
so when George jumps out of his car and comes to the window. He explains that this is quite a good place to leave the
cars. We can shoot Fingal first and, returning by another way,
have our lunch comfortably and go on to the lower slopes in
the afternoon.

Tony points to a large rounded hill with a jutting shoulder
and says, "Is that Fingal?"

"Yes, sir," replies George smartly.

I notice—not without amusement—that George is on his
very best behaviour today and is very much the junior
subaltern. I cannot determine whether George is really awed
by the superior rank of his two fellow shooters, or whether
he is being careful not to take advantage of the fact that he is
their host.

Tony says, "We go across the moor, do we, and up over the shoulder?"

"Yes, sir," agrees George, "and we come back at the other side of the fir plantation."

"That sounds all right," says Tony, "and anyhow you're O.C. Troops—so lead on, General Craddock."

George blushes, "Well, I mean that's what we usually do, sir . . . you see, the birds usually fly across the shoulder of Fingal and we get another chance at them on the way back."

By this time we have all got out and are standing in the road. Pinkie and I have no arrangements to make, so we hang about waiting for them to start. The wind has a knife-edge to it, and they take ages to settle matters . . . coats are removed and stowed in the cars; guns are taken out and examined; bags of cartridges are produced—and empty bags for the game—and Symes is loaded with haversacks. Symes looks quite dazed at all the advice he receives, and is completely out of his element. Finally, when all is ready, we start off across the moor—the three shooters in front with the dogs, and Pinkie and I and Symes behind. We have been told not to speak or—if speak we must—in whispers only, but somehow we do not want to speak. It is so quiet and peaceful here, the springy turf and the heather beneath our feet and the cloudless blue sky above our heads, and all around us the upstanding hills, peeping over each other's shoulders. There is no sign of man, nor of man's work; we might be hundreds of miles from anywhere. Every now and then we come to a burn, full of brown peaty water, which meanders lazily across the moor, or to a clump of pine trees, or a low stone wall. . . . Then we begin to climb the lower slopes of the hill, and here the heather grows higher and thicker, and the hoar frost, melting with the sun's rays, sparkles upon it like diamonds.

We have been walking for about twenty minutes when the

dogs put up some grouse—they fly off squawking and the three guns speak almost simultaneously. I have been expecting this for so long that I have ceased to expect it and the noise is so loud and so sudden that I almost jump out of my skin. My two companions are equally startled. Pinkie says "Oh!" and Symes drops a game bag . . . he picks it up at once and looking at me somewhat sheepishly says that it slipped out of his hand. Tim is now signalling to us to keep back until the birds are retrieved, so Symes spreads a mackintosh on a convenient boulder and we sit down.

"Does the colonel want me to fetch the grouse?" enquires Symes anxiously.

I reply that the dogs will find them, but that he will probably have to carry them.

He smiles and says, "You'll keep me right, won't you?" and I promise to do what I can in the matter.

"It's grand fun," says Symes. "I never did anything like this before. There seems a lot in it . . . and I don't want to let the colonel down. I've read about shooting grouse, of course, but I never thought I'd be doing it." Symes is so pleased with himself that I have not the heart to point out that he is not shooting grouse, but merely carrying the ammunition. Instead, I suggest that he will have to write to Miss Ebb and tell her about it. He agrees that he must do so, and opines that she will be very much surprised when she hears about it . . . "She's having a good time too," adds Symes. "What with Naval Officers and being taken to see over ships . . ."

Pinkie says, "I've never been out with guns before either. I shall write to Aunt Elinor and tell her."

There is a short silence, and then Symes says in a thoughtful voice, "War is funny, isn't it?"

"But this isn't war!" exclaims Pinkie.

"It's my war, Miss," says Symes firmly—an oracular statement which gives me food for thought. If it were not for the war, if it were not for the fact that a megalomaniac in Central Europe had run amok and turned the world into a cockpit, Symes would be packing china in a London basement. . . .

The birds are now collected, and we are invited to admire them before they are stowed into the bag. There are three birds, two of which have fallen to Tony's gun and one to George Craddock's . . . I feel absurdly sorry for Tim, but manage to refrain from showing any sympathy, as I am aware that Tim would hate it.

Now we are off again, the three guns in front spreading out fanwise and keeping level with each other. It is much warmer, for we are sheltered by the hill. Symes looks very hot in his thick battle dress, but he plods on manfully and refuses to allow Pinkie or me to lighten his load by a single bag. We have now nearly reached the top of the ridge and Tim signals to us to wait, so we sit down again—very thankfully—and watch the shooters until they disappear over the top. We hear four shots and then another two—Symes looks at me enquiringly, but I shake my head, for I am aware that it is better to obey orders to the letter than to display initiative.

Pinkie asks what time it is and, on being informed that it is eleven o'clock, she groans and says, "Only eleven? I'm simply starving."

"It's the fresh air," says Symes, and he produces a large slab of milk chocolate and shares it with us . . . I compliment him upon his forethought, and he replies modestly that he often feels hungry himself in the middle of the morning and chocolate is easy to carry and very filling. We talk in a desultory way. Pinkie, harking back to our previous conversation, asks Symes whether he likes being a soldier or would rather be back at his usual job, and Symes replies that he likes being a soldier. "I never thought I'd like it," he declares, "but I like it so much I couldn't go back—not to the packing room, I couldn't. Gertie says the same—well, I don't know what's to happen to us after the war. It's difficult, isn't it? Gertie says not to think too far ahead, but just win the war first . . . still, you can't help wondering."

It certainly is a problem, and I am so interested in it that I ask Symes why he feels that he could not go back. He replies that packing china doesn't seem important now—not the kind of job for a man—"but it's the colonel, really," adds Symes thoughtfully. "I never knew there could be anyone like the colonel. If you'd told me I'd be happy as an officer's servant I wouldn't have believed you—no menial work for me, I'd have said—but it's a pleasure to do things for a man like him. Sometimes I wonder . . . well, sometimes it just crosses my mind that I'd like to carry on with the colonel after the war . . . if he'd find any use for me . . . but then there's Gertie . . . it's a problem and no mistake."

Pinkie says, "Everyone likes Colonel Morley, don't they?"

"*Everyone,*" agrees Symes, enthusiastically. "Why the whole Battalion would follow him through hell—and he'd be in front, too, *he* wouldn't be shoving the men on from behind—in the very front is where you'd see *him* . . . We're off to Egypt soon," adds Symes.

"Really?" I enquire, somewhat surprised to hear this piece of news, for Tony has not mentioned it.

"Yes," says Symes. "Oh it's quite right, Miss. Everyone knows about it in the Battalion, only of course we're not supposed to talk about it to outsiders. It will be interesting to see a bit of the world . . . the Sphinx and the pyramids . . . wonderful they must be!"

Tim is waving to us, so we move on, and I am glad to find that Tim has two birds to his credit this time . . . . We take

a cast round the shoulder of Fingal and come back through a
wood, and George Craddock has timed his manoeuvres so well
that we arrive back at the road and the waiting cars at one
o'clock precisely. Everyone is ravenous by now, so no time is
lost in finding a sheltered spot, spreading mackintosh ground
sheets and opening the picnic baskets. Tony has provided an
excellent lunch with ample food for everyone—but not too
much—and I realise afresh what a capable person he is, for I
know from long experience how difficult it is to steer a course
between the two extremes. Symes is given a large packet of
sandwiches and a bottle of beer and goes back to the cars to
enjoy his meal in solitude. The morning's bag has been spread
out on the ground in front of us—nine and a half brace of
grouse, a pigeon and three hares—and the shooters admire the
results of their efforts as they eat . . . "but we ought to do
better in the afternoon," says George Craddock hopefully.

"We ought to have another gun," Tony says, "and I suppose
we could have got Jack MacDougall or Ledgard—but I just
felt that it would be much nicer without them—"

"It *is* much nicer," agrees Tim, "and if only I were pulling
my weight . . . I mean I should have got a brace out of that
last covey that broke back over my head . . . in fact I missed
several absolute sitters. I haven't done any shooting since last
year," he adds apologetically.

"You have been otherwise engaged, sir," points out George
with a smile.

"Bigger game—" murmurs Tony.

"Yes," says Tim with a sigh, "Bigger game . . . you
wouldn't think there was a war on, would you?" and he waves
his arm round the peaceful hills.

It is so peaceful and friendly and pleasant that I am glad to
be alive, and I wish we could stay here forever amongst the
hills—where the only other living creatures are the birds and

the black-faced sheep—and never return to the world and its cares. Nothing here is troublesome or confusing, there are no problems here . . .

I am thinking about this, and wishing that I had been born a black-faced sheep, when Tony suddenly remarks, "I wish we need not go back."

"So do I," agrees Tim. "It's simply heavenly. It's all the more delightful because it's so unexpected . . . we appreciate it more . . . we've snatched a day from peace-time if you know what I mean."

"Oh yes!" cries Pinkie. "That's just what I've been feeling all the morning—you've put it into words, Major Tim."

"Peace all round us," says Tony.

"Yes, sir," agrees George, "But there's more in it than that. Don't you think that the reason we're enjoying it so much is because—well, because we all like each other?"

Tony smiles and says, "Good companions—eh? I believe there's a good deal in that."

"We could have another day, sir," says George eagerly, "I mean any time that you think we could get a day's leave . . . the moor needs shooting badly—"

"But you're going off to Egypt, aren't you?" I enquire.

Tony looks at me in amazement.

"Well, aren't you?" I ask, and add a trifle diffidently, "I thought you were."

Tony says "Well . . . well, that beats the band. How on earth did you hear that, Hester?"

Everyone is looking at me and I feel somewhat uncomfortable, but I pull myself together, and inform Tony that Symes told us, and that the whole Battalion is under the impression that it is destined for the land of the Pharaohs.

"Good Lord!" exclaims Tony. "It was only last night that I

heard it myself . . . and it's supposed to be strictly confidential
. . . How *do* they get to know these things?"

Tim says, "They always know before we do."

George Craddock exclaims, "Do you mean it's *true*? We're
really going . . . Gosh, how marvellous! I bet we'll show the
ice cream merchants where they get off . . . Active Service at
last . . . Gosh, how absolutely super!" He rolls over on to his
back and waves his legs in the air.

Tony is looking a trifle grim; he says, "Well, keep it under
your hat, Craddock—though I don't suppose it's much good
if the whole blinking Battalion knows—"

"Yes, sir," replies George, sitting up and trying to look
serious and reliable. "Oh yes, sir, of course, sir. I won't say a
word . . . d'you know when we're going, sir?"

Tony says, "Strange though it may appear, I *do* happen to
know the approximate date of our departure."

There is a short but somewhat strained silence, which is
broken by Pinkie saying, "Oh look!" and pointing at a tiny
speck in the sky just above the shoulder of Fingal.

"An aeroplane!" says George (somewhat unnecessarily, for
the speck has approached and lost height so rapidly that its
nature is now quite obvious).

Four of us look up at the plane with casual interest, but
Tim leaps to his feet and clamps his field glasses to his
eyes . . .

"What—" begins Tony.

"It's a Jerry, that's what!" exclaims Tim, " . . . yes, it's a
Jerry. I saw too many of the brutes in France to make any
mistake."

"It's coming down!" cries Pinkie excitedly. "It's coming
down . . ."

By this time the plane is less than half a mile away and is
losing height rapidly. Its engines are making a loud laborious

noise—entirely different from the cheerful hum to which we
have become accustomed—but I have no sooner noticed this
than the engines peter out, and the plane does a gentle nose
dive into the ground and tilts over with its tail pointing sky-
wards. Somehow or other it reminds me of a slow motion film,
and the noise of the crash, which reaches our ears a second or
two later, adds to the illusion.

Tony has already assumed command, "Come, Tim—" he
cries, "Craddock can stay with the girls—we must take Symes
because he's the only one in uniform—," and he starts running
across the moor towards the wreckage. Tim picks up his gun
and follows, shouting and beckoning to Symes.

The unfortunate George, who has leapt to his feet and
seized his gun in readiness, remains standing beside us with
an expression of disappointment upon his face, which makes
me want to laugh. I suggest that he should go with the others
—Pinkie and I will be perfectly all right without his protection—but George says that he daren't; the colonel said he was
to stay . . . "and I like staying, really," adds the miserable
youth, "I mean it's an honour in a way . . . it's only . . . well,
as a matter of fact it's the first time . . . I mean I've never
seen an *enemy* before . . ."

Pinkie gasps and says, "An enemy *here!* Isn't it—isn't it
amazing to think of?"

I have been watching the plane with Tony's field glasses,
and, as it is only about five hundred yards away, I can see it
very clearly indeed . . . . Two figures crawl out through an
opening in the roof and slide down on to the ground. They
appear somewhat dazed. When they see our party approaching
they turn towards the plane—perhaps their first thought is to
destroy it—but Tony calls out to them in German and they
immediately hold up their hands.

Pinkie, who has been hopping with excitement, suddenly

announces that she must be there, she can't wait a moment longer and, as I feel the same, we start walking towards the scene of action with George fluttering round us like a motherly hen and begging us to remember that "the colonel" said we were to stay where we were . . .

"You can't trust them!" cries George. "And there may be bombs . . . and I'm responsible for you . . ."

The two airmen are now being disarmed, and as we approach I can hear Tony enquiring, in somewhat stilted German, whether there is anyone else in the wrecked plane. They shake their heads and say "Nein," and one of them points over the hills and says that their two companions descended by parachute. Tony translates this information—otherwise I should not be in possession of it—and adds that he will just make sure. He climbs on to the sloping wing, which has come adrift in the crash, and peers through the smashed window. As he turns to come down his eyes light upon us and he exclaims, "What are you doing here? I thought I told you to stay near the cars," but there is a twinkle in his eye as he says it—and a twinkle in his voice as well—and I hear George give a long sigh of relief.

"I suppose this is the end of our shooting," says Tim regretfully—and of course it is, for the prisoners must be taken to Donford immediately, and the plane must be guarded until the proper authorities can be informed. After some discussion it is agreed that Symes shall be left to look after the plane, Tony and George will take the prisoners to the Barracks and report the matter to Air Force Headquarters, and Tim will drive us home in George Craddock's car.

This settled we walk back to the road—and what a curious little procession it is! The two dour-looking Germans in their airmen's uniforms and our own men in sporting kit. (In spite of their clothes, however, there is no doubt of their profession; they stride along with their guns over their shoulders and their faces have assumed a soldierly mien—stern and unsmiling.) Pinkie and I bring up the rear, and have some difficulty in keeping up with the main body of troops. We rustle through the dried heather, we scramble over walls, we leap from tuft to tuft of grass through the boggy places. The sun is shining as brightly as ever and the wind is blowing billowy white clouds across the azure sky; a lark springs up from our very feet and soars into the air, and from afar off comes the plaintive bleat of a sheep, but the whole atmosphere has changed, for the day's peace has been broken . . . there is an air of unreality in the scene.

Pinkie pinches my arm and says, "Hester, I don't know whether to laugh or cry . . . or whether I'm dreaming . . . what do you feel?"

"It's war," I murmur sadly.

"But war—here!" she says, fumbling to express her meaning, "I can't believe it . . . it's so utterly *silly,* somehow . . ."

WEDNESDAY 18TH SEPTEMBER

Donford is all agog with a rumour that the Germans have actually attempted an invasion—the rumour arrives at Winfield through the medium of the butcher's boy. I have just succeeded in persuading Annie that there is nothing in it, and that the butcher's boy has been pulling her leg, when Grace arrives with an armful of chrysanthemums and a large cabbage and says she has brought them for me, as a present to my body and my soul, and that a proper present should always be of this dual nature. I am delighted with the gifts and agree that a double present is more than twice as acceptable as a single one. Annie takes the cabbage and carries it in triumph to the kitchen, and I proceed to arrange the flowers.

Grace says have I heard about the invasion. The Germans set sail in their flat-bottomed boats and we allowed them to come within five miles of the shore before opening fire . . . it is "absolutely authentic," because she heard it from the lift boy at the Donford Arms and his cousin was actually *there* and saw the whole thing with his own eyes. Our Air Force and Navy simply finished them off, and there was not a German left to tell the tale.

Grace's eyes are like saucers, and I feel as if my own eyes were enlarging rapidly, but I manage to pull myself together and enquire why this extremely reassuring piece of news has not been broadcast to the world.

Grace says, "We don't want the Enemy to know what has happened—that must be the reason. It's an absolute fact that hundreds of German soldiers have been washed up on the south coast of England. I *know* that's true because Nannie's sister's husband is a commercial traveller and when he was down there he saw people digging graves."

"Oh Grace!"

"You needn't believe it if you don't want to," says Grace crossly. "As a matter of fact nobody seems to believe a word I say. Jack is most annoying at present; he listens to Haw Haw and believes what *he* says."

"You shouldn't let him."

"I don't," says Grace promptly. "We had a blazing row last night over that horrible oily man—his voice makes me quite ill—I wanted to listen to the B.B.C. Orchestra, and Jack wanted Haw Haw . . ." she smiles reminiscently as she speaks, and I feel sure she got her way, but I make no enquiries for I do not want to hear about the row.

"You aren't going to the Depot, this morning, are you?" enquires Grace. "There's no need for you to go because we sent off all the parcels yesterday . . . By the way, how did the shoot go off? Did you get a good bag?"

"Yes, it included two German airmen."

"Hester!"

"It's perfectly true."

"Tell me all about it," says Grace. "Tell me *everything*," and with that Grace, who has been on the verge of departure, settles herself in her chair and prepares to listen with all her ears. Unfortunately this does not suit me at all, for I have not been to the town to do my shopping, and, as I was unable to shop yesterday, I am in possession of a list of goods which are required for the household. I explain this to Grace and she rises with manifest reluctance. "Oh well," she says, "as a matter of fact I ought to pop in and see Ermyntrude this morning. You had better come to tea and tell me about it."

In the last fortnight or so the little town of Donford has undergone a strange metamorphosis; it has become "Polarized," so to speak. There is a large camp of Polish Troops on the golf course, and there are dozens of Polish officers billeted in the town. There are officers' wives, and a few children— though how they managed to get here nobody seems to know. Pinkie spoke no more than the truth when she said that the place was "teeming with them", they seem to outnumber the natives by a proportion of two to one. As one walks down the High Street one hears the staccato sound of the Polish language on every side, for the streets are always full of soldiers, hurrying past on some errand, or gazing into the windows of the shops. They are a cheery lot, and there is plenty of laughter amongst the little groups which congregate at the corners of the streets, but even in the middle of the greatest joke they do not fail to make way for a passerby—their manners, from the oldest colonel to the youngest private, leave nothing to be desired. Sometimes as one goes upon one's lawful business one sees a meeting between old friends. A man will stop and gaze at another in joyful amazement, and they will shake hands firmly and cordially and burst into excited speech. I have seen this happen not once, but several times, and it has always given me a thrill of pleasure. It is curious to see how this small Scottish town has taken these foreign soldiers to its heart. The somewhat dour Scottish faces break into friendly smiles, there are bows and signals and gallant attempts to overcome the barrier of language. The Donford girls have all got Polish friends—some of them have two or three—they seem to be able to overcome the barrier more easily than the older people. In most of the shops notices in Polish have appeared; there are Polish newspapers on the bookstalls and Polish dictionaries are selling like hot cakes. . . .

I turn into Simpson's (the draper) to buy a card of buttons for Betty's pyjamas and find the whole shop disorganised and business at a standstill. There is a Polish lady here—very smart and nicely dressed—and she is surrounded by shop assistants who are endeavouring to understand what she wants. Mr. Simpson himself has been fetched, but is unable to solve the problem, the counter is piled with goods of every description, but apparently none of them is what she requires.

"It's shirts—I'm sure it's shirts," declares the first assistant earnestly.

"We've tried shirts," replies the second assistant. "We've tried pyjamas too . . . and vests and pants."

"Try collars," says Mr. Simpson, wiping the perspiration from his brow, and one of his myrmidons rushes away to carry out his behest.

Somewhat diffidently I approach the little group and enquire whether the lady speaks French. . . . She turns to me at once, with a delightful smile, and overwhelms me with a torrent of such fluent French that I am completely sunk. I shake my head and say in my halting manner that if she will explain her requirements slowly and simply I will do my best to help her. While this conversation is taking place Mr. Simpson and his assistants are standing by ready to receive instructions; they are gazing at me reverently, and I realise that my stock has gone up a good deal. It is to be hoped that I shall be able to play my part as interpreter in a worthy manner or my stock will slump pretty seriously.

The lady spreads her hands and says it is very good of me to come to her aid. She is so grateful. It is very simple really. She requires a "robe de nuit" for her son. It must be of the best quality flannel, because he suffers from the cold. In Poland it is cold—yes—but here it is so damp as well. "That is understood?" she enquires, smiling.

Fortunately for us both it is understood quite easily, and I explain to Mr. Simpson that the lady wants a nightshirt for her son—a flannel nightshirt of the best quality.

"A flannel nightshirt?" says Mr. Simpson. "How old is the child?"

I translate this to the Polish lady, "Quel âge a votre fils?" I enquire.

She looks at me in surprise . . . and then laughs heartily and announces that he is twenty-eight years old and six feet tall. The mystery is now solved and everyone is happy. I explain to the lady—as best I can—that the mistake arose owing to the fact that she looks too young to have a grown-up son. She acknowledges the compliment with another delightful smile, and we part on the best of terms. Business in Simpson's shop is now resumed, and several people who have been waiting, more or less impatiently, to be served are attended to without further delay.

FRIDAY 20TH SEPTEMBER

I have often thought Jack MacDougall an annoying sort of person and today he is more annoying than usual. He comes in with Tim to have a glass of sherry on his way home from the Barracks and, instead of drinking up his sherry and going home to his own wife and children like a sensible man, he remains to pester us. There is no stability in Jack. Sometimes he is cheerful and pleasant as any man could be and sometimes he is gloomy and irritating—and today, unfortunately for us, he is in the latter condition. "Oh yes," says Jack, "Oh yes, the Greeks are doing well, but wait till the Italians get going—"

"I was under the impression that the Italians got going first," says Tim.

"They thought they were going to have a walk-over," explains Jack, waving his glass, "and now they'll bring up reinforcements. They've got immense reserves, of course . . . I can't understand all this optimistic talk."

"But things *are* going better . . ." I begin.

"I don't see it," says Jack. "I see no improvement at all . . . our R.A.F. goes over and batters Berlin, and their fellows come over and batter poor old London. What's the good of that?"

"That's war," says Tim, and I can see that he is getting cross.

"Of course it's war," agrees Jack, smiling unpleasantly, "but that is *no* argument."

"No," replies Tim. "There *is* no argument for war. It is utterly foolish; it is wasteful and wicked . . . the only point that seems to have escaped your notice is that we didn't choose war. War was forced upon us by Hitler . . . but mark my words, he'll be sorry for it before we've finished with him."

"Let's hope you're right," says Jack. "We have no means of

knowing how things really are. We aren't *told* . . . we aren't told *half* . . ."

"You've been listening to Haw Haw!" I tell him.

"Why shouldn't I?" Jack enquires.

"Because he's poisonous," I reply. "He exudes venom like a rattlesnake. You wouldn't drink something that Hitler sent you in bottle, so why should you allow him to poison you with words?"

"That's nonsense, Hester—" begins Jack.

"No, it isn't nonsense," I assure him. "You *are* poisoned, Jack. A little while ago we talked about the war and you were quite cheerful about it, and now, when things are much brighter, you are as gloomy as you can be. It's Haw Haw poisoning you're suffering from."

Unfortunately Jack is not in the mood to take my teasing in the right spirit, he evades the point and declares that I am indulging in "wishful thinking," and hiding my head in the sand like an ostrich . . . "Look at the U Boats!" says Jack gloomily, "Look at Egypt! Look anywhere you like . . ."

Tim is becoming more and more irritated with Jack, and so am I for that matter, so we are both pleased when his jeremiad is interrupted by the appearance of Bryan, who erupts into the room in his usual violent manner. (Bryan is going back to school on Monday, and is spending his last few days advancing the education of his Polish friend.) I am in great hopes that Bryan's advent will hasten Jack's departure, but Jack seems in no hurry to depart.

"Hullo, is this Bryan?" exclaims Jack in mock surprise. "Is this Bryan that I see before me? And what has Bryan been doing with himself, may I ask?"

Bryan hates this sort of nonsense—and I hate it on his behalf —but he answers quite pleasantly that he has been out in the woods.

"In the woods?" enquires Jack. "What do you do in the woods? Play that you're fighting the Germans, I suppose."

"No," says Bryan. "Sometimes we play hide and seek, but most of the time I've been teaching a Pole to talk English."

Jack seems amused at this, "Dear, dear!" he says, "what a strange way of spending your holidays! I suppose you are qualifying for the teaching profession, are you?"

Bryan is no fool, and knows that Jack is teasing him; he replies gravely that he is going to be a soldier.

"I see!" says Jack. "You're going to be a soldier, but meantime you're a professor of English. Does your Polish friend teach you to speak Polish, or is it a one-sided affair?"

At this Bryan smiles to himself in a secret sort of way. "No, it isn't one-sided . . ." says Bryan slowly. "He's teaching me . . . something."

There is a moment's silence, but Jack has not finished with his catechism yet. "Oh!" says Jack, rather nastily. "Oh, that sounds very mysterious . . . he's teaching you something, is he?"

I am aware that the matter cannot be left like this, and am about to try to clear it up when Tim takes a hand in the proceedings. He looks at his son in a friendly manner and says, "You've told us too much or not enough, old fellow. What's the mystery?"

"It's wrestling," says Bryan quickly. "I didn't mean it to be a mystery at all. They do a lot of wrestling where he comes from . . . I'll show you, if you like, Dad."

Tim does not accept the offer. He smiles at Bryan and says "Good!" and as far as he is concerned the subject is closed, but Jack is not content to leave it there and invites Bryan to show what he can do.

"Don't be an ass," says Tim, who has now lost patience completely. "How can he show you what he can do? You don't propose that he should try out his wrestling on you, do you? I thought you'd had enough unarmed combat when you tackled me on the shore."

"I thought he might *show* me," Jack replies with a careless laugh, "but, if you don't want him to show what he can do, I don't mind in the least . . . I wouldn't hurt him of course . . ."

Bryan is watching and waiting anxiously for the end of the argument and I can see by his face that he is eager for the fray, but, as Bryan is only twelve years old and slightly made and Jack is a full grown man, I am not in favour of the idea and I say as much quite plainly, adding that in any case my drawing room is an unsuitable arena for a wrestling match.

"I'll show you one of the things he taught me," says Bryan at last. "Please, Mum, let me . . . I'll just show him quite gently, shall I? It's like this you see . . ." and advancing suddenly upon Jack he seizes Jack's arms and holds them.

"Ha, ha!" cries Jack. "That's what he's taught you, is it! I knew that trick at school. You think you've got me cold, but . . . I do *this* . . ."

Nobody knows what Jack does (unless he knows himself) and nobody knows what Bryan does—whether it is what he intended to do or something quite different—but the result of their combined efforts is most astonishing, for the next moment Jack is lying on his back underneath the piano and Bryan is standing in the middle of the room, with an expression of utter and complete amazement upon his face.

It is extremely difficult not to laugh at this modern version of David and Goliath. I can hear Tim give a smothered snort, and I know that I must not look at him, or we shall both lose control of ourselves and burst into shrieks of laughter.

"I say!" cries Bryan, rushing to the aid of his fallen foe, "I say, I'm most awfully sorry . . . I'd no idea it would work like that . . . you see I've only done it with *him* . . . and of course he *knows*. I mean he knows what I'm going to *do,* you see . . . and does something else to prevent it happening . . . Gosh, I *am* sorry!"

Jack takes it uncommonly well—indeed the fall seems to have improved his temper—he crawls out from beneath the piano and allows Bryan to help him to rise.

"I *say!*" exclaims Bryan, "I say, you *have* got a lump on your head! It must have been the piano. We should have done it outside—"

"Yes," agrees Jack, "but I didn't know we were going to do it at all . . . Oh well, there's no serious damage done . . . no, I don't want antiphlogistine, Hester, I'll just go home."

"I *am* sorry," declares Bryan earnestly.

"It's all right," says Jack, "But you better be careful you don't kill someone by mistake."

"Oh, I *will.* I'd no idea it was going to happen . . . it was like an explosion or something."

"Dynamite wasn't in it," agrees Jack, feeling his head tenderly. (He is *really* going now, for he is gravitating towards the door, and we do not urge him to delay his departure. Bryan fetches his coat and helps him to put it on.) "Where is my cap?" he enquires. "Not that I can wear it, of course, but I had better take it with me . . . thank you, Bryan . . . no, it's all right. It wasn't your fault, really. Oh well, that's the last time I shall indulge in Unarmed Combat with the Christie family."

Tim murmurs—*sotto voce*—that perhaps Jack might like to try a fall with Hester, and with that we both rush into the drawing room and throw ourselves into chairs . . .

Bryan follows us more slowly. "I couldn't help it," he declares. "Honestly, I couldn't. I didn't *mean* to knock him down . . . and I *wouldn't* have knocked him down if he hadn't

done what he did . . . I mean it was him doing what he did
—whatever it was—that made it happen. As a matter of fact
I don't know now what *did* happen, but . . . Oh, you're
laughing!" cries Bryan, in great relief. "Oh, you're laughing!
I thought you'd be angry."

"I am angry!" sobs Tim, burying his head in a cushion, "Oh
goodness, I'm sore all over! Look at your Mother, she's crying!"

"I suppose it *was* rather funny," says Bryan with a little
chuckle. "Well, I mean it must have been . . . I must tell
Voicheech about it. I wish he could have seen it."

Tim has now recovered from his paroxysms, he sits up and
blows his nose with a trumpeting sound and agrees that
Bryan's instructor would have got a kick out of the affair. He
then enquires what Bryan would do in the unlikely event of
his receiving five bob—not in payment for his unwarranted
assault upon his father's guest, of course, but merely as a token
of affection.

Bryan listens to this with a satisfied smile and says, "Well,
I think it would be fair if I gave Voicheech half of it, don't
you?" and holds out his hand for the money.

SUNDAY 22ND SEPTEMBER

Bryan is going back to school tomorrow, and during the
afternoon while we are engaged in packing his trunk, the
following conversation takes place.

"Mum!"

"Yes, Bryan?"

"Mum, I say. Will you be kind to Voicheech when I've
gone?"

"Bryan, I simply couldn't. I've got more than enough to do
already. You know quite well that I've got the 'Comforts' to

run, and now I've been roped in to visit soldiers' families. You *know* that, Bryan."

"I know, but one hour a week isn't much, is it?"

"I can't take on anything else."

"One hour . . . say every Wednesday afternoon."

"No, Bryan. I'm sorry, but I simply couldn't."

Bryan sighs. "He's going to miss me awfully. He hasn't any real friends except me. The other chaps come from quite a different part of Poland . . . you wouldn't think that would matter, would you?"

"No, you wouldn't."

"But they're mostly from towns. He's a country person, you see."

"Yes, but I can't do anything for him."

"He used to live with his mother in a little cottage on a farm,—I showed you the picture, didn't I?"

"Yes, but I haven't time—"

"I know. Well then the Germans came and he joined up, you see, but of course his mother was left. He doesn't know what happened to her *at all*. He doesn't know . . . she may be *dead*. It must be *awful* for him, mustn't it? I mean I couldn't think of anything worse than that . . . I couldn't bear it."

"Couldn't you?"

"No, I just couldn't . . . so that's why I'm so sorry for him, you see."

"Yes, I see."

"So you *will* be kind to him, won't you?"

"Yes, Bryan."

"I knew you would!" cries Bryan, giving me a hug. "I *knew* you would when you understood about it . . . just one hour every week . . . it isn't much, is it?"

"No, it isn't much."

"Just one hour. He'll come here every Wednesday afternoon at three—I told him to—and you'll talk to him and cheer him up . . . and then, when I come home at Christmas . . ."

Part 4
November—December

Open my diary and discover that I have written nothing in it for the month of October. This is due to the fact that I have been busy with the accounts of the "Comforts Fund" which have been handed over to me in an almost inextricable muddle by the former Treasurer. Tim who promised to help me with them gave them up as hopeless and pronouncing them "a pig's breakfast" advised me to draw two thick lines and begin again. What with this, and Bryan's Pole and various other matters, domestic and otherwise, I have had little time for writing and my diary has suffered accordingly. October has been a placid month at Donford, nothing of any importance has happened to me or mine, and during its thirty-one days we have had no air raids. It has been very different in the South, and I have worried a good deal about Mary, who is living alone in Winteringham Square. Richard is in camp on Salisbury Plain and seems to think he will be there all winter. I have had a letter from Mrs. Loudon, saying that she intends to spend the winter at Avielochan instead of returning to her house at Kiltwinkle. She says she prefers snow and darkness to the visitations of the enemy and adds, "I am no use to anybody anyway and all I can do is to make socks, and I can do that as well here as there."

It is unlike Mrs. Loudon to be sorry for herself, and I feel somewhat guilty. She is lonely and anxious—a bad mixture—and I have done nothing to help her. She has asked me so often to go and stay with her, but somehow or other I have never felt free to go—perhaps it would be more true to say that I have not wanted to go—and now that Tim is back I am even less inclined to leave home.

Grace comes in while I am writing and exclaims, "Is that your diary? I thought you had given up writing a diary *long* ago."

I reply that my diary is of an unusual kind. Sometimes I write in it daily and at length, and at other times I neglect it for months.

Grace says, "I believe I could write a diary like that, and as a matter of fact I believe I *should*. I could put in all the clever and amusing things that the boys do and say . . . Oh yes, I know you're laughing at me, Hester, but you know quite well what I *mean*. Of course they can't talk yet, but I've told you before I like to make plans for the future . . . that reminds me," says Grace eagerly. "That reminds me. I *knew* I'd come on purpose to tell you something tremendously important— it was you talking about your diary that put it out of my head —what do you think has happened, Hester?"

"Ian has cut a tooth." I reply at once.

"How did you know?" enquires Grace (looking so crest-fallen that I feel rather a brute for having stolen her thunder). "How did you know, Hester? As a matter of fact it isn't Ian at all, it's Alec . . . but how did you know?"

I reply that I have had babies myself and have served a long, and at times somewhat painful, apprenticeship at the Regimental Welfare Centre, so I happen to know a little about their ways.

"Yes," says Grace. "Yes, well of course I know they're a little backward; Nannie says her last baby had a tooth before he was six months old; but twins are often backward, aren't they? and anyhow it's the sweetest darlingest little tooth you ever saw, and he never lost a wink of sleep over it."

WEDNESDAY 6TH NOVEMBER

News today most cheering. Roosevelt in, the Greeks doing well, and London free from air raids. I put on my coat and trip down to the Barracks, feeling on top of the world. Discuss my feelings with Grace, who has arrived at the Mob. Store before me and is already knee-deep in mittens, and find that Grace shares my sensation. She says that in the last few weeks she has "felt much better about the war" and she thinks it is because she has been able to grow a protective covering to her feelings. I suggest that the magnificent stand made by the Greeks has helped, for it has shown that the Axis Powers are vulnerable. Grace says, "Of course the Greeks have done well. There has been a recrudescence of all the splendid courage which helped them when they fought against Xerxes. They were outnumbered then, and they are outnumbered now. Thermistocles said in the hour of victory, 'It is not we who have done this, not we, but the Gods and Heroes who would not endure that one wicked man should become master of Asia and Europe.'"

I am so dumbfounded at the aptness of this that I can make no rejoinder, and Grace continues, "So you see it's the Gods and Heroes who are helping them now . . . but you needn't look at me with awe, Hester. I'm not so well-versed in Greek History as you may think. I just happened to come across it in a book I was reading and it seemed to fit the occasion so well that I learned it off by heart."

I cannot help feeling that it is very noble of Grace to give me this explanation, and am about to say so when the advent of Mamie puts a stop to all interesting discussion. Mamie's conversation seldom rises above the level of servant-troubles, and children's ailments, and clothes—though she has been known to include regimental gossip in her repertoire. Mamie is in the middle of a long story about Jane's tonsils, when Stella walks in and says, "Hello everybody, what's the news?" and Mamie, who had almost arrived at the end of Jane's tonsils, starts at the beginning again.

"Poor little Jane," says Mamie dolefully, "I was just telling Hester and Grace that she may have to have her tonsils out . . . but Herbert says he's determined to have further advice. Herbert says it's just a craze taking out children's tonsils. Herbert says—"

"But what's the *news?*" enquires Stella, interrupting with an absence of sympathy which seems almost inhuman. "Hasn't *anybody* heard any news this morning? The papers hadn't come before I left home, and our wireless died on us last night—"

"Roosevelt's in," says Grace shortly. She has no use for Mamie, but her dislike for Stella is active and profound.

"Roosevelt!" echoes Stella.

"Splendid, isn't it?" I exclaim.

"Why?" enquires Stella, "Why is it splendid? The other man might have been just as good, or perhaps even better . . . a new broom sweeps clean," adds Stella triumphantly.

I am completely squashed and can find nothing to say, but Grace comes to the rescue at once, and with admirable presence of mind retorts that you should never change horses when crossing a stream, and she thinks the American people are extremely sensible not to attempt this difficult and dangerous feat.

Stella says, "Where are the sticky labels? Has anyone seen them?" To which Grace, who is now on the warpath, replies, "Never mind the sticky labels you can write on the parcel."

Mamie now joins in the conversation and enquires why

Symes is not here this morning. It is so much easier when we have Symes.

I reply that Symes is away on leave—Embarkation Leave—as the 4th Battalion is under orders for foreign service.

Grace says, "Yes, I heard that. I hope Symes is having a nice time with Miss Gertie Ebb. Did he show you her photograph?"

Mamie says, "Oh dear, d'you mean we shan't have Symes any more? How perfectly sickening!"

Stella says, "We can do without him quite well. As a matter of fact I never liked the man."

"I think he's perfectly sweet," declares Grace.

"He was very *useful*," bleats Mamie, "He was so good at doing up the parcels . . . the string hurts my fingers. I wonder if Herbert would detail someone to come and help us to do up the parcels. Shall I ask him?"

Stella says that Mamie is to do no such thing. An ordinary soldier would be worse than useless to us. She adds that for her part she enjoys her work here; she feels she is doing something useful, and she would have thought that Mamie might feel the same. Mamie replies that if Stella would like to do up the parcels, she will undertake to address them. "The string hurts my fingers," repeats Mamie fretfully.

Grace and I have now finished our share of the work and, as it is still quite early, Grace suggests that we should take our usual walk along the shore. I agree at once, for the atmosphere of the Mob. Store is stuffy and dusty, and it will be pleasant to get a breath of fresh air before lunch.

"It isn't the dust, I mind," declares Grace, striding along and breathing deeply. "It's those women . . . they make me tired. I'd like to—I'd like to knock their heads together," declares Grace fiercely ". . . and you needn't giggle like that, Hester. You know you'd like to do it, yourself."

"That's why I'm giggling," I reply.

"Mamie is a sheep," continues Grace. "She looks like a sheep and she bleats like a sheep, and her brain is like a sheep's brain . . . and Stella is a cat, of course. I don't like cats . . ."

"Neither do I."

"They do nothing but bicker—Mamie's bleating annoys Stella, and drives her mad—and yet the two of them are always together, they are in and out of each other's houses at all hours of the day—a practice which I detest."

"So do I."

"They dislike each other, and yet they live in each other's pockets. Odd, isn't it?"

"Extremely odd" I agree . . . "but perhaps they don't really dislike each other."

"I think they do," replies Grace reflectively—her ill temper is vanishing rapidly under the influence of exercise and fresh air—"Their natures are incongruous and they get on each other's nerves. There might be some fun in bickering—I mean it is conceivable that they might get a kick out of it if they did it cleverly—but they just bleat and scratch. It's *too* dreary."

THURSDAY 7TH NOVEMBER

I am visited, in the small hours of the morning, by a frightful dream in which a sheep and a cat are locked in mortal combat . . . the cat, being more agile, appears to be having the best of it, when the sheep suddenly produces a tin hat and bashes the cat on the head with deadly effect . . . I awaken damp and trembling and am thankful to find myself in my comfortable bed and to see Annie arranging my morning tea on the table beside my bed. The day has started badly, but, contrary to the usual rules, it proceeds peacefully upon its appointed course and nothing worth chronicling occurs until teatime when Guthrie Loudon makes an unexpected appearance in my drawing room. As I am always delighted to see Guthrie I welcome him warmly and compliment him upon his robust health—which is apparent to the most casual beholder —and ask him where he has sprung from; Guthrie, in answer to my question, replies that his ship is in port for minor repairs and he has managed to wangle ten days' leave.

"Your Mother is still at Avielochan?" I tell him.

"Yes," says Guthrie, "but as a matter of fact I don't think I shall be going to Avielochan just now."

"Not to Avielochan?" I ask in surprise.

"No," says Guthrie. "At least . . . well, I don't think I will . . . not just now. I was there in June, wasn't I?"

It is obvious that there is something in the wind—can it be the red-haired nurse? . . . and if it is the red-haired nurse, what am I to do about it? Am I to go behind his back and wire to his mother, or am I to lie low and say nothing? On thinking it over I decide that I shall pursue the latter course, for I find that I am a little tired of Guthrie's love affairs.

While I have been engaged in arranging my plan of action (or inaction), Guthrie has been looking round the room, and now he enquires, "Are you alone, Hester?" in the tones used by the villain in a melodrama.

I reply instantly that Tim is hiding under the sofa and Pinkie behind the curtains.

Guthrie says, "Good. I wanted to speak to you alone."

"Have a scone," I say, waving the plate before him.

"No thank you, Hester."

"Well, have a cookie, then."

"No," says Guthrie. "No, I want to speak to you seriously."

As I have decided to abandon Guthrie to his fate I have no wish to be made the recipient of his confidences, so I try again to head him off and enquire how many "U" boats he has sunk since his return to duty. Guthrie says he doesn't know—

possibly none—and anyhow he has come to speak to me about something important . . . or at least something very important to *him* . . . "as a matter of fact it's about . . . about a girl," adds Guthrie blushing furiously.

I exclaim, "Oh Guthrie, not *another!*" in accents of dismay.

"But this is quite different," declares Guthrie earnestly. "This is the real thing. Honestly Hester—I wish you would listen—"

I interrupt him by saying firmly, "Not if she has red hair," at which Guthrie laughs and says, "But she hasn't red hair . . . Oh Hester, I wish you would be sensible for five minutes!"

"But why choose me?" I enquire. "Why not confide in your mother or your cousin, Mrs. Falconer, or any of your other relations? Why should I be singled out like this and forced to listen to Love's Young Dream?"

Guthrie giggles and says, "If I didn't know you, I should think you were horribly unsympathetic," to which I immediately reply that, if he didn't know me, he would not be in a position to judge whether I was unsympathetic or not, and that as a matter of fact I am as hardhearted as a plum—especially where he is concerned—and wish to have neither part nor lot in any more of his affaires de coeur.

This touches Guthrie on the raw—as indeed it was meant to do—and he replies, somewhat heatedly, "I wish you wouldn't keep on about—er—that other time, Hester. It sounds as if I were a sort of Don Juan . . . Besides this is quite a different matter—absolutely different. It's as different as night from day. If only you'd listen sensibly for a few minutes . . . you're the only person who can help me."

"Why am I?"

"Because Mother will listen to you. She likes you—and she will listen to what you say—and you could explain the whole thing calmly and sensibly to her—but that's only one reason. Do *please* be decent about it, Hester."

Seeing that there is no chance of escape I resign myself to listen, and Guthrie leans forward and begins his tale.

"The first time I saw her I thought she was beautiful," says Guthrie dreamily, "I thought she was the most beautiful creature I had ever seen, but after that I forgot she was beautiful because she is so much more. She is lovely in the sense that Americans use the word, she is adorable from the crown of her gorgeous head to the tips of her toes. She is perfect, Hester. She is what I've been looking for all my life. If I can't marry her, I shall never marry anyone—that's all."

Guthrie pauses and looks at me, and I reply that she sounds fairly satisfactory and enquire when I am to have the pleasure of making her acquaintance.

Guthrie says, "But Hester . . . it's Pinkie."

This simple statement is so entirely unexpected and so utterly amazing that I am absolutely overcome. My mouth falls open and I find myself gaping at Guthrie like a codfish.

"But Hester . . ." says Guthrie, in a reasoning sort of tone, "but Hester, who else could it be? I mean there isn't anybody else in the *world* so absolutely perfect and adorable. is there?"

"Does Pinkie—"

"Yes," says Guthrie, nodding, "Yes she does. Darling beautiful Pinkie! Isn't it—isn't it simply too marvellous for words?"

"But Guthrie, how did you—"

"It's Mother that's the difficulty," declares Guthrie. "Mother will kick up a most awful dust . . . Mother always does," adds Guthrie somewhat ingenuously.

"You think she will?"

"Sure of it," says Guthrie with conviction. "You don't know Mother as well as I do . . . but as a matter of fact I've got one pretty good shot in my locker, *it was Mother who introduced us.*"

"Really?"

"Yes, really," declares Guthrie laughing, "Rather comic, isn't it? Mother brought her to see me at the hospital. *What do you think of that?*" He pauses and looks at me, but, as I haven't the least idea what to say, I say nothing, and Guthrie continues, "That was the first time I saw her, and I thought she was beautiful. She was so beautiful that it was like having the sun shining in my bare little room—I hardly dared to look at her. I can't tell you how surprised I was when she came back again to see me . . . we got on better by ourselves . . . without Mother, I mean. After that she came nearly every day . . . and then we wrote to each other. We're engaged, now," adds Guthrie firmly.

I am so busy trying to readjust my ideas that all I can say is "Are you?"

"Yes," says Guthrie, "And we're going to be married no matter what anyone thinks. Pinkie's father has never taken any interest in her, and her aunt seems a most extraordinary person . . . they seem to be wrapped up in their own affairs. They don't understand her at all. I want to take her away," says Guthrie, earnestly, "I want to try to make up for all she has missed. I want to spend my whole life making Pinkie happy . . ."

He continues in this vein for some time and, as he talks, I am assailed by the strange feeling that I have heard it all before . . . where and when have I heard it? The problem nags at my mind until suddenly I remember Bill . . . poor Bill, it seems a little hard, but these things just happen, and nobody has found a reason for them yet.

Guthrie is still enumerating Pinkie's charms and painting their joint future in rosy colours. He seems to have forgotten that there is a war raging, and that he is only temporarily released from the combat. "You don't think I'm too old, do you?" Guthrie enquires anxiously. "Pinkie doesn't think so, but I just wondered. I don't *feel* old, of course, but I'm thirty-one. My birthday was the day before yesterday . . . You'll do what you can with Mother, won't you, Hester? It isn't that I mind what she says—I mean to marry Pinkie whatever she says or does—but it would be nicer for Pinkie if Mother could be brought round—if Mother could be made to see it in a sensible light. You're the only person who has the slightest influence with her."

"I don't think I have any influence with her."

"Oh, you *have*. I thought perhaps you might go and see her and explain everything to her."

"To Avielochan!"

"I know it's a lot to ask," declares Guthrie, "but there's so much at stake. It might make a difference to our whole lives—couldn't you, Hester?"

I reply firmly that I could not, and that there is no need for such extreme measures.

Guthrie says, "Will you write to her, then?" and I agree with feigned reluctance.

The truth is I am bursting to write to Mrs. Loudon and inform her that her scheme has worked, and my one idea is to get rid of Guthrie so that I can start my letter without delay, but Guthrie is not an easy person to get rid of. He suggests that he should stay while I write the letter and help in its composition and, when I refuse to write at all under such circumstances, he begins to tell me what I am to say and what I am not to say until my brain positively reels.

There is nothing for it but to tell him quite firmly and plainly to go away and leave me to write in peace. He rises, somewhat reluctantly, and says, "Have it your own way, but don't forget to tell her that I should never have met Pinkie if it hadn't been for her . . . where is Pinkie?"

I reply that Pinkie has gone to play badminton with the Polish officers.

Guthrie says, "Oh, has she?" in a surprised voice.

I add, quite casually, that she plays badminton with them three times a week and that if he cares to take a stroll down to the Town Hall he will be certain to see her.

Guthrie walks towards the door.

I accompany my guest into the hall, and remark that when Pinkie is not playing badminton at the Town Hall with the Polish officers, she is to be found at the Barracks playing squash with our own subalterns—unless of course she happens to have gone to the pictures with one of her other friends.

Guthrie looks at me sideways and says, "You *are* a little devil, Hester!"

The letter to Mrs. Loudon writes itself—my pen flies over the paper—and it is just finished when Tim returns from the Barracks. Tim is very much interested in my news, and suggests that we should send Mrs. Loudon "one of those night telegrams" so that she will receive the tidings of her son's engagement tomorrow morning . . . "and you must write to Elinor Bradshaw too" adds Tim.

"I suppose I must."

"Of course you must," says Tim. "Pinkie is in our charge . . . but there's nothing to worry about. Loudon is a damned good fellow—nobody could possibly object to him. They're both lucky," adds Tim reflectively, and I agree with him.

We compose a Night Telegraph Letter to Mrs. Loudon, and Tim telephones it for me . . . reflect that it is extremely pleasant to have a husband at home again to undertake these small but troublesome duties.

Guthrie, who has spent the night at The Donford Arms, turns up immediately after breakfast (I have had no chance to speak to Pinkie privately, and have been looking forward to an interesting chat, so Guthrie's appearance at this early hour seems premature to me). He is no sooner seated than a telegram arrives from Mrs. Loudon saying, "Send them both here immediately," and as there is no need for subterfuge I pass the message to Guthrie without remark.

Guthrie reads it and pales visibly beneath his tan, "Good Lord, how frightful!" he exclaims. "Great Scott, how did she hear about it? You don't mean to say you *wired* to her . . . you couldn't *explain* in a wire."

I reply that I wired and wrote, and explained everything that required explanation. I point to the telegraph form which has fluttered on to the floor from Guthrie's nerveless fingers and add that there is no need to worry, as his Mother is delighted at the news of his engagement.

Guthrie says, "How do you make that out?"

I reply that the fact is self evident since she wishes Pinkie and Guthrie to go to Avielochan for the remainder of Guthrie's leave.

Guthrie picks up the wire and reads it again and says, "She's simply furious. She wants to get us there and make us change our minds."

I seize the wire, and reread it, and point out that there is nothing in it to support Guthrie's theory. Guthrie retorts that there is nothing in it to support mine. If she is pleased why doesn't she say so? I reply that it is not her way to go all out upon a telegraph form. Guthrie says she could have put "delighted" without extra cost. I reply that it is not a question of cost, but a question of character. Guthrie says do I imagine that I know his Mother better than he does. I reply that I do.

At this point—when we are both becoming somewhat heated—Pinkie chips in and remarks, "You know, I think Hester's right. She wouldn't want us both to come, unless she was pleased about it."

Guthrie says, "Why wouldn't she?"

Pinkie replies, "Because it would be so unpleasant."

Guthrie says gloomily, "You don't know Mother at all—either of you."

After some more discussion, during which Pinkie sticks to her guns with commendable tenacity, it is agreed that Mrs. Loudon's invitation is to be accepted—or, rather, that her command is to be obeyed—but that it is to be understood by all parties that nothing Mrs. Loudon says or does is to make the slightest difference to the engaged couple . . . "As long as we make up our minds to that," says Guthrie firmly, "as long as Pinkie promises faithfully that whatever Mother says or does it won't make any difference."

"But what could she say?" enquires Pinkie, in reasoning tones, "What *could* she do to separate us?"

"She'll do all she can," declares Guthrie. "You don't know Mother . . . Oh well, I suppose we had better wire and say we'll go tomorrow."

Pinkie says, "Why wire? Why not just go today? We can catch the 3:30 train, if Hester will take us over to Breck Station."

This surprises Guthrie and he enquires why Pinkie is in such a desperate hurry, to which question Pinkie replies by snatching the telegram and pointing out the word "immediately."

Guthrie says, "Yes, but why should we?"

"Because she's your Mother, Guthrie darling," says Pinkie firmly.

I am so delighted with Pinkie that I could hug her, but I manage to refrain from showing my feelings, and suggest that, if the 3:30 is to be caught, Pinkie must pack her things before lunch. Guthrie says he must pack too, but, instead of departing forthwith, he keeps me standing in the hall for at least five minutes while he rhapsodises over Pinkie and repeats that nothing his Mother can do or say will induce him to give her up . . . finally I push him out of the door by main force and follow Pinkie to her room to help her with her packing.

It is just as well that I have decided to help Pinkie for when I open the door I find her standing in the middle of the room with her hands clasped in front of her, and her packing not even started . . .

"Oh Hester!" she says, "Oh Hester, I'm frightened! I'm not grown-up enough, or something."

I enquire anxiously whether she has changed her mind about Guthrie, and assure her that if she *has* changed her mind she must tell me at once and I will put everything right.

"Oh no," says Pinkie earnestly. "Oh *no,* I'm quite grown-up enough for *that* . . . it's Mrs. Loudon . . . I've never had to do anything important . . . like this . . . before."

"You needn't be afraid of Mrs. Loudon."

"She may not like me," says Pinkie anxiously.

Fortunately I am able to reassure Pinkie as to her reception by her prospective mother-in-law and although I refrain from disclosing the actual facts, I am able to tell Pinkie enough to give her confidence.

We start to pack, and, while we pack, Pinkie talks excitedly and somewhat incoherently, "Darling, I hate leaving you," she declares, "but you'll let me come back when Guthrie goes to sea, won't you? I could bear it better if I was here with you . . . no, I won't take that frock, it's too tight for me and I look like a pincushion. Perhaps Annie would like it . . . Oh Hester, I feel full of bubbles, only it's a nice feeling and it wouldn't really feel nice if you were full of bubbles, would it? . . . I wanted to tell you ages ago, but I *couldn't,* because there wasn't anything to tell . . . it wasn't until Guthrie went away . . . and then he wrote to me and of course I answered, and then we went on writing. Of course I knew from the very first moment I saw him lying in bed with his poor hand bandaged . . . and so brave and everything . . . yes, I *must* take those stockings because they go so well with my tweeds . . . I know, but I'll darn it . . . darling, you aren't cross with me for not telling you? Say you aren't. I couldn't tell you until I knew whether Guthrie . . . well, as a matter of fact I *very nearly* told you. Guthrie is thirty . . . yes, I'll take that jumper . . . thirty is the most perfect age . . . but of course he's thirty-one now, which is even more perfect. You're *sure* Mrs. Loudon won't hate me? You're perfectly certain, aren't you? I mean she won't think I'm far too young and silly, will she? . . . Oh Hester, you are a *comfort* to me . . . Yes, I *must* take those brogues; we must make a place for them somewhere, because I shall be walking on the hills with Guthrie . . . Oh dear, how happy I am! . . . and it's all you're doing, Hester . . . I can never never thank you, not if I kept on saying thank you night and day for weeks, so it isn't any use trying . . . I mean if it hadn't been for you I should never have met Guthrie . . . it just seems too awful to think of," says Pinkie, pausing with a pair of knickers in one hand and a single silk stocking in the other, "it just seems too awful to think that I might never have met Guthrie!"

"Where is the other stocking?" I enquire anxiously.

"I don't know . . ." says Pinkie, in a vague sort of tone, "I must have lost it . . . but Hester, do you realise that if I hadn't gone to the hospital that morning with Mrs. Loudon I *wouldn't* have met Guthrie? . . . I didn't want to go," declares Pinkie, looking at me wide-eyed, "I very nearly said I wouldn't . . . and then I was sorry for her because she seemed awfully lonely, somehow, and she seemed to be so anxious for me to go . . . Fancy if I hadn't gone! Fancy if I hadn't met Guthrie! Fancy if I had married somebody else! Not that I ever really thought of marrying anybody else—but still . . . No, Hester, those bedroom slippers are absolutely dead. They had better be buried, I think. I just wondered if you could possibly lend me your blue ones . . . I would be frightfully careful of them . . . darling, you are a perfect *lamb!* . . . Can you find room for this blue scarf because Guthrie said it matched my eyes. He is the sweetest thing, Hester . . . don't you think so, *honestly?* There couldn't ever be anyone else so perfect, could there . . . so absolutely right . . . Won't it shut? Oh, but it simply *must* shut . . . No, there's nothing I could leave behind . . . No, I must take that suede jacket . . . Look, I'll sit on it! . . . There!" cries Pinkie triumphantly. "There, I thought it would! That's one advantage of weighing about a ton!"

Feel very flat tonight without Pinkie, and I can see that Tim misses her too. He says, "It's very quiet, isn't it?" and then, after a prolonged silence, he remarks that it will be nice when she comes home. "We shall have to cheer her up of course," adds Tim thoughtfully. I agree to this. Presently he says, "It will be rather nice when Betty is grown-up, won't it?" I agree to this also.

TUESDAY 12TH NOVEMBER

Am obliged to take the car over to Breck Station to collect a crate of oranges which I have ordered from a fruit merchant in Edinburgh. The crate is larger than I expected, and there is a good deal of discussion between the porter and myself as to how it is to be got into the car. The porter suggests that I should open the sunshine roof and drop the crate in from above, but I do not welcome the suggestion, for I do not see how I shall be able to get it out again, and envisage the possibility of being obliged to keep the crate in the car until its contents are consumed. We could put the crate on the luggage grid, of course, and this would be the most sensible thing to do if I could get the luggage grid open, but it has not been opened for so long that it has stuck and my efforts to turn the key are unavailing. I am still struggling with the key, and trying not to bestow upon it any of the unladylike adjectives which I have picked up from time to time during my thirteen years of Regimental life, when I am hailed by name and turn round to find Captain Baker standing at my elbow.

"Let me do that," he says. "Perhaps it needs a little oil . . . just a drop of oil sometimes works wonders . . . there . . . no . . . frightfully stiff, isn't it . . . yes, there we are!"

I thank him heartily and, complimenting him upon his resourcefulness, enquire whether he always carries a can of oil in his pocket.

"Yes, I do," he replies, laughing. "I find it most useful when the balloons are recalcitrant, and it creates an impression of efficiency. Is this crate to go on? Let me lash it on for you."

He lashes it on in a most professional manner and again I have cause to thank and praise him.

"Funny, isn't it?" he says, surveying his handiwork with satisfaction.

"Why is it funny?" I enquire.

"Because I used to be so helpless," replies Captain Baker frankly. "I used to be an absolute footler, and I accepted the fact philosophically and never made the slightest attempt to train my hands to serve me better."

"But you were a professor . . . and clever people—"

"A lecturer," says Captain Baker smiling. "There's a good deal of difference, you know. I was merely a lecturer on zoology and not particularly brilliant—or at any rate not brilliant enough to excuse incompetence." He hesitates for a moment and then adds, "I'm awfully glad I met you, Mrs. Christie. We're going away on Friday and I wanted to say good-bye."

I am sorry he is going away, and tell him so, and ask if he could come and have supper with us some evening before he goes. Tim would like to meet him again, and I might hear the end of the cricket match, but Captain Baker replies regretfully that he has not an evening to spare.

"I suppose I mustn't ask where you're going," I enquire.

He smiles and says that he has not the least idea . . . "I'm glad I met you," he says again. "I've often thought about that talk we had at the MacDougalls'. I've often wondered whether you considered me a pessimist of the deepest dye."

"You *were* a trifle gloomy," I tell him. "But you were right and the optimists were wrong."

Captain Baker acknowledges this and adds that he wishes it had been otherwise. "I *felt* gloomy," he continues earnestly. "I had a horrible feeling of apprehension. Everyone seemed so pleased and so convinced that things were going well . . . but I could not believe them. If I had been a Celt I might have thought myself 'fey', but nobody could be psychic with a name like mine . . . no, it was just a feeling of apprehension, no more and no less. It lay over my spirits like a black cloud . . . and then, when the worst happened and France collapsed and we were left to face the enemy alone, my spirits rose and I felt like a different being. Wasn't that strange?"

"I can understand it."

"Can you?" enquires Captain Baker. "That's very interesting. Perhaps you felt the same. It was a most extraordinary feeling. I went about saying to myself, 'now we know where we are; now we can face up to it,' and we *have* faced up to it, haven't we? It takes something pretty grim to stir us up, and set our feet on the Warpath, doesn't it?"

"Yes . . . how do you feel about things *now?*" I enquire anxiously.

Captain Baker laughs and says, "I believe you think I'm 'fey' in spite of my name!"

"Well, you were right before."

"Yes, but I might not be right again . . . however, if it's any consolation to you I can tell you this: I feel grand."

"Do you?"

"Yes, *grand*. The jackal is getting his tail twisted by the Greeks, and we're going to get at him soon—I feel quite sure of it."

"What about the tiger?" I enquire.

"Ah, Sher Khan!" says Captain Baker. "It will take a bit longer before we can hope to see his skin spread upon the Council Rock . . . but the day will come."

The conversation has been extremely interesting, but time is getting on and I must get home to lunch. We shake hands cordially, and Captain Baker says he hopes we shall meet again.

"Good hunting!" I exclaim, as I climb into the car and drive off, and Captain Baker echoes the Jungle cry. I have only met him three times, but I feel as if I knew him quite well.

MONDAY 18TH NOVEMBER

Letters received from Bryan and Pinkie.

"Dear Mum, How are you getting on? There was an air raid in the middle of the rugger match so we all had to go in. Old Parker said it was a draw, but it was not a draw because we were 3 and they were 2 and we could have socked them. It was a swizz. Edgeburton's father came and he took me out two. We had a fine old blow out. We did not have baken because of the rashons and their were no eggs because they are not laying still it was a good blow out. He is only a captain so Edgeburton need not swank. The wressling is useful. Snodgrass is 13 and bigger than me a good bit but I could not bare his cheek any more. It was not quite such a good show as when I nocked Captain McDoogle down but it might have been worse. Snodgrass was serprised. Please tell Wojciech it is being useful. I wish we had a nice house where we could ask people for the hols sometimes. Some of the people ask me for the hols but I like coming home but I wish we had a big house and then we could ask people sometimes don't you? Its passed half term. I hope their will be snow in the Xmas hols. Would anyone give me a tobogan? I mean if anyone wants to know what I want thats what I want. Love from Bryan."

Avielochan.

"My darling Hester, I never seem to have time to write letters, but I have just told Guthrie that he is to be quiet until I have finished. It is lovely here, I think it is the most beautiful place I have ever seen and we are so happy. Guthrie and I just suit each other. We like the same things. We go for long walks over the hills and Guthrie takes his gun and shoots for the pot. He shoots anything we happen to see, but we do not see very much because we talk too much. Guthrie shot a grey hen in the woods and we are going to have it for dinner. I have had one or two nice talks with Guthrie's mother. I was frightened of her at first, but not now. She is very shy, I think, and that makes her fierce. I think she likes me because I like her so much and I am sure I should not like her if she did not like me. It is lovely to hear all about Guthrie when he was little. Guthrie says he wishes there was someone to tell him what I was like when I was little, but of course there isn't anyone. Guthrie's mother has given me a sweet photograph of him when he was five. Hester darling, I am trying to write *sensibly,* but it is difficult because I can't think of anything except Guthrie. Of course we both know that he has got to go back to his ship—we have only got five days—but the main thing is we have found each other. It is awfully kind of you to say I am to come back to Winfield when Guthrie goes away. It will make all the difference. Guthrie wants me to go out now so I must stop. Lots of love from Your loving Pinkie.

P.S.   Guthrie sends his love.

P.P.S.   Guthrie has just heard that his leave has been extended until the 10th December!!!"

SUNDAY 24TH NOVEMBER

We have not seen much of Tony Morley lately, for he has been busy giving his Battalion its final polish before its departure for Egypt, and has had no time to visit his friends. Today, however, Tim and I have been invited to lunch at the camp and we walk over in good time for the meal. There are only ourselves and George Craddock and Tony himself, but he gives us a "Party" lunch and excuses the extravagance by explaining that he wishes to leave an impression of good cheer behind him when he departs to warmer climes. Tim is asking Tony all sorts of questions about the Battalion, so George and I have a conversation to ourselves. He enquires for Pinkie and says he has received a letter from her and is delighted to hear of her engagement. He says it so frankly and sincerely that I believe his words and realise that, in George's case, Pinkie's method has been successful.

"Pinkie is simply splendid," declares George, smiling cheerfully. "It's been grand having her as a friend . . . and of course we shall go on being friends. There's no reason why we shouldn't, is there?"

"None whatever," I reply with conviction.

"We're going to write, of course," says George. "Pinkie has promised to write. I hope she will."

"Pinkie always does what she says—keeps her promises I mean."

"Yes," agrees George. "There's no nonsense about her. When she says a thing she means it."

It is my turn to talk to Tony now; I ask him how he likes the idea of Active Service, and he replies that he is looking forward to it very much. "You see, I've made something and I want to try it out," he explains quite gravely. "I've made a fighting weapon and I want to see how it works. I've created this Battalion out of a rabble—well, it was *almost* a rabble when I took it over—and it hasn't been all beer and skittles. Sometimes I've been in despair over it. Sometimes I've cursed the day when I took on the job. I've laughed over it and I've cried over it," declares Tony, with one of his comical sideways looks, "I've torn out my hair by the roots . . . but gradually the thing has taken shape . . . it's been *very* interesting."

"You're satisfied with it?" I ask.

"Good heavens, *no!*" cries Tony, screwing up his face in emphasis. "Satisfied! Good heavens I should think *not*. I told

you before it would take me five years to do the job properly.
That was in March, wasn't it?"

"Yes, I think so."

"Well, this is November, so I've had eight months. It's a
Battalion now—that's about all that can be said—it's got co-
hesion, and quite an idea of the purpose for which it is intended; its esprit de corps is . . . well, as a matter of fact it's
pretty good . . . Have some more lamb?"

"No thank you. Tony, tell me this, is it better or worse than
you expected?"

Tony's eyes twinkle, "It's better," he replies, "but I chose the
piece myself. I went to the butcher and said, 'Show me the best
piece of lamb you've got, because there's a very particular lady
coming to lunch with me,' so he showed me a piece of loin
and this is it."

"Tony, you know quite well I didn't mean the lamb—it's
perfect—it melts in the mouth. I asked you about the Battalion—"

"It's tough," says Tony promptly. "Tough as blazes . . .
that's one thing I can say about it, cross my heart."

"Perhaps I'd better go, if you'll excuse me, sir," says George,
consulting his watch in an anxious manner.

"Oh!" says Tony. "Oh, there's no hurry . . . Church
Parade," he explains. "We've got our padre now. A brand new
one, very young and keen, so we've got to live up to him,
haven't we, Craddock."

"Yes, but he's awfully decent," declares George. "I'm sure
he'll be splendid when he gets into the way of things . . . I
mean it's difficult at first."

"Yes," agrees Tony. "He hasn't been used to Jocks. Last
Sunday he preached too long a sermon, didn't he, Craddock?"

"Forty-seven and a half minutes," says George in hushed
tones.

"Was it?" enquires Tony with interest. "Was it really, Crad-dock? Oh well, I think he realises his mistake. I wondered," continues Tony somewhat diffidently, "I wondered if you and Tim would like to come this afternoon. The service is to be in the village church—"

"I don't think we can," declares Tim, looking at me in a beseeching manner. "I mean it would be better . . . you see I'm sure to go to sleep and it's a bad example for the Jocks."

"It will be all right, sir," says George quickly, "He's only going to give us ten minutes."

Tony smiles. "It was like this," he says. "Walker asked me how I liked his sermon and I told him I liked it immensely. It was an excellent sermon, well thought out and well ex-pressed."

"Was it, sir?" enquires George in surprise. "I never heard a word after the first quarter of an hour. I was thinking of the Jocks and wondering how long they would stand it."

"You needn't have worried," Tony replies. "They were all asleep. You worry too much about the Jocks. You should have listened to the sermon. It was after the pattern of John Stuart Mill and exceedingly interesting and original. I told Walker that, and he was as pleased as Punch; he said 'Then you didn't think it too long?' I replied that it wasn't too long for me, and that if he wished to deliver his sermons to me he should con-tinue exactly as he had begun. He's a trifle slow at picking up the more delicate shades of meaning," continues Tony thought-fully, "and I realised I should have to make the point clearer. I repeated that if my salvation was his chief concern he should go on as he was doing, but, if he wanted to get at the Jocks, he must make it short and snappy."

"What did he say?" enquires George eagerly.

"He smiled . . . he had got it, you see . . . and he said that he had noticed some of them had gone to sleep. 'I think I shall have to abandon you to your fate,' he said in his slow Scottish voice. He has quite a healthy sense of humour, has Walker . . . . Oh well, to make a long story short, I gave him a few hints. I told him I knew a good deal about soldiers and ten minutes was all they could stand without going to sleep. I told him to cut out philosophy altogether. I said 'Take a Bible story—just a simple story out of the Bible and tell it in your own words. Use your imagination. Make it real to them. They'll listen to you if you do that.' "

We are all gazing at Tony wide-eyed.

"Well, he asked for it," says Tony, laughing. "If someone asks my advice they get it. I'm old enough to be his father— or very nearly."

When we come out from lunch the Battalion is on parade, and we stand and watch it march off. Tim grabs my arm and says, "By Jove they're marvellous . . . Couldn't have believed it! Morley must have sweated them properly. Fine-looking fellows, aren't they?"

The Battalion is an inspiring sight as it marches past in serried ranks. It is a sight which brings tears to my eyes and a lump in my throat. A Battalion of soldiers always affects me in this peculiar manner and it affects me more strongly than usual today for these men have given their bodies to be trained to fight. They are going to fight for freedom and justice; they are going to fight for their country; they are going to fight for me. Yes, it comes to that. They are going to fight—and perhaps die—for me and mine, and I can do nothing to show my gratitude. I cannot do anything at all for them. If I could supply them with "Comforts" it would be something, but they will not need warm garments in Egypt . . . but I realise that this thought is more than a trifle absurd and endeavour to smile at my foolishness.

We watch the Battalion march off and follow it to the little village church where the service is to take place. The road is lined with villagers and their children, and they wave to the men as they pass.

Tony has arranged for us to have seats in the gallery and Symes is waiting for us at the church door to show us where to go. I shake hands with Symes and wish him good fortune, for I may not see him again before he goes; Tim shakes hands with him too and thanks him for helping me and Symes murmurs that he liked it, and he didn't do anything really, and he'd have done a lot more if he could.

The seats are in the front row of the gallery and we look down upon a sea of heads; black and brown and yellow and ginger, but all neatly cut—in fact they are almost shaven. Tim has noticed this too, he whispers, "Well barbered, aren't they? None of your long-haired lounge lizards here . . . that's Morley, of course. Morley was always keen on short hair."

Tony himself is sitting in the front pew with some of his officers. He looks stern and withdrawn and I wonder what he is thinking . . . Tony has been a good friend to me, and I shall miss him very much when he goes away.

The organ booms out and the men stand up and sing "Oh God Our Help in Ages Past." It is magnificent to hear all these men singing; their deep-throated roar is enough to lift the roof. My eyes are stinging again—Oh Hester, what a fool you are!

The little padre has a round shining face. He does not look much older than Bryan, but he has a good resonant voice and his accent—thought it might grate upon ears accustomed to B.B.C. English—has a pleasant homely sound. There is a prayer and a metrical psalm and then comes the sermon, and it is at once obvious that Mr. Walker has taken his colonel's advice to heart, for, instead of announcing a text, he takes out his watch, lays it beside him on the edge of the pulpit, and says that he is about to tell us a story and it will take ten minutes. The effect of this statement is electrical. The Jocks have prepared themselves for a lengthy nap by disposing their limbs as comfortably as their cramped quarters will allow, but now they sit up and cock their ears. Some of them nudge each other.

What a curious thing it is to look at these men! They are exactly like regular soldiers who have been in the army for years. They have the same habits, they have the same faults. A year ago—or less in some cases—these men were clerks, bakers, chauffeurs and a hundred other things, but they are soldiers now. They are cheery, irresponsible, vocal and sentimental; they grumble and swear; they laugh, they swagger a little—and why shouldn't they swagger? Tony says they're tough, and I can believe it.

While I have been thinking these things, Mr. Walker has plunged into the story of the flight of the Israelites from Pharaoh, and is declaring that it was the first known case of "mass evacuation." They move out from the hovels where they have lived beneath the tyrant's hand and set forth upon their long and hazardous journey into the unknown. Their leader, Moses, is pictured very vividly by Mr. Walker. He is a busy man, for all the organization rests upon his shoulders. The people stream eastwards, old and middle-aged people and young children, and Moses is everywhere up and down the line encouraging, directing, commanding. Pharaoh has said they may go, but they have not gone far before he changes his mind and sets out after them with all his army to bring them back. Mr. Walker describes the passage of the Red Sea and the destruction of Pharaoh's hosts with considerable gusto. He has stuck to the story closely and, if he has embroidered it a little, he has merely embroidered it with details which his fancy has suggested. Thus far he has spoken from notes, but the notes are finished now and the story is finished too . . . but the story has excited him, it has gripped his imagination—as indeed it has gripped mine—and the ending does not satisfy him. The waves have rolled over Pharaoh's head, but drowning is too easy a death for such a monster. . .

". . . and the wotters rrolled over them and they were all drrowned," declares Mr. Walker (rolling his R's more fiercely than ever the waters of the Red Sea could have rolled). He hesitates here for a moment and then continues, "but Pharaoh himself came up to the surrface and he cried out, in a loud voice 'Moses, save me!' . . . and Moses answered neverr a wurrd. Then Pharaoh got a mouthful of wotter and down he went, but he came up again, and again he cried out louder than beforre, 'Moses, save me!' . . . and Moses answered neverr a wurrd. Then Pharaoh went down down to the verry bottom of the Red Sea, to the verry bottom of it, but he strruggled up to the surrface of the wotter, and he cried in the loudest voice he could, 'Moses, Moses, save me!' . . . and Moses answered, 'I haird you the furrst time.' "

We stand up to sing—and there is no need for anyone to be nudged awake—and we sing the metrical version of the hundred and twenty-fourth psalm.

> Now Israel may say and that truly
> If that the Lord had not our cause maintained . . .
> When cruel men against us furiously
> Rose up in wrath to make of us their prey,
> Then certainly they had devoured us all. . . .
>
> Ev'n as a bird out of the fowler's snare
> Escapes away, so is our soul set free;
> Broke are their nets and so escaped we.
> Therefore our help is in the Lord's great name
> Who heav'n and earth by his great pow'r did frame.

The fine tune, the brave words, go rolling out together—everyone is singing as loudly as he can. Everyone is at one in this expression of gratitude for past favours and in hope for the continuance of help against the powers of evil.

We emerge into the chill pale November afternoon, and I am quite exhausted. During the short service I have run the gamut of emotions; I have struggled with tears; I have struggled with laughter; I have been lifted to the heights. I cling to Tim's arm and we wait until the Battalion has formed and marched away for we want to say good-bye to Tony, and this is our last chance.

Presently Tony comes up to us and asks, with a sideways glance, how we enjoyed the service.

"It was magnificent," replies Tim. "It was a splendid service . . . and the sermon was grand."

"It *was* good, wasn't it?" Tony agrees. "I told him to use his imagination, but I didn't realise he had so much to use . . . he enjoyed drowning Hitler, didn't he?"

We talk for a few moments in the cold bleak little church yard. The wind is sweeping round the corner of the church, and the bare trees are bending to its blast.

"Well . . . good-bye," says Tony. "Write to me sometimes, Hester."

"Yes," I say huskily. "Yes, of course . . . Take care of yourself, Tony," I add—could anyone have thought of a more foolish thing to say?

"Oh, rather," says Tony. "I'll be all right . . . see you again when we've drowned the dictators in the Red Sea . . ."

He salutes me gravely—and, somehow, the simple action which has become so commonplace assumes the dignity and importance of a sacred rite. I realise for the first time what a salute should be. I realise all that it means . . . ("We salute thee Caesar, we who are about to die.") . . . and I wish that I could return his salute, but I am only a woman and women have no brave gestures such as this . . .

Tony holds the salute for a moment and then turns smartly and walks away . . . shall I ever see him again?

WEDNESDAY 27TH NOVEMBER

Great discussion at the "Comforts" this morning anent the Christmas Party which is to take place at the Barracks on the Saturday before Christmas Day. Mamie announces that she will do the decorations with the help of Stella, if Grace and I will undertake to buy the toys for the tree. Grace agrees to the arrangement with enthusiasm, and I agree reluctantly (I have done the job before and she has not). Mamie then goes on to say that Herbert is letting her have fifteen pounds for the party, but perhaps we ought not to spend it all. It seems a good deal, doesn't it? We are told to practise the strictest economy, aren't we? . . . but then, on the other hand, the children ought not to suffer because of the war, poor little things.

Stella says, "The toys must all be British made, of course."

Grace says, "Oh, of course."

I enquire how much money we may spend on the presents for the tree.

Mamie says, "Well, what about eight pounds?"

This is quite ridiculous, because there are at least eighty children to be provided with toys, and I am aware from past experience that no reasonably decent toys can be bought for less than an average expenditure of three shillings. I explain this in detail and, doing a hasty sum, I point out that I shall require twelve pounds at least.

Stella says, "Twelve pounds! You can't spend that on toys. We shall need five pounds for the decorations."

I point out that cheap toys are no use—it would be better to give them none at all—and add that the decorations can be done with flags, which can be obtained on loan from the Quarty, and with holly from our own gardens.

Stella objects to this. She says decorations properly done give the bare hall a festive appearance, and add to everyone's enjoyment . . . "streamers of coloured paper and chinese lanterns," says Stella earnestly, "tinsel and candles for the tree . . ."

"That's all very well," I reply, "but children don't really appreciate decorations. They would rather have decent toys. Don't you agree, Mamie?"

Mamie has children of her own. "Yes," she says reluctantly. "Yes . . . well . . . as a matter of fact I think they would . . ."

Stella pounces upon her at once, "Mamie!" she exclaims. "Mamie, you know we agreed that five pounds was the very *least* we could manage on."

The wretched Mamie swithers helplessly, for she is one of those people who, like Reuben, are unstable as water . . . indeed she is like soapy water, for she slips through one's fingers in a lather of words. "Oh well," says Mamie. "Hester will just have to manage. We can't give them cheap toys of course because, as Hester says, they just get broken. It's a waste of money giving them cheap toys . . . but of course we want the decorations to be nice too, and you can't do really good decorations for nothing . . . the children would rather have toys, I daresay, but . . . well . . . Hester must just manage somehow. It's war-time, isn't it?"

"That's just why we should make a special effort to have really good decorations," says Stella firmly.

"Yes, of course," agrees Mamie.

"But Mamie," I object. "You said we were to think of the

children first. I can't possibly get decent toys for them unless I have the money to buy them with, can I?"

"No, of course not," agrees Mamie.

"You can get quite good toys for two shillings each," declares Stella, who has been doing sums on the blotting paper.

Grace has contributed nothing to the argument, but has continued to slave away at the parcels. She now looks up with a sweet smile and enquires whether it would not be better if she and I were to undertake the decorations—which we could easily manage with two pounds—and Mamie and Stella could buy the presents with the rest of the money.

There is a short but dismayed silence.

"Oh!" says Stella. "Oh, but I'm sure you could choose the presents better. Hester has done it before . . . so have I, of course, but . . . but I think you and Hester should do it. I daresay Mamie and I could manage the decorations on three pounds, really."

As Grace and I walk home together I think about the argument and begin to chuckle.

"It *was* funny," says Grace.

"We were haggling like a lot of women shoppers," I declare.

Grace nods, "Thank Goodness she didn't take me at my word. I *hate* doing decorations, don't you?"

"Loathe it," I reply with conviction.

"Holly!" says Grace with a shudder. "Nasty little spikes of holly sticking in one's fingers for days! Dusty flags twining themselves round one's neck, as one struggles to nail them up! *Nails,* Hester! D'you like nails?"

"No."

"I can never get the things to go in straight, can you?"

"Never. They always bend their necks when I hit them."

"I can never hit them," declares Grace.

We walk on in silence for a few moments.

"It was Stella," says Grace. "Stella wanted slap-up decorations, so that everyone would say, *"Who* did the decorations? It's like fairyland!"—that woman makes me sick. . . . It will be fun choosing the presents, won't it?"

I cannot agree with this, so I refrain from any rejoinder, but Grace insists upon one. "It *will* be fun, won't it?" she repeats, squeezing my arm.

"It would be fun if one had unlimited money to spend," I reply in sombre accents.

"It will be fun," says Grace with conviction. "You'll let me choose the presents for the boys, won't you? Because I know the sort of things Ian and Alec will like when they're older. You don't mind, do you?"

"No, of course not."

"And we'll take Betty with us to help to choose the presents for the girls."

"Betty!" I exclaim in amazement.

"Yes," says Grace, warming to her plan. "Yes, we'll go on Saturday afternoon—it's a marvellous idea. She will know exactly what little girls would like—and it will be so good for her to help to choose presents for other children."

"Will it?" I enquire in doubtful tones, for somehow or other I cannot visualise Betty performing this labour of love.

"Yes," says Grace firmly. "It will bring out all the *best* in Betty. Of course we must take her."

SATURDAY 30TH NOVEMBER

Grace calls for us at two o'clock, and we set out together to choose the presents for the tree. I have taken pains to explain the matter to Betty and, somewhat to my surprise, she seems to have grasped the idea. Grace explains it all over again as we walk down the long road to the town and I must admit that she explains it more fully than I have been able to do. The substance of Grace's lecture is that it is more blessed to give than to receive, and Betty listens with astonishing meekness.

"Will I be giving them the things?" she asks at last.

"No," says Grace. "But when you see how pleased the children are you will know that you have helped to choose the toys . . . and of course you are giving up your Saturday afternoon to choose them . . . and you can choose your own present, too."

By this time we have reached Miller's shop and we are escorted downstairs to the Toy Department by Mr. Miller himself. I have provided myself with a list of the children divided up into sexes and ages: Infants, girls from three to six years old, boys from three to six, girls from six to ten, boys from six to ten—and so on—and, beside each group, I have written the number of toys required and the amount which is to be spent upon them. I show the list to Grace and explain that I must start with the infants' rattles and woolly balls, but she can do the boys, and I advise her to start at the bottom of the list and work up gradually, for I have found, to my cost, that any other method produces absolute chaos.

Miller's Toy Department is an attractive place. It is stocked with toys of all sorts and sizes and, as we descend the stairs and the full beauty of its bursts upon our gaze, I am not surprised to hear an exclamation of rapture from my daughter.

"Oh, how lovely!" she cries, prancing forward. "Oh, how beautiful! Oh, it's like Aladdin's Cave!"

I am still talking to Mr. Miller and explaining our requirements when Betty seizes upon a doll's bed and announces that she will choose her own present first, and this is it.

"No, you can't have that," I reply. "It's too expensive—and you must choose the other presents first."

Grace says why not let her have the bed? After all it is only ten and six and we can easily economise on the other presents, but I refuse to consider it for a moment.

"Seventy-six toys at an average of three shillings each," says Mr. Miller, figuring out the sum in his note book.

Grace has now found a trumpet and says that it will be the very thing for Tommy Brown—whose father is in the band—she is sure he would like it.

I reply that we ought to keep to our programme and work up from the infants.

"Yes," says Grace, "but just let's put this aside for Tommy."

"Well, can I have this bow and arrow?" enquires Betty, tugging at my coat. "Can I have it, Mummy?"

Grace says, "Why not let her have it and then we can get on?"

I agree and begin to choose rattles.

Betty disappears, but returns a few moments later and says "Look at this lovely tea set, Mummy! I think I would rather have this."

Grace says, "Here's a drum. Don't you think it would be nice for the other Brown boy?"

I reply that I do not think it would. Mrs. Brown is expecting another baby shortly and will be driven quite mad if her offspring are provided with drums and trumpets.

Grace says, "Well, what about this box of soldiers?"

Betty says, "Oh Mummy, I would *love* a box of soldiers! Mummy, can I have a box of soldiers for my present?"

Grace says, "Wouldn't you rather have a doll? Look at this sweet little baby doll, Betty!"

"Oh *yes*," cries Betty ecstatically. "Oh *yes*, it's just like Ian, isn't it? Oh *yes*, I'll have *that*."

I enquire how much it costs, and Grace looks at the ticket and exclaims in horrified tones, "Hester, it's sixteen and six!"

I go on choosing rattles and woolly balls.

"Look!" says Grace. "Here's a box of bricks and it's only two and eleven. Shall I put it aside for one of the six-year-old boys? . . . Oh no, it's made in Germany! Here's a little cart . . . Oh bother, it's five and ninepence!"

"Look at this lovely Teddy Bear!" exclaims Betty. "Look Mummy, can I have this Teddy Bear?"

"No, it's too expensive," says Grace.

"Well, can I have a pedal motorcar?"

"No," says Grace firmly. "No, you must choose something for *other* little girls. You remember what I told you, don't you? Choose something that you think a little girl of seven would like."

Betty looks round and flings herself upon an enormous stuffed donkey on wheels, "Oh, isn't he sweet?" she cries. "Oh, she would love this donkey . . . and so would I . . ."

"It's too expensive," says Grace wearily.

"Well, what about a train?" enquires Betty. "Look at that lovely train in the box with three carriages. I'm sure she'd like *that*."

"It's for a girl," says Grace.

"I know," agrees Betty. "I know it is, but I'm a girl and that's what I would like . . . or a pistol that fires caps."

I leave them to fight it out between them and forge ahead through my list. I have finished the infants now and am looking at picture books and Teddy Bears for the four-year-olds when Grace returns to my side.

"I think we should let Betty have that bed," she whispers.

I reply firmly that Betty is not to have the bed. She is to have something quite cheap—or, at any rate, no dearer than any of the other children. Grace says she sees what I mean but she wouldn't mind making up the rest of the money herself. "Betty really *wants* the bed," says Grace earnestly.

I reply more firmly than before that Grace is not to do anything of the sort . . . it is very kind of her to think of it, but it wouldn't *do*.

Grace sighs and says it's very difficult indeed. All the really nice toys are so dear. She has chosen presents for the six-to-ten-year-old boys, but has exceeded the money allocated for that particular group. What had she better do?

I reply that she had better choose them again.

Grace says, "Couldn't you economise on the babies?"

I reply that it is quite impossible to do so; I refuse to give the babies cheap celluloid rattles, as they are unsafe.

Grace admits this, and, after a moment's thought, produces another plan. "We don't need to give the babies *anything*," she says delightedly. "They wouldn't notice, would they? I mean Mrs. Mackay's baby is only three months old."

"The mothers would notice," I reply. "The mothers would be frightfully insulted."

"Mummy!" cries Betty. "I've *quite* decided. I want this uniform for my present. It's a ticket collector's uniform and it's got a dear little punching machine for punching the tickets. Look at it, Mummy!"

"Hester," says Grace. "Hester, d'you think this book would be suitable for the youngest Craven boy?"

By four o'clock we are only half way through our list, and are utterly exhausted. I suggest that we should go home to tea and complete the task some other day. Grace agrees to this suggestion at once, and says Tuesday afternoon would suit her . . . and she thinks we would get on quicker without Betty.

WEDNESDAY 4TH DECEMBER

It is eleven o'clock on a cold and windy night, and Tim and I are about to leave the comfortable warmth of our drawing-room fire and betake ourselves to bed, when suddenly the front door bell rings . . . and rings with a loud and imperative pull. The servants have gone to bed long ago, so Tim rises and goes away to answer it . . . and, shortly after, I hear angry voices in the hall and rush out to discover what is the matter.

Tim is talking to a strange man with Air Raid Warden equipment, and I gather that the conversation is not proceeding on friendly lines.

"He says we're showing a light," says Tim. "I thought you said our black-out was perfect, Hester."

As I have taken every conceivable precaution to make our "black-out" satisfactory I am somewhat surprised at this information, and I explain that our own warden has been round the house several times and could find no chinks at all.

"I don't know about *that*," says the man. "That's nothing to do with me. There's been a swap round and I'm your warden now. It's me you've got to satisfy, and I'm not satisfied."

The somewhat hectoring tone is annoying Tim, and he enquires rather crossly what we can do about it at this time of night.

"That's your lookout," replies the man. "The black-out has to be complete or else you'll be fined. You're a danger to the community, that's what you are."

This is such a frightful accusation that I seize Tim's arm, and say that we must do something at once.

"Yes, you'd better," says the man. "You'd better come out and I'll show you . . . can't have lights showing, you know."

Tim points out that it is extremely cold and windy, and that we are just going to bed, but the man refuses to accept this as an excuse and waits impatiently while Tim and I put on our coats.

"*You* needn't come, Hester," says Tim. "There's no sense in both of us getting pneumonia . . ." but I reply firmly that as I am responsible for the black-out I must see where it has failed.

We follow the man round the house to the drawing-room window. It is dark and cloudy and we are met by a piercing wind which seems to penetrate to our bones.

"*There!*" says the man, pointing to the drawing-room windows.

"Where?" enquires Tim.

(I feel inclined to echo Tim's question, for I can see no light at all.)

The man replies that there *is* a chink of light, and that if Tim will kneel down on the path and put his face close to the glass he will see that a chink of light is showing at the left hand top corner above the curtain . . .

"Kneel down on the path?" asks Tim, incredulously. "Do you mean to say you've brought us out here to show us a light —and we've got to kneel down on the path to see it?"

"It's orders," replies the man smugly. "There's to be no lights at all."

"It's orders, is it?" enquires Tim in furious tones. "It's orders that you're to go round Donford and kneel down at every window?"

"Oh well . . ." begins the man, somewhat taken aback.

"But it isn't *well*," cries Tim, more furiously than before. "It's very *ill*. You seem to have constituted yourself a sort of Gestapo. You're exceeding your duties in a ridiculous way."

"If you kneel down . . ."

"But I'm not going to kneel down," declares Tim. "I've more respect for the knees of my trousers than to kneel down on a soaking wet path. Nothing will induce me to kneel down. The whole thing is absurd and ridiculous. Do you realise the reasons for the black-out? The black-out is intended to baffle aeroplanes—not worms."

"We're supposed to—"

"Yes!" cries Tim. "You're supposed to use your common sense, if you have any to use . . . look at that light over there!" he continues, waving his hand towards a square of brightly illuminated blind in a house down the road. "Look at that window! Why don't you go and get *those* people out of their house? Why don't you get onto *them* instead of crawling about on my path?"

The warden straightens himself and looks round. "Gosh!" he exclaims. "Gosh, that *is* a light! I'll need to go over at once."

"I should think you'd better," agrees Tim in calmer accents. "That light could be seen for miles . . . I don't envy you your job, but you needn't carry it to extremes. We'll stick up a bit of black paper tomorrow . . . here, have a cigarette!"

I cannot help smiling as the cigarette changes hands for the incident is so typical of Tim; he is always resentful of bluster and bullying, but can never be angry for long.

"You like happy endings, don't you?" I ask, as we grope our way back to the house.

"Happy endings?" says Tim. "Oh, I see what you mean . . . Yes, I suppose I do . . . hate falling foul of people, really."

MONDAY 9TH DECEMBER

I am busy ordering food when Annie comes and says that I am wanted on the telephone. Pick up the receiver expecting to hear Grace's voice, but find to my surprise that it is Richard . . . Enquire anxiously where he is and whether anything is the matter. Richard says he's in London, of course, and this is a trunk call, and why on earth have I been so long in coming to speak to him. I apologise humbly and explain that I had no idea it was a trunk call, but was under the impression that the call was being made by a friend of mine who is getting up a Whist Drive in aid of the Donford Spitfire Fund, and has been making my life a burden by ringing me up at inconvenient moments. Richard says people ought not to use the telephone for inessentials—he never does—but women seem to make a hobby of telephoning to their friends. Can't help feeling that Richard has now wasted more time than I did, but decide not to point this out, for it would only lead to an argument and waste still more time. I enquire anxiously whether everything is all right; Richard replies that he does not know what I mean. I point out that we have been worrying about him and Mary. "Oh, you mean about the Blitz!" says Richard, "No need to worry. The old house is still standing. Mary is busy with canteens and all that sort of thing."

So far Richard has given me no indication as to why he has rung me up, and I am about to ask him the reason for his unwonted extravagance when he suddenly comes to the point. "We're going overseas", says Richard, "so that's why I'm here . . . Embarkation leave . . ."

"Oh Richard!" I gasp.

"Don't fuss," says Richard's voice in matter-of-fact tones. "There's no need for you to go up in the air. Mary is being very sensible about it . . . . no, I haven't the slightest idea where we're going, except that I've got to get a topee with a thingummy round it, so I suppose that means it will be hot."

"A puggaree," I put in.

"Yes," says Richard, "but the point is I want to see you before I go. That's why I rang up."

I pull myself together and say that I will consult Tim and let Richard know, but Richard says there isn't time. His leave is up on Thursday, so I must make up my mind whether I want to see him or not.

Of course I want to see him.

"Good," says Richard. "You can travel south tonight and I'll meet you in the morning. The train will probably be hours late, but I can find out—so long, Hester."

The line goes dead; I lay down the receiver and look round the room. I feel as if I had been on a long journey. The room looks quite strange to me—strange with the peculiar strangeness of a familiar room visited after a long absence. I notice the shabby furniture and the large darn in the carpet with reawakened eyes. I say aloud. "I am going to London tonight," and somehow or other the sound of my own voice carries conviction and I begin to believe it, but there is so much to do that I have no time to analyse my feelings . . . I am conscious only of a pleasant excitement stirring through my blood.

Tim says that he wishes he could come too, but this week is hopeless because Herbert is on leave. "I might manage the weekend," says Tim thoughtfully.

"It would be lovely."

"We ought to go to Winch Hall," continues Tim. "Uncle Joe keeps writing and saying he wants to see me on business. I don't know what he means, because the lawyer manages all his business affairs, but if we're in the south I think we ought to go and see them. We could meet there and spend the weekend with them and come home together. How would that do?"

The express train to London stops on request at a small wayside station about five miles from Donford. Tim says he will take me over to Breck in the car, but we must start early because it is so dark.

It is very dark indeed, cloudy and wet; the road is narrow and winding and our dimmed headlights give us little help. To me the drive seems unending and fraught with dire possibilities, and I enquire more than once whether Tim can see anything at all.

"You're practically blind in the dark," replies Tim a trifle irritably. "It's a question of visual purple . . . I have more of the stuff in my eyes than you have . . . Good Lord, what's that?"

"It was a cow," I reply meekly as we shave past the obstacle and bump over a stone at the side of the road.

"A cow!" exclaims Tim, peering ahead and decreasing his pace from fifteen miles an hour to ten, "It couldn't have been a *cow*. Nobody would leave a cow out on a night like this. Cows are kept in byres . . . at night . . . in winter . . . Isn't there a road block here?"

A dim red light marks the road block and helps Tim to negotiate it successfully, and in another five minutes we arrive at Breck in good time for the train, only to learn that the express is two hours late. Tim suggests that we go home and return two hours later, but the idea does not appeal to me at all, for one thing the drive in the dark has been sheer torture, and for another—and this is an even more cogent reason—I dislike leaving home even for a few days, and am always upset when it comes to the last moment. Having keyed myself up and said good-bye to Winfield and taken leave of Betty, I shrink from the prospect of doing it again . . . in fact I feel that if I return home now I shall be unable to go to London at all.

I explain this to Tim, but he does not seem to understand, "I'd no idea you were so fond of Winfield!" he exclaims in surprise.

"I'm not," I reply quickly. "I mean it isn't exactly Winfield, it's *home* . . . it's wherever we happen to be . . ."

"Dash it!" says Tim, "Do you mean to tell me we've got to sit here for two solid hours? There isn't even a fire in the waiting room."

We stand upon the dark deserted platform arguing the point, and the keen wind whistling through the arches argues very forcibly on Tim's side. I am about to give in and allow myself to be driven home, when a man appears out of the gloom. He is old and bent and is carrying an oil lantern, and he reminds me of one of the dwarfs in Betty's beloved *Snow White*. He holds up the lantern and has a good look at us, and apparently we pass muster for he invites us to come and warm ourselves in the lamp room. It is a small bare cubby hole of a room, and it smells very strongly of paraffin, but a gorgeous fire is leaping and crackling merrily in the big old-fashioned fireplace. The old man brings a chair and wipes it before inviting me to sit down, and Tim lights a cigarette and heaves himself on to the table.

We are warm and comfortable now and there is no more talk of going home. The old man seems pleased to have our company. He sits on an oil keg near the fire and converses with us in an agreeable manner. He is the night-watchman, he says, and he is here every night all by himself and goes home to sleep during the day . . . He has been in the railway all his life—most of the time as a signalman—but he retired some years ago and started a small duck farm. Now the war has brought him back to the railway and he has taken the place of his nephew who has been called up for military service. I suggest that it must be a lonely sort of life, but he replies that he likes it fine, and he often has company—interesting folk—to share his hours of vigil. His accent is so broad that sometimes it is difficult to understand what he says, and we are obliged to ask him to repeat himself.

"There's Poles comes here whiles," says Cameron—for such is his name—"They fair mak' me hairt-sick for they canna mak' oot a wurrd I'm saying, nor me them . . . nice enough fellers they are, the maist o' them. There was yin the ither nicht, he was an officer like yersel' and no unlike ye eether, and he sat on yon table the way ye're sitting the noo. He says tae me, 'You talk slow and simple me understand.' Sae then I talked slow and simple d'ye see—the way ye'd speak tae a bairn—and we got on fine. He'd been through a wheen o' adventures, yon feller. It was like a story-buik, no less. He says tae me, 'I speak English good, yes?' Sae I nodded and said he was daeing fine, and he was too, and then he says, 'But I want learn Scotch now' . . . Aye, they're grand chaps, yon Poles!"

"Yes," agrees Tim, "and they're pretty hefty fellows too, most of them. Strong, upstanding fellows, they are."

"That's so," nods Cameron, "Tough's no the wurrd for them . . . it'll be a bad day for any Jerry that comes their gate. They're wanting a bit o' their ane back, and it's tae be hoped they'll get it."

Just then the telephone bell rings and Cameron goes away to answer it. He returns almost immediately and says in a matter-of-fact voice, "It's a purrple. I'll need tae dowse the lichts."

The lights in the station are oil lamps, so it takes him a little while to hobble round and "dowse" them.

Tim goes out to see if he can hear a plane, but there is nothing to be heard. It is very dark and very still, but every now and then a goods train chugs through the little station, clanking and rattling, or a passenger train goes flying past with a terrifying roar . . . The old man explains that the trains do not slow down for a "purrple" warning (which means that there are enemy planes in the vicinity) so my train will be here in another twenty minutes.

Tim asks whether he gets many warnings, and he replies, "Och aye, but they seldom come tae much . . . there wus ane nicht," he continues, tapping out his pipe at the fire and smiling thoughtfully. "Maybe ye'll mind the nicht the bombs fell at Donford? . . . Aye, I wus here, masel' as usual, and I haird the bombs burrsting—a fine noise they made—sae I took ma lantern and away I went along the line. I wus feart the line micht be damaged, d'ye see. I'd no gane that far when I haird the engines o' a plane . . . and it wusna' ane o' oor planes, fur it wus a deeferent soond a'together . . . and then I saw the Jerry coming towards me ower the trees. It wus braw moonlicht, d'ye see. He wus that low doon he looked the size o' a hoose. Weel, I dowsed ma lantern, and I crooched doon, for I wusna' wantin' him tae see me . . . on he came, diving low, and his engines just roaring . . . the noise fair lifted the bunnet aff yer heid . . ." He pauses, and is obviously reliving the terrifying experience . . . "Aye," he says, "I thocht I wus for it that time, he came ower me and he wus that low . . . and he was that big. If I'd had a rifle I could ha' got him as easy as easy. My, I wus wild! I wus wilder the next morning though, for when I got hame I foond he'd dropped ane o' his bombs in the burrn at the back o' ower hoose—it's the burrn where I keep ma ducks, d'ye see—and fower o' ma best burrds wus deid. There wasna' a mairk on them, but they wus deid nane the less. . ."

We are still sympathising with the old man when another train is heard. He rises and says, "That's herr . . . and we'll need to look nippy for she doesna' wait ower lang."

As we follow him out of the warm room on to the pitch-dark platform Tim hugs me suddenly and fiercely, "Oh Hester!" he exclaims. "I wish you weren't going . . . or that I was coming. For God's Sake take care of yourself!"

My heart sinks into my shoes, and I decide that I can't go. I can't possibly leave Tim . . . not now . . . not if he feels like that. Try to explain this to Tim, but find that I cannot speak . . . am bundled into the train by Tim and Cameron and despatched to London willy-nilly.

TUESDAY 10TH DECEMBER

London surprises me, not because it is different from usual, but because it is so much the same. Richard meets me at the station and drives me through the familiar streets in his car. It is eleven o'clock in the morning; the sun is shining brightly in a cloudless sky and people are walking about doing their shopping.

"Empty, isn't it?" remarks Richard.

I agree a trifle doubtfully; the traffic is certainly less than usual, but "empty" is not the word I should have chosen to describe the streets. To a country cousin like myself London seems thronged, and the noise and movement is bewildering. The route to Wintringham Square is well known to me, and I point out to Richard that he is making a detour. Richard replies that there is a time-bomb in the vicinity and Fulton Street is closed to traffic. Sometimes they remove the bombs and sometimes they cover them up and leave them to explode —it all depends.

I murmur "How awful!"

"Yes," agrees Richard, "but as a matter of fact they don't do a great deal of harm. They're more of a nuisance really." The old house looks exactly the same—except for the windows which, like those of its neighbours, are covered with close white netting. Richard and I were born and brought up in this house, and it retains my affection and respect. Although it is one of sixty houses, all exactly the same, number thirty-two has a certain character of its own and a very real dignity. Built in Victorian times—in days of peace and plenty—it has now found itself in the middle of a war and remains solid and unmoved by war alarms. I am still looking at the old house and musing over the past, when we draw up at the door and Mary runs out into the street to welcome me.

Mary is a nice creature and a very satisfactory sister-in-law. She is a sensible, practical-minded person, cheerful and amiable and extremely good-looking. She was quite beautiful as a young girl; it was her beauty that attracted Richard, and I have always thought it a very fortunate accident that she is exactly suited to Richard in temperament.

As I follow Mary upstairs an air raid siren sounds and I notice, to my surprise, that it is the "All Clear" signal. When I point this out to my hostess, she replies that nobody takes much notice of the siren now, and that for her part she never knows whether there is a warning in progress or not. This seems strange to me, but I make no comment upon it, for I have already decided that while I am in London I shall do as Londoners do. Mary apologises for giving me a room on the second floor, she wanted to give me the best spare room, but it is full of Richard's kit.

"Hester will feel much more at home in her *own* room," says Richard firmly, "and she won't be sleeping here anyhow, so what does it matter?"

I find this remark somewhat difficult to understand, but I assure my host and hostess that I would much rather have my old room, and, when they have gone and left me to settle in, I find my statement is even more true than I had thought. There is something very appealing about a room which one occupied as a child; it brings back one's childhood more vividly than anything else I know.

Mary has not changed this room at all, for the house is large and they have no children. The furniture, the pictures, the carpet, are those I remember so well. I am supposed to be resting after my journey, but I do not want to rest, I want to renew my acquaintance with old friends. First I examine the light maple suite and I discover the dent in the wardobe which was caused by my efforts to improve my service at tennis. The dent is not large and not noticeable to a casual observer, but I can feel it with my fingers . . . it will still be there when the girl who made it is dead and gone! The stain on the carpet seems to have vanished . . . but no, the carpet has been turned so the stain is in the other corner of the room. It was made when I upset a bottle of nail varnish and all my efforts to remove the mark were without success. The carpet was new in those days and now it is old, but the stain remains (it resembled the map of Australia and still does so) and it gives me a strong link with that other Hester who inhabited the room.

The long mirror reflects me again as it reflected me in my most intimate moments . . . as it reflected me ready for school in a navy blue coat and skirt and a black felt hat. I can see that schoolgirl now . . . she gives herself a cursory glance in the mirror, tugs at the front of her coat—which seems a trifle short for her—and runs downstairs. The girl grew up and the mirror saw her dressing for her first dance—it saw a thin girl with large frightened eyes arrayed in a white lacy frock; it saw her practising her curtsy for her presentation; it saw her in white satin and orange blossom. The dressing-table mirror is spotted with damp, and I am not sorry to see its degeneration, for it was never a kindly friend. It was like the friend who is in the habit of saying, "I feel it is my duty to tell you . . ." and it did its duty well. It was always candid about spots or blemishes or untidy hair. I glance into it as I pass to the window and find that its nature is not ameliorated by the passing years . . . I have been travelling all night, but the mirror refuses to make any allowances for me!

The bars are still at the window, for this was our nursery —Richard's and mine—before I was promoted to a bedroom of my own. The bars take me back even further, and I remember a terrible day when Richard wanted to see a Punch and Judy show which was giving a performance in the street below. He put his head between the bars and was trapped there, howling and kicking his legs wildly in the air. It was not until Father was fetched that anything could be done to release Richard—but Father did it easily. I can see him now taking Richard's head in his hands and turning it sideways and withdrawing it from between the bars . . . "There," said Father, in his quiet voice, "you would have had no difficulty in doing it yourself if you hadn't been frightened. Never lose your wits in an emergency, Richard, or you may lose your head, too." Good advice! Does Richard remember it still?

The view from the window is very familiar, and by pressing my forehead against the pane I can see the trees in the square, their branches swaying with the wind. I can see over the roof tops to the spire which still dominates the surrounding houses. High in the air hang the barrage balloons—strange modern monsters.

During my inspection of the room I have discovered that my bed has not been made, it has no sheets nor blankets nor pillows, and I am surprised at the delinquency on the part of Mary's staff. The housemaid appears with a can of hot water in her hand and in answer to a somewhat diffident enquiry on the subject she exclaims, "Oh, but you won't be sleeping 'ere, ma'am! You'd never get a wink with all the planes and sirens and the guns. Mrs. Fanshaw gave orders for your bed to be made in the lib'ry . . . none of us sleep up 'ere."

I endeavour to show no surprise at this information, but cannot stifle a slight feeling of alarm, for now it is indubitable that I have arrived at the theatre of war.

Mary and I spend the afternoon knitting and chatting and picking up the loose threads of our friendship. She is having a holiday from her canteen work on account of Richard's leave, and I gather from what she says that she needed a holiday pretty badly, and that her post at the canteen is by no means a sinecure. Sometimes she is on duty all night and returns home to sleep in the day time. "But I like the work," says Mary thoughtfully, "it's useful work and I am the right person to do it."

"He wants me to go to my people—they live near Taunton now—but I simply couldn't go down there and vegetate. I should go mad. If I had children, of course," says Mary, with rather a sad little smile, "if I had children it would be different. I should take them away to the safest place I could find and keep them there. It's dreadful to see the little children in the tube stations!"

"Tell me about your work," I urge her.

"It's a mobile canteen," she replies. "A sort of glorified coffee-stall; we go wherever the bombs have fallen and give the people hot meals."

"Is it true that everyone is very brave?"

Mary smiles, "No, not everyone," she replies. "Some people are very brave and some aren't; but on the whole they're wonderful. A woman came up to the canteen the other day with her face all cut with glass. She said, 'Hitler has smashed my house, so now I'm going to make munitions to smash *him!*'— that's the sort of spirit they show. Then there was another woman; she said, 'We were so happy in our little house and now it's gone!' It *had* gone. It was one of a little row of houses and the others were untouched, but these people's house had simply vanished—it was like a gap in a row of teeth."

"Poor souls!"

"Yes," agrees Mary, "but there are worse things than losing your house—she had her husband safe. You know, Hester, I think we could learn a lot if we took it in the right way. One thing we could learn is to put first things first—to see life in proper proportion. Some of us love *things*—I mean possessions like furniture and houses—and some of us love people too much."

"But we are told to love each other!" I exclaim.

"Yes, but not first," says Mary thoughtfully.

I am turning the heel of my sock, so there is silence for a few minutes, and when we begin to talk again the conversation is in a lighter vein. I hear about Bryan's visit to Wintringham Square, and Mary has some amusing tales to tell me of his sayings and doings while in the Metropolis. Mary is not only very fond of Bryan, but also very proud of him; she assures me that he is very clever—a fact which I have suspected at times, but which, unfortunately, is not borne out by his school reports.

"Oh, school reports!" cries Mary scornfully, "I don't mean *that* sort of cleverness. Most of the greatest men in the world were dunces at school. Bryan's kind of cleverness is much more important. He is clever with people—you should have seen how he managed Richard—Bryan has wit and humour and the knack of expressing himself. . . ."

The experience of listening to someone else waxing lyrical over the good qualities of my offspring is unprecedented, and I cannot help thinking that Mary is an exceedingly perspica-

cious woman, and that her conversation is intensely interesting
. . . but fortunately I am able to smile at myself. . . .

At tea time Richard returns; he is worried over his business
affairs, and declares in a gloomy manner that the office will go
to pot while he is away. He has been trying to fix things up,
but has not been able to complete the job and will be obliged
to visit the City again tomorrow morning.

Spend the evening helping Richard to pack and suggesting
various comforts which he may find useful in the tropics, and
while we are so engaged the telephone bell rings and I discover that it is Tim.

"How are you?" enquires Tim's voice. "What sort of journey
did you have? There was a raid in the Midlands and I couldn't
sleep a wink for thinking about you."

I assure Tim that I got on splendidly and that there is no
need to worry about me and, while I do so, I cannot help smiling, for Tim is always so scornful when I worry about *his*
safety, and now he is worrying about mine with far less cause.

"When are you going to Winch Hall?" he enquires. "You
had better go on Thursday. I don't like you being in London
at all. I shall arrive at Winch Hall on Friday morning, but you
had better go down on *Thursday.*"

This sudden change of plan is somewhat inconvenient, for I
had intended to visit the hairdresser on Thursday afternoon.
I review my arrangements hastily and try to make up my mind
whether it is more important to have my hair done, or to fulfil
my marriage vows. Tim, who is still at the other end of the
line (and how strange it is to think of him standing in the hall
at Winfield with his head a little on one side and the receiver
glued to his ear) says, "Hester, you *must* go on Thursday . . .
I suppose you had arranged to have your hair waved or something . . . but, if so, you must put it off," and I am so flabber-
gasted by his prescience that I meekly agree to do so.

"That's right," says Tim. "That's splendid . . . yes, we're all right here. Pinkie has come back, and she'll look after things while we are away . . . yes, she's quite cheerful . . . yes, she seems very happy . . . yes, Betty is perfectly well . . ."

After some more conversation with my host and hostess I retire to my bed—which has suddenly and mysteriously appeared in the library—and go off to sleep at once.

WEDNESDAY IITH DECEMBER

Am greeted at breakfast by anxious enquiries as to what sort of a night I have had, and reply that although I was wakened several times by sirens and gunfire and other "noises off" I managed to obtain a reasonable amount of sleep.

Richard says, "You'd soon get used to it. I never hear anything now, thank goodness," and having thus expressed his gratitude to Providence he goes on to enquire what Mary and I propose to do with ourselves this morning and whether we can meet him at Weston's for a slap-up lunch. Mary replies that this will suit us admirably, and explains to me that Weston's is the last word—lovely food, a splendid band, and amusing people to see—and that is has taken the place left vacant by various Italian Restaurants which have had to close their doors.

"Don't be late," says Richard as we bid him good-bye.

Mary and I have a prowl round the shops which are as fascinating as ever. I buy a doll's bed for Betty—as I am aware that this is what she wants—and Mary buys a pair of wool-lined boots. As we pass through the millinery department I am tempted to buy a hat—Mary assures me that is not really extravagant, as a new hat is as good as a tonic, and this particular confection suits me admirably and makes me look about five years younger. I buy it and put it on, and my conscience tortures me for about half an hour.

As we leave the large store and walk through the streets Mary points out several places which have been bombed, but they have been cleared and partially rebuilt, and there is little damage to be seen. We pass a small tobacconist's shop and stop to read a large notice in the window. It announces:

IN THE EVENT OF AIR RAIDS THESE PREMISES WILL REMAIN OPEN. IN THE EVENT OF A DIRECT HIT THESE PREMISES WILL CLOSE IMMEDIATELY.

I am so delighted with this that I decide to buy a cigarette lighter for Richard here (Mary says that he does not possess one and it will be a useful present to give him) so we go inside and spend some time selecting one which will please him.

While we are in the shop we hear the noise of gunfire, and two shattering thumps which seem uncomfortably near. Several people come in from the street and one woman—somewhat pale and breathless—declares that "one came down on the next block." Two fire engines rush madly down the street. The noise of gunfire and the roar of aeroplanes is simply terrific. I look at my companions and wonder whether they are as frightened as I am. They show no signs of alarm, but then (I hope) neither do I. The tobacconist, who is a dear old gentleman with snowy white hair, suggests that we should all come into his back room as it is safer there, so we follow him through a door and find ourselves in a snug little parlour. The walls are lined with shelves and the shelves are stocked with packets of cigarettes, but there are two easy chairs in front of a pleasant fire. Our host stirs up the fire and asks us to be seated. By this time the company has been augmented by a taxi driver, a young man in Air Force Pilot's uniform and an errand boy with a basket. There is also a fat woman, who seems to have risen out of the ground. In spite of the noise, which continues as violently as ever, our companions seem anxious to converse.

The taxi driver remarks that there's a crater down the street big enough to hold a bus.

"The wickedness of it!" exclaims the fat woman, rolling her eyes. "The wickedness of it! If I could get 'old of 'itler there wouldn't be much left to bury."

The pale woman (who looks like a music teacher, though I really don't know why) replies with spirit, "Berlin's worse— that's the main thing. It's easy to bear if you know they're getting it too."

Everyone looks at the Air Force Pilot, but he does not take the hint, and it is left for the errand boy to address him directly. "Could I get into the Air Force, sir?" enquires the boy in an unnaturally gruff voice.

The Pilot does not smile, he replies quite kindly, "Yes, we'll be glad to have you when you're a bit older."

"I'm eighteen", declares the boy, sticking out his chest . . . but unfortunately his voice goes back on him and the statement ends in a squeak.

"You've got to show your birth certificate," says the Pilot promptly.

"Never mind," says the taxi driver, "You'll be 'ere when we've gorn west . . . that is, if a bomb don't get yer."

He has scarcely spoken when there is an appalling crash, the house rocks upon its foundations and all the ornaments leap off the mantelpiece and strew themselves over the floor . . . several people scream, and I cannot tell whether I am one of them . . . I am absolutely dazed for a moment and, when I recover, I am quite surprised to discover that I am whole. Nobody is hurt though everyone is pretty shaken. The Air Force

Pilot is heard to remark that it's a bit thick and he prefers the air any day of the week. . . .

The gunfire has slackened now and the noise of the planes diminished; everyone is preparing to depart on their business when it is discovered that the door has jammed, and at this the music teacher, who has been extremely courageous, begins to laugh hysterically—"We can't get out—we can't get out—we can't get out—" she exclaims.

Mary seems to be familiar with these symptoms of strain and, taking her firmly by the shoulders, gives her a little shake. Meanwhile the combined efforts of our male companions have enabled them to burst open the door, and we are at liberty to depart.

The front shop presents a scene of desolation impossible to describe; the windows are in fragments and packets of cigarettes are strewn all over the floor. The proprietor surveys the débris with a grim expression, but has very little to say. Mary and I are the last to leave the shop, we shake him by the hand and thank him for his hospitality,—and I feel so sorry for him that I slip a pound note into his pocket when he isn't looking—it is not much, but it is all that I can spare.

We step over the rubble which blocks the door of the shop and find the taxi driver waiting for us outside. He touches his cap and grins and enquires whether we would like him to drive us home, and adds that his taxi is round the corner and hasn't been touched. This reminds us that Richard will be waiting for us, and after a short consultation we decide to drive to Weston's. Personally I am thankful to climb into the taxi and sit down for my knees feel as if they were made of cotton wool and my heart is still beating irregularly . . . am quite glad to see that Mary is pale, as I should not like to think that I am less brave than she is.

We look at each other and smile. Mary says, "We ought to

powder our noses, but I can't be bothered," and I reply that what I need is a bath.

Richard is waiting for us in the doorway, he rushes down the steps and opens the taxi door, and enquires whether we are aware that he has been waiting for three quarters of an hour, and has nearly lost his reason with anxiety on our behalf, whereupon the taxi driver turns round in his seat and says, "If these two ladies belong to you, I can tell you they're made of the right stuff."

Richard seems to understand. He replies that he knew that before. He gives the driver a ten shilling note and, taking Mary and me firmly by our arms, he leads us into the restaurant. Mary says that we want to wash, but Richard refuses to allow us to do so . . . "No," says Richard, "I'm not going to let you out of my sight again, so you'll just have to remain dirty."

We sit down at a corner table and Richard orders cocktails—I murmur feebly that a cocktail is just what I need, but I don't want much to eat. Richard replies that he is about to order an enormous meal, and that Mary and I have got to eat it; we can tell him what happened when the meal is safely inside us.

"Nothing happened, really," says Mary. "Nothing serious, I mean. We took shelter in a tobacconist's, and when we came out there was a crater in the street."

Richard says, "That's quite enough—I wish to goodness you would go away to some safe place and stay there."

When I have had my cocktail and drunk a plate of very hot soup, I begin to feel more like myself and become somewhat self-conscious about my appearance—Mary's hat has a rakish air, and there is a large streak of dirt across her cheek, and I feel sure that I am even less presentable than she is. . . . I catch sight of myself in a long mirror and my worst fears are confirmed.

Several letters are waiting for me on the hall table at Wintringham Square. I seize upon them eagerly and turn them over and gloat upon them as a miser gloats upon his gold, for, although I have only been away from home for two days, I am longing to return. There is a letter from Betty in the little pile, and I open that first, for Betty's letters, though less newsy than Bryan's are always a joy.

"Dear Mummy—we met the twins and they new me. She let me wheel the pram. She sed will you come to tea becos Mummies away so you must be dull so I sed yes. She sed will Daddy come two so I arskt him and he sed not if I no it. I plade with Artha in the bern and he fell in. He shoodent have sed I pusht him becos it was an axident. Pinky ses thats a sneek annyhow and noboddy likes them. Pinky has a dimond ring. Guthry gave it to her. It issent her burthday its becos they are going to be marrid. She told me so its troo. Pinkie ses I mussent arsk you what your going to by me in London. I was wundring if your going to by a bed for Rose but Pinky ses wate and see. It will be nice when your home agen. Your loving dorter, Elizabeth Christie.
Miss Clark ses thats the rite way to end a letter so I did."

Grace's letter comes next.

"Hester darling, When are you coming home? This place is a wilderness without you and there isn't a creature who can understand the simplest joke. First of all, my dear, I must tell you, the Ledgard—Browne Winters engagement is definitely *off!* Thank heaven we aren't going to have *that awful woman* in the Regiment! I can't think what T.L. saw in her. She came to tea with me yesterday and behaved in the most extraordinary way—stalked in like a tragic muse and said that 'all was over' between her and 'Captain Ledgard,' and that she had made a *great mistake* about him. Then she went on to say that it was not T.L. whom she knew and loved in the Days of the Great Pyramid. T.L. is a new soul, and she has nothing in common with him. When I suggested that she might have discovered this sooner, she replied that the whole affair was *my fault! ! !* Naturally I was annoyed and asked her what on earth she meant whereupon she replied that I had presented T.L. to her notice in a false light—I ask you! ! ! ! Fortunately Tom is taking it very well, and in fact if he were not so *intensely stupid* one might almost suspect that he had *engineered* the break with Ermyntrude. Jack says that Tom goes about the mess telling everyone that he is a new soul, and standing drinks all round. Betty is coming to tea today. I asked Tim also, as I thought he might be feeling a little dull, but apparently he is too busy. I suppose it is quite impossible to buy silk stockings in London. If you happen to see any (my size is 9) you might get them for me, and I will pay you when you come home. I went to the Comforts Depot this morning, Mamie and Stella were squabbling as usual. I must stop now as there is no more news. Much love, Yours, Grace "

Mrs. Loudon writes:

"My dear Hester, I would have written you before, but have been too much taken up with the engaged couple. Guthrie has now gone to sea and Pinkie back to Donford. Guthrie behaved like a lunatic while he was here, the two of them might have been ten years old for all the sense they had. However we were all young once. Pinkie is just the girl for him. I said it before and I see no reason to change my mind. She is thoroughly sound and sensible at heart for all her daft carryings on. The only fault I have to find with the creature is that she is a great deal too good-looking, but she cannot help that. She is devoted to you, but I daresay you knew that already. It shows her sense. I am worried about Millie Falconer. I have written her twice and told her to shut up her flat and come to Avielochan, but I can get no sense out of her. If you have the time you might go and see her and tell her she is to come away; it is quite unsuitable for a woman of her age to remain in London by herself. Your affectionate old friend Elspeth Loudon.

P.S. Maybe you will think I sound a bit halfhearted about Guthrie's girl. It is not my way to go into raptures, but I am fully aware that I am a lucky woman."

As this is Richard's last night before sailing to an unknown destination I feel that it will be kind to leave him alone with Mary; so, after supper, I announce my intention of visiting a friend.

Richard asks, "Who is he and where does he live?" and I answer that the friend is of the female sex and inhabits a small flat in Queen's Gate. Richard then enquires whether she is young and attractive, to which I reply that on the contrary she is old and somewhat foolish. Richard says he does not know why I am so secretive about my affairs. Any information about them has to be dragged out of me by wild horses, but of course if I prefer to spend the evening with a silly old woman, rather than remain here with him and Mary, I am at liberty to do so.

Mary says "Richard!" in a horrified tone, but I know Richard too well, and am too fond of him to be annoyed by these unreasonable approaches. He is tired and worried and the prospect of leaving his wife alone in London—perhaps for years—has upset his equilibrium. I therefore reply quite mildly that

Mrs. Falconer is a cousin of my old friend, Mrs. Loudon, and that I met her at Avielochan when Betty and I were there for a holiday, and I add that Mrs. Loudon has asked me to visit Mrs. Falconer and to persuade her (if I can) to shut up her flat and go north.

Richard looks somewhat ashamed of himself and says that he will walk along to Queen's Gate with me and leave me at the door, because the streets are as black as Old Sam.

I find Mrs. Falconer sitting over a comfortable fire. Her flat is just as I had expected—full of odds and ends of furniture and liberally sprinkled with china ornaments and knick-knacks of all descriptions.

Somewhat to my surprise Mrs. Falconer knows who I am and welcomes me warmly . . . "So nice of you to come," she declares, "I *would* have asked you to tea. I always say that tea is the best meal of the day. Of course it is rather different now, so I daresay it was just as well that you could not come, though you cannot get cream cakes anywhere and crumpets do *not* taste the same with margarine. It was so peaceful there, wasn't it?" enquires Mrs. Falconer in her usual vague manner, "and nobody could have imagined that the next time we met it would be war-time. I would not have believed it possible that there could be war again, but now it seems quite natural.

I search hastily amongst this rag bag of talk for something to answer, but before I have found what I want, my hostess is off again.

"Dear, dear," she says, shaking her head, "who would have thought that we should *all* be in the war? Not even Guthrie or that strange Major Martin who came to the house so frequently. I declare one could not turn round without finding him there—it was really very strange."

I murmur feebly that Mrs. Loudon encouraged Tony Morley to come whenever he liked.

"He did not come to see Elspeth," declares Mrs. Falconer firmly, "I do not know to this day *why* he came. But you must not think that I dislike men—and in fact it is always a great deal nicer when there are men about the place. Dear Mama always used to say that *that* was one of the advantages of daughters."

As usual Mrs. Falconer is having the effect of making my head swim. When I was at Avielochan I became used to her and sometimes was able to follow her train of thought, but I am out of practice and am completely bewildered.

Mrs. Falconer has paused to poke the fire; she now continues, "Of course, dear Elspeth has no daughters, so it was not that in *his* case . . . I wonder what became of him—Major Morgan, I mean".

I tell her that Tony Morley is now a colonel and has gone to Egypt.

"Fancy!" says Mrs. Falconer, "I wonder if he has seen the Sphinx. It struck me as being a very large monument. Now I should never have thought of making him a colonel, but perhaps he does not talk so much when he is on parade. Dear Papa used to say 'Much noise, little speed'—but aeroplanes were not invented then and the truth is we got on very nicely without them. I often wonder," continues Mrs. Falconer with a thoughtful air, "I often wonder what dear Papa would have said about this war. His remarks were always so illuminating. He was very much interested in the progress of the South African War and we often used to say that if Papa had been younger nothing would have kept him from volunteering . . . 'Cook's son, Duke's son,' says Mrs. Falconer reminiscently, "*that* was the song in those days and dear Papa was extremely patriotic. He often told us girls that we were fortunate in having been born British subjects. He had a large coloured map hanging upon the drawing room wall and moved the pins every day after he had read the newspapers."

"It would be difficult to do that with this war!"

Mrs. Falconer agrees. "Difficult certainly, but I have no doubt Papa would have managed it. He was fond of saying 'Where there's a will there's a way.' However I am really quite thankful that neither he nor dear Mama are still living—you may think this a very *heartless* thing to say, but I feel sure that they would not be happy if they were alive now. Papa liked bacon for breakfast *every* morning and Mama was very much alarmed at the idea of fire. I remember once when we were shopping in Bond Street and a fire engine went by at a great rate poor Mama was upset for the rest of the day. We found out afterwards that it was only a practice and there was no fire at all which comforted Mama greatly."

As I am here with a definite object, I make a determined attempt to break into the conversation and, sitting forward in my chair, I say urgently, "Mrs. Loudon wants you to go and stay with her."

"Yes, dear," says Mrs. Falconer, moving her hands vaguely. "Elspeth wrote. I cannot remember where I put the letter. She seems very much pleased with that girl—I mean Guthrie's fiancée—but perhaps you did not know that Guthrie is engaged again . . . quite good family, I believe, and nice-looking into the bargain. Elspeth seems to think that Guthrie is going to marry her, but I think they should wait for a little in case he changes his mind again . . . these war weddings—are you enjoying your visit to London?"

There is some connection here, but none that I can find, and the question itself is so odd and unexpected that I find some difficulty in answering it. Am I enjoying my visit to London? Yes, in some ways I am. I am enjoying the feeling that I am in the thick of things. I am enjoying the feeling of kinship which unites the whole population of London into one vast family, so that the Queen and the flower woman at the corner are both my sisters. It is an uplifting feeling and a strong aid to courage, and in it lies the explanation of many a brave deed. Having come to this conclusion I am able to reply quite truthfully that I am enjoying my visit to London very much.

Strange to say, Mrs. Falconer has waited for my answer, and now she comments upon it quite sensibly, "Yes, dear, I am so glad," she says. "There is something about London, isn't there? It is very kind of Elspeth to invite me to go to Avielochan and stay with her, but I do *not* feel that I can leave here at present."

"I think you should," I murmur.

"No," says Mrs. Falconer, "no, in times like these it is better to be in one's own home with all one's own comforts . . . not that Elspeth's house is uncomfortable of course . . . but still . . . and another thing to be considered is what would happen if a bomb fell through my roof and I were not here to see to it?"

"But what could you do?" I ask.

"I have a thing with a long handle," replies Mrs. Falconer promptly, "and the lady next door has a stirrup pump . . . we have filled a pail with sand and put it upon the landing. Perhaps you saw it when you rang the bell."

I decide to try again, "It would be wiser . . ." I begin.

"No," says Mrs. Falconer firmly, and with a total absence of her usual muddled vagueness, "no, dear, it is better to remain at home. London is my home. It has been my home for many years, and I should not care to leave it now . . . I believe you understand," adds Mrs. Falconer, with a sudden knowing smile. "I believe you understand my feelings, so perhaps you will be good enough to explain them to Elspeth. I find it extremely difficult to explain things to Elspeth . . . she has such strong prejudices."

THURSDAY 12TH DECEMBER

I arrive at Winch Hall at teatime which is, I think, the right hour for a guest to arrive on a visit . . . the right hour not only for the guest, but for the hostess. At teatime the day's activities are over, and the hostess is ready for conversation, and there is an intimate quality about teatime which makes the guest feel at home. Uncle Joe and Aunt Posy are the best kind of host and hostess (they do not fuss over one, but simply accept one into their household as an active member) and Winch Hall is a lovely place to stay. I have stayed here before, of course, but not very often, for Tim and I have moved about so much that we have not had much time for visiting.

The house is not very large; it is old and comfortable and a trifle shabby. The drawing room is early Victorian—a period piece—not of set purpose, but merely because it has not been altered since early Victorian times. It is not very comfortable, of course, but that does not matter, for Uncle Joe and Aunt Posy use the morning room to sit in and the morning room is the cosiest room imaginable. Brown is the predominant colour here; the carpet is beige and brown, the heavy curtains are brown and blue, the deep leather chairs shine like horse chestnuts. The bow window has a wide window seat upon which one can sit and look down the sloping garden and over the wide fields and trees. There are books on the shelves and magazines on the side table and baskets for the spaniels, in which they are supposed to lie, but never do, preferring the hearth rug, where they can be near the feet of their gods and the warmth of their gods' fire. It is a peaceful room, a friendly room. You could not imagine loud harsh voices here, nor ugly scenes. I feel this more strongly than ever this cold frosty evening when I arrive and am welcomed to the fire which blazes merrily in the wide old-fashioned grate. Uncle Joe insists that I shall sit in his chair because it is warmer there ... Aunt Posy's plump hands busy themselves with the tea equipage which stands on a round gate-legged table before the fire. There is much to talk about, for they want to know all my news, and they want to see the latest photographs of the children, and they want to hear details of Tim's adventures in France. Uncle Joe is particularly interested in the details of the retreat for he is an old soldier and a distinguished one. Most of his service was done abroad—he was attached to the Egyptian Army, and was afterwards in India—he looks like the peppery old colonel beloved of Punch, but his heart is of gold. Aunt Posy was with him in India—for he never married—she followed the drum for years and now she is settled with him at Winch Hall running the house in a capable manner. Although he is slight and quick and somewhat excitable and she is plump and placid, there is a strong family resemblance between the brother and sister.

I am still trying to satisfy Uncle Joe and to answer his searching questions anent the Retreat to Dunkirk when an Air Raid signal breaks the peace. While I was in London I became quite hardened to the eerie sound and learned to take no notice of its import, but it seems different here; I look enquiringly at my host and hostess to see how they are reacting.

Uncle Joe smiles and says, "We've got an excellent shelter in the wine cellar. We used to go down whenever the siren sounded, but we got a bit tired of it."

"Perhaps Hester would like to go down," puts in Aunt Posy, looking at me anxiously.

I reply that I am perfectly happy where I am, but merely wished to know the local rules.

Uncle Joe laughs. "That's the spirit!" he declares. "As a matter of fact planes pass over constantly on their way to London, but they are making for more important objectives than Cobstead. If you happen to see a plane when you're out it's a different matter, of course. You should make for the nearest ditch."

Aunt Posy lifts her head from her embroidery for a moment and says, "And if there isn't a ditch you must lie down perfectly flat . . . not in the road, of course, but in a field. There is usually a gate."

"Is it necessary?" I enquire, for somehow or other I cannot imagine myself taking cover in this manner.

"Necessary!" echoes Uncle Joe, "It may be necessary or it may not, but it's better to be on the safe side. They've been known to machine gun people on the roads."

"You must always do it, dear," declares Aunt Posy firmly. "You must take shelter whenever you hear their engines. The engines say 'For *you*, for *you*, for *you*,' so it is quite easy to know the difference. There is no need to be ashamed of taking cover—all good soldiers do."

Uncle Joe chuckles and says, "I was talking to the Vicar this morning—just by the lych gate—and a Jerry came over the trees. We were both in the ditch before you could say Jack Robinson. He's younger than I am, but I beat him by a short head."

"Joe, you never told me!" cries Aunt Posy reproachfully.

"I've only just remembered it this moment," replies Uncle Joe. "It was damn funny, and I thought at the time how amused you would be . . . and then I forgot to tell you. Old Brooke rolled into the ditch like a cannon ball—it was full of brambles too!"

"Mr. Brooke is very fat," explains Aunt Posy.

". . . and very pompous," adds Uncle Joe grinning wickedly.

"He moves rather slowly as a rule, and wears such a dignified air that you can almost see his prospective gaiters."

"Joe!"

"Well, it's perfectly true . . . but this morning," says Uncle Joe, laughing heartily at the recollection, "this morning when I saw him come crawling out of the ditch on his hands and knees with brambles clinging round his neck . . . and mud in his hair . . ."

"Joe, you didn't laugh!" cries Aunt Posy in alarm.

"Of course I laughed. Anyone would have laughed. I nearly split my sides."

"Oh dear, I hope he wasn't hurt. I shouldn't like to hurt his feelings. He really is so very kind and nice—and so good to the village people—"

"He laughed too," Uncle Joe assures her.

It is now nearly six o'clock, and Aunt Posy takes me up to my bedroom and talks to me while I unpack. I have always noticed that she likes to get me alone, and she talks more and faster when Uncle Joe is absent, but the reason for this is not because she is in awe of her brother, but because she is of the generation which was taught to keep women's talk for women's ears. I hear domestic news now—servant-troubles and the scarcity of sugar for jam-making—and am urged to retail my own experiences in this field; I comply by telling Aunt Posy about Annie's marriage and various other domestic details which would be of no interest at all to Uncle Joe.

"It is so lovely to have you, dear," says my hostess with a sigh, "but I do hope you won't be frightened. We really *are* in the front line, you know."

"Aren't you frightened?" I enquire with interest, for I have never felt that kind plump Aunt Posy is the stuff of which heroes are made.

"Not now," she replies candidly. "I was very frightened indeed two years ago. The Munich Crisis frightened me so dreadfully that I was quite ill. Then, when the war started, I was so miserable about it that I wanted to die . . . but now I want to live and see the end of it." She hesitates for a moment, and then adds with a little smile, "If you had told me eighteen months ago that German aeroplanes would fly over this house, and that I would not take any notice of them but just go on as usual, I should have thought you were mad!"

I ask her what has changed her outlook and she replies, "I think we have got beyond being frightened for ourselves. We don't matter, Hester. It is Britain that matters now. We are all soldiers now . . . I have seen a great many soldiers in my time and they are cheerful people; they don't trouble about the past or the future, but just do their jobs. Don't you agree?"

I do agree. Strangely enough the idea of Aunt Posy as a soldier of Britain is not in the least comic.

"We had a bomb," continues Aunt Posy quietly, "and I believe *that* helped me more than anything. It fell in the rose garden and made a deep hole and smashed all the drawing-room windows, but nobody was hurt and it was not nearly as bad as I expected. You shall see the hole tomorrow," she adds, smiling at me.

I make further enquiries about the bomb, and am informed that Joe was very angry, but has now quite recovered from his rage and has decided to use the bomb crater and make a little rock garden there—a sunk garden where they can grow plants requiring shelter and warmth . . . "Don't change, dear," adds Aunt Posy, as she goes away. "We never change for supper now. Joe is in the Home Guard, of course, so he goes out at night, and he prefers me not to change either."

Supper is a cheerful informal affair and for my part I like it much better than the ceremonious dinner which was de rigueur at Winch Hall before the war. We have fried fish and cauliflower au gratin, cocoa and toast and marmalade, and we finish with apples and pears from the Winch orchards; we rise from the table feeling comfortably fed.

Nine o'clock is now approaching and Uncle Joe puts down his paper and looks at me enquiringly, "The news," he says, "you'd like to hear it, wouldn't you? I have a feeling there may be important news tonight."

The wireless is tuned in, and almost immediately we hear Big Ben—it seems curious to hear the familiar strokes reverberating in this quiet country room—then comes the news and Uncle Joe is more than justified in his expectations. It is great news, tremendous news, news of a splendid victory. Sidi Barani has been surrounded and captured by British and Imperial Troops. It is a victory of British Generalship and of British courage and endurance. Thousands of prisoners have been captured, guns and tanks and other war material have been seized, and the Italian Army has been put to flight.

Uncle Joe is so excited by the stirring news that he is obliged to get up and walk about the room. "Grand!" he cries, his eyes flashing fire, "Splendid! Magnificent! That's the stuff to give them . . . wish I was there. Capital! This is what I've been hoping for. I know that coast . . . been up to Buk Buk myself . . . wish I was there now. We've got 'em cold unless I'm very much mistaken . . . the Italians can't take it . . . haven't the bulldog strain . . . they're all right as long as things go well, but now . . . shouldn't like to be Graziani. He's in a bit of a hole, if I'm right. That escarpment—what do they call it, "Haggag es Sollum"—narrows down their line of retreat to a bottle neck . . . and the Navy's there, (the splendid chaps that they are!) and they can blow the road to bits . . . hell, why aren't I twenty years younger?"

I have seized a map from Uncle Joe's table, and have been following his commentary closely.

"Keep 'em going!" cries Uncle Joe. "Keep 'em on the trot with no time to collect their wits! Not easy, of course, in that sort of country—sand and stones and scrub—transport difficulties must be enormous; but we've been preparing for this for months. I knew it. I felt Wavell had something up his sleeve —something pretty good—and Wilson, splendid fellow! We needed this. It'll have tremendous effect all over Africa—Italians won't be able to dominate Abyssinia much longer—it'll have repercussions in Senussi territory, in Libya, too. Well, well, it's the best news we've heard since the war started . . . might be the turning point . . ."

While he is still talking Uncle Joe is tying a huge knitted muffler round his neck, and struggling into an ancient British Warm which has recently been decorated with an emblem of the Home Guard; he is about to sally forth upon his nightly round of duty. I enquire somewhat diffidently if it would be comme il faut for a mere female to accompany him.

He looks at me in amazement and says, "You? D'you mean you want to come? . . . Well, I don't see any reason why you shouldn't. I just go round the posts and see that everything is all right, you know—just look in and have a bit of a talk with the fellows—"

"It is dreadfully cold!" murmurs Aunt Posy.

"Won't hurt her if she's warmly clad," declares Uncle Joe firmly. "Won't hurt her at all. It's a fine frosty night and there's a splendid moon. Run and get your coat, Hester."

"Wrap up warmly, dear!" cries Aunt Posy, as I dash out of the room.

Uncle Joe and I set out together, and a funny couple we make—he is clad in his British Warm and a steel helmet and is armed with an old Service Rifle; I am wearing my fur coat and a woollen bonnet, and am armed with a stick. Aunt Posy comes to the door to see us off and beseeches Uncle Joe to take good care of me . . . "Don't let her get lost," says Aunt Posy earnestly. "Take his arm, dear. Keep moving and don't hang about . . ."

"Go in, go in!" cries Uncle Joe shooing her away from the door, "You'll catch your death of cold standing in the draught with nothing on."

It is a glorious night, clear and frosty, and the moon is so bright that only the planets are visible in the dome of heaven. The moonlight sparkles on the crystals of frost; and the shadows of the trees and walls and hedges are black and sharply defined. It is very quiet and peaceful. A cow moos softly in its byre as we pass the home farm, and far away there is the sound of a dog barking.

"I like moonlight," says Uncle Joe in a reflective voice. "The world is very beautiful clad in moonlight . . . reminds me of a woman in black velvet and diamonds . . . always thought a beautiful woman looked her best in black velvet and diamonds . . . Glad you came?" he enquires, shooting a sideways glance at me as he speaks.

"Very glad," I reply.

"It's good for us," he says, as we leave the road and begin to mount a slight rise. "Much better for us than cooking ourselves over the fire. Nobody but a fool wants war, but it's good for people like me to be shaken up. Alice and I were getting awful old fogies, you know. We were in a rut. We did the same things at the same hour and were upset if anything happened to disturb the routine. If it wasn't for this war I should be sitting before the fire toasting the soles of my slippers . . . and my pipe going . . . and a whisky and soda at my elbow. Then bed at ten-thirty, regular as clockwork. Instead of that here am I prowling about my fields looking for an enemy."

"Sometimes I can't believe it, Uncle Joe."

"Neither can I," he admits. "I've soldiered all over the place, and I've seen some fighting in my time—I was on the North West Frontier for years—it seemed natural there . . . but here, in England, the idea of an enemy seems unnatural. We're actually on the lookout for men landing on our shore with guns in their hands! Sometimes, like you, I can't believe it . . . and then suddenly I realise that it's true. England is threatened with invasion—my own fields are threatened—my own house. That makes my blood boil, Hester. It isn't *new* of course. England's been threatened with invasion before—the Spanish, the Dutch, Napoleon—and there have always been men to guard her shores . . . just as we are doing today."

"I like that thought!"

"It's a good thought," he agrees. "We're guarding England. We're part of England's history. It stirs the blood, doesn't it? The old war horse hears the bugle."

By this time we have reached the top of the little hill—which boasts the delightful name of Mellow Rise—and we stand still for a few moments gazing out over the moonlit sea and the foreshore. Uncle Joe points out the defences which have been erected, and I notice that they look a good deal more business-like than the defences in Donford Bay. There are two concrete pill boxes—one at each end of Uncle Joe's property—where the Home Guard keeps watch, and there is a camp of artillery hidden in the wood beyond the stream.

Hitherto we have been sheltered by the hill, but now that we are standing upon the top of it we can feel a faint breeze stirring from the east, and it is suddenly very cold. Just beside us there are two old oak trees, stunted and gnarled by a thousand storms, and between them is a small ruined hut, made of rought-cut stones. It is roofless and overgrown with ivy and the cement is crumbling, but the walls have been so strongly built that they are still standing.

"Look at this little house," says Uncle Joe, laying his hand on the crumbling wall. "I've often wondered what it was. It's too small for a dwelling house—even for the meanest peasant —it isn't even big enough for a good sized cow. It has often puzzled me and I've tried to find out when it was built, and why—but without success. Now I know."

"Why was it built?" I enquire.

Uncle Joe does not reply at once—he is enjoying my curiosity—"Come inside and look through the window," he says. I do as he tells me, bending my head as I pass through the low doorway and looking round with interest at the thick stone walls. The window is a small square opening which gives on to the sea, and through it can be seen the wide sweep of Cobstead Bay.

"That's what it's for," says Uncle Joe, "It's a lookout post. It's the right place for a lookout post—you couldn't find a better—and the little window is at exactly the right angle. I got one of the gunners to come and have a look at it and he measured it out, did a lot of calculations and found that he couldn't have bettered it, himself."

"Do you know who built it?" I enquire, looking round with even more interest than before.

"My great grandfather built it. There's no doubt about that. You can tell the date of a building from the cement. He must have had it built when Boney was massing his armies to invade England. Interesting, isn't it?"

"More than interesting. Tell me all that you know about it."

Uncle Joe laughs, but he is pleased. "I don't know much more about the little house," he replies, "But I can tell you a bit about the old boy who built it. He was a fine old chap— a Joseph like myself—Joseph Christie. We've got his portrait (perhaps you've noticed it over the fireplace in the hall), a big upstanding man with humourous eyes, and wearing a white stock. Well, that's Joseph Christie who built this little lookout post and used it when he was guarding England's shores. I use it too, it keeps the wind off, but I'm going to have it repaired and a new roof put on."

"I think he would like you to have it repaired."

"Do you? I believe you're right . . . as a matter of fact I have a queer feeling when I come up here at night . . . a queer feeling that I'm not alone," says Uncle Joe a trifle shame-facedly. "I don't believe in ghosts or anything like that, you know, but I just have that feeling. It's a pleasant feeling, mind you. I'm an old campaigner, and pretty hardened, but I never *did* like visiting outposts in the dark by myself. Well, I don't visit them by myself. The old boy comes along . . . silly, isn't it?"

"No, it isn't silly," I reply quickly.

"Some people would think it silly," Uncle Joe points out.

"Some people don't believe in Drake's Drum."

There is a little silence and then Uncle Joe murmurs, "H'm, Drake's Drum . . . same sort of thing . . . h'm. Well, we'd better be getting along, Hester."

FRIDAY 13TH DECEMBER

Tim arrives at lunch time. It is lovely to see him again, and so much has happened since Monday that it seems more like four weeks than four days. After lunch the two men are left to chat, and I am conducted round the garden by Aunt Posy. She is particularly anxious to show me the bomb crater and the Christmas roses.

"There!" she exclaims, as we stand on the edge of the deep jagged hole, "There, Hester—don't you think it will make a

delightful sunk garden? Joe has promised to get some large
stones, and I thought of a lily-pool at the bottom. There will
be stone steps, of course, and I shall make little crevices for
the plants . . . I can see exactly how it will look when it is
finished. I have always wanted a sunk garden," adds Aunt Posy
with a little sigh of satisfaction.

I congratulate her on the attainment of her ambition, and
we walk on together.

"I hope you don't mind," says Aunt Posy, after a short
silence. "I hope you don't mind coming out with me like this.
Joe wanted to talk to Tim on business, but it won't take very
long."

I assure her that I am delighted to walk with her at any time,
and especially in such beautiful surroundings.

"It *is* pretty," agrees Aunt Posy. "Some people dislike the
country in winter, but to me it has a beauty all its own. I like
seeing the fields under plough—the earth is such a fine rich
brown—and you can see the shape of the trees when they are
bare."

This is what I have often thought myself, and I say so, adding that I prefer the country to the town at any time of the
year.

"Do you really?" says Aunt Posy, "I am very glad, dear. I
always thought you were a town person. Usually, when people
are born and brought up in London, they prefer the town. I am
so *very* glad."

It is difficult to see why Aunt Posy should be so glad,
"so *very* glad," to hear of my predilection for country life, except that she is the kind of person who enjoys being in accord
with those around her. Argument or disagreement in the mild-
est form would make Aunt Posy uncomfortable. We walk on
together in great good humour, Aunt Posy chatting cheerfully,

and presently I find myself being escorted through a gate which looks like the entrance to a house.

"We aren't going to call on anyone, are we?" I enquire in some alarm, for having been invited to come for a stroll in the garden I have come in an ancient tweed coat and my woollen bonnet—quite unsuitable garb in which to call upon a complete stranger.

Aunt Posy smiles and shakes her head, "No, dear, I should have warned you if I had thought of paying an afternoon call —though as a matter of fact you look very nice indeed—this house is empty at present. It belongs to me and I thought I should like to walk round and satisfy myself that it is in good condition."

"It belongs to you?" I enquire, somewhat surprised to discover in Aunt Posy a woman of property.

"Yes, my father left it to me. It has been used as a dower house. I have always been very grateful to my father for leaving me Mellow Lodge—it has been pleasant to know that I have a place of my own to live in if Joe should marry . . . He is not likely to marry now," adds Aunt Posy naively.

"Has it been empty for long?" I enquire.

"No," she replies. "The tenants left last month. They had several small children, and Cobstead is not a suitable place for small children just now. They were pleasant people and I was sorry when they went away, but perhaps it is all for the best."

"All for the best?" I enquire.

"Well, dear," says Aunt Posy vaguely, "Well, dear, sometimes when one thinks at the time that a certain event is a misfortune one finds that it is not . . . There was the bomb crater, for instance."

Mellow Lodge is quite a small house, but it possesses a character and dignity of its own. It is old and solid and is built of the same grey stone of which Winch Hall is made. It is a cheerful-looking house with good-sized windows. There are large trees round it, sheltering it from the north and east but, towards the southwest, the prospect is open and the garden slopes gently upwards to Mellow Rise. We do not enter the house, because Aunt Posy has not brought the key, but we walk round it and peer in at the windows. One of the gutters is choked, and we make a note that this must be cleared at once, otherwise the place seems in good order. The garden is in good order too, and Aunt Posy explains that the Winch Hall gardeners look after this garden for her and that vegetables have been put in so that the ground shall not be unproductive . . . "and that is most important at any time, but especially just now," declares Aunt Posy firmly.

Having satisfied ourselves that all is well, we return to Winch Hall in time for tea.

The evening is spent in conversation, and it is not until Uncle Joe has departed on his rounds that Tim and I retire upstairs to bed and find ourselves alone. Somehow or other I have had a feeling all the evening that Tim had something on his mind. I know him so well, and we have never had secrets from each other. Tim shuts the door and comes over to the fire, which is a luxury that Aunt Posy insists upon providing for her guests; he sits down on a chair and looks at me.

"Well?" I enquire a trifle anxiously, "Well, what's the matter?"

"Nothing," replies Tim. "Nothing's the *matter* exactly. I've been wanting to talk to you, that's all. I've been bursting to talk to you all the evening, but now I don't quite know how to begin."

"Tim!" I cry, "Tim, what is it? Is it something to do with business—the business that Uncle Joe spoke of in his letter?"

"Yes," says Tim.

"Tim! Don't say that they have got to sell Winch Hall!" I cry. "Oh Tim, that would be frightful!"

"Would it?" enquires Tim.

"Of course it would. They've been here for centuries—all your family—and old Joseph would hate it."

"Old Joseph?" enquires Tim, but I cannot stop to tell him about old Joseph Christie now. I shake his arm and ask him again whether or not my foreboding is true.

"No," says Tim, smiling. "You're wrong for once, Hester. So far there is no need to sell Winch Hall, and I'm particularly glad of that because Uncle Joe has made me his heir."

"His heir!" I exclaim in amazement.

"That was what he wanted to discuss," says Tim thoughtfully. "That and something else, but I told him I couldn't settle anything without consulting you."

"But Tim—"

"I wasn't really surprised," says Tim quite candidly, "because, of course, I'm his nearest relation and he's always been frightfully decent to me, but the other idea *was* a bit of a surprise."

"What other idea?"

Tim hesitates. "It's like this," he says. "Uncle Joe and Aunt Posy are getting old. They want us to come here and settle down near them. He suggested that I should retire—after the war, of course."

"Tim!"

"I know," says Tim nodding. "It's a bit of a surprise, isn't it? I mean I had never thought . . . but Uncle Joe says he is getting old, and there is a good deal to do, managing the estate . . . he would teach me how to manage it."

I am so amazed that I am speechless and can only stare at Tim.

"Yes," says Tim, "Yes, I was afraid you wouldn't like the

idea. Uncle Joe thought you would—but I was afraid you
wouldn't. I told him I must talk it over with you. It would
mean leaving the Service, of course. You wouldn't like that,
would you?"

"But Tim—" I gasp.

"There's a house," says Tim. "It belongs to Aunt Posy, and
they would do it all up for us . . . but it would mean leaving
the Service."

Mellow Lodge! Mellow Lodge for us . . . a home in which
we could settle down and have our own furniture which has
been stored for years. A home for Bryan to come to in his
holidays, where he could bring his friends . . . a proper
nursery for Betty . . . a garden of our own . . . a home at
last . . . but Tim, what does Tim feel about it? Does Tim
want to retire? I can't believe that he wants to give up his
career. He has often talked about "when I get command," and
the day when he will command the Regiment is drawing closer
now. I pull myself together and say, "It's for you to decide."

"No, it's for both of us to decide," declares Tim, squeezing
my arm. "We're partners, Hester. The firm has got to make an
important decision . . . we've got to look at the whole thing
sensibly. I see two roads and there is good in both."

I see the two roads also, and I see that there is good in both,
but for me the good in one far outweighs the good in the
other.

"I know you like the Regiment," Tim is saying, "You're
Mrs. Tim of the Regiment—and I've always been proud of
your popularity. You're the right kind of soldier's wife—not
terribly G.S. as some of the wives are—you enjoy all the fun
of moving about, of seeing new places and meeting new people.
You'd be sorry if I retired before I got command, wouldn't
you?"

"Don't you want to get command?" I ask.

"Yes," says Tim. "Yes, of course I do . . . it's only . . ."

"Only what?" I press him, because I must know for certain. I am so terrified that we may take the wrong turning.

"Only . . .", says Tim slowly and with difficulty, "Only I *do* love this place . . . it's in my blood, I think. We've moved about so much . . . it would be nice to have a real home. We shouldn't be very well off, but we could live here quietly . . . it would be dull for you, Hester."

I seize Tim's arm. "It would be perfect!" I cry, "It would be absolutely perfect!"